Aphonea en
ily. Even with
to avoid touching the men, or making any inex-
plicable sound.

A fat, hairy little guardsmen lurched up to her,
reeking of wine and foul odors.

"Who're you?" he demanded, small red eyes
glittering, "What're you sneakin' around for?"

Aphonea blinked. Then she reached out with
one finger and touched him in the center of
his forehead.

"You do not see me," she said, gazing into his
eyes compellingly.

He slapped her hand away.

"I do too!" he insisted.

Reaching out he snatched her headscarf off
and his face brightened in appreciation of her
beauty. He looked around happily, as though
expecting applause for this conjuring trick. But
his fellows were lost in their own exploits.

Perhaps I can lure him into the corridor, she
thought, wondering if he was unaffected by her
magic because he was so drunk. She smiled at him.

Encouraged, he grabbed her breast and gave it
a playful squeeze.

Changing her plans, Aphonea punched him in
the nose, knocking him onto his fat behind.
Then she tried to leap over his prone body. His
hand flashed out and caught her ankle, bringing
her down on top of him.

"Theeeve!" he bellowed. "Thieeeeeefff!"

BAEN BOOKS created by CHRISTOPHER STASHEFF
Dragon's Eye
The Gods of War
The Day the Magic Stopped

With L. Sprague de Camp
The Enchanter Reborn
The Exotic Enchanter

With William R. Forstchen
Wing Commander: End Run

THE DAY THE MAGIC STOPPED

EDITED BY
CHRISTOPHER STASHEFF

THE DAY THE MAGIC STOPPED

This is a work of fiction. All the characters and events portrayed in this book are fictional, and any resemblance to real people or incidents is purely coincidental.

A Baen Books Original

Baen Publishing Enterprises
P.O. Box 1403
Riverdale, NY 10471

ISBN: 0-671-87690-2

Cover art by Larry Elmore

First printing, October 1995

Distributed by Simon & Schuster
1230 Avenue of the Americas
New York, NY 10020

Printed in the United States of America

Table of Contents

Prologue by Bill Fawcett   1
Pride and Puppetry by Christopher Stasheff   4
Now You See It by Morgan Llywelyn   38
Loyalty by S.N. Lewitt   55
Flicker by Jody Lynn Nye   85
The Thief of Eyes by S.M. Stirling   110
Facts of Life by Laura Anne Gilman   150
Elemental Tactics by Roland Green   167
disIllusions by Mike Resnick and
      Lawrence Schimel   186
What Price Magic? by Teresa Patterson   196
The Scam by Brian Thomsen   219
Alternative Medicine by Judith R. Conly   252
The Beggar's Revolt by Michael Scott   270
Jacus the Slug by John Mina
      and William R. Forstchen   281

PROLOGUE

Bill Fawcett

The mate settled back and relaxed. They were miles from shore, too far out for most ships, but not the *Nyad*, not anymore. The last smudge of land had disappeared an hour before, a situation that would have made the Egyptian captain's mate extremely nervous only a few months earlier. Now it meant they were safe from pirates, and the lean, dark-haired seaman was just glad that the route they now took cut two days off another boring crossing. They would be in Byzantium tomorrow, the richest port in the world. He relaxed and inhaled the sea air contentedly. The deck smelled of salt and drying hemp accented by hints of the valuable spices and exotic spell components stored in amphorae below.

Over the sailor's head the bright red sail was pushed taut by wind striking it, as always, at just the ideal angle. He still found himself occasionally wondering at the source of that constant breeze, attracted by a very expensive spell the ship's master had purchased in Byzantium. Above and beyond the mast the wind swirled and fought, but somehow always each bit of air decided to push perfectly against the wards inscribed in its exact center.

1

"Smooth passage," a voice commented over the dark-tanned seaman's shoulder. It was the owner and master and he sounded pleased with himself. "Rough beyond, but Lord Thraik's spells . . ."

He never finished the sentence. Nor did he need to. The mate had served with him since they were both boys scrabbling along the docks of Alexandria. They'd fought the sea for most of their lives, losing too much and too many friends. They were both content to never have to do so again.

The mate observed again how the new magics were certainly a wonder. They were traveling forward so smoothly a sling pellet left on the deck would not roll. But less than an arrow's shot away, waves nearly as high as the deck surged and subsided. Above them the dark sky was filled with low clouds and passing squalls. A wall of glittering darkness was advancing toward the small merchant and passed to either side of them, but inside their bubble of magic the deck under the two men's feet remained dry.

To the two shipmates, protected by those powerful spells, the storm seemed almost distant and more entertaining than ominous. Even the crew, mostly Egyptians like their officers, lounged near the bow enjoying the spectacle, and more so the novelty of being able to do so. Near the merchant's wide hull the water was so calm that when the enchanted sail was down they could see their own reflection in the deep green of the Aegean.

The spells woven around the ship were newly developed and costly. Both facts her captain invariably enjoyed pointing out to the less fortunate masters he met in the dockside wineshops. He always took the sting from such bragging by buying the next round. Sailing in the rough weather meant he would get a premium price for his cargo and he would show a profit on even the outrageous cost of the spells in four or five voyages.

The self-satisfied smile both men were sharing ended abruptly as the ship lurched, tumbling the master against the railing several paces away. Before the mate could hurry over the now surging deck to pull his old friend to his feet, both heard the unmistakable sound of the fully set sail tearing as it took the full force of the storm.

Obscenities relating to undependable wizards mixed with prayers as the master and his crew fought to save the ship. They had been too confident that the magic would protect them. Lines were loose and the deck strewn with extra cargo packed on at the last minute. They were still struggling when the calm returned.

The mate grabbed onto a line as the enchanted smoothness returned so abruptly that it nearly threw him off balance. Soaked and with one hand bleeding, it was several minutes before he cleared his way to where the master sat surveying the damage and deciding they had been lucky to survive at all.

Overhead the winds, once more tame, pushed against the two halves of their sail, moving them very slowly through the smooth water. The sky cleared as the last of the storm moved ahead of them.

"The spells are working again," the master assured both the mate and himself.

"What happened?" the mate wondered. "Thraik's spell was guaranteed to survive even his death."

"The spell is fine," the owner repeated. "Something in that storm nullified it."

"Stopped the magic?" the mate wondered aloud. "What could counteract those two powerful spells?"

"We've sailed off course and there is food suddenly spoiled as well," the master explained. "Whatever it was affected the compass and preservation spells, too."

"All the magic stopped," the mate marveled.

The captain shook his head. "It may be an interesting landfall tomorrow. That storm was moving directly toward Byzantium."

PRIDE AND PUPPETRY

Christopher Stasheff

"I thought show business was going to be fun," Cairn muttered as he eyed the gateway to the city—the gateway, and the two huge guards who stood by its pillars, their spears glittering in the late afternoon sunlight.

"We didn't come to enjoy ourselves," Prince Orlin hissed. He wasn't visible at the moment. "The business of entertainment is nonetheless business."

That was enough to remind Cairn of his duty to his prince—and to the king who paid him to keep his son out of trouble. He sighed, hitched his large rectangular pack high on his shoulders, and stepped forward to see how far through he could get by looking innocent. One step changed the angle of sight just enough to see around the right-hand guard to the pretty girl who sat just behind the gate on a folding stool, hands in her lap. Brown hair tumbled about her shoulders, framing an oval face with eyes that were large, brown, and gentle. Her nose was small, her lips full, and her robe tan. Cairn caught his breath; suddenly, brown was his favorite color. On the surface, she was only pretty—but there was

4

something underneath that glimmered in her eyes and transformed her into a beauty.

She gave him a reassuring smile, and he plucked from it the confidence to go ahead through the gate as though he had every right to be there.

The guards took exception. One caught his shoulder with a wide, hard hand. "Your pack has an odd shape, stranger. What's in it?"

"My stock in trade, sir." Cairn shrugged out of the straps, lowered the pack to the ground, unbuckled the top flap and flipped it back. The guard scowled down. "I see nothing but red wooden slats."

"Yes, sir—it's a puppet stage, hinged and folded for traveling. The puppets and curtains are inside the frame now, but they'll be outside it as soon as I set it up in your marketplace."

"Puppets, eh?" The guard's eye glinted, and the second stepped over to peek down, too. "Make the children happy for a few minutes, huh?"

"I certainly hope so, sir." Cairn hoped even harder that they weren't going to make him take out the puppets—but in the few weeks he'd been performing, he had already become used to everyone and anyone taking any excuse they could find to demand a free show.

"Clever stuff. Good for the little ones," the second guard opined.

Yes, good for the children. All the fathers and mothers brought their little darlings to see the puppet show, because it was so right for children. Of course, the grown-ups laughed as loudly as any of the "little ones," but that was just because they were happy that their children were happy, wasn't it?

"Well, there's no harm in dolls," the first guard said with a smile. "No weapons, though, of course."

Cairn smiled and spread his hands. "I haven't any."

The girl leaned forward. "Even the dirk in your boot is a weapon, young sir. Pray yield it to the guard."

Cairn stared at her, his mouth open, as the guard

reached down and slid the dagger from his boot. *Now, how in the name of Hermes did she know I kept a blade there?* More to the point, how had she known he had a right to be called "sir"?

The guard glanced at the girl; she nodded, and he stepped aside. "The marketplace is down the avenue and south of the palace. Our city is open to you."

The girl seemed open, too—even friendly, in fact. Cairn shouldered his pack again and stepped past the guard, dragging his steps as he came even with the young woman, searching frantically for something to say. "Your pardon, lady. I don't really think of a carving knife as a weapon."

"Nevertheless, it might kill a man." The words were firm, but the eyes were mischievous.

"I am called Cairn, and I am a puppeteer, as you know. Who are you, lady, and what is your office?"

"Well, you are forthright, at least. I am called Lira."

"The lady is a magician, fellow," one of the guards called. "If you think to court her, think again."

Lira flashed him a glare. "I thank you for your concern, Hugo—but I am in no danger."

To say the least! If she could work magic . . . "Are you really a magician, lady?"

Lira heaved a sigh. "I am, goodman, though not the greatest. Those few among us who own some skill must each take this post for three hours each week, to find hidden weapons, and be here in case of need." The way she said it made it seem as though "need" could never happen, and with two human mountains guarding the gate, Cairn was tempted to agree. Still . . . "I have heard that some merchants have sought to bring magicans of their own into this city."

Lira nodded. "And they are welcome, if they are well-intentioned."

Hugo shuddered, and Cairn remembered one or two tales he'd heard about magicans who weren't so well-intentioned, and had tried to battle it out with the city's wizards. A few had come close to winning, but the city wizards, never vindictive, had given them quick deaths anyhow. "And is it true, lady, that magicians like you can read a man's heart?"

"Only if he wishes it read." Lira lowered long lashes, turning her head to watch him out of the corners of her eyes. "Yet few have heard that rumor. You seem somewhat better informed than most."

Cairn bowed. "We who live by the public's pleasure, lady, must always know the news to tell them."

Lira smiled. "Is your news truth, or rumor like this?"

Cairn smiled back. "I, at least, am always careful to say which is rumor and which fact."

"Then be welcome to our bazaar." Lira gestured toward the interior. "And remember my name, if you have need of it."

"Lady, I shall always have need of it." Cairn bowed and turned away, hurrying so that he wouldn't have to look at her face again after that last comment.

"Coward," Prince Orlin's voice chided. "Would you flee when you have finally plucked up the bravery for a compliment?"

"I would." Cairn swallowed thickly. "Highness, I fear I may not be well; I feel somewhat light-headed."

"I should think you would; the lady was beautiful. Yet even I would think twice ere I put out my hand to a magician."

"You don't mean I have fallen in love again!"

"Again? I didn't know you had ever fallen in love before at all!"

"Only once," Cairn confessed. "It was much more intense than this, though."

"That only means that you are still in the early stages. Do not let it bother you—it happens to the best of us," Orlin assured him. "Come to think of it, it happens to the worst of us, too. In fact, I suffer an attack of romance at least once a month."

"I defer to your greater experience. Myself, I don't quite know what to do about it."

"Have at her, of course! What else is the urge for?"

"I had the notion that it had something to do with living together all your lives, and a side effect involving children . . ."

"Nonsense! Such bondage is for peasants! Have at her, and let her worry about the consequences!"

"Consequences, yes." Cairn cleared his throat, striving for tact. "Isn't your current . . . situation . . . one such consequence, Your Highness?"

"Well, if you're going to quibble about the fine points, there's no use talking to you," Orlin grumbled, and subsided into muttering under his breath. Cairn sighed, reflecting that consequences for the prince were consequences for him—His Highness might have been able to get into trouble by himself, but he wasn't much good at getting out of it.

Cairn only had to ask directions twice before he found the marketplace—oddly, right behind the temple. The place was a regular warren, rows of stalls forming a maze. They all had a very temporary look to them, but the wooden poles were so weathered that Cairn couldn't help thinking they'd been there longer than he'd been alive.

He followed the twists and turns of one lane until he came to a large open space in the center. Breathing a sigh of relief, he dropped his pack and began to set up his stage.

"Laboring like any slave!" Prince Orlin sniffed, still invisible. "Is this charade really necessary?"

"I'm afraid it is, Your Highness," Cairn sighed. "After all, how are we to pose as puppeteers if we never perform?"

"Are you sure you know how to make the dolls dance?"

"Well, not dance, really, no," Cairn demurred, "but to make them walk about and move well enough to act out their tale? Yes—I made the old puppetman train me that well, at least, before I gave him his money. You forget that we have had to perform several times in the last two weeks."

"No, I don't," Orlin grumbled. "That's why I asked."

Cairn wisely declined comment. He finished hanging the curtains, then went inside the booth to take two exquisitely-carved marionettes out of their cloth bags. "It cost us a small fortune to buy this whole show from the old fellow!"

"My father will reimburse you as soon as we see him again," Orlin grumbled.

"When we *can*," Cairn amended.

Cairn unwound the strings, hung the puppets up, and checked for tangles or breaks, but there were none—the old puppeteer had trained him well. "I'm ready, then. Are *you*, Your Highness?"

"As ready as may be," the prince growled. "How demeaning! That a man of royal blood should have to stoop to entertaining in the marketplace!"

"Clean living would help," Cairn said dryly. Before the prince could answer, he took the tambour and went outside the curtains. He began to beat a tattoo, shouting "Hola! Come one! Come all! The tragical farce of Pyramus and Thisbe is here enacted for your enjoyment! Come one! Come all! Come see!"

Strollers looked up, then strolled over, looking interested. Children turned eagerly, then set up a clamor, begging their stall-keeper parents for a penny, pestering their customer-parents for a few minutes to watch. When a dozen people had gathered, Cairn turned his tambour over and passed it around. The spectators grudgingly dropped in their coppers. "Thank you, one and all!" Cairn managed a bow without spilling the change. "Wait just a moment, and you shall see Pyramus in miniature!" He dodged around inside the booth before anyone could protest the delay, hopped up on the bridge and called, "Ready, Your Highness!" Then he pulled the cord. The curtains opened to show a garden at the height of summer. Pyramus stepped out onto the stage; the children oohed and aahed, and one mother said to another, "He moves so naturally!"

A wall stretched down the middle of the stage—a wall with a rather large (by puppet standards) hole. Pyramus went right to that chink in the wall and called, "Thisbe! Oh, Thi-i-i-i-sbe!" in a voice remarkably like Prince Orlin's.

And there she came, fluttering out onto the stage, skirts touching the ground (for of course she had no legs), calling in a falsetto, "Oh Pyramus, my love!"

Some of the men grumbled and began to move away. "Give it a chance!" their wives hissed, and insisted on watching as the lovers set an appointment to meet at Ninus's tomb.

For a love story, it had quite a few humorous lines in it—in fact, it was quite witty; but all the wit and amusement were lost on this particular audience. The children laughed and clapped with delight, but they would have applauded anything the marionettes did. They protested loudly when the curtains closed, but Cairn called out, "No, it's not done! Only a moment, to change the scene!" He pulled the backdrop up and flipped it over the leaning rail, then pulled the cord again.

There it was, Ninus's tomb—or somebody's, under a sky painted dark blue to show that it was supposed to be night—for after all, the scene was lighted by the late afternoon sun. But there was noise outside the booth, some loud guffawing and belching, and young drunken voices sneering, "Hey, puppets!" "Come on, that's for tads!" "No, I wanna shee!"

Just what Cairn needed—a group of drunken apprentices! But he gritted his teeth and brought Thisbe on, to proclaim her fear and worry because her Pyramus wasn't there yet. Then the lion bounded onto the stage—nowhere nearly as well as the people walked, if the truth be told, but Cairn had only been a puppeteer for a few weeks—and pounced on Thisbe, who screamed and bolted. This was tricky—managing to drop the lion onto the trailing end of her cape before Cairn yanked her off the stage—but it worked, and the cape fell. The lion buried his nose in it while he roared and bellowed, and Pyramus came on in time to see the beast worrying the cloth. He gave a dreadful cry, and the lion bounded off-stage (to hoots of drunken laughter, and some angry growling in more mature voices). Pyramus rushed to catch up the fabric and weep and wail at the sight of the rips in it. He announced to the audience that Thisbe was dead, so he might as well kill himself. The young drunks agreed loudly, and the older voices snarled at them, whereupon the youngsters began to heap abuse. Pyramus turned his back on them, gave a dreadful cry, and fell with sword point sticking up between his arm and his side. Thisbe came on, gave a cry of horror, and announced that if Pyramus was dead, she had to leave this earth.

"On the mark!" a drunken apprentice laughed, and scooped her up in a hard hand. Cairn gave a shout of dismay, but had the sense to let go of the control stick, so that the thief didn't break the strings as he turned, laughing—but sure enough, he tripped on those strings, and the older men gave a shout of anger at having their show interrupted. The younger men answered with a shout of defiance, and Cairn hung Pyramus's control stick over the backdrop while he jumped down and dashed out of the booth to see older men squaring off against younger. So far, no fists were flying, only abuse . . .

"Peace!" a voice thundered, and a watchman appeared from nowhere, half as wide as any of the men and a head taller. "Stop this brawling!"

Actually, it hadn't started yet, but Cairn wasn't about to quibble. The watchman took in the stage and the stolen puppet in a glance, then glared at the thief and said, in a voice of doom, "Is that yours?"

"Wh . . . yes!" The young man—a teenager, really—straightened up, looking as truculent as he could while weaving on his feet. He blinked bleary eyes and said, " 'Tis now!"

"And whose was it a minute ago?" The watchman looked over at Cairn.

"His, watchman!" One of the older men pointed to Cairn. "The boy yanked it right off the stage!"

The watchman didn't say anything, just held out a hand. The boy glared at him, then slapped the puppet into the broad palm and turned away, grumbling—but the watchman stopped him with a broad hand. "I told you boys not to drink so much! Home with you, now, and don't come back to this marketplace today!"

Looking sullen, the teenagers retreated, leaning on one another. The watchman turned to give the puppet back to Cairn. "Drunken apprentices! They're my biggest trial. They'll grow to be good men, though, so we must put up with their antics and not be too harsh on them."

"Very true," Cairn said, surprised at the man's understanding.

The audience members were moving away, with exclamations of disappointment. "No, wait!" Cairn called. "I'll finish . . ."

"No, you won't." The watchman clapped his other hand on Cairn's shoulder. He gave the puppet back, but demanded, "Where's your license?"

Cairn stared blankly. "License?"

"Surely, a license," the watchman said. "None can vend their wares in this marketplace without permission from the temple, whose land this is! Go and get one straightaway, or *I'll* shut you down myself!" Then he frowned. "What's that growling?"

"Only my stomach," Cairn said quickly. "I'll go for that license right now, sir, and thank you!" He turned away, spinning the marionette to twist its strings, then wound them around the control stick. As he dropped it into its bag and pulled the drawstring, Orlin snapped, "Your stomach indeed! You knew I was about to give that watchman the tongue lashing he deserved!"

"Yes, and that's why I went out of there so quickly," Cairn told him. "Besides, he *didn't* deserve it—he was just doing his job, part of which was getting my puppet back! How could we do the play with no Thisbe?"

"We shouldn't do it at all! You wooden-headed lunk! How dare you endanger my royal person!"

"I didn't endanger you." Cairn began to take down the curtains. "Only Thisbe."

"But it could have been me! You'll have to be a great deal more careful in the future, Cairn! What will you tell my father if I've been kidnapped?"

That you couldn't keep your hands to yourself, Cairn thought, but he didn't say it. Instead, he packed up the stage and went to find a monk.

He found two, and they insisted on seeing his play to make sure it contained nothing immoral. Cairn went along with it philosophically—just two more people trying to sneak a free performance. The monks seemed rather disappointed to find the play so completely moral, but they made a valiant try. "Kissing, right there in front of the audience? No, doll man, that will never do!"

"Well, I suppose the play can manage without the kiss . . ."

"And the word 'bloody,' when Pyramus picked up her cloak! In fact, the blood itself! Obscenity, Master Cairn, obscenity!"

Cairn stared. He had heard that "bloody" was an obscenity in a land far away, but certainly not here. "Without the bloo—excuse me, the mauled mantle, though, there is no reason for Pyramus to slay himself!"

"You really shouldn't show that onstage," the other monk sniffed.

"But without it, I'd have no show!"

"Don't be an ass, Cairn," Prince Orlin whispered. "Grease their palms!"

Cairn stared at the monks, shocked. Bribes for holy men?

"There is also the matter of the license fee for our

holy temple," the older monk said stiffly. "Do you truly have a single gold piece to your name?"

"No gold, but several silvers." Cairn pulled them from his purse and counted twelve into the monk's palm, accidentally letting two more drop in. "Twelve silvers is equal to one gold in value."

"Very true, very true," the monk sniffed, and the money vanished up his sleeve. "Well, if you're careful to keep all obscenities from your little farce, Master Cairn, you may perform in our marketplace."

The younger monk nodded, made a flourish with his pen, and handed Cairn the finished scrap of paper. "Show that to the watchman if he asks. You may have the fourth space in the second row—the carpet seller who had his stall there died last week, without an heir. You should do good business just from customers who come looking for him."

Cairn thanked them and turned away, somewhat shaken. In fact, he was so unnerved that he didn't even notice his surroundings until a gentle voice asked, "What troubles you, puppetman?"

"Whuh!" Cairn looked up, startled—and saw the pretty magician at his elbow. "Oh! Your pardon, lady. I had not seen you come up."

"No, nor seen me watching that performance you gave the monks just now, either—had you?"

"I had not," Cairn confessed. "I was too much concerned with their carping."

"They will bend many rules for the good of their temple. Does that bother you so badly?"

"I'm afraid it does. Still, it's not for themselves, I suppose . . ."

"For themselves, they have very little concern, which makes them all the more intent on the good of the temple."

Cairn nodded. "Certainly they don't look as though they're wasting any great sum of money on themselves—

even their robes are threadbare, though I have to admit they're scrupulously clean."

"Their robes, or themselves?" Lira asked with a smile.

"Both." Cairn found himself returning her smile—and wishing he could stare at it all day; it was certainly the best thing that had happened to him since he had become Prince Orlin's companion.

"But I could see, by watching your performance, that you are not very skilled," Lira told him. "You haven't been a puppeteer very long, have you?"

"Not at all,' Cairn admitted. Alarms coursed through him.

"In fact, you bought this show only a few weeks ago, and learned barely enough to pretend to your craft, didn't you?"

Cairn stared, appalled.

"Come, I will not betray you," Lira's voice sank low. "You certainly didn't come to this city to make money, when there are many puppeteers here, and all of them much better than yourself. Why *have* you come?"

Cairn gave her a long look, deep into her eyes, and felt his heart turn over. Trustworthy or not, he knew he was going to confide in her. Still, he hedged it as much as he could. "You have found me out, lady. I have come to the city to find a magician who can break a spell cast by another of his profession."

Her face didn't change, but somehow Cairn knew she was disappointed, massively disappointed. Amazed, he wondered why. She forced a smile, though. "Breaking another's spell requires a rather powerful magician, puppetman. In fact, those who have gained that much knowledge and skill have usually retired from commerce, and work only by special arrangement."

"Which means very expensively." Cairn felt his stomach sink.

"Very," Lira agreed. "I doubt that a simple puppeteer could afford the services of such a one."

Despair struck. "Then what am I to do?"

"Seek out a middle-ranking magician with a very different kind of magic," Lira counselled.

Cairn frowned. "What kind would that be? And where could I find such a one?"

"I may be able to arrange a meeting," Lira told him. "Do you need to counter a love philtre, or an anti-love philtre?"

Cairn gazed at her for a moment, impressed by her insight but also by how far she was from the mark. "It does have to do with love," he admitted.

"So I had thought," Lira sighed. "Well, if you will excuse me, I must go back to the temple, for it is in their hostel for single women that I lodge."

"Oh, of course!" Cairn said. "I'm sorry for having taken you so far out of your way."

"I hope you are lying," she said, with one last half-hearted attempt at a smile, then turned and was gone.

Cairn stared after her, wondering, "How did I offend?"

"By saying you needed a counterspell for love, you ass!" Prince Orlin's voice hissed. "Can't you see the woman's intrigued with you?"

"Intrigued?" Cairn stared at the retreating, slender back. "A magician, a *beautiful* magician, intrigued with *me?*"

"There's no accounting for taste," Prince Orlin grunted. "Still, I would have said the lady was pretty, but scarcely beautiful."

"Oh, no! A beauty, surely!"

"Perhaps to *you*," the prince grumbled, "and you seem to have some magic of your own, for her to be interested in your ugly countenance. Take my advice, lad, and exploit that interest while you may. Who knows? Perhaps you can exploit it all the way into her bed before you leave this city."

Cairn recoiled from the suggestion, and hot words sprang to his tongue—but he swallowed them, reflecting that he would surely have indigestion as a result, and ignored the prince's cynical advice, saying only, "The sun is low. We had better seek an inn."

"You already have an in—with her," Orlin chuckled, "and if you aren't a total fool ..."

Cairn did the best he could to ignore the very detailed advice that followed.

If there was one thing to be said for Orlin's father, it was that he had given the two young men plenty of money—and knowing them both, he had given most of it to Cairn. "Let your knight-companion be your beast of burden, boy," he had told Orlin. "Why should you be vexed with keeping watch over your own purse?" The prince could accept that, so even though Sir Cairn now masqueraded as Cairn the Commoner, he was a very well-heeled commoner indeed.

Nonetheless, they had to keep up appearances, so Cairn set up his stage one more time that evening and beat his tambour as the sun was setting. This time he attracted a very different sort of crowd, if a dozen people can be called that—all adult, all well-dressed: merchants and master artisans, out to enjoy the evening air and buy a few trinkets if they found anything to their fancies. But when Pyramus set foot on the stage, one of the "merchants" raised a tipsy cry of delight. "Orlin! Surely that puppet is a caricature of Prince Orlin!"

The puppet froze in place.

"Oh, well done, puppetman! You have caught him perfectly—the perpetual leer, the effeminate gestures, even the mincing gait that we see as he comes into the Great Hall!"

"It is Lord Natherby," Prince Orlin's voice hissed.

"What is he doing *here*, dressed like a merchant?" Cairn hissed back.

"Slumming," the prince grated.

Lord Natherby didn't hear, of course—he was having much too much fun ridiculing his prince. "You have shown him for what he is—the quintessential fop! Your puppet lacks only the sneer he gives at the slightest hint of disagreement!"

The puppet turned slowly, as though searching for its tormentor beyond the stage, and the unseen nobleman gave a shout of delight. "There it is, the very sneer! Oh, bravely done, showman! But how? What magic is this, that you can make a puppet's face change its expression?"

The other audience members began to grumble, and one said, "Ask him after the show, graybeard! We want to see how it ends!"

"For that matter, we want to see how it begins," said another.

The aristocrat turned to face them, drawing himself up to his full height and looking down his nose at them in haughty disdain. "I am Mosaht Lord Natherby, and you will hold your tongues until my curiosity is satisfied!"

A couple of other men stepped up beside him, drawing back their cloaks to show the swords at their hips. The commoners muttered in surprise and drew away. Lord Natherby gave a bark of laughter and turned back to the stage. "Now, puppeteer! How did you bring about this change of expression?"

Cairn had hung up the control sticks and come down, leaving the puppets sitting limp and lifeless on the stage. "It is an old trick, sir." He thanked heaven that the old puppeteer had told him about it. "One side of the face is carved into a smile." He held up Pyramus's head in profile. "The other side is carved into a frown. To make the puppet change expressions, you merely turn him around." Gently, he rotated Pyramus's head, and sure enough, the puppet was no longer smiling, but frowning.

"And when you look at him from the front, he sneers!" Lord Natherby clapped his hands like a child. "How wonderful, puppeteer! And how simple! Come now, finish your show! The audience is waiting."

"Uh—no longer, Your Lordship." Cairn looked up to find that the spectators, bored or frightened, had faded away.

"No matter! I wish to see it!" Natherby declared imperiously. "On with it, puppetman! Show me a show!"

What choice did Cairn have?

Natherby applauded and hooted all the way through, so loudly that Cairn was amazed the man could hear the dialogue—but when it was done, the lord's silver in his pocket, and the man himself gone away, Cairn wasted no time in dismantling his stage. "You were the very picture of self-control, Your Highness! Not a line missed, not a word out of place!"

"The old puppeteer told us that the show must go on," Orlin grated, "though he didn't say why. Still, I knew I would be in danger if I gave away the whole imposture. I wonder how the puppets can stand it!"

Cairn wondered how the puppeteers did. "How did you make it through?"

"By imagining all the revenges I'll heap on Lord Natherby when I've regained my rightful place in the world! Hurry, Cairn—I wish to be safe in our room at the inn, where I may swear and rage in peace!"

Peace, however, they were not about to have. As Cairn trudged back to the inn, his steps dragging with weariness and the weight of his pack, a hulking form stepped out from behind a booth to block his path. "There's gold in your purse, puppetman," the thug snarled. "I want it."

Cairn looked up with a thrill of fear—but with it came the knight's savage delight in a fight fully justified. "I have no gold."

"Silver, then! There must be a lot of that, for we saw all those rich merchants around your stage! Give it here!"

A fighting grin tugged at Cairn's lips. "Come and take it."

"You heard him, boys," the thug said, and footsteps sounded behind Cairn. Adrenaline rushed through his veins; he pivoted aside and caught up a stick of firewood lying beside a food vendor's stall. As the first thug bore down on him, Cairn feinted at the man's head, then shoved the club into his stomach. The man doubled over with pain, but his mate came in low and swinging hard, left-right-left. Cairn met the first two blows with his club, trying to pivot aside, cursing his heavy and cumbersome pack—and the third blow caught him square in the chest. Breathless for a moment, he swung his club high anyway—and felt hands on his back, felt the straps abruptly give way and the pack's weight vanish. He spun about, shouting in anger—a double shout, for the unseen prince howled, too. Cairn leaped after the third thug, seeing the whetted knife, the cleanly-cut straps—and a mallet seemed to hit him from behind. He clutched at the nearest stall, trying to do nothing but hold himself upright while the world swam around him. Confused shouting filtered through the pain with the sound of running feet, and another blow doubled him over with pain.

Then a fireball exploded, clearing his head amazingly. He saw the thugs fleeing and started after them, knowing he could never catch them when he was still hobbled by pain—but they suddenly stopped to swat at something unseen, howling with agony and pressing hands to their faces, their bellies, their buttocks.

"Bees!"

"Draw their stingers! Kill them!"

"I can't see them! They're not there!"

Invisible bees?

Never mind! Cairn sprinted, caught up with them, and wrenched the pack out of the hands of the biggest thug. The man turned to him in a rage, then arched backward with a howl of pain. "My feet! What's wrong with my feet?" He fell, and his two comrades followed him, holding their feet and bellowing.

Cairn stared in amazement, leaning against the pack and heaving deep breaths.

"Kick them! Club them!" Prince Orlin raged. "Hurt them while you can, for what they would have done to me!"

Cairn only shook his head, still gasping.

"Can't you protect me any better than that, idiot?" the prince raged.

"With all ... due respect, Your Highness," Cairn panted, "you can drop ..."

"Now, now! Is that any way to thank me?"

Cairn turned, staring. A chubby, graying man stood at his elbow, nodding toward the thugs. "Their feet are full of the jabbing of pins and needles, puppeteer. It might be a good time for you to make your escape."

"Good idea!" Cairn hefted the pack by the remains of its straps and hurried off into the night—or at least, hurried as much as a man can with a pack that's both large and heavy. Cursing under his breath, he reminded himself to invest in a barrow.

When he was sure he had put enough space between himself and the thugs, he dropped the stage and leaned on it to regain his wind and tell the chubby graying man, "I can't thank you enough. You *are* the one who saved us?"

"The same," the man said, with a slight bow. "I am Yakob. My young friend Lira told me that you were in need of magical assistance." He chuckled. "I see that she was right."

"Yes, well, I hadn't been thinking of those three baboons when I told her that," Cairn said. "Thank you from the depths of my heart, Master Yakob."

Yakob waved away the thanks. "It was nothing—or at least, very little. Lira tells me you have a far more challenging task for me, eh?"

"I do," Cairn admitted, "if you're willing to undertake it."

"Ah! So I had hoped!" Yakob nodded briskly, his eyes gleaming. "Therefore I came looking for you, and seem to have found you at the right time."

"Right time indeed," Cairn agreed fervently, "and very grateful I am, too." He reached for his purse. "May I show you gratitude in more tangible form, Master Yakob?"

Yakob laughed and pressed his hand away. "It is little

enough, Master Cairn. I will include it in the price of whatever more exotic spell you need, for it's sure to be far more costly—if it works. If it does not, *then* I will charge you for this minor bit of warding. But come, let us discuss it at my house!" He clapped Cairn on the shoulder and led him away.

His house was quite modest, but it was close to the temple and the marketplace, and radiated a feeling of warmth and security even as he closed the door behind them. He led Cairn into the big central room, then laid out bread, cheese, and wine. "Dine, young fellow! For surely, youth has keen appetites, and you have the look of one who has not fed well in some time."

"Thank you, Master Yakob!" Cairn set down the puppet stage and fell to. Yakob sat by, sipping wine and watching him eat with a pleased smile. When Cairn sat back with a sigh, Yakob said, "Now, about this spell you are needing . . ."

"Yes, the spell." Cairn got up, went to the pack, and opened it. "It's a rather unusual situation, Master Yakob." He took out the puppet Pyramus and brought him back to the table. "Your Highness, somewhere we must trust someone, and you'll just have to take the risk of trusting Master Yakob."

"Well, if I must, I must," Orlin's voice grumbled. The puppet sat up, slipped the bracelets that were attached to the strings off its ankles and wrists, and stood up, hands on hips, to face Yakob, giving him an imperious glare.

"You see, Master Yakob," Cairn said, "we need to break a spell that shrank a tall man down to a height of a foot and a half."

Yakob simply stared.

"Don't you *dare* laugh," the diminutive Prince Orlin commanded.

"I assure you that I never laugh at magic," Yakob said, recovering from his surprise. "May I ask your name?"

"Master Yakob," said Cairn, "may I present His

Highness, Prince Orlin of Vagratin, Knight of the Anklet and heir to the throne."

Yakob went back to staring. Finally, he said, "A prince under so doughty a spell! This will be a weighty business indeed!"

"He does weigh considerably more than most puppets," Cairn admitted, "though nowhere nearly as much as a grown man, thank heaven!"

Getting down to cases seemed to revive Yakob a bit. "Are you stronger than your size would lead you to expect, Your Highness? Do you seem to have boundless energy?"

"Oh, yes!" Prince Orlin balled a diminutive fist. "And my muscles have never been so hard!"

"It is to be expected." Yakob nodded. "When you cram all the mass of a grown man into a body the size of an infant's, the flesh will be compacted, growing much harder. Even then most of it will evaporate, though, and take the form of energy. I take it there was pain?"

"Pain! It was sheer agony!" The prince shuddered at the memory.

Yakob nodded. "He may weigh only a fifth as much as he used to, Master Cairn, but I dare say he could carry his own weight, and the whole stage, too!"

"*Sir* Cairn," Prince Orlin corrected, just to be difficult.

"Sir?" Master Yakob looked up at Cairn. "Well, well! A prince and a knight both! I am honored!"

"We will be more honored," Cairn told him, "if you can break the spell that binds His Highness."

"Well. As to that, I must know more about it." Suddenly Yakob became all business again. "You must tell me how you came to this predicament, Your Highness, for I cannot treat you if I do not know all I can about the spell, and the conditions under which it was cast."

"Must I really?" Orlin demanded pettishly. He looked up at Cairn. "It's bad enough having you know about it, but a stranger?"

"I don't see how he can possibly help if he doesn't

know the whole story," Cairn sighed. "We had better tell him, Your Highness."

"Well, if I must, I must." Prince Orlin turned back to the magician. "You see, I made overtures to Lord Thraik's daughter—"

"Lord Thraik!" Yakob's eyebrows tried to climb into his vanished hairline. "The most powerful magician in the kingdom? He whose power is so great that he defended the realm from an attacking navy all by himself? He who was born the son of a knight but ennobled because of his services to the Crown? He who has become the most powerful lord in the land, whom none dare defy?"

"Yes, *that* Lord Thraik," Prince Orlin admitted. He actually had the grace to look embarrassed.

"You're very right," Cairn told him. "*None* dare defy him."

"So I see! And what form did this defiance take? Surely not mere overtures!"

"I'm afraid my prince went well beyond the overture," Cairn said. "He was past the intermission and almost to the finale when Lord Thraik walked in."

Prince Orlin grumbled. "I should have expected a wizard to put some sort of watchdog spell on his daughter! I'll wager that when I touched her knee, it started alarms clanging inside Lord Thraik's head. He came on the run and waved his hand, changing me to the size of a doll just as I was about to make a woman of her!"

"To break her heart, you mean!" Cairn couldn't keep his tongue still any longer. "Just as you were about to finalize your seduction of her, you told her that this would be all there would be to your romance!"

Yakob stared, aghast. "Why?"

Prince Orlin shrugged impatiently. "It is the final sauce to the banquet of seduction."

"A sauce of great cruelty! Can you have pleasure only by another's pain?"

"Pain? What mattered her pain? She was being honored by a prince!"

Yakob's face settled into stern, forbidding lines. "I doubt that she thought of it as an honor."

"The maiden burst into tears," Cairn said grimly.

Yakob nodded. "Tears which were the alarm that brought her father, I doubt not." He looked up at Cairn. "How do you know such details?"

Prince Orlin grumbled, "I was rattled enough right after the event to tell it all, and Cairn was the one to talk to, since he is a knight by rank, and paid to be my drinking companion besides."

Yakob nodded, eyes still on Carin's. "If I were you, I would consider a change of occupation."

"So I shall, when this is ended—but I cannot leave my charge in such a predicament."

"Even if it is the consequence of his own crimes?"

"It was not I who did it, but Lord Thraik!" Prince Orlin shouted.

Yakob fixed him with a penetrating stare. "I know Lord Thraik by reputation, at least. The man is said to be hard, but fair. Has he set no term to your punishment?"

"Well—yes," the prince admitted. "I am to stay this size until I marry one of the women I have seduced—and I would rather die than wed!"

"But not stay small?" Yakob asked.

"Well—no," Prince Orlin admitted. "Marriage can't be worse than this!"

Yakob looked up at Cairn. "Is there no alternative?"

"Oh, yes," Cairn said. "He can stay a mannikin until he has learned enough of the pain of the weak and lowly so that Thraik can be sure he won't commit so calloused a crime again!"

"From which pain you seek to shield him," Yakob pointed out.

"Well . . . yes. But I don't succeed completely."

Yakob gave him a bleak smile, then transferred his gaze to the puppet prince again. "I'm surprised that your father the king has not commanded Lord Thraik to undo the spell."

"Well—he hasn't," Orlin grumbled. Yakob raised a questioning glance to Cairn, who admitted, "His Majesty hasn't been told; my prince feared that his father too would insist his son marry."

"Yes, I had thought the king was just," Yakob said, with a grim nod. "So that is why you have no bodyguards, no other royal train, and are going about in disguise?"

"Yes," Cairn confirmed. "It was a stroke of great good fortune to find an old puppeteer who was seeking to sell his show—it's the ideal hiding place for a man of Prince Orlin's new size, especially since his flesh has become as hard as wood. Can you help us, Master Yakob? Or must my prince suffer humiliation and poverty to earn his proper size again?"

"I *should* say that he must," Yakob growled, "for I am most inclined to agree with Lord Thraik. But I told Lira that I would help if I could, so I will try—though why she would wish to aid such a reprobate as this, is more than I can understand!"

Cairn's pulse quickened as he remembered that it was he whom the lady had wished to help, not the prince of whom she knew nothing—but under the circumstances, he didn't think it politic to mention it.

Yakob stood up and beckoned, leading the way into a back room—but what a room! It was easily as large as the rest of the ground floor put together, and the walls were filled with shelves crowded with jars and bottles of liquids and powders in all manners of colors and textures. A long workbench stood at one side of the room, filled with bowls of metal and stone, mortars and pestles, and other items of metal and glass of which Cairn couldn't possibly have guessed the purposes. The floor, surprisingly, was sand, except for a narrow wooden walkway around the edges.

Yakob took a staff and began to pace around the large open area in the middle, jabbing the foot of the pole into the sand. "If my magic were based on inborn gifts alone, Your Highness, a very ordinary, middling magus like me would never be able to dream of breaking a spell cast by a master like Lord Thraik."

"But your magic is of another kind?" Cairn remembered what Lira had told him.

"A very different kind," Yakob confirmed. "A little bit of talent, but a great deal of knowlege—yes, I have studied all my life—knowledge of numbers and figures, geometrical figures, of the harmony underlying all of creation and the ways of expressing that harmony in sums and differences . . . well, there is a chance. If your diminutive size is *out* of harmony with the rest of the universe, Your Highness, then perhaps I can restore you to your true size. If not, well . . ."

"You mean if my present size is my proper size?" Prince Orlin cried, outraged.

"I did not say that," Yakob hedged, "and certainly the size of a person's body very rarely has anything to do with the size of his soul. Still, there is a chance, however slight—but mind you, it is only slight in any case, for Lord Thraik is a magician of formidable power." He strode out into the center of the floor and inscribed a circle with the foot of his staff. "Now! Stand there, Your Highness, while I light the brazier."

"What for?" the prince asked, taking his place with trepidation.

"To establish the proper mood, the ambiance that will render the fluidity of the dynamics of the universe more apparent, more open to adjustment . . . You said there was pain when you shrank to your present size, Your Highness?"

"Pain? Agony! Agony unbearable! I would have gone mad from it, if it had endured much longer!"

Yakob nodded, seeming satisfied somehow. "Then be prepared for such pain again, for as you shrank, so must you grow. . . . Now!"

Flame sprang up from the brazier with a whoosh, and

the room seemed to darken. Yakob held up his hands, the staff level between them, and began to recite an incantation, one that went on and on in a language that seemed to be spoken straight from his throat, filled with l's and gutturals. The room continued to darken, and Cairn held tight to the nearest bookshelf. Surely it was only his imagination that a feeling of tension was building in the room, building and growing; surely it was his imagination that Yakob seemed to be having greater and greater difficulty holding that staff above his head, as though it were growing heavier and heavier . . .

Sparks jumped from the sand all about the room and met above the prince's head in a soundless explosion—but Cairn felt the impact of their meeting even though he didn't hear it: a crack like the breaking of a staff, but Yakob's pole remained intact. He staggered under the sudden release of weight, though, as light returned to the room and the flames in the brazier died.

The magician leaned on his staff, panting and trembling. Cairn rushed to his side, but Yakob waved him away. "Not me—him! Be sure the prince is well!"

Cairn whirled and rushed out into the sand. Prince Orlin still stood, but was shaking so hard that Cairn thought he might come apart. The knight dropped to his knees. "Highness! Are you well?"

Orlin moved trembling lips, but no sound came out. Cairn felt panic surge, but Yakob's weary voice stilled it. "He is badly shaken, but nothing more—as any of us would be, with an implosion like that right over our heads."

Cairn turned slowly. "The universe likes him this size?"

"No," Yakob sighed. "A larger prince would be more harmonious, though I can't think why. It is simply that Lord Thraik's spell is too strong. Even approaching it from the different orientation of my numerology, I have succeeded only in disrupting the fringe of the spell—for which, praise heaven! If that was the power unleashed by the edge, spare me from thinking what the center would be!"

"It is hopeless, then?" Oddly, Cairn felt a sense of relief—a relief that died as the magician said, "No. It is only that my magic is not strong enough. There is one magician who might help us, however—a senior cleric in the temple, who has been studying magic for a lifetime. I will take you there—but I promise nothing. The cleric may not choose to help you—or may not be able to. Lord Thraik is, after all, a most powerful adversary indeed!"

"Nonethelees, we are grateful," Cairn assured him. "Especially after you have worn yourself out for us already! However can I thank you, Master Yakob?"

"You cannot." The magician mustered hidden reserves and straightened, pointing at the miniature prince. "*He* can!"

The trembling lips moved; a sort of cawing came out, that modulated into words. "I . . . I thank . . . you, Master . . . Yakob."

The magician nodded slowly, a gleam of approval in his eye. "And you are welcome, Your Highness. However, the senior cleric will choose thanks that must be expressed in deeds, not words alone. Come, to the temple!"

Yakob led them to the temple, the prince in a large pouch that Cairn slung over his shoulder; Orlin complained about the bumping, but it was certainly a load off Cairn's back. They joined the line of worshipers who were filing in for evening prayers—but once inside, Yakob split off from the stream and moved toward a small stairway that led downward. A bald-headed guard who wore a breastplate over his monk's robe came alert and raised his spear, frowning, but Yakob only smiled and waved at the man, and he lowered his weapon, though he still looked unsure as Cairn went past him.

"You're known here," the knight commented.

Yakob nodded. "As I say, my magic is different from

that which the clerics know, and I come to discuss metaphysics with them from time to time."

He led his charges though an inconspicuous passageway to a chamber whose door stood ajar. Nonetheless, Yakob knocked, and a female voice called, "Who is it?"

"Yakob, lady," the magician answered, but Cairn's blood was already thrilling at the sound of her voice. "Enter," she called, and Yakob pushed the door open, leading him into a small room lighted by several tiny windows and lined with books. Under a lamp sat Lira, with a volume in front of her. Cairn's heart leaped, but he managed to keep his smile from growing too broad and said only, "I thank you, lady, for sending your friend to my aid."

"Cairn! How delightful to see you again!" Lira laid down her book and rose, almost seeming to float as she went to meet him, hand outstretched. He caught it; he couldn't help himself, he had to kiss it, and the skin was marvelously soft. So was her laughter. "You are quite the courtier, sir!"

Cairn released her hand and couldn't keep the grin from growing. "I think you know more about me than I would like, lady."

"Do I indeed! And what would you want me *not* to know?"

Prince Orlin saved Cairn from answering by clearing his throat loudly. Lira frowned. "Your pouch seems to have a touch of catarrh, Sir Cairn."

How had she known he was a knight? "I fear it holds a burden of impatience, lady."

"Burden of impatience indeed!" Orlin snapped. "Will you cease your blithering and let me out of this lightless hole?"

"Yes, do release him, whatever he is." Lira was frowning as she resumed her seat. "What have you brought me, puppetman?"

"I would not thrust my burdens upon you, lady," Cairn began, but she cut him off with a gesture. "Would or not, you have. Let him out." Cairn sighed, set his pouch on the desktop, and opened the flap. Prince Orlin leaped out and stood glowering at Lira, hands on his hips, nodding at her start of surprise. "Aye, Prince Orlin himself, the victim of a villainous spell! Be so good as to summon your master, girl, for I have important matters to discuss with him."

Anger flashed in Lira's eyes, but only for an instant before she became all puzzled innocence. "My master? But why would a prince want to speak to the Chief Priest? Are you thinking of making a huge donation? If you aren't, surely he would be as likely to auction you off as a curiosity, as to talk with you!"

"Girl, you speak to the prince of Vagratin!" Orlin thundered.

"Of Vagratin, perhaps," Lira responded cooly, "but not of myself, or of my city."

Orlin began to swell with rage, but Yakob interrupted quickly. "The Lady Lira is herself one of the senior clerics, Your Highness."

"A senior cleric?" Orlin stared. "This slip of a girl?"

Lira smiled at his discomfiture. "This 'slip of a girl,' Prince, could turn you to a toad in an instant—aye, and conjure up a snake to eat you, too."

Prince Orlin paled. "You wouldn't dare!"

Again, Yakob interrupted smoothly. "Lady Lira was raised in the temple precincts, due to her piety—and her dying father's huge donation. She began serious study of magic before she was twelve. Accordingly, she has been learning for fifteen years, and has gained so much knowledge, and controls so much power, that the senior clerics were forced to count her among their number."

Cairn suspected that Lira had also inherited her father's wealth when she turned twenty-one—but surely that could have had no bearing on the clerics' decision!

Prince Orlin stared, quite taken aback and, for a wonder, silenced—but Lira demanded, "Why have you come to me, Prince?" Cairn started to explain, but she silenced him with a raised hand. "No. He must tell me himself, or I'll not aid him in any way."

Anger brought Orlin out of his trance, but he needed Lira's help, so he throttled the emotion and began to explain. She held his gaze with her own, and as the tale progressed, Cairn could see that the prince began to try to glance away, but somehow couldn't—he had to look straight into the lady's eyes even as he told her what he had done to Lord Thraik's daughter. Then, somehow, he was telling her what he had done to other women before the lord's daughter, and others, and others, until his tale began to take on much more the tone of a shamed confession than a history. Lira only listened, asking a question from time to time—but at the end of it all, demanding, "And are these deeds to boast of, Prince?"

Orlin admitted, "No. I see now that in every case, I preyed upon one far weaker than myself, who was really within my power, and could scarcely say 'nay' even if she wanted to."

Lira nodded slowly. "Is this the way a monarch protects his people?"

"No." Finally, Prince Orlin hung his head. "I see that now—that these were not conquests, but exploitations. There is nothing to be proud of in this." His mouth twisted, and Cairn realized with a shock that the prince was filled with self-contempt. The lady really did have powerful magic!

"You should indeed be ashamed," Lira agreed, "and Lord Thraik's punishment is just. Why should I help you escape it?"

"Because I am a prince?" But it was a very half-hearted attempt at an excuse.

"Because you shall some day inherit the crown of Vagratin? But your conduct thus far makes me doubt that your people will be well governed by so selfish a prince. Still, I shall try to help you for Cairn's sake, and Yakob's."

"Will you truly?" The prince looked up, amazed, then

glanced at Cairn and Yakob as though wondering what magic *they* possessed.

"As to Lord Thraik's daughter," Lira went on, "and the other women you have debauched, I suspect they are probably better off free of you. They may know anguish for a few months, but if you wed any one of them, I am sure you would give her far more grief in the rest of her life than pleasure or even relief now."

Prince Orlin winced.

"Yes, I will try to break Lord Thraik's spell after all," Lira sighed, "but there is grave risk in it. Even if I succeed, you will feel great pain—and if I fail, the magic may kill you. Do you still want me to try?"

Orlin's face showed inner turmoil as he debated the matter briefly within himself. Finally, he said slowly, "All I have ever wanted from life is pleasure, and there is a great deal of that even for one who is only eighteen inches high."

"There is some truth in that," Lira said, her voice colorless. "A prince does, after all, have many privileges."

"But pleasured or not, I would always be at other men's mercy," the prince went on. "My words, my commands, would never be taken seriously even if I *did* inherit the throne. My courtiers would fight for possession of me, then terrorize me into ruling as they wished. . . ." He shuddered. "Death is surely better than being a slave king!"

"And?" Lira said inexorably.

"And . . ." Orlin continued reluctantly, ". . . besides . . . I now begin to feel that there might be something more to life than mere pleasure—or, rather, pleasures other than those of the flesh."

"Such as the satisfaction of a wise decision, or of governing well?" Lira nodded, satisfied. "Yes, I will try to break Lord Traik's spell. Come, I shall lead you to the inner sanctum."

She rose—and above them, they heard a sudden, tremendous groaning. In the distance, voices shouted in alarm and terror; huge piles of masonry crashed. Prince Orlin screamed as his puppet costume ripped assunder, torn by ballooning muscles as he swelled, growing fantastically right before their eyes. He howled, he bellowed, "Make it stop! Please make it stop!"

Yakob and Lira were both sawing the air with their hands, shouting incantations, but Cairn couldn't hear them over the prince's wailing. "My finest spell for easing pain!" Yakob shouted. "It doesn't work!"

"Nor mine!" Lira cried. "The magic has gone away! I feel it! There is no longer any power for me to draw on! Quick, massage him! Lessen his pain! I must go to see what I can do to help protect the temple!"

She ran from the room; Yakob and Cairn set themselves to massaging. "You are whole; you are not injured!" Yakob cried. "The pain is only the soreness of muscles suddenly grown!" He kept exhorting and reassuring as he kneaded limbs shuddering with spasms, and the prince's screams began to lessen, finally ceasing, and he was able to tell them to stop. "You can do no more! Your pummelling hurts now!" They stopped, and the prince lay inert, groaning.

Yakob rose and went to a little worktable at the side of Lira's chamber, where he gathered up herbs and mixed them with water. He brought it back to the moaning prince. "Drink!"

"What good will it do?" Orlin groaned. "There's no more magic to ease my pain!"

"This doesn't require magic!" Yakob snapped. "Only knowledge of herbs! Drink!"

Any chance was worth taking. Orlin drank, and began to relax as the potion soaked into him. He was almost able to sit up when Lira finally came back, dishevelled and exhausted—but she held out her hands, making passes over the prince's inert body and muttering a brief incantation before she collapsed into her chair.

"What good can your spell do," Cairn asked, "if magic no longer works?"

"We don't know why it stopped—so it might come back at any moment," Lira told him. She raised her head at the distant clash of arms. "Robbers seek to loot the temple, but the guards are stopping them. Let us hope the magic comes back before the robbers triumph!"

"*I* don't," Prince Orlin groaned.

"Oh, don't worry, Your Highness," Lira said, with a flash of anger. "Even if the magic comes back, the spell I cast should hold you in your present form."

"Should?" Orlin asked in a hollow tone.

"Should," Lira repeated firmly. "There is no certainty—but when the magic went away, it broke Lord Thraik's spell, and he will probably have to recast it—if he deems you worth the trouble."

Prince Orlin looked up indignantly, but just then, the clash of arms stopped, and even more distant shouts and cries began. Lira stiffened, staring, then ran from the room without a word.

"What's the matter with her?" Prince Orlin groaned.

"I think the magic has come back," Cairn answered.

The prince stiffened, braced against pain, then stared in amazement. "It's true, even as she said! The spell's broken!"

"Let's hope Lord Thraik doesn't remember you," Cairn said.

Lira came back, her smile radiant through her exhaustion. "The magic has begun again! There has been much damage and many lives lost, but the city will return to its normal self!"

"I hope that's good," Orlin said with apprehension.

"If it weren't, your father would have no power; his rank depends on the strength of the city." Lira looked him over as though just noticing him, and the prince, unclothed, blushed and turned away. "My spell is holding," Lira said, "which means that the purpose of Lord Thraik's spell is fulfilled. Yakob, will you assist the prince out, to find some sort of clothing? I must have a few words with his companion."

Against all logic, Cairn's heartbeat increased. He knew she only wished to discuss the prince, but a man could hope. . . .

Lira saw the prince go out the door and nodded with satisfaction, then turned to Cairn. "Do you think he has learned anything?"

"Something," Cairn said slowly—more slowly still, due to disappointment, "but respect for the poor, or for women? No, lady, I cannot be sure of that."

"He has gained a little," she told him, "by feeling the pain he used to cause others, and by experiencing their humilation. He has gained that much at least, or Lord Thraik's spell would have returned."

She spoke with the authority of one who knows magic, but Cairn knew his prince. "I hope you are right," he said slowly, "but I doubt Orlin can ever be anything but self-centered, even with the example of your compassion and selflessness before him."

Her smile was radiant, but she assured him, "I want things for myself, too, Sir Cairn." Her eyelids drooped, and the way her gaze seemed to pierce through to his core made Cairn's pulse quicken with hope again. "Then you are human after all, lady—but surely a mere knight should not aspire to the hand of a lady who is so powerful that she could obliterate him with a word and a gesture."

"Very true," Lira said, her voice low and husky, "but a knight who has kept a prince safe through such misadventures as Orlin has had, and even found a way to save him from the revenge of Lord Thraik, must surely be raised to the nobility. Come back to me when you have been given your nobleman's coronet, Sir Cairn."

Cairn felt her gaze almost physically; suddenly her presence overwhelmed his senses, and he knew she was doing it by magic. His mind whirled, his brain was in turmoil, but he dared to reach out toward her hand . . .

And was saved by Prince Orlin's limping appearance, cloaked in the rough robe of a novice and attended by Yakob.

"Have you recovered, Prince?" Lira's voice was suddenly severe again.

"I will live, at least," Orlin groaned, "which may be painful, but is very satisfying." Then, with massive reluctance, "I thank you, lady."

"Well. That is quite pleasant," Lira said with a curt nod. "But the thanks I wish, Prince, is for you to treat every woman you meet with respect, from this day forth—*every* woman, no matter how high or low her station."

The prince stared at her for a long minute, then said, "Well, I can do that much."

"Can you indeed," she said, with icy sarcasm.

"Oh, yes." Prince Orlin grinned wickedly. "After all, I still have the great satisfaction of knowing that I have thwarted Lord Thraik's plans for me."

"Really?" Lira said, with a smile of amusement. "I thought they had succeeded remarkably well."

NOW YOU SEE IT

Morgan Llywelyn

Weary beyond weariness, Joklyne rubbed his burning eyes for the ninth time. Bed! If only he could tumble into a soft bed and sleep for a week. But to do that he must have a bed, and his most recent landlord had just evicted him for being too far behind in his rent. Right now the only home he had was the Men's Toilet in the Grand Concourse. He had to have money. The only way he knew to get money was through magic, in a city where almost everyone practiced magic.

No, Joklyne amended ruefully, the others don't practice. Almost everyone but me can work magic, at least some degree of genuine magic, the manipulation of natural forces through supernatural agency. The smallest child in the street can make toys materialize or pets vanish. I'm the only one who has to practice, rehearsing basic legerdemain that wouldn't fool any citizen of Constantinople. To the rest of them I'm a fraud. My tricks are only good for earning a few coppers from first-time visitors to the City of Magic, credulous tourists eager for sorcery but not really knowing what it is.

Joklyne knew what sorcery was. And he had long ago accepted the sad fact that his best efforts were only a pale imitation of the genuine abilities of the Magically Gifted.

It was not much of a life.

The Men's Toilet was not much of a home, either. But at least it was solid, being part of the Grand Concourse, one of the very few solid and permanent structures in Constantinople. Most of the city's buildings were magicked, dreamed or conjured into being by some denizen of the place to fulfil the desires of the moment, and likely to burst as effortlessly as a soap bubble when they had served their purpose. Magic did not require solidity or permanence. Men who could not work magic did require a substantial setting, however. Joklyne longed with all his weary being for a real wooden bed with a real feather mattress, standing on four firm legs on a solid floor.

The Grand Concourse had to be solid because it was the hub of Constantinople, the terminal that welcomed visitors—and their money—from the mundane world. Built of red marble and rose quartz, it towered dome upon dome above the apparitional city. Amid flux and flow, the Grand Concourse offered newcomers a place to catch their breath upon arrival and adjust themselves to the heady air of illusion ... and to have their arrival as tourists officially certified so the appropriate fees could be extracted from their assets in the mundane world.

"Meet me at the GC, Jo," a friend might say, and no matter how the city changed, Joklyne could always find the Concourse and the waiting friend. But friends were pretty thin on the ground. A man with no money had limited social prospects. Life was a matter of struggling to survive, while watching the Magically Gifted effortlessly supply themselves with crystalline palaces or silken pavilions or shimmering sailplanes.

It was enough to make a man bitter.

Joklyne strove not to be bitter, to accept his lack of

talent with good grace. He was the first to laugh at himself—a grown man living in the Men's Toilet.

It was just that this morning his eyes burned and his neck was stiff and he was finding it hard to laugh at anything as he stared into the mirror above the basin, then shuffled out through the varnished oak doors to look for some arriving tourist he could impress with a bit of sleight of hand. Make their shoes appear to turn into silver. Create a shower of rice from empty air.

Or his old standby, the Seven Marble Shuffle. That one was usually good for some coins tossed into his battered hat.

As he stepped out onto the gleaming marble floor of the huge lobby he was digging in one of the countless pockets of his custom-made, but shabby coat, looking for his seven marbles. Nine, really. That was the heart of the trick. Anyone with manual dexterity and a bit of patience could learn to perform it.

Joklyne's stomach was growling ominously. If he was dizzy from hunger he might not be able to do the Seven Marble Shuffle. Better use the last coppers he had, he decided, and buy something to eat in one of the shops and stalls sure to be found, however briefly, out on the streets of the city.

Noting regretfully that there was no current influx of new arrivals, Joklyne made his way to the broad front entrance and went out beneath the pillared portico at the top of a sweep of imposing stone steps. At once the city assailed him with myriad sounds. Bells, chimes, peals of thunder, the laughter of unicorns, the squeal of clouds being knotted, the tinkling of crystal and clanging of gold. Joklyne turned up the collar of his coat as if he had stepped into a deluge.

He disliked being abroad in Constantinople. The environment of the City at the Center of the World was hostile to its few unmagical citizens. Although he had been born and bred in the city, Joklyne had always thought of himself—or been forced to think of himself—

as an outsider. He was different; he was handicapped by his lack of magical talent. He could only deal in tangible realities, which were frequently painful and did not cushion his way through life. "Why don't you go where you belong?" some of the more cruel inhabitants of the city occasionally taunted him. "Why don't you go out in the mundane world where they're used to your kind."

How could he answer? The truth was, Constantinople was home, the only home he knew. Uncomfortable as it might be for him, he found the idea of the mundane world even more uncomfortable. At least here he knew the rules.

The rules, as the Emperor Dagus enforced them, were that the Magically Gifted were pampered and privileged, and much less likely to incur one of Dagus' savage and arbitrary persecutions. The Thirteen Families, those most in the Emperor's favor, were the people most likely to tyrannize the less gifted. Those Who Could, Joklyne thought to himself, trampling without a care on Those Who Could Not. But it was probably the same in the mundane world, he reasoned. The strong always stood on the backs of the weak. Being one of a tiny and oppressed minority had made Joklyne philosophical. It had also made him wary, and now, as he stepped out onto the streets of the city, he braced himself out of long habit.

Anything might happen. In Constantinople the unexpected was everyday fare and a man's only protection was a quick wit, if he had no sorceries at his fingertips.

Joklyne descended toward street level. A beggar near the foot of the steps glanced up at him. Joklyne knew the man by sight as another of the ungifted, who made a precarious living by soliciting alms from tourists. His clothing was even shabbier than Joklyne's threadbare garments. "Is there a train in?" the beggar enquired hopefully. Joklyne shook his head. "Not yet. Quiet as a tomb in there. Give it a few more minutes."

"A few minutes real time, or a few minutes Constantinople time?"

Joklyne forced a smile. "There is no time in the Magic City," he replied. The ancient saying tasted dusty and shopworn in his mouth. The Magically Gifted could avoid aging, but he was aware that his hair was turning gray and his face was seaming.

The beggar shrugged and turned away. Joklyne watched with casual interest as the man made his way down the Central Avenue in the general direction of the Cathedral. Perhaps the begging would be better elsewhere.

Joklyne stopped watching him and glanced up and down the street instead, trying to decide whether to go to the left or the right. Eventually he ambled off to the left, but the only eating places he found were glittering and costly restaurants that had sprung up overnight to satisfy the whim of the inhabitants for some new exotic food. They would be gone tomorrow. And Joklyne knew he could not afford them anyway.

He turned, listening to his stomach growl, and made his way back toward the Grand Concourse, intending to search for some affordable shop on the other side—if one existed today.

He had just spotted a little booth with a striped awning that looked promising when the sun went out.

To be precise, there was no sun, as the Magic City did not depend on solar illumination. Someone had once magicked a great golden globe in the sky above the GC, which shed glittering rays of gold dust that fell like rain and sparkled in rivulets in the streets. It had been such a success that it had been allowed to remain there for as long as anyone could remember, kept in place almost unconsciously by the collective desire of the Magically Gifted.

But on this day it went out. Ceased. Vanished.

Joklyne rubbed his eyes, fearing for a moment that he had gone blind.

Then he perceived, dimly, through an unfamiliar twilight, the outlines of the shops and stalls along the street.

One moment they were there.

The next moment they were gone.

In itself this was not unusual, as structures were continually being refashioned in the twinkling of an eye. But no eyes twinkled. The buildings were not replaced. Joklyne heard the sound of something very heavy collapsing with a great crash in the next street over. At the same time, a sailship fell out of the sky just in front of him. The sorcerer's wind that propelled the craft had ceased abruptly. With a rending of silken sails and a splintering of ebony planks, the vessel disintegrated before Joklyne's astonished eyes.

Its occupants, two women and a man who belonged to the Thirteen Families, sat dazed amid the wreckage. The man pulled himself together enough to wave his hands and make passes through the air, but nothing happened. One of the women said something contemptuous to him and began trying to extricate herself from the wreck, which was rapidly fading into nothingness.

Only light streaming through the great glass doors of the Grand Concourse illuminated the scene. Throughout the city, buildings that owed their tensile strength to magic were simply falling apart. Pleasure pavilions perished. Trees of emeralds shrank into brittle weeds devoid of leaf. Roses of rubies withered and died. Dead vegetable matter made blotches on lawns suddenly sere and brown.

The splendor of Constantinople was ... gone.

In its place was a sprawl of ancient, noisome tenements that had been given no upkeep for centuries. Walls had crumbled, roofs rotted, paint peeled away like flesh from a dead skull. Alabaster streets faded to reveal muddy trackways beneath their illusion, where open sewage ran.

Compared to the real Constantinople, Joklyne realized, the Men's Toilet in the Grand Concourse was a palace. He stood thunderstruck, trying to comprehend the incomprehensible. This was the place in which he had been born and spent all his days! This slum. Was it possible?

Yet he knew it was. The bone-deep intuition of a native told him that he was seeing his true birthplace, his real habitat. This slum . . . was the Magic City. As it really was.

Then he heard the rumble of a train beneath his feet, approaching the terminal through one of the railway tunnels leading into the city. Within minutes a crowd of tourists would be swirling through the lobby and twittering with anticipation, eager for their first glimpse of magic.

Joklyne took a long look at the destination that awaited them. The magic had failed. He did not know why; having no understanding of true magic he could not begin to speculate either on its motive force or the loss of same.

But he was no fool. He knew opportunity when he saw it. Joklyne spun on his heel and ran toward the Grand Concourse. He took the steps three at a time. As he ran he fumbled with his clothing, bringing up his full bag of tricks from the capacious pockets he had once designed. As he hurried into the light he felt the darkness of the city behind him as if it were tangible. He could hear the first screams of the citizens of Constantinople as nightmare descended on them. Their world had fallen apart and they were helpless, more helpless than any wild animal, for they had no survival skills apart from their magic. They did not know how to heal the wounds they were suddenly suffering as buildings fell on them before dissolving. The buildings vanished, but the wounds remained, bleeding. Hundreds were dying in the shockingly altered streets. Their voices rose into one mighty wail of terror.

"Serves you right," Joklyne whispered to himself. "Thought you were gods, didn't you? Thought you were better than anybody. Hah!"

He felt pity, but sternly thrust it aside. He would not

allow himself to be tormented by sympathy for people who had shown no sympathy to him.

At least, not now. Maybe later. He knew he would grieve for them later, because he had a tender heart.

But now he was going to do something for himself, because he knew that if he failed to do so he would regret it for the rest of his days.

Joklyne strode briskly across the marble lobby just as the double doors that led to Platform C swung open. An influx of tourists poured through. They wore expensive clothing and had the sleek, well-fed look of businessmen and their wives. Some sort of convention, perhaps. Constantinople was the ultimate convention site. Visitors were willing to pay a fortune to riot amid mansions of amber and chalcedony and lapis lazuli.

But those mansions were gone now. Suddenly, incredibly, gone.

Joklyne wondered briefly if the great gold and jade palace that was home to Emperor Dagus had also disappeared. Or was it real, substantial enough to withstand whatever had just happened? As the lowest of the low, he had never got close enough to the royal palace to find out. Joklyne shook his head. No time to think of such things now, not with a fresh tide of visitors flowing toward him. Habit took over and he moved forward to intercept them, wondering how to comport himself in the changed circumstances. The Magic City they were expecting had gone, but surely there was still some way for a clever man to make money from gullible strangers.

With a practiced eye, Joklyne selected the most likely target. A portly man with a florid face was just patting his coat to be certain he still had his wallet in an inside pocket. That sort of nervousness was a dead giveaway; the fellow was unsure of himself. Joklyne adopted his customary expression for such occasions, a humble, hopeful smile, the offering of a man who has learned to expect rejection. He walked forward with his hand outstretched. "Welcome to Constantinople, good sir!"

"Don't need a guide," the portly man said dismissively. "We know what we want to see."

At this, a dumpy woman in a costly but unflattering print dress came forward to stand beside him, brushing a wisp of graying hair out of her eyes. She gave Joklyne a diffident smile. "It's our first holiday together in years, really," she said in a rather plaintive voice. "I've been so looking forward to this."

"Ah." Joklyne filled his voice with sympathy, as if the loss were his. "What a pity."

The couple hesitated as other visitors brushed past them, heading toward the doors.

"What do you mean?" the portly man demanded to know.

"The Magic City is, alas, no more," Joklyne replied.

The man gave him an incredulous stare. "You're joking."

Joklyne sighed. "Would that I were. But I'm telling you for your own sake, the city you came to see isn't out there any more."

"No magic?" the woman asked plaintively, beginning to fuss with the string of pearls she wore around her plump neck.

"Pay no attention to this . . . this person," her husband ordered. "Come on, Hazel, we'll see for ourselves what this is all about." He caught her by the arm and pulled her toward the doors.

Joklyne swiftly interposed his body between them and the exit. "If you once go through those doors," he advised, "the electronic eye buried in the doorway will scan the ticket fixed to the bracelet on your arm and report back to your travel agent that you have indeed visited Constantinople. Once that happens, as you were surely told, the full sum charged for your trip will be deducted from your credit account back home. There will be nothing you can do about it then, even if you are totally disappointed with your trip."

"How do you know that?" the man asked suspiciously.

"We in the Magic City know a great deal about our visitors," Joklyne replied, his smile reflecting genuine concern. "It is our business to know about them, and to make them happy. We are here for their pleasure. Or rather, we were here for their pleasure. Now that the magic has gone, I cannot imagine that tourists will be flocking into Constantinople to see what remains. It isn't very prepossessing, I'm afraid."

The portly man was watching him with a dubious expression. But his wife was increasingly distressed. "Oh, Herbert, if it's as this man says, we should turn around and go home, you know? We don't want to be charged for magic if there isn't any."

"We only have his word for that," Herbert replied. Just at that moment, however, the first of the tourists who had gone out into the city came back through the doors of the Grand Concourse They looked dazed and frightened.

"It's chaos out there!" one cried. "No lights, no buildings, people running everywhere screaming . . ."

Joklyne nodded. "I told you," he said to Herbert.

"So you did," the portly man agreed reluctantly. "Well, friend, I guess I owe you one. At least we won't be charged."

"But I did so want to see some magic," his wife murmured, almost to herself. "Something to remember and tell the children about."

Joklyne turned toward her. "We hate to have our visitors disappointed," he said in a kindly tone. Any mention of children always touched him, he who lived alone with neither wife nor child, and hated his loneliness. Though how could a man with no talent offer a wife anything? "If you want to see magic, of course you shall," he promised. "The best we have to offer. Oh, it may not be quite what you expected, but you won't be charged thousands of credits for it, and at least you can go back home and tell your children that you saw, ah . . . the Dancing Scarves!"

He promptly wriggled his fingers in the direction of his chest, then closed his hands into fists. When he opened them a rainbow of silk scarves fluttered around his head and shoulders. The dumpy little woman gave a squeak of pleasure.

"Don't be ridiculous, Hazel," her husband snapped at her. "That's a parlor trick, nothing like what we came here for."

"Ah, but that's only the beginning," Joklyne assured them, warming to his performance. He flicked his wrists and tossed his head and the scarves began to writhe with a life of their own, bowing and dancing on an invisible wind. At his apparently magical behest they formed themselves into flower shapes, tulips and irises and great full-blown roses. Hazel clapped her hands together like a child. "It is magic," she breathed, determined to believe.

Joklyne smiled modestly. "In a small way," he replied. "Now watch this." He tossed the scarves into the air, caught the end of one, and snapped it. At once they disappeared, and in their place Joklyne was holding a silver chain. He offered it to the woman. "Put your fingers through this loop," he instructed.

"Should I?" she asked her husband.

Joklyne frowned in momentary annoyance. The poor creature was obviously very much under Herbert's fat red thumb. The spurious magician knew how it felt to be a nonentity. Without waiting for Herbert to give his permission, Joklyne twisted the chain and it suddenly knotted itself around the woman's wrist. There it sparkled like diamonds. A snap of Joklyne's fingers and it doubled and trebled itself, paving her entire arm with glittering silver. Her eyes opened wide in wonderment.

The tourists who had ventured out into Constantinople and returned in shock were milling around the lobby, trying to decide what to do next and talking among themselves in anxious or angry voices, depending upon their various characters. A few of them wandered over toward Joklyne and watched, curiously, as he ran through his repertoire for Herbert and his wife. They saw the Shower of Rice trick, the Disappearing Ball, Three Pieces of Cloth, and Joklyne's *pièce de résistance*, the Seven Marble Shuffle.

With this one he won Herbert over. It had always been Joklyne's best trick, and he had never done it so well as today.

Soon a crowd was gathered, watching. Herbert became quite proprietary, explaining, "This man kept us from going out there. Instead he's been working magic in here for us, and it isn't costing us anything, either." He clapped a meaty hand on Joklyne's shoulder.

Joklyne had never had such a large and appreciative audience. A few of the tourists, feeling cheated, had made their way back to the trains, but most of them stayed to watch, determined to see at least a few small wonders after having come so far. And strangely enough, the tricks were not as insubstantial as Joklyne considered them to be. Warmed by his audience, he found himself taking more chances, enlarging his repertoire as variations occurred to him. What he was doing was not magic, not magic as the gifted of the City would have performed it, yet there was a certain feel about it, a tingle, a rush, as if somehow a fragment of the sorcerer's gift had entered Joklyne's fingers after all. He found himself enlarging the Seven Marble Shuffle to Nine and never missing a beat. The Shower of Rice was transmogrified into a Shower of Apples. It was as if he could think the magic into being.

And it was magic. At some point he could never remember afterwards Joklyne's tricks ceased being tricks, and became the manipulation of natural forces by supernatural agency. For the first time in his life, Joklyne began to experience what the Magically Gifted had enjoyed, the sense of power. His heart sang in him. Outside in the city there was no magic, but within the rosy walls of the Grand Concourse one small and humble fraud had become a true practitioner. Best of all, his abilities were appreciated.

"You've saved me a lot of money," Herbert conceded. "I think it's only fair that you have, ah, some small percentage of what this trip would have cost me if you hadn't stopped me from going out through those doors." He pressed a sheaf of credit notes into Joklyne's astonished hands.

Meanwhile, others in the impromptu audience were digging into their own wallets and pocketbooks and taking out, not coppers, but similar notes which they bestowed on the delighted Joklyne.

They had come for magic and he was giving it to them, even if it was not the magic they had expected. But they were not thieves, these visitors. They were prepared to pay for value received. And Joklyne was giving them considerable value. He essayed, and to his own astonishment achieved, the Vanishing Tiger Trick. And the Clouds of Flame. And materialized a fountain of perfume in the center of the lobby of the Grand Concourse. Twittering like birds, a bevy of women rushed to dip their fingers in the fragrant scent and splash it on their temples and wrists.

Joklyne felt as if he were flying.

Another train arrived. A fresh influx of visitors elbowed aside the first, and to these newcomers Joklyne repeated his warning. Some ignored him and ventured outside the GC, only to return a few minutes later, as angered and disappointed as the first group, and satisfy themselves with gathering around Joklyne and watching his performance. By now he had set his hat on a stair rail and people were stuffing money into it. When the hat would hold no more, someone produced a shopping bag and gave it to him. Or perhaps Joklyne materialized the shopping bag for himself.

Meanwhile, as confusion gripped the city outside no one was paying any attention to what was happening within the Grand Concourse. Constantinople was like a giant animal in its death throes. Tourists were the last thing on its mind. Nor was Joklyne any longer concerned about the fate of the city beyond the walls. He occupied a magical sphere of his own, a world he had never thought to inhabit. His wildest fantasies had become reality.

A tiny blond girl with bouncing ringlets tugged shyly at Joklyne's arm. "Please sir," she said, "I was promised trees covered with jewels. And unicorns. Can you make unicorns?"

Joklyne gazed down at her earnest little face. "I can't make anything as wonderful as a unicorn," he started to tell her, but then he found himself falling helplessly into the stars in her eyes, and heard his voice say, "I shall do my best, sweetheart."

He waved his hands. He closed his eyes in a moment of intense concentration. He ... clenched ... his mind in a way he had never known he could. And suddenly, in the distance, he heard a distinct rumble of inhuman laughter.

The voice of a unicorn.

The beast came trotting toward them across the gleaming marble floor, its golden hooves clattering metallically. When it reached the little girl it stopped, dipped its gleaming single horn to her in salute, and knelt before her, pressing its great head against her small bosom while a beatific expression stole across its face.

The watching crowd cried out in wonder.

In that moment, Joklyne the humble, Joklyne the insignificant, owned the world and all its treasures. Standing at the center of what seemed a vast and bedazzled audience, he performed feats of magic beyond his wildest dreams. He could do anything. Whatever he attempted, succeeded. It was as if the sum total of magic that had been subtracted from the substance of Constantinople had been conferred upon one man, who now flung it into the air like a shower of stars and brought forth wonders on demand. People shouted out the names of magical accomplishments they had only read about, and Joklyne obliged. The Swimming Salmon, the Levitating

Lady, the Guillotine—he did them all. Effortlessly. Feeling confidence rich as marrow in his bones.

Sometimes the balance shifts, he thought to himself. And even the weak may stand on the backs of the strong.

He grinned at his audience. With a single wide sweep of his arm he produced, for their delight and delectation, a genie almost as tall as the great dome of the Concourse, an exotic figure with gleaming green skin and gleaming white teeth and a pair of voluminous pantaloons made of crimson silk, tied at the waist with ropes of pearls.

It had occurred to Joklyne that having the genie grant each member of his audience three wishes would make an unforgettable climax for his performance. He wanted to give these people something special; their admiration was giving him so much.

"Now you see it!" Joklyne cried gaily, gazing up at his masterpiece, "and now . . ."

In that moment, the balance shifted again.

Joklyne felt sorcery drain from him as if someone had opened his veins. The tingling flowed out of him, leaving him exhausted and slightly nauseous. As it faded, the genie faded, becoming as translucent as his silken pantaloons and then disappearing with a loud pop.

"What happened?" cried one of the tourists, aware of an unsettling change in the atmosphere.

"Listen," said another. They listened. The screams and death cries from beyond the walls of the Grand Concourse had ceased. In their place was a startled silence. Then something like a faint, uncertain cheer.

The visitors stared at one another, unable to interpret the sounds reaching them. But Joklyne could. Born in Constantinople, he knew the city thoroughly, knew its moods. As surely as if he had gone to the great front doors and gazed out, he knew the magic had returned.

Whatever the Magic City had lost, she had, in one blinding flash, regained.

Joklyne drew a shaky breath. He could not tell how much time had passed; while revelling in his power, he had lost any sense of time. It might have been an hour, it might have been a day that he held his audience in the palm of his hand.

But whatever time of sorcery had been vouchsafed to him, he realized with a wrench of pain that it was not enough. He had tasted the magic now, had shared the incomparable feeling of being able to create with the simple force of his mind and his concentration. No matter what happened outside, how could he ever go back? How could he ever be content, knowing so clearly what he lacked?

His brief period of magic had been, not a gift, but a curse that would make him throughly miserable for the rest of his life. He saw it so clearly, with eyes that could look beyond illusion.

Pain welled up in him like a pool of tears.

The tourists were no longer thronging around him as densely as they had been. Already they were beginning to drift away; some wandered toward the doors to peer out cautiously. Joklyne knew what they must see: the crystal towers returning, the golden globe shedding its gold dust on the alabaster streets.

In a moment they would abandon Joklyne altogether and rush outside to experience the real thing.

Joklyne sighed very softly to himself.

A small hand seized his large one and tugged, hard. He looked down. It was the tiny girl with golden ringlets.

"Oh please," she said to him, "won't you make the unicorn come back? Just for a moment, just to tell me goodbye."

"I cannot," he told her. If he spoke even one word more he thought the pool of pain inside himself would brim over and spill out.

The child shook her sunny head. "Of course you can," she said with the assurance of total belief. "You just did it. Do it again."

In her voice was the command of an empress.

Expecting defeat, but unable to deny her, Joklyne waved his hands; closed his eyes; clenched his mind.

And even as the magic returned, without reason or explanation, to the Magic City, the man who had once lacked the sorcerer's skill heard the clatter of metallic hooves dancing across the marble floor.

LOYALTY

S. N. Lewitt

"I need to know who is trying to poison me." I tried to keep the anger out of my face. This sorceress, a street magician I did not quite trust even if she did come with a recommendation from Brother Michael, was not responsible. I knew that for a fact, since Brother Michael was my usual healer and he had found the traces of poison.

"I cannot tell you who is doing it or why, Commander," Brother Michael said when I visited him this morning. "I can only tell from your condition, from what I can see in your organs, that it has been going on for many days. Some substance that is being fed to you in very small bits daily, so that you will eventually store enough in your body that you die. It will look slow and natural, like a disease, but there is no doubt that this is poison."

Brother Michael is the best there is. He has consulted for the emperor and his father-in-law, the general, several times and still has his head. If his hands holding steady over my body for so long that I fell asleep revealed poison, then indeed there was no doubt in my mind.

Besides, Brother Michael was once the head of the medical faculty of the Lyceum Magus before he took orders. There are rumors that he might even be a saint, though all of his cures can be ascribed to meticulously performed spells and good diagnoses. Besides, a saint wouldn't see someone like me, a commander of the Varangian Guard, unannounced in the middle of morning prayers. Which Brother Michael has done more than once.

And saints rarely attend emperors and rulers regularly, or keep their old friends and acquaintances from the days before they took orders. Brother Michael was holy and quite brilliant, and he had lost none of the worldly shrewdness that had made him the terror of the court before he had retired to the monastery, from where he still held invisible strings of quiet influence.

"Well, can you do anything about it?" I had asked when he gave his diagnosis. I assumed it would be very easy, a few incantations, some incense, and the cramps would leave my belly and the whole thing would be over.

But Brother Michael only shook his shaggy head and waved his hands in the air uselessly. "Lucius Arsenius, there is nothing I can do. You have to find the poisoner. And very soon indeed. The poison has entered your system and I am surprised you are alive even now. But be careful of activity. Too much activity will speed the evil in your body and give you less time to track down the poisoner." He seemed distraught by it all, having such a thing walk through the monastery door.

As if it were his problem. As if he were the one who had moaned all day in bed and had passed blood and felt as if his insides were on fire. As if there were nothing at all he could do about it and he wished he didn't have to be reminded of the nastiness of the world he left behind.

"Fine," I said through clenched teeth. "But can you give me any relief? Can someone help me until I can see justice done?"

That seemed to confuse the poor brother even more. He blinked his watery eyes and looked out the window, as if awaiting inspiration. "Perhaps I can give you the name of someone who can help," he said hesitantly. "I am not certain, you understand. She is only a witch, a street sorceress. Probably half her income comes from the crimson mantle. But she has some knowledge of poisons and the like, and has a good reputation, for someone who never studied properly."

I snatched the name up and read it over seven times, though that didn't change the facts. I did not like the idea of leaving my fate, my life, and the protection of the Empire, in the hands of some street witch who used her talent merely to supplement that other one.

But I could not risk a proper licensed magician from the Lyceum. They are all too politically connected, owing favors to this noble or that minor prince. It is a wonder anyone can trust a proper magician at all. Even the most innocent love potion could have political consequences.

Everyone knows the story of Irene Herekonos, who was married to John Mylos of the not-quite-noble Arsenius family only to consolidate lands and to take over her fortune. Poor Irene was an orphan, after all, and without brothers. And all of sixteen years old and very lovely besides. But John had never been moved by a woman's youth or beauty and he was far more interested in Irene's fortune than in Irene herself.

So Irene bought a love potion and slipped it to her new husband the third day after their marriage. Within weeks, Irene not only controlled the family finances, but had gotten the ear of the old empress as well. She became a serious influence on Imperial policy while John was off fighting the Rus and the Huns at the borders, though even with all her power at court her husband continued on the battlefield.

John died when Irene was twenty-five. She was considered the most beautiful woman in the Empire at the time, and on her husband's death became the wealthiest as well. And the most important. Rumors are that she was the emperor's mistress for a while, though the stories became vague and I have never been sure which emperor it was. Or whether my branch of the family is descended from one of her legitimate children or from an Imperial bastard. It was a very long time ago, and she always claimed that all of her children were her third husband's.

Though of course we know this is not true. Even today, four generations later, my cousins and brothers and I all bear some resemblance to the old royal family. Enough that many of the older officers in the Guard remarked on it when I began my career. And, of course, they had all heard of Irene. Who hadn't?

Ah, but that isn't the point. The point is that I dared not approach someone who might be in the pay of one of the Helios or the Teklos, or who might have heard a bit of gossip whispered or who knew that this daughter had purchased thus and such a spell. No, I had to go to someone without connections, a minor streetwalker who picked up something on the side with her healing talents.

I had been afraid to send for her at first. Afraid that she would be toothless and ugly, that she would be incompetent as well. Brother Michael may be quite reliable, and being in the Church, at least his agenda is clear, but he does have this undeniable tendency to help out those he considers worthy. Which means that he could easily send me a second-rate witch who had children at home to feed or who was generous to the quarter or who had come to him to discuss the matter of her vocation among the sisters.

So I was at least pleasantly surprised when she arrived. Christa was not a common streetwalker with a few midwife skills. No, even without the mantle and her rich crimson gown, it is obvious that this woman is a properly trained hetaira, an educated courtesan of the highest rank. She wore the cloak that Theodora once wore, and it folded over her shoulders like it did Justinian's bride, with the same modesty of drape and subtle ornamentation as the wife of an ancient ruling family might wear. Her sandals were inlaid with tiny yellow stones and her servant followed behind her with a businesslike satchel.

I met her in my study. Her eyes went once around the room, carefully noting all the details. Yes, it is a very old house and built in the Roman style around a garden. All the rooms have beam construction as they did in ancient Rome, before spellbuilding became an art practiced outside of sacred precincts. And the paintings on the walls are old-fashioned, perhaps, not the currently popular hanging fabrics from the Eastern part of the empire. I knew that she noted all these things carefully before her gaze went to the library. I could almost see the itch in her hands to reach for the oldest scrolls and the bound vellum.

She looked, she sighed, and then she became all business. I had never dealt with a hetaira in any capacity except as entertainers at parties, where they gave opinions like men and conversed like learned doctors. Always very amusing. I had thought them very funny, well trained in imitating their betters.

Facing down Christa, I suddenly realized that she was not merely an imitator. There was something in the set of her eyes, in the way she studied me that reminded me of Brother Michael.

"If you would permit me," she said, and her voice was low and melodious and carefully groomed.

I nodded and she came to me, touched my wrist lightly and then placed her long fingers on my temples. I felt as if cool water invaded me and I knew she was searching as Brother Michael searched, the way a truly trained healer analyzes the body. Her eyes were closed and she was deep in concentration, with the same look that Brother Michael has when he is deeply involved in some healing work.

"It is poison indeed," she said. "A slow one, where a little is added each day. Your body cannot rid itself of this evil, and so it builds and builds as you sicken." She turned away and her expression filled with disgust. "They use this to make death look natural, as if any child with a wild talent for healcraft couldn't detect it! I suppose the idea is to prevent the victim from seeking a competent healer in time."

"And for me?" I asked. "What can you do?"

She sat down uninvited and ran her finger along the top of my desk. "You are very close to the critical stages. Another dose or two or heavy physical exertion and you will be dead. There are several possibilities. There is a spell that can protect you from the effects as long as the poison is not increased. Then, when your body is sufficiently recovered, we can begin the treatments to draw out the evil humors and restore you to health. It is not an easy or pleasant course of action, but it is the only thing that is effective. Or you could choose to leave this place entirely. That would probably be most healthful in any event. But if you ingest much more, there is nothing we can do. Magic can only go so far. If a man is intent on killing himself, there is nothing we can do to prevent it."

I looked at her and wondered where her loyalties lay. "I need to know who is poisoning me," I said evenly. "Can you discover this?"

Her eyes fluttered. "I am not sure," she said. "Maybe. I have never tried anything of this nature before."

To be honest, she did not panic or play the weakling. Hetairae are known for being competent and reliable individuals, but I had always thought it was because such an anomaly was amusing in a woman trained for pleasure. Perhaps I had been wrong. Or maybe this one was more healer than hetaira, who had entered that other sisterhood when the Lyceum Magus was closed to her. Surely enough women had entered convents because there was so little desire for wives who were well versed in Homer and the writings of St. Augustine. There was the great poetess who was also a great beauty and nearly chosen as empress. But as she reached out her hand for the apple, the emperor said, "It is by women that evil has come into the world." And she replied, "And it is by woman that that which is greater than evil came into the world." She became a nun and a mystic and a great writer, though I think the emperor had little to regret from his choice.

"Well, we must try it now," I said. "I have to know. It is important to the general."

She arched one eyebrow, but did not ask the obvious question. Why the general and not the emperor? The one with the crown or the one with the power.

We of the Guard have never abandoned our general. We made him and he made us and together with his wisdom and our might we had expanded and secured the empire. The young Emperor Constantine VII, married to the old man's daughter, was no more than a figurehead. He had never campaigned, never led the Guard to the borders to fight even the barbarian tribes or the sea pirates who lurked in the Mediterranean. No, there was in truth only one ruler, and it seemed that this healer-witch-hetaira was astute enough to know that.

"Lucius Arsenius, there are things you are not saying," she said softly. "Things that I may well need to know to find out who is poisoning you. Can you go away for a few weeks for your health's sake, perhaps to the mountains for the cooler air?"

I shook my head. "Whoever is behind this cannot know that I suspect," I insisted. "If I leave on whatever pretense, it will become obvious. No, do whatever is needful to keep me alive for a few more days until we find this poisoner, and then you and Brother Michael will be able to draw out the evil and I will be able to recover in peace."

She cocked her head as if thinking about something distant. "You might want to be careful of Brother Michael," she said, and her words were as silent as spring rain in the garden. "He is an abbot, but that does not remove him from the ranks of advisors."

I snorted. Everyone knows that he's one of the General's

advisors. It is why I feel more comfortable with him in any event. "And what about you?" I asked. "What faction or interest do you favor? You're not without politics yourself."

She smiled, and her whole face filled with sparkle and promise. I could see well why any man could want her when she was in this frame of mind. Though she was pretty enough while serious, the conflict between face and thought was difficult to digest and I found myself seeing her as a man as I listened to her speak. Now she was all seduction again.

"I am completely without politics," she said, her perfect teeth flashing. "I have never had dealings with the Imperial family or the Guard or any of the higher nobility. Mostly I have attended to merchants, foreigners who ply the silk road. I know more about Samarkand than about the Palace. And I despise the entire thing and everyone who deals in politics."

I nodded as if I accepted this, though it was obviously a lie. No one of her training and intelligence could be without politics and opinion in Byzantium. But I did not think that, whatever her leanings, she was any threat to me.

One does not grow gray hair in this city without some instinct. Mine, which I had always trusted, told me now that I could trust the healer. Or at least, I would come to no harm from her. For the time being, in any case.

"How shall we begin the investigation?" I thought aloud.

The witch thought the question was directed at her. "I have a young apprentice," she said slowly. "She could be introduced to your kitchens as a maid, or maybe a serving girl. She is very pretty. I have taught her already to use her talent to detect this poison in its raw form and in food. This is not difficult to do if an apprentice knows what she is looking for. The real problem is when one doesn't know and thinks that the belly cramps and bleeding bowels are the result of disease. Which is the natural assumption. It is very well done, this poisoning."

So the girl will be introduced to the serving staff. That was a good place to start. I liked that and told her so.

"Now," she said, "first we have to take care of you. The spell will not be very pleasant, but there is no help for it. It will bolster your body until we can begin a proper cure."

"Yes, indeed," I agreed.

She had me lie on a couch facing east, just as Brother Michael always does. She spotted my brazier immediately and threw some herbs on it. The smell was sharp but agreeable. And she started with a prayer that I had learned for my first communion and bade me join in, so I knew she was decent in her devotion to the Church. Not that I thought Brother Michael would send me to less, but it was reassuring.

I do not really like magic. It is the opposite of soldiering. Magic is akin to politics, everything moving unseen beneath the surface, nothing plain to the eye. I am a plain enough man and like to see my enemies and know my friends. People may say that in this city that is impossible, but among the Guard it is still commonplace. We are still Roman soldiers who protect our general. And we make him if he leads us well and unmake him if he ignores our good.

But magic is something else again, and even though the Church permits its practice, I still do not quite trust that which I cannot see. Saving the mysteries of the Incarnation and the Resurrection and the Mass, of course. And my own hope of salvation, which I trust is far off in the future, though clearly someone wishes it much closer.

The hetaira witch began to chant in a language I thought was Aramaic, though I was not certain. I didn't like the foreignness of it. The words sounded harsh and cruel and had neither the fluidity nor the beauty of our native Greek.

I closed my eyes. I did not wish to look as she did her work. I heard her hard leather soles against the mosaic floor as she circled the couch and I felt . . . something.

All imagination, I thought. Just a trick because I was trying too hard not to think of it. But as she chanted again I could not ignore the energy that poured into me.

The pains in my belly, which had been constant for several days, lessened. At first I thought I imagined that, too, but as she came to the end of her last wail the pain abated completely.

Then a hand touched my shoulder. "It is done," she said. But she shook her head and sighed, and her carefully disarranged black curls shook all down the front of her robe.

"I feel wonderful," I reassured her. "The pain is all gone. I feel like I could ride all day and drink all night and wench all week. You've done very well."

But she kept her eyes on the floor. "It is only an illusion," she said. "I cannot repair any damage to your body until we leach the poison out of you, and we cannot do that here. It will be a hard working." Then she looked up and her eyes met mine. And I have seen such determination in the eyes of an enemy with a sword in his hand. "You are not healed. And remember, this only gives you a little time of health to evade your enemies. In the end the poison is still lodged in your organs, eating them away. It will kill you whether you feel fine or not, if you do not leave here and come under the care of a master healer. Immediately."

I nodded. "You explained that all very clearly," I reassured her. "But I cannot afford to leave until I have the poisoner in hand and his employer dead. I don't like it, but it is necessary."

She looked down at the mosaic as if the old piece of a dove with an olive branch were the most fascinating piece of art in the world. "I will send the girl Alexa to you today," Christa replied. "To watch over the kitchen and find out where the poison is. And please, if you can, avoid that food. The less damage the more likely it can be healed, though I do not like this at all. A sick man should not play well and walk around with all the symptoms masked. It only makes for bad times later."

She gathered up her satchel and gave it to the servant who had followed her. Before she closed the case, I had noticed several dark herbs and strange symbols within. Then, with barely a nod, she left.

"Ummm," I cleared my throat to remind her of unfinished business.

She hesitated and turned. "Yes?"

"Your fee," I said, feeling stupid. "We have never discussed your fee for this work."

She shuddered delicately, as if even the mention of money were abhorrent to her. "I will send my servant to your majordomo," she said. "I assume that you have sufficient funds." That was not a question and she did not wait for an answer as she left my house.

The girl arrived not two hours later. The porter was amazed that she arrived in a sedan chair like her mistress, but this was merely a kitchen wench. Not much to look at with a round face and unkempt hair, she would go unnoticed among the pots and vegetables. Still, there was something frighteningly calm and assured in her eyes, as if under the serving girl's shift and plain features there was all of Holy Wisdom veiled and waiting.

She was uncanny and disturbed me. Everything disturbed me. Even feeling healthy again and knowing that the poison still ate at my bowels made the bright daylight seem unreal.

It could not possibly be late afternoon of the same day. Eternities had come and gone between now and when the sun had risen. And yet this seemed unlike the sun. The brightness was a mockery of my murder.

My murder. I had not thought of it that way before. I did not want to use the word so plainly. But there was no other word that was correct. And there was no doubt in my mind that the young Constantine or one of his supporters was behind it.

He was weak-willed and as weak of mind as of character. If he ruled, all Byzantium would break apart. The great gathering of nations under the single throne would fragment and dissolve. Like Alexander's empire before us, all the civilization and culture, all the learning and elegance we have achieved would fall back into barbarism.

It takes more than courage to hold together such a strange mixture as occupies our borders. It takes cunning and diplomacy, understanding mixed with firmness, clear vision and singular good luck. And the blessing of God, of course, though as His instrument to spread His Holy Church we hope we deserve Divine Favor.

The old general, who has never been able to retire, has all these qualities and more. His son-in-law is a figurehead who wishes to be more. It would make good sense for the younger to destroy the loyal officers who brought his father-in-law to power in the first place. And it was among his entourage I intended to look.

After all, Constantine keeps his elderly father-in-law in the field, fighting barbarian Rus, instead of at home. And the emperor had never taken the field himself, a thing for which no solider will forgive him.

The sun was still in the sky. I would have to act quickly. Surprise is an old tactic but it is still useful.

Full of energy, I sat at my desk, an old Roman–style desk that belonged to my great-grandfather when he was an officer in the Guard, and began to write. I could have had a secretary do this chore. There are three in this house who are capable. But I do not trust them. I do not trust anyone. And so I wrote out the invitations myself.

The guest list was perfect. Seven is the correct number for an old-style formal dinner, but I only really suspected two. And I needed no more to test my plan. It was late enough that dinner would be under way, and while the cooks would be worried about adding the necessities for a formal dinner, some could be bought from a cookshop and they could surely handle the rest. Adding two to the evening meal would be no strain on them.

But I had to get to them after whatever poison had already been cooked into the food or added to the wine. And so I had to tell them late, so that nothing could be changed. Of course, I do not have to tell the kitchen the identity of the guests, though at times I have done so to impress the servants to get the very best from them. This time I deemed it unpolitic.

I asked the porter where my wife was. She would not be present at a political dinner in any event. Only a hetaira was considered a proper dinner companion in such discussion.

My wife, the servant told me, was exactly where I expected her to be. Waiting on the young empress. As she should be. The girl is able to influence both her husband and her father, and I am fortunate enough that my wife was among her ladies. Not that the girl wanted proper wives for companions. She would rather have surrounded herself with her girlhood friends and other inappropriate associates. No, I was quite honored that my wife was among those women entrusted with keeping the girl in line.

She was not expected home for dinner. I wondered who she planned to dine with. And as the only appropriate feminine dinner companion anyway, I suddenly thought to ask Christa.

Of course I would have to pay for her services as an entertainer tonight. But with her special skills and observation, she might well be able to gather enough information that we could find the culprit by sunrise and I could be properly purged of the poison. And live.

So I wrote another invitation, this one to the hetaira witch. I hoped she had no appointment this evening. Even if she did, I was prepared to pay handsomely for her to break her engagement.

How much easier it is to plan and think when the body is not in pain, when the mind is freed from constant thoughts of lingering agony. I actually enjoyed planning this little dinner. The thought of my enemy delivered on a platter, so to speak, filled me with unspeakable pleasure. I whistled as I strolled past the courtyard garden to the kitchen, to tell the cooks that there would be guests to dine.

"What in St. Helen's name do you mean by this?" Christa demanded, fuming. "I sent you the girl. I told you to keep away from the kitchen. And I had an important client tonight, a very important client."

"I mean to find out the murderer tonight," I said for the second time in the same conversation. "Whoever does not eat of the poisoned dish is the man, that is quite simple. All you have to do is tell me which dish is poisoned."

The hetaira's face went red with rage. "That is the stupidest plan I have ever heard," she finally exploded. "Do you want to know why it is stupid? Let me tell you. First of all, the kind of poison that is being used can be ingested in small quantities. As you have done over a period of weeks. It would be no trouble at all for the poisoner to eat whatever dish it is without ill effect. And where is your vaunted plan then?

"Then there is the matter of needing me in this plan. My apprentice was sent here to identify poisoned food. She is capable of doing this. She cannot cure or give the illusion of health, but she can certainly identify something tainted. Which is why I sent her here in the first place.

"Then there is the matter of your guest list. Five people, only two of whom are actually suspect. Why on earth you invited Brother Michael I cannot fathom."

"Because he's a good dinner guest," I said firmly. "And because I didn't want to just invite from one faction. And you must stay and be a proper hetaira and make conversation with my guests."

Her eyes widened. "Absolutely not. I am not about

to break an appointment with this particular client in any event."

She stood in my study with her satchel and her robes drawn close around her. Unlike this morning, her curls were perfectly arranged and her face was elaborately made up. Under the deep red robe I was certain was a gown of the finest fabric cut to the empress' style of the month. But Christa was not about to let me see it.

"So if this plan is so bad, you tell me one that's better," I shot back at her, just as I would to a junior officer in training.

Christa closed her eyes as if she were very tired. "Oh, all right," she relented. "If you will ask Alexa in here. Have her come in and I'll see if something can be done. To salvage this whole thing. What a fiasco. Indeed, Lucius Arsenius, you are a soldier. You think like a soldier, you plan like a soldier. And you have all the subtlety of a steel sword and a legion."

I sighed and snapped my fingers. The porter arrived, and I told him to fetch the new girl from the kitchen. He seemed surprised, but left without a word.

Two minutes later Alexa arrived. She barely spared me a look and went directly to her mistress. They conferred in voices so low that I could not hear them even in the same room. I looked out across the old-fashioned atrium garden. It was so peaceful and lush as the last bright rays of the afternoon sun illuminated the splashing fountain against the flowers. Soon the sun would sink rapidly and the garden would darken like a candle being snuffed. But just now the classical arrangement and the sounds of insects and birds seemed a gruesome contrast to my present state.

Finally I forgot about the women whispering in the corner, about the guests coming to dinner, even about tracking down my would-be murderer. I passed into a state where I thought about death alone, about how all the life around me masked only its own end and how nothing ever escaped Judgment. I became melancholy and serene together, a very odd state, and yet it felt as if I had touched something true.

I wondered if this was true meditation and made a note to ask Brother Michael this evening when he arrived. The old man had asked about the state of my soul so many times that I felt bound to discuss what seemed like the one glimpse of spirit I had had in a year.

"We can do something here," Christa announced, and suddenly I was thrown back into the study, the world, and my own personal predicament.

"Alexa tells me that there is already a dish made and laced with the poison," she went on. "She has identified it as the fish, the one in cream sauce that you like so well. Which makes sense, the white sauce would mask the color as well as any flavor. Whoever has done this is cunning. Anyway, I can go and set a spell on the dish, on the dose intended for this evening. As I explained, it is safe for everyone else to eat, as there is only a very small amount in the food. It is you who are in danger because this has been building in your body for a long time.

"Anyway, I shall set a spell that will affect only the person who is behind the plot. This is because they are connected in another way to the food, and so the spell is completely defensive and will only recoil. It cannot touch anyone who is innocent. It will not kill the man; I refuse to do that. I will not use magic to harm. I am a healer, healer trained and healer vowed. The spell will only mark the man, and in such a way as you will know sometime tomorrow. The backlash will hit and you will know."

She stood proud, her chin jutting forward and her eyes flashing. Even though she is small and fine-boned, in such a mood I would not like to meet her in a fight. There was much about her that made me think of the fiercest Varangians, those who came from the north countries and talked of nothing but their honor and their alcohol.

She was only a hetaira and a street sorceress, but I had to respect her. It was a new feeling. I had never thought of such worthy of anything save use. And yet this street corner witch undoubtedly had her own version of honor. I was impressed.

"Then do whatever you think best," I said. "I'll pay whatever you ask."

She turned to follow Alexa, but at the door stopped and looked at me. "Of course you'll pay," she said softly. "But I'm not doing it for money. I'll do this because we resolve things too easily with death and too little with debate. I'll do this because I believe that God has given me what power I have to uphold His law, and because murder is against everything holy. And I'll do it for my honor and for God and my patron saint. But I don't do this for money, and I don't do it for you. You're just another plotter treating lives like chess pieces, not caring about what is right or good or just. Just about your own advantage. I despise you all."

I wanted to say something, to make her call back those unfair words, but she had already left the room.

She was wrong. Who was she to judge me, anyway? What did she know? Suddenly I wondered if she would make some other spell of her own and hurt us all because she did not like who we were or what we did. Because she could not understand. She was only a hetaira, a courtesan and entertainer. Her opinion meant nothing, except in the theater and at dinner parties.

And I knew I was wrong even as I thought those things. This courtesan was something much greater than she appeared. Otherwise, what would it matter what she thought? Still, far better that she had hated me and for much less reason.

Who was she anyway? And why did I care?

I pressed these matters to the back of my mind. They were not soldier's questions. They were not important. I had important things to do, a very political dinner to arrange and a death to contemplate. I couldn't spare the time for one little whore.

So I let her go with Alexa to do whatever magic they had planned while I went to do important things. Like argue with the porter about how to set the couches until my guests arrived.

Brother Michael was the last to arrive, as befitted a man of his calling and station. Caius Lucianus was the first, an old comrade from my days as a junior officer. He had since become a political creature and I distrusted him. But he was a good dinner guest, full of witty conversation and humor and all the latest gossip. Still, I was distressed to see how heavy he had grown, all those years of eating rich court food and no exercise. Fat and lazy, like the young boy who claims the throne.

Nikolas Patros and Nikolas Helios arrived together. We always called them "the Nikoli" and though they were unalike physically, they were inseparable in every other aspect of life. Patros was a court secretary and was privy to the entire correspondence of the emperor, as well as much of the diplomatic material with our tribute states. Helios was better positioned with the Navy, who generally go undernoticed because the Guard has more power. But the Navy holds the key to the seas and it is by the seas that we are most vulnerable. Byzantium is surrounded on three sides by water. Salt water. If it were not for Justinian's great foresight in building the cistern system, we could be cut off by land and brought low by the lack of fresh water. But we have the cisterns.

I had even been to a floating party once, hosted by Emperor Constantine. Down in the main cistern the pillars are old Roman statuary. One has a Medusa head, though in its proper place because such things are unholy. The whole is like the greatest palace chamber, all arches and fine marble, but the whole of the thing is covered in water and we sat in shallow boats with our picnics as the torchlight reflected in the great lake below us.

Decadent, I thought. That was when I decided I could not support him, even if the Church had crowned him and his father-in-law declared him ruler. The drunken boys peeing into what was the city's supply in case of siege was the last straw. He could not control his courtiers, the pup didn't even try. I could no more follow a man like him than I could follow a donkey.

These thoughts filled me while I watched my guests.

As I said, Brother Michael arrived last. He was shown to the couch of honor and wine was offered to him before any of the others. Inviting a churchman of his stature always makes entertaining simpler. I do not have to be concerned over who will feel slighted and who will feel his dignity threatened. Only the general, or maybe his son-in-law, would be a better choice for easy etiquette, but Brother Michael is easier to get. Besides, he loves my cook's fish in white sauce.

Which is properly famous. I could live without honey, without meat, without wine even. I could not live without this fish in white sauce, so rich and complex and satisfying to the tongue that I have it almost every day in Lent and all the rest of the year besides. Two serving girls, very pretty but demure, brought around the platters for the guests to serve themselves. The Nikoli and Caius took generous portions. Brother Michael took very little, which I found curious. He usually eats heartily of the fish and forgoes the meat, as becomes a man who is a walking saint.

I half listened to my guests' conversation. About the races again, the Blues and the Whites and who had the better teams and which charioteers were superior. I am partial to the Greens myself, so I listened a little more carefully and served more wine.

The meat came, and the garnishes, and the boiled eggs and the lentils that were a reminder of simple solider fare. I liked having lentils. They are honest food, and I am not ashamed that I have risen in rank and still enjoy the things I was born to enjoy. Lentils, and bread, and wine. Plenty of wine until the honey cakes were served around with yet another large unwatered pitcher.

Talk was freer now. "What do you think of the Cappadocian procession?" Patros asked.

"It was in poor taste," Caius replied. He is a snob, and out of shape to boot. I wondered through a haze of wine why I had invited him as his voice droned on in the background. "And it held up traffic patterns. They should have been content to go from the Hagia Sofia to the Palace like everyone else, or if they had to march around for an hour it should have been at the Hippodrome. Not through the streets and especially not on a market day. These people just do not have urban sensibilities. . . ."

"We should never have accepted the Cappadocians as allies," Nikolas Helios stated flatly. "They don't even know how to be decently defeated. They behave like they're doing you a favor after you've broken their necks. Impossible people."

"They need much more humility, and to be taught decency as well," Brother Michael added. "There is too much influence from that new religion of Muhammad and the Fatimids are becoming a real danger. And our general cannot supervise two fronts at the same time."

I shuddered. I had been on campaign to Persia and that had been enough. It had won my loyalty to my general forever, but the scars had never healed.

"Still," Caius interrupted, "we should have simply crushed them and treated them as a defeated colony. The emperor gives them far too much respect as it is."

I managed a polite smile and nod and then one of the Nikoli, Helios, used mention of the Hippodrome to turn the discussions back to racing again.

If Christa had not intervened, the entire party would have been a dismal failure for my purposes. All my guests ate heartily of every dish, excepting Brother Michael who should provide us worldly creatures with a model of restraint. The hetaira was right; my plan would have discovered nothing. I hoped hers would.

I said goodnight to my guests at the door with old Roman manners instead of permitting the porter to see them out. Brother Michael left after Caius but just before the Nikoli. I thought his parting glance to me was odd. Perhaps he was assessing Christa's work. I could not tell and I felt a cold chill as he studied me, and relief when he crossed the threshold.

The next day dawned beautiful, perfect and clear and bright, and not too warm to stand guard outside on the battlements without extra water. I awoke with more energy than I had had in ages, it seemed. There was no pain; there was no weariness. I had not slept so well in what seemed like ages, and now I was bursting with vigor and ready to start on my search.

Hours away still before the spell worked its insidious way through the food, just as it had taken weeks for the poison to accumulate in my body. I wondered for a moment whether Christa had done anything at all, or if she had merely given me a sop so that she could get out of my house.

For a moment I did not trust her. No one should trust anyone in Byzantium. There are too many plots and too many spies and more danger in the dining room than on the field of battle.

But Christa had been recommended to me by a respected churchman. If I could not trust Brother Michael, who left the maelstrom of politics for the monastery, I could not trust my own hands.

And so, for the morning, I went about my duties at the Palace. I made up guard rosters, I supervised training, I sat down with the commanders of another division and discussed our parade route strategy. I mentioned that there was some displeasure with the route for the Cappadocians, that even the most astute had not realized that we were trying not merely to impress the procession, but wear them out before they arrived at the Palace. We would have to find an alternative tactic.

And after I had done all the interesting and important things, there was the paperwork that had accumulated during my illness. Beloved of bureaucrats, there were so many documents to sign, others to examine, and more than just a few to write. Including a complete report to the Palace security agents about possible threats to our true ruler during negotiations with the Latins. Being crafty and wise was not always enough. The Franks and the representatives of the Pope of Rome were as perfectly capable of a full-out frontal murder attempt as an elegantly prepared and meticulous delivered assassination. It is quite frustrating that they are more deterred by large numbers of men in uniforms and swords than by the knowledge that our Lyceum Magus is superior to any training available in the Latin states. And by the fact that only a very few Frankish and Florentine and Venetian students have ever stayed out the full course there. No other foreigners, to my knowledge, have ever been accepted. Perhaps they think that their crude witchcraft is a match for anything we can teach. In this they are quite wrong, and even I understand how great an error it is to underestimate the enemy.

We are enemies. Though of course we never say so directly. And for which I am just as glad. I would rather openly be their enemy than to have to pretend to be allied to those unwashed, uncouth foreigners. I much prefer dealing with the Arabs. At least they bathe. And their magical academies in Fez and Damascus are worthy rivals to our own (though of course ours is the superior institution, and Christian besides).

I did not spend so long on paperwork as perhaps I ought. I did not finish more than a few pages of the pile my secretary had left on my desk and told me was of the most urgent character. I pushed away from the desk and surveyed the stack. It was only for the bureaucrats after all. And it was already past noon.

Past noon. This time yesterday I had been in conference with Brother Michael. Today I felt hearty and strong, and very soon I would know who was attempting to poison me. Unless it was someone not at my party.

A sudden chill ran over me. Perhaps it was none of the obvious candidates. Perhaps it was some foreign embassy that had been insulted by a parade route, or a cousin I have not seen in years who wanted to inherit, as my wife has never seen fit to have children. There could be so many people, so many reasons, and I had only considered the simple and political.

And it was past noon. Soon, very soon if Christa's expectations were correct, I would know my murderer. If Christa's spells worked, if I had invited the right people.

As if I had summoned her with my thoughts, Christa swept into my study, the porter trotting behind her to announce her, or at least keep her from invading my sanctum.

"It's all right, Theodos." I waved him away.

Christa did not sit down. She stood stark still in the middle of the floor glowering at me. Her courtesan's mantle was draped elegantly from the shoulder and fell in rich folds over her feet. Her hair was simply dressed and heavy black curls hung free to her waist.

"So now what?" I asked her. "How do we know who it is, or do I have to sit here and pretend that everything is normal until someone dies?" I'll admit that my tone held a nasty edge.

She looked at me for a long minute, her eyes snapping. "No," she said finally. "I put a compulsion on the spell. The person affected will have to come here. Whoever shows up in your study this afternoon is the murderer."

"Why did you come then?" I asked, genuinely curious. "Why didn't you just tell me last night and stay home?"

She sighed heavily and the mask of avenging fury dropped from her face. "Because I am honestly curious myself," she said. "Because as much as I despise the kind of person you are, all your blind loyalties and assumptions, I also do not think that slow poison is admirable. And I admit it, I am curious. Brother Michael told me that there was no reason anyone would want to attack some mid-ranked officer in the Guard. There are too many of you, and you have far too little power to matter."

She might as well have stuck a knife in my gut. Not enough to matter. But I *did* matter to someone, enough to risk the killing.

"Well, we may have to wait a while," I said. "You might as well sit down. Or would that be demeaning to someone in as exalted a position as yourself, to sit in a mere mid-level officer's chair?" I couldn't keep the sneer from my tone.

She did have the grace to blush slightly, and seated herself on the couch where she rearranged the folds of her mantle so that they retained their rich shape and flowed over the furniture like water. No matter how infuriating or rude, I had to admit that she was beautiful. And there was something in her venom that added to her attraction.

I sent to the kitchen for some light refreshments, with the order that the new girl Alexa serve. There would be argument, I knew. The more senior girls would grumble that they were not able to escape the heat and the hard work and the critical eyes of the cook. And I would have to hear it later when the cook complained to my wife about me choosing which kitchen wench served, hoping that she would find it in her heart to be angry and jealous. While my wife would not be at all jealous, she would still report the entire thing to me in miserable detail. If she had to suffer the moans of the cook, she would make sure I suffered as well.

Alexa came in with a platter of honey cakes stuffed with pistachios and an ewer of wine. She behaved almost like a real serving girl until she went to kneel at her mistress' feet. They chatted quietly.

I knew I should return to the paperwork. There was so much to do and I had avoided it far too long. Christa and Alexa were being quiet. I should be able to concentrate. But I would honestly rather do anything than the required reports and signatures, especially not on such a fine and still afternoon. The light shimmered in the garden and I could hear the water in the fountain dancing brightly.

And suddenly I panicked as I had never done in battle. Christa's spell wouldn't work. I was wasting time, wasting what little was left of my life. I was terribly afraid. We could sit all afternoon and no one would come. And I would never discover the murderer. And even if I were cured of this poison there would be another, and another. And if those didn't work there would be a young girl to slip a knife between my ribs in the hours before dawn.

The porter interrupted my morbid musings when he announced Brother Michael had arrived to see me.

I will admit I was startled. Brother Michael has rarely visited, and never uninvited. If he had some message for me he could easily have sent a servant, and had done so on other occasions. So I could not help but wonder to what I owed the honor of his visit.

He swept into the room, his black church robes sweeping the clean mosaic behind him like the emperor's train. His high black headdress covered his bald scalp and his white beard shone like bright silver against his priestly garments. His eyes were steady and easy and he smiled as he saw Christa and Alexa and the tray of honey cakes. He took two of the cakes before he sat down in the larger armchair and sighed deeply.

"To what do I owe the honor of this visit, sir?" I asked, perplexed.

Brother Michael's eyes sparkled. "I was at St. Luke's for a christening and on the way home I realized I was very close to your house. And I thought you might not mind an old man resting out of the sun for a minute or two before going on home. It is a long way back to the monastery."

"After you are rested, I hope you will let me send you the rest of the way in the sedan chair," I offered. It is pleasantly warm, but a long way back and Brother Michael's robes are heavy.

He nibbled at the honey cakes avidly and took a third while Christa asked about whose baby had been christened and who had been present, all the gossip that a hetaira was supposed to know. Though the family turned out not to be noble—no surprise. A noble infant would not have been baptized at St. Luke's, though it was quite impressive that a family of little wealth and less standing could draw the likes of the old abbot.

He took two more cakes, and the platter looked a little empty. I asked Alexa to return to the kitchen and get some more snacks. Obviously Brother Michael was hungry.

She smiled and obeyed. But I did not see her return.

Suddenly, sharply, the pain lanced through my body. My stomach was pierced by a hundred lances. I burned with Greek fire coating my innards. I dropped to the floor and screamed, curled up to try and ease the pain.

But the pain did not ease. It raced through me and doubled itself, worse than it had ever been before. "Help me," I moaned.

I saw Christa stand over me, her face white and shocked and her mouth drawn. "I can't," she said, her tone distressed and amazed together. "I . . . *can't*. The magic is gone. Oh dear Lord, it's gone!"

She started keening and wringing her hands. Brother Michael took a handful of the new cakes and the almond-stuffed dates and then consumed four pieces of toast covered in goat cheese and herbs before he even looked at me.

Or at Christa. I was in too much pain to make it out clearly.

"Help me," Christa pleaded with him. "My magic is gone. It's gone." She still seemed panicked.

I was well beyond caring.

Brother Michael smiled, the warm sincere smile of a saint in Heaven. "I really can't help you, my dear," he said, patting her fondly on the shoulder. "I have to be going now."

"But he's going to die," Christa wailed.

And Brother Michael turned and smiled again. This smile was just as warm and just as winning as the earlier one. "Just so," he said. "It is God's will. There is nothing you can do."

And then it was all a jumble that seemed like a dream. Brother Michael eating and eating as if he had never seen food before. Though he had just come from a christening, and he could hardly have failed to stay for the party. Even poor people have parties with the best food they can offer.

"You," she screamed, and lunged for him. "You've taken my magic away."

Her nails reached his face and he mumbled something, made a pass that even I recognized as a spell. Protecting himself.

But nothing happened. Christa's long nails reached his nose and tore skin from his cheek.

Brother Michael turned white.

"Stop it," I yelled in my parade command voice.

And they did stop. Without their magic they were— ordinary. And though their magic was stripped, my years of training and drilling and command were still intact.

Slowly, painfully, I drew myself up. I managed to get to my chair, to sit, to lean back and uncross my arms from my belly. I thought of the great traditions of the Roman legions. We are the new Rome, the center of the universe. All roads lead to Byzantium.

And I knew I was going to die. I could feel the poison eating my insides out. The pain had become so great that I could hardly feel it. It overwhelmed so that I could not acknowledge the greatness of it, and so I could not respond.

All I could think of was to die well. Romans did not succumb to mere agony, did not surrender merely because they were doomed.

Both Christa and Brother Michael looked at me in amazement as I got up from the floor and arranged myself decently in the chair. They did not seem to believe I could do even this much.

I looked at them, one to the other. I knew, it was all so clear, and yet I could not believe it or face the truth. Dying was easier.

"Tell me, please, Brother Michael, why you have had me killed," I said softly.

The old churchman looked past me, to the icon of the Madonna on the wall behind me. "This blocking of our magic is God's will," he started. "Otherwise you might survive until Christa could save you. But I knew that there was no choice. You see, Lucius Arsenius, your Roman loyalty is far too simple. You make up the guard schedules, you are privy to everything in the Palace."

"But I am loyal to the general," I said.

"Yes," Brother Michael said. "I know. And so does everyone else. And you would still guard the young emperor and save him from death. You would not join in an assassination plot."

My eyes widened. "Nor would the general," I protested. "He would have nothing of it. And there is no need, young Constantine is only a figurehead and a boy anyway."

Brother Michael waved his hand. "The general would not know. It was perfectly planned. The Cappadocians would take the blame, and they are a treacherous people in the best of times. We cannot trust them as allies in any event. Better to simply beat them thoroughly and teach them to fear the empire. And so we would have no young emperor and a good solid war against the Cappadocians and Milos Kalkaines would be ready to marry the widow when the time came. It was perfect. It was God's plan. I was only the instrument of Divine will. And it will save the general in any case, because two of young Constantine's plots against the general have failed due to us in any case."

He chuckled and glanced around the room. "You invited all the wrong people, Lucius Arsenius. The Nikoli and Caius are all part of my faction to keep the general safe. We are very discreet, you understand. But since you will die soon I can tell you these things safely."

"And where do I fit into this will of God?" Christa demanded.

Brother Michael looked at her with amazement. "Child, you would not have saved him. You hate his kind, and in the deeper forms of healing there can be no hatred. No, you would have done very well and still it would have done no good. Then he would die and you would learn to be humble about your minor talent as a woman should, and keep it for the amusement of your clients."

Christa sprang up, ready to attack the old man again. I ordered her to sit. "If anyone is going to kill Brother Michael, it's me," I said, perfectly calm and rational. "I am already a dead man, so it makes no difference. You would die for this murder, I would already be dead."

I did not know how I could do it. I rose and grasped the sword that hung at my side. That sword that had fit into my hand every day since I was a boy now seemed too heavy to lift. And yet I saw myself raise it to my waist and lurch forward. I watched as the short blade thrust into the old abbot's chest and the blood spurted out as I withdrew the blade.

I smiled at Christa. "We are both avenged," I told her.

I think I collapsed. I lay on the floor, aware only of the burning running through me again and of Christa standing over me, crying. Trying to say magical words to no avail. Perhaps it was God's will, I truly do not know. But the exercise was dead. Christa could have been reciting Homer's catalog of ships for all the good it did.

And then she knelt next to me and took my hand. "I

misjudged you, Lucius Arsenius," she said. "I was wrong. There is much that is admirable in you, and I shall try to remember always."

"And the Emperor," I said.

"What?" she asked.

"The plot," I reminded her. "It must be exposed. I do not like the young emperor and I do not like the Cappadocians and I have never made a secret of either. But I will not permit them to be smeared unjustly. God knows, there is surely enough good cause."

The end of the magic for that time surely must have been God's will, though Brother Michael would not understand. If he had been able to use his great power we never would have known about this plot. And I might have lived, or might not, but that was less important than the truth. And with his magic about him Brother Michael would have been unassailable.

"What shall we do?" she asked. "I have several clients in very high places."

"Yes," I encouraged her. "Let them dig out the whole plot."

Then I shuddered and sighed. The last act of my life, and it was one I hated. "Bring me a parchment and pen," I said. Paperwork.

My head spun. I could not write much. My hand was not steady and the letters did not look like my own. And yet I forced myself to go on, to put all the words down.

I, Lucius Arsenius, a commander of the Varangian Guard, have this day killed Brother Michael upon his admission of guilt in a plot to destroy our young emperor and blame the deed upon the Cappadocians. This is a true statement. The hetaira Christa is witness to this.

Then I signed my name and sank back to the cool tile.

She took the page from the floor and read it slowly. "I will show this to everyone at the Palace," she said. And I knew she would. Without magic she was no less intimidating than she had been before.

I had my revenge, I had my victory. And it was enough.

FLICKER

Jody Lynn Nye

Binyamin ben Gibb stood on the stage of the amphitheater and waved his hands in the air. "You see, my lords and ladies, not a flicker of magic about me. Ask your neighbor if you're not certain of it yourself. Go on. I like my audiences to become acquainted."

There was a hubbub of low murmuring in the audience, punctuated with giggles. A few patrons reached out their hands toward him, eyes closed or open, sensing. Ben Gibb nodded.

"Satisfied?"

There was a roar of approval from the crowd. "Then where did these fine birds spring from?" He raised his hands on high so his long, purple-banded sleeves dropped to his shoulders, to reveal eight white doves perching on his hands. The audience applauded and cheered. He smiled, showing brilliant, square, white teeth.

"You are too kind. In tribute, therefore, I release these birds to the gods!" He shook the doves off. They fluttered about him for a moment, then scattered hastily to the skies. Ben Gibb wasn't worried about their well-being, nor their return. They'd congregate backstage in a short while, where Vasilius, his assistant, waited with handfuls of bread crumbs rubbed with fat.

His entire act consisted of such ruses—the merest trickery—and yet ben Gibb played to full houses day and night. For all their fine powers, the wealthy and powerful ones had forgotten the skills of their own humble bodies. These people could buy and sell him a hundred times over, but he had something they did not. Hand-eye coordination, misdirection, duplication, the careful placement of wires and trapdoors and smudge pots gave him the ability to create wonders without the use of magic, a gift which—alas—he had been denied. Children usually saw more of the hidden side of his act than the adults, but they all watched in wonder.

"And now, my cherished patrons, I wonder if I might beg your cooperation?" ben Gibb asked, stepping to the edge of the stage and leaning forward engagingly toward the sea of crisp white and purple cloth. "Would one of you consent to be the subject of my next miracle? I swear before all the gods that there will be no affront to your honor, nor embarrassment of any kind. Will one step forward?" He'd had his eye on three or four togaed matrons in the crowd. Older women made good subjects and were always grateful for the attention. "You, madam? Or perhaps you?"

The sea of linen heaved as men turned to the women they were with and tried to persuade or forbid. Ben Gibb smiled. He knew that in the heart of the shyest woman was a secret wish to be bold, and here was the safest of exposures. To participate in a theater trick was not at all dangerous nor harmful to the modesty, and yet it guaranteed every eye would be upon her. Ben Gibb waited respectfully, then bowed deeply in the direction of an excited cluster of patrons.

One of the women had been persuaded by her companions to mount the stage. She must have been fifty or so, but her eyes were shining and hopeful as a girl's. Ben Gibb took her hand as if it were made of thinnest glass, and led her to the pedestal table where his equipment had been replenished by a swift-footed Vasilius.

"I am indeed most honored, madam, for such distinguished a patroness as yourself to participate in my poor show," ben Gibb said. The woman gave him a gracious smile, and he returned it, taking great care to look humble. He took a brass bowl from the table. The heavy smell of oil rose from it. From the scent he could tell that Vasilius had once again mixed the solution flawlessly. What an apprentice the boy was becoming! "Take this here in your left hand, my lady. It is not too heavy, is it?"

"No," the matron twittered. She fixed a nervous smile on her mouth as ben Gibb walked around to her other side with another bowl and laid it on her other upturned palm. He moved around behind her, spreading his hands out, ready, judging the timing.

"And now raise them on high!" Ben Gibb threw up his arms toward Heaven. "I call upon the gods to show here the favor they have for this honorable woman and the line of her house!"

As the woman thrust the bowls upward, the thin film of oil in each sloshed enough to expose the Greek fire underneath to the air. Whoosh! Flames shot upward, red on one hand, and blue on the other. The woman gaped, nearly dropping them, but not quite. She *was* brave. Ben Gibb had not misjudged his subject. Nor had he misjudged the amount of Greek fire in the bowls. Her hands, when he removed the magical impedimenta from them, were no more than warm. Her cheeks, too, were glowing. Ben Gibb smoothly transferred both bowls to one hand and used the other to pick up the trailing hem of her toga. He bowed deeply to the floor and kissed the fold of cloth.

"I thank you, patroness. The gods do indeed favor you." And me, he thought gratefully. With care, with luck, I've been spared another beating. Perhaps there'll even be coins afterward. He pledged a third of all gifts tonight to Mercury.

The woman beamed at him, and was helped off the stage by her family, all chattering excitedly about the magic. The young girl who took her grandmother's arm glanced up at ben Gibb through thick eyelashes. How lovely she was—ah, but how unobtainable. Such a high-born lady of such fabulous beauty as that must have suitors galore among her own class. Ben Gibb recognized her with a start. It was Eupatia. The older woman was not her mother, so it must be an aunt or the mother of a friend.

Shaking, he retreated to center stage. For a moment, the persona of ben Gibb the magician retreated, and that of Binyamin, second son of Gibb ben Yelia, the wealthy cloth merchant, peered out. He and Eupatia had been neighbors and friends all through their childhood. She was an attractive girl who had no idea how beautiful she was, nor would she believe Binyamin when he told her so. When she had manifested magical talent, she'd used it to enhance her face and form until she was nearly goddesslike. Binyamin, gawky, thin, teenaged, only a second son, was intimidated, almost terrified, by such perfection. He waited in vain for his own talent to emerge so he might one day approach her from a position of equal strength. It never happened. He was dextrous, he was intelligent, but painfully devoid of any hint of magic. Both his parents and his elder brother, Ruven, had good skills. Though they didn't say so, Binyamin felt they were ashamed he was so talentless. They never understood why Binyamin had chosen to leave.

He'd made his own way, traveling out into the far reaches of the empire with a few tricks he'd worked out and a packful of fabric lengths from his father's ware-houses. Over time, he had increased his repertoire of illusions and refined the quality of his stage show. In a modest way he'd become famous, though earning bread and lodging wasn't always a certain thing. He'd worked

his way back to Constantine's city two or three times,
but none of his family had ever come to a show. They
didn't connect ben Gibb the wonderworker with their
son. And now Eupatia was here. She was blinding, breath-
takingly beautiful, and just as forbidding as before. He
strained after her, until an impatient shuffling of feet in the
front rows reminded him he had a show in progress.

"My lords and ladies, another wonder, if you please?"
He returned to center stage, drawing every eye with a
sweep of his purple sleeves. Vasilius trotted out from
behind the curtain, his arms loaded with silk cloths. Ben
Gibb kept a close eye on the flambeaux at the edge of
the stage. He'd commissioned those cloths in the great
Eastern markets at colossal expense. The brilliant jewel
colors in them were real, and the weaving of such a fine
web cost a fortune. A single ember could send his whole
investment up in noxious smoke.

"My lords and ladies, know you of the wonders of the
East? A man there may divest himself of his outer body
and walk in the midst of the crowd invisible! Only his
spirit passes back and forth, bringing back to the earthly
form the experience it has had. I have learned this skill
from the most learned of the Eastern wizards. Shutting
out all light, I shall now put my body into a state of
suspension, and walk among you, describing secrets that
I find. When I return, I shall reveal them. Ah, ladies,
fear not for yourselves," he said slyly, to the twitter that
arose. "I am a man of honor. As for you gentlemen, I
can be persuaded with a coin or two." He raised his
eyebrows and pantomimed the counting of money.

There was a burst of appreciative laughter. As ben
Gibb described the miracle of invisibility, Vasilius began
busily to drape the veils over his master's shoulders and
arms in a prearranged pattern. It looked like the boy was
strewing them at random. It was meant to. First, two
whole layers of black silk went on, then came heavy draperies of colored cloth with hidden wires inside to create
the appearance of a body standing with its arms outflung.

His hands now hidden from view, ben Gibb removed the rods from the inside of his robe that would hold the whole exoskeleton upright. The outer layer of black would prevent anyone from seeing through the disguise. Then, under cover of the inner layer of black, ben Gibb waited for the dancing girls to whirl across the stage. When every eye had locked onto their beauty, he crept slowly backward through the curtain.

He stripped down to the short tunic under his toga and stole, and ran out of the stage entrance. His sandals flapped on the loose pebbles of the brick street as he dashed into another entrance. Servants and patricians alike ignored him as he made his way politely through the rows, offering dates and figs from a tray. Clad in an ordinary servant's tunic, he was invisible.

On the stage, Vasilius, stocky in his white robe, flitted around the brilliantly colored figure on stage, chanting. Occasionally he would draw near and cock his ear toward the "face," as if listening to something that he, the Magician ben Gibb, had to say.

Ben Gibb glanced around him. Most eyes were still fastened on the silk-draped framework. Quickly, he picked out a few likely subjects. The woman in the yellow-patterned toga—he'd seen her before. There was a slight heaviness about her face, but she did not seem unhappy. With child? If not, he could at least hint at good news. But wait—she leaned backward to hear the words of someone seated behind her. The loose gown dropped across her midsection. Yes. Very slight, but unmistakeable. It would perhaps be news to her neighbors.

He watched as two youngsters, barely into manhood and womanhood, met in a steeply sloped aisle to exchange love tokens under the light of a flambeau. They parted, and hurried back to where their families sat in the amphitheater. Ben Gibb smiled. No, he wouldn't spoil their joy. First love comes only once, he thought with a sigh. The youths were equally well-dressed. It was likely their parents could be persuaded to make a match between them someday, if he did not ruin their secret with his intervention. He thought of Eupatia, and sighed.

A tidbit of information here, an observation there, an overheard word or two gleaned from a low conversation between two very highborn men, a purse untied and the contents counted, as ben Gibb was out of the door and running for the stage again.

In a moment, he had assumed his magician's robes, and signalled to the dancing girls to whirl out and distract the audience once again. Trying to ignore the compelling rhythm of sistrum and drum, ben Gibb scurried forward under cover of black silk to fill out the dummy figure. He began to sway as if coming to himself.

Vasilius sprang forward to remove the cloths from his master's face. Ben Gibb let his head drop backward. He addressed the crowd in a ringing voice.

"I have seen! The gods have given to me many visions."

One by one, he enumerated his observations. The husband of the woman in yellow beamed around at his neighbors as a nod from his blushing wife confirmed that there was a baby on the way. The audience sighed with happiness. A matron at once began to scold the son whom ben Gibb revealed had torn a large hole in his embroidered tunic while roughhousing in the aisles. The man whose pocket the magician had picked was so impressed that ben Gibb knew to the last sesterce how much he had with him he threw a good handful of coins onto the stage. Vasilius ran forward to gather them. The magician stood looking out over the crowd with dignity, ignoring his servant as if such things as money were beneath him, although he was aware of the count and kind of the gift. Such would feed his company for a week!

With the greatest daring, ben Gibb warned the two senators that the measure they planned to introduce was unfavorable to the gods.

"Perhaps sacrifice would help propitiate them!" he finished, his voice booming to the outermost pillars.

"How do you do it?" a man called from the middle distance.

"I but use the gifts given me by the gods," ben Gibb said, bowing humbly. "I learned the skills in many places around the world, so that I can bring them here—to you!" From a concealed pouch in the heavy robe, he produced rose petals and flung them out over the heads of the crowd as if they had appeared just then in his palm. The audience laughed. He thought it was with delight, but there was an unfamiliar edge to the sound. Ben Gibb looked anxiously in the direction of the loudest murmur. He'd thought when he had examined his audience that the family on the eighth tier was one of wealth, but now that he looked again, he wondered how he had misjudged them. The regal purple trim at the edges of their togae was of the cheap imitation made with grape extract, not Tyrian snails. And the woman's gold necklace was dross. Her fine linen was not so crisp, nor the jewels so bright.

But it was not only those patrons whose appearance had suddenly slipped in value. Nearly everyone in the best seats looked shabbier than they had. What's more, they were noticing the change in one another. Some of them glanced down at themselves, and were horrified at what they saw.

Ben Gibb was offended. Some wag in the audience had decided to use his art to deprive those around him of their illusions, thereby upstaging *him*. Unless the perpetrator ceased his practical joke at once and restored the semblance of beauty and wealth, there'd be a riot. Already he noticed that one of the ladies was leaning over, covering herself with her veil. Her ample, round bosom, just concealed by the thinnest of gowns, had attracted his attention when she had entered the theater. Now her breasts seemed to be drooping precipitously toward the floor. Her cheeks burned with shame, and her husband was looking around him with his hands clenched, searching for someone, anyone, who was grinning at his wife. Binyamin looked around, too, but saw only confusion and anger.

An old man sagged backward in his seat, gasping for air. His wife and children rallied around him, fanning his face and slapping his wrists. He waved them away, but his skin was touched with a blue tinge. Ben Gibb had seen enough men with weak hearts to know that here was another. If he could relax, his humors would rally, returning healthy color to his cheeks.

In desperation, ben Gibb clapped his hands. The dancing girls, their scarves no longer peacock bright but still pretty, dashed onto the stage and began whirling around. The audience, distracted, looked up at them.

"Good ladies and gentlemen," the magician called. "May I not please you? I present yet another of my celebrated miracles! My assistant, Vasilius!" He flourished his long hands back and forth, and the servant ran forward. Ben Gibb heard a faint clanking. Clever boy, he'd understood the cue.

"You have servant problems at home, do you not?" ben Gibb asked the audience. He heard a murmur of response. Too many people were still eyeing one another, or looking down at themselves. "I have nothing but trouble, nothing! I am a good master, and yet this lad steals from me. Yes, steals! I shall prove it."

He turned to Vasilius, who pretended to tremble. Ben Gibb shook Vasilius's right sleeve. It seemed empty, but a handful of coins slipped clattering from it onto the stage. The magician shook harder. A brass lamp, handsome but cheap, fell between their feet with a crash. He grabbed the boy's other hand and shook both of them. He was rewarded with a knife, handfuls of necklaces, and a very small dog that dropped to the floor and scrambled to its feet. It ran around them, barking.

Ben Gibb had regained the audience. They were staring at him, and many were laughing. Vasilius's sleeves and tunic produced clay cups, one after another, a length of chain, a small shield, and a pair of caligae. Ben Gibb released the boy's hands and turned to appeal to the audience.

"What am I to do with such a thief?"

"Dismiss him!" a man shouted.

"Beat him!"

Ben Gibb shook his head.

"Kill him!" cried a woman's voice, harsh with some emotion.

"I will," the magician said. "I shall put this wretch to death as a lesson to others who might steal from their good masters!" He clapped his hands. One of the girls ran out from backstage, bearing a pair of light, bronze swords. Ben Gibb took them from her and clashed them together. He aimed the points at Vasilius, who had fallen to his knees with his hands clasped together under his chin.

"Mercy, master!" the boy quavered.

"You deserve none!" Ben Gibb announced, in stentorian tones.

Exaggerating every movement, he stalked toward Vasilius. The crowd began to chant.

"Kill him, kill him, kill him, kill him. . . ."

By the gods, ben Gibb thought, I hope they don't swarm over us when they find out it's only a trick.

Using the volume of his sleeves for cover, he crossed the swords in a certain way. He shoved the juncture of the two shining blades under the boy's chin, then yanked them outward. The swords flashed underneath the boy's ears, flew outward.

The audience gasped. Ben Gibb stood back and turned slowly, holding the swords aloft, to reveal Vasilius, still with his head on his shoulders. There was a moment of silence, then the audience broke into thunderous applause. As soon as he could be heard again, the magician spoke to the crowd.

"Good help is *so* hard to find, my lords and ladies."

"Magic!" a man cried from the high tiers of the amphitheater. "How could you do that?"

"Just skill, good sir," ben Gibb said, bowing. He handed the swords to Vasilius, careful to conceal the wire hinges that allowed the blades to fold.

"My mother's eyesight depends on a spell. It ceased to work just a few moments ago. We've tried and tried to restore it but no one's skill remains. How is it you can keep on going with your wonders?"

Ben Gibb was confused. "I told you, good sir, my miracles have nothing to do with magic. Everything I do can be explained by the skillful passage of hands."

"It's a lie!" shouted the husband of the woman in the thin dress.

"Why do you accuse me of lying? I seek only to entertain," ben Gibb said, now feeling desperate. He swept his gaze across the audience. They did not look happy.

"You have stolen our magic!" the first man shouted. "Restore it at once!"

"Yes, give it back!" Others took up the cry.

"I've taken nothing!" ben Gibb said, his hands outspread, now worried. His heart pounded wildly as he looked out across the crowd but he forced his voice to remain calm. So this was no single man's prank. No one had the power to suppress so many talents at once. He straightened up, commanding the audience with the patrician stance his father had so often used when someone questioned *his* integrity.

"Ask yourselves. Did you not look into your hearts when I first spoke to you? Didn't I say that I had no magic, that my wonders were illusions? Didn't you find that true?"

"Well . . . yes," said a few patrons, reluctant to admit they *had* been monitoring him.

"Then how could I steal your magic, which would surely take more skill than *you* have. I am but a humble illusionist."

The murmuring rose again, as the good people

debated his words. The angry husband leaped up and thrust out an accusing hand.

"He seeks to twist our minds to agree!" he shouted. "Kill him, and our magic will return!"

The mob took up the shout, just as it had preceding Vasilius's mock execution. "Kill him! Kill him! Kill him!"

Ben Gibb's blood turned cold. "Gentle ladies, I appeal to you . . ."

But he couldn't get another word out. The crowd had risen to its feet, and swept toward him. They were buoyed on the rage and shame of having their secrets turned inside out so everyone could see the seams. Ben Gibb was no fool. He turned on his heel and ran.

Vasilius and the dancers were offstage already, fleeing to safety, wherever that may be. Ben Gibb pushed his way past the flutter of falling veils that the women had thrown off so they would not be hampered while running. Above him, the white doves fluttered to the top of the wall, emitting coos of fear. The magician realized that he wouldn't have a chance at life if the frightened crowd recognized him. He hastily pulled off the sumptuous purple robes, and with real regret, stuffed them into the properties chest next to the door. The chest he shifted so it blocked the door swinging inward, in hopes of giving him a few seconds more ahead of the mob.

"I know not if I will ever see you again, my treasures," he muttered, with a sad glance, as much to his absent assistants as to the magical apparatus. Behind him, the sound of chanting voices grew louder, and he heard the slap of sandals on stone. The boldest of the men in the audience had decided to take action. If the magician had stolen their magic, and the only way to release it was death, then they would kill him. But the magician had no intention of remaining to die quietly. Ben Gibb grabbed a pair of Vasilius's disreputable sandals and put them on. His good shoes he tossed out the players' entrance to the left, then hotfooted to his right, the side away from the patrons' gate.

What had happened? ben Gibb asked himself as he dashed down the alley. Surely nothing *he* had done had deprived his patrons of their abilities! He'd never had a legitimate spell in his life. The great God knew he had been born singularly devoid of magical talent, else he would never have begun such a career. So it was someone or something else taking action against the supernaturally talented—but what? Who?

Ben Gibb ran along the alley toward one of Constantinople's markets. It should be easy to lose himself here. At nightfall, he intended to sneak out of town and seek his fortune elsewhere. Too bad, he told himself, thinking of the patrons who threw handfuls of coins on a whim. It would have been nice to stay another week and lay in a small store of wealth. Perhaps he would have bought silk scarves for the dancing girls, and new shoes for Vasilius. And he'd have welcomed another glimpse of Eupatia.

He skidded to a halt at the mouth of the alley, looking around him with horror. Had everyone gone mad?

The street was full of mobs of angry men, most of them wearing fine robes that were torn and stained with blood. Groups of them leaped forward to pull down the awnings over booths. They kicked at piles of oranges, scattering the fruit all over the muddy street. If any of the merchants protested, the men dragged them out and beat them, leaving them gasping on the cobbles. What frightened ben Gibb most was the wild look on all the faces. One woman ran screaming past him. She skidded to a halt for a moment, looking up at the sky. Her hands waved up and back in a complicated pattern. Whatever she was expecting to happen, didn't. She burst out crying, tearing at her hair. Ben Gibb stepped forward to put a hand on her arm.

"What's wrong?"

She shook him off, and ran away, shrieking and crying. Ben Gibb didn't have time to wonder what was happening. The sound of running behind him alerted him that his own problems were not far behind him.

"There he goes!" a voice shouted. Ben Gibb recognized it as the angry husband. A wild cry went up as the others spotted their quarry. He took only a glimpse back at the mob, as disheveled and dirty as the crowd in the market. Survival lay ahead. He plunged into the forest of awning poles.

"Stop him!" the man yelled.

Ben Gibb flung aside stolae hanging from a rope and dashed into a booth from the side. A young girl looked up at him with huge, dark eyes. A small child huddled with its head in her lap, too frightened to move.

"I won't harm you," he said, holding his hands palm out to show he held no weapon. The girl continued to stare as he scrambled over the pile of garments on the floorcloth, and out the other side of the booth, brushing aside more scarves. Poor quality, he thought, as he ran. His father wouldn't tolerate the stuff in the lowest of his shops.

"Out!" the proprietress of the spice stall ordered, as he appeared between the hanging scales. She was a stout matron with a shawl over her hair and shoulders. When he didn't move immediately she came after him with a huge bronze ladle. She swung the big spoon at his head. He sidestepped, knocking his shoulder on one of the measuring pans. Orange cumin powder spilled in his face, making him sneeze. The woman snarled as the precious spice scattered all over. Ben Gibb eluded another blow from her ladle, and ran out into the street.

Unluckily, he found himself almost in the midst of his pursuers. The men greeted his sudden appearance among them with open mouths. Without his costume it took them extra moments to recognize him. By the time they realized the slender man with red hair was their quarry, he had taken to his heels again. They shouted their hunting cry, only making him run faster.

"Stop!" they shouted. "Stop him!" Ben Gibb paid no

attention. As long as the rest of the city was going mad, too, no one else was going to pay attention to one running man.

A rock hit him between the shoulder blades. More stones whizzed past him, splashing in the sewer trench that ran down the middle of the street. He covered his head with his arms and ducked into the nearest shopfront.

It was a mistake. He knew it as soon as he did it. The low shop had no other exit to the street. Two young male slaves glanced up startled from the bread dough they were shaping. Ben Gibb looked around frantically for an escape route. To run out the door into the windowless courtyard would only trap him in an enclosed space large enough for the mob to corner and beat him. He cast his gaze about.

"In here!" he heard his pursuers shouting. The door darkened with their shadows just as he threw himself over the barrels of flour into the corner of the brick walls just under the hot ovens. One of the slaves turned to stare down at him. He pantomimed pleading, clasping his hands together, and the servant nodded.

Ben Gibb huddled against the rough bags of unmilled grain, trying to make himself seem like a half-filled sack. He pulled a fold of his tunic up over his bright hair and shut his eyes, hoping that a stray gleam of light from door or window wouldn't give him away.

The men streamed into the bake shop. They were too far gone in rage to make a careful search. Instead, they rocked the barrels, kicked the sacks, and slammed the doors. A hard toe took ben Gibb straight in the belly, but he swallowed his exclamation of pain. He just concentrated on keeping his head down. One of them discovered the entrance to the courtyard behind, and some of them followed, shouting. Others pulled open the iron doors to the bread ovens, to the dismay of the wailing bakers.

"They're gone," the servant whispered, as the shouting

receded. "The morning's bake ruined! My master will be furious."

Ben Gibb raised himself carefully from the floor. His tunic was covered with chaff.

"My . . . my thanks for saving my life," he said, as he climbed over the barrels. The two servants bowed, their eyes on him, expectant. He fumbled for his purse. It was still there, and a few coins remained in it. He jingled the bag and handed it to the young men. "Give this to your master to make amends." They bowed. That was the last grand gesture he could make, so he hoped it would do. The servants glanced at each other, and he knew the money wouldn't get to the baker. That was all right. These men had earned it. With as much dignity as he could, he straightened his tunic and stepped out into the street.

It looked like the poets' description of a war zone. Men and women wandered aimlessly, their eyes focused on nothing. Pickpockets and looters, knowing that their crimes would go unremarked in the general chaos, thrust their way boldly into the press of people, emerging with pouches and necklaces almost under the noses of the overrun centurions. It hadn't taken the criminal element long to seize opportunity. Binyamin ben Gibb realized that he, too, should have come to his senses long since. He was reacting to crowd hysteria, instead of working with it.

The patrons stumbled out of the fourth shop along the street from the bakery.

"I told you there was no magician in here!" the angry woman who followed them shouted, her voice audible over the usual market hubbub. "I've enough to deal with, if the milk turns sour!"

Before they should turn and see him, ben Gibb slipped into the crowd and strode off in the opposite direction. The mob could go on rampaging through disappointment after disappointment. If they didn't catch him, eventually their rage would abate, and they would go home.

He walked as fast as his legs would move. Changing from one side of the street to the other, he checked to see if anyone was on his trail. So far, no one. Good. He wove his way out of the market, not able to believe the decline that had happened almost in the flicker of an eyelash. What had happened? Was magic gone for good? Had all magic around the world vanished at the same time? If so, he would have to find himself a new act. It would be too perilous to perform his miracles. He was used to the jealousy of young men whose women he captivated by his skills at prestidigitation, but this fear and murderous rage that had manifested itself in the theater terrified him.

He could go home! He would never have considered such a choice before, but without magic, he and his brother were equals. Binyamin still wouldn't inherit, but perhaps Ruven would take him as a junior partner. A bright future wove itself for his inner eye. There was still Eupatia, he thought, and the tapestry faded. He couldn't face her, not after all these years.

The mad city was no longer safe for visitors. With any luck at all, the theater should have cleared out. Ben Gibb had lost his pursuers. He decided to retrieve what he could of his belongings, and go.

The great, echoing hall stood open to the streets as well as the skies. Servants wandered aimlessly in the tiers, as confused as everyone else as to what had happened. Nothing had changed for them, Binyamin thought. Nothing had changed for him, either, but these hadn't lost their livelihood as a result of this magical catastrophe.

Without their spell to keep them burning and smoke-free, the flambeaux in the sconces were at last guttering out. Binyamin took the passage through the stage-left side of the house almost by feel, heading toward backstage. He heard a faint scratching. Probably rats, he thought. The anti-pestilence spells were gone, too. Pray he could find some fleabane before the bugs ate him alive.

Two more doors. He'd take the small chest with him on his shoulder. If he could find his mules, he could return for some of the heavier and more valuable props. If nothing else, he could sell the valuable silk to feed himself.

No light shone in the rest of the passageway. Binyamin sighed. He'd have to haul his goods out into the alley to pick out what he wanted. He stepped into the backstage area, felt his way past the curtains that led out onto the stage. The large, carved chest wasn't where he'd braced it; of course not. It had been flung wide by the mob. He patted the curtains, the door, the wall, then his hands touched something warm in the dark. He jumped backward, falling over a pile of props. It was human flesh.

"Bring the torch, Gritus," a woman's voice ordered. The outer door opened, and a huge man in a servant's tunic entered, bearing a stick with a dripping, flaming cloth around the upper end.

"I borrowed some of your Greek fire," the woman's voice said, turning toward Binyamin in the dark. "Nothing else seems to be working."

The servant lit his way to his mistress, and stood over her, massive, protective. The torchlight illuminated the lips, cheekbones, and eyelashes of a flawless profile glowing rose and ivory. It was Eupatia.

"That is you, Binyamin, isn't it?" she asked.

He let out a croak of surprise, and scrambled to his feet. The torchlight shone on him, and Eupatia smiled. Her lips, round and plump wreathed, and her small teeth, translucent as alabaster, gleamed with the whiteness of snow. Binyamin found his heart was pounding, constricting his throat. Her beauty was an oppressive, physical force, stronger than he.

"What are you doing here?" he asked, weakly.

"My aunt enjoyed your performance," Eupatia said. "So did I."

"Thank you," Binyamin said, backing away more carefully, putting out a hand to feel for obstructions. She took a step forward, and he felt his face flush. "Now I must go. I . . . I just came for a few things."

Eupatia started to speak in a rush of breath. "Bin . . ." The sounds of sandals clattering down the alley interrupted her.

"They're coming," she said, wide-eyed.

Ben Gibb felt panic, and started to pick up whatever was around him on the floor to stuff into the small chest.

"I have to leave," he said, avoiding looking directly at her. "They blame me." The two large servants moved to stand on either side of him, leaving Eupatia in shadow. What was this? He turned to face her.

"Are you going to give me away?" he asked.

"Oh, no, not at all," Eupatia said, her lovely mouth forming an O. "One never gives away what one wants for oneself." She lowered her head and looked up at him through her eyelashes, a pet gesture of hers since childhood. "I'll show you a trick of my own: I want to make you disappear."

She reached out and took his hand. Her small, smooth fingers intertwined with his, and clasped firmly.

Ben Gibb immediately felt the sweat spring up on his palm and between his shoulder blades. He had never dreamed of having her so close. Now that she was, he was terrified instead of elated.

"What do you want, my lady?"

Eupatia frowned. "Don't call me that; we used to bathe together."

"That was a long time ago," Binyamin said, with real regret. The thought of climbing naked into a bath with this goddess made his manhood shrink right up and try to hide against his body.

"I know! You ran away, and never wrote to me."

"I . . . I couldn't," he said, helplessly.

"Come home," she said, impulsively holding out a hand to him. "Right now, and I'll save your life."

"No," Binyamin said. "I don't belong there any more."

Eupatia stamped her foot, and her eyes sparked. The effect devastated Binyamin. He stood with his mouth open, unable to do anything but stare.

The sounds of the mob outside grew closer. They both looked toward the door. Binyamin glanced down at the bundle of clothes in his hands.

"What can I say to you to let me escape?" he asked.

"Nothing," said Eupatia. "Not a thing. I could call for help, right now. I could say you used your power to draw me back here. What do you think of that?"

"You wouldn't!"

She smiled, a half smile, a cat's smile. "I might." The mob noises grew louder, and they could hear the rattle of stones. The young woman's eyes widened, and the coy expression vanished. "They're coming. If you swear you'll come home with me, just for a little while, my guards will defend you. Things have changed. They'll accept you now. They'll welcome you. Quick now, swear! Your wretched pride, or your life! Swear it!"

Just like the children they had been together, Binyamin thought. He put his hands between hers and recited the ancient formula, swearing faith by the God of his fathers. Eupatia looked satisfied, and nodded the guards to the door.

"Can you hide?" she asked, looking around at the small room.

"I'd be a poor illusionist if I couldn't change my own appearance," he said. He selected a few lengths from the armful of silk fabric he used in his soul-projection trick, and arrayed them around him like a formal robe. The outfit was gaudy, black silk sleeves and back, with a rainbow cloth masquerading as an undertunic, with another as a scarf. He grabbed one of the small squares used by his dancers, knotted it on the end, and secured it on his head like a nomad's cap. Binyamin accomplished his transformation in only a few seconds, the brief time he had before the door burst open on the gang of angry men armed with torches and staves wrenched from who knew where. Eupatia looked at him, and that slow smile that made him quiver inside touched her lips.

"Clever," she murmured, and turned to face the men.

"I *thought* we heard something in here," said the leader. He was the angry husband whose wife had lost her retaining spell. "What are you doing here, lady?"

"I was waiting, hoping the magician would return," she said, careful not to stand directly in front of him. "But as you see, there's no one here but me and my servants, and my friend."

The men looked at the two burly men in short tunics, and the stranger in the silk robes. Ben Gibb did his best to return their gazes impersonally. He changed his expression to the patrician glare, and held it until the man glanced away. Instead, he pointed at the heap of belongings Binyamin had bundled into the small chest.

"What have you found?"

"I was looking through his possessions, trying to find the spell that robbed me of my magic," Eupatia said, with just the right amount of defensiveness. "Nothing so far, or I would have informed you."

The man backed away, knowing she was of a rank equal to his. He treated her with more respect. "I'd give a lot to know that, too," he said. "My wife . . ." his voice trailed off. "I'd give a lot to know. Who are you, sir?" He turned to Ben Gibb. Eupatia hastened to intervene.

"This is my neighbor, Binyamin ben—ben Yelia," she said, faltering only a little over the name, and quickly substituting his father's. Her mind had always been swift-moving. "The loss of magic ruined his clothes, as you can see, proving his tailor was criminally inept." She turned to Binyamin. "Look at you. Your father will be furious," she said.

He did his best to look shamefaced but still maintaining the patrician air.

"I know," he said. "I thought the bargain was too good."

That sounded plausible to the mob, who by now were beginning to calm down in spite of themselves. A few of the men retreated out of the door, melting away down the alley. Only a few held on, as if they hoped the wizard would appear out of nowhere and give them satisfaction.

Eupatia decided to see them on their way. "Will there be anything else?" she asked, with a touch of asperity.

"No," the man said, now uneasy. "Well, no. I suppose not." He lowered his torch so that the flame flashed in the bronze mirror suspended on the wall. Eupatia, her eye distracted, looked over his shoulder at the mirror, and caught a glimpse of herself. The man turned his head, but saw nothing but the pretty young woman's reflection.

Eupatia continued, though her voice was faltering now. "So you see, the magician is not here. If he returns, my servants will deal with him. You must seek him elsewhere."

The man blinked at accepting an order, but even without her bespelled supernatural beauty Eupatia had the charm to drive it home. "That we will, lady."

The rest of the mob withdrew, and pattered down the alley more quietly. Binyamin let out a sigh of relief. He was safe, for good and all. He bent once more to pick up his possessions. Now he had time to put them in order. He dumped the tangle of cloth out of the small chest, and began to repack from the beginning.

Eupatia remained with her back to him. The servants, now both holding torches, still loomed, but now they weren't so threatening to him. Hmm, he thought. Heavy props first. Cloth, wires, plates, bowls. The folding swords went into their proper sheaths, and into the top of the small chest. He secured them with leather straps so they wouldn't snag the folded silks. All these tricks would still be good for the provinces, providing the madness hadn't spread out of Constantinople. A little sound brought his attention back to the mirror. He looked over Eupatia's shoulder at her reflection. She was crying. His heart melted.

Just as he had years and years before, just as if they still lived next door to one another, he hurried forward to put his hands on her shoulders, to squeeze his cheek next to hers.

"What's the matter, dear one?" he asked.

"I'm not beautiful anymore," she sobbed. He felt his sleeve and produced a small cloth with which he dabbed away her tears as if she was a child.

"Oh, no, you're wrong," he said, his eyes meeting hers in the mirror. The spell had gone, true, but she still glowed like a pearl. The loss of magic had restored her normal features. He was shaken to see how little difference it made in her, but now she looked more like the girl he remembered. He was drawn back half a dozen years to the days before her magic had matured, when she had the promise of true beauty. This is what it was meant to be in its full flowering, not the fearsome enhancement.

"How things change," he said, keeping his voice light. "Just think. An hour ago I was the most famous conjuror in the empire, and now here I am, a boy again."

"And I was pretty," she said, miserably. A loud squeal erupted from somewhere behind them, and the flambeaux lit up all at once. Binyamin and Eupatia looked around in surprise as three rats, moving as if their tails were on fire, scurried out of the dressing room and out into the alley.

"It's over," he said. "The spell is broken. Whatever the curse was, it's gone."

"It's over," Eupatia breathed.

Just for a second, the harrowing goddess-beauty flickered over her features like the hard glint of jewels. Binyamin felt dismayed. His emotion must have showed on his face in the mirror, because Eupatia let the spell fade.

"I'd lose you again, wouldn't I?" she asked, and her lovely eyes were stricken.

"It ... I ... You don't need the spell, Eupatia," he said. He shed all his artful manner, and he was indeed the boy Binyamin again. "You're so very, very lovely all by yourself, without falsely enhancing it."

Eupatia shook her head, refusing to believe. "It isn't true."

"It is," Binyamin insisted. "I always thought that the rainbow paled beside you, that you look like what ... what birdsong sounds like. What honey tastes like." His long, thin hands tried to pull the images out of the air, and she laughed.

"You're quite a showman, Binyamin ben Gibb," she said, turning around and wrinkling her nose at him. He bowed, with a flourish of his long hands.

"I always try to impress when I need to make a point," he said. "If I were to escort you out that door right now, there's not a man in the city whose eyes wouldn't follow you, whose heart wouldn't feel the utmost jealousy that I'm the one walking with you and not he. And the reason is fully natural, without enchantment."

"It isn't true," Eupatia insisted.

"It is. That spell you use is like the illusion I use to prop up the draperies on the stage." He took the black cloths off his shoulders and molded the wires into the shape of a man's body. "It's all exterior. My audiences think they see the form, but there's no substance inside."

"No substance," she said thoughtfully, staring past him at the flambeaux. Binyamin gazed where she gazed, trying to guess what she was thinking, As an adult, a man with experience behind him, he could now look back and see what had troubled him. He was mature enough to make his own way in the world, and to say what was in his heart.

"I have always loved you," he said. The soft words fell like drops in a pool. He felt the reaction radiate through the young woman at his side, and felt at last confident enough to tell her the truth. "In my position I never could feel worthy of you. I would never inherit my father's wealth. I have no magic."

"I never cared about any of those," she said, turning to him with her hands out. He took them, kissed the backs of the fingers tenderly.

"But the combination of circumstances, I couldn't aspire to such a star."

Her gaze dropped to their clasped hands, and up to meet his eyes in earnest appeal. "I drove you away."

Binyamin grinned. "No, I drove myself away. If I hadn't had such a chip on my shoulder about being the second son and a magicless freak, I might have made something of myself. You frightened me, but that's all in the past. What I say now is that you don't need the spell to make you beautiful. You are already as lovely as it's possible to be."

Her eyes went wary with fear. "I don't know if I can let it go. Everyone expects me to look this way now."

"Please try. Let them see you as the gods made you." He studied her face, and was struck again by the perfection of her browline, the piquant sweetness of her small chin. "It's much, much better than the illusion. And believe me, I know. I'm an expert on illusions."

"Will you be with me, then?"

"I will," he said.

She smiled, and he caught his breath in wonder, the force of six years' lost love catching up with him in an instant. "You have magic of your own, Binyamin ben Gibb."

He shook his head, a playful glint in his eye. "My wonders are all worked without magic. I told you so during my show."

THE THIEF OF EYES

S.M. Stirling

Aphonea the Sorceress drew in her breath with an impossibly long inhalation. Sitting cross-legged within her circle, she kept her slender back straight, eyes closed, palms open upon her thighs. Incense burned in a small dish of black jade, the dull crimson glow of the ember the only light in her sanctum. Its bitter herbal scent filled her lungs, lifting the eyes of spirit free of the prison of flesh.

She had the ancient Hellenic face, grave and serene of expression, full lipped, with deep-set eyes and a rounded chin. Her blond hair was coiffed in an antique style that emphasized her classical looks. The other-worldly looks impressed her patrons no end; this was how a sorceress was *supposed* to look, though few did.

If there was one lesson she'd learned during her grindingly poor childhood, it was to please those with money to spend.

A full minute after filling her lungs, she exhaled through her mouth, blowing out a long, cool stream of air. It began to turn white and to curl in on itself, forming

110

a ball of sparkling fog that floated before her without dissipating. After a time, figures could be dimly seen within the glittering mist, accompanied by the sound of voices—far off and barely heard.

Aphonea opened hyacinth-blue eyes and spoke a *word*. Instantly the fog cleared and the voices rang clear.

She was looking at two men, an older and a younger, in a room halfway across the metropolis. They lay on couches of ivory-inlaid sandalwood carved with the curious designs of Hind, cushioned in samite, sipping a thick dark Kheftu wine from rhytons of fancifully blown glass decorated with strings of gold embedded in the material. Servants cleared the remains of a meal from the table between them, set out sweets, and withdrew silently. Malagyros filled the cups with his own hand.

Automatically Aphonea calculated their cost. The vintage within was worth more than the cups themselves; Malagyros was that kind of host, from the rumors. *Or perhaps he just doesn't know the value of such things,* she thought with a trace of malice.

She'd never seen her rival before, and she studied him with some disappointment. Aphonea had imagined him small and skinny with receding hair and a nose half as big as his whole face. He should be pock-marked too, and cringing with the shame of his father's slave birth.

In reality he was quite good looking, about her own twenty-five years, with a craggy face and shrewd, narrow brown eyes. He was lean and of average height, but muscled like an athlete. His dark hair hung to his shoulders in elegantly pomaded curls and he wore a gentleman's silk evening robe with an embroidered yoke of pearls worth . . .

Aphonea frowned at herself. *Stop that.* The fury was beginning to cloud the cool perfection of the vision itself; magics of clear sight required clear thought and melted like ice before the warmth of the passions.

Bastard son of a slave, she thought—and the worst of it was that that was *true.* Lolling on sandalwood couches while she, daughter of nobility older than the City itself, had to scrabble about *earning* her keep.

She spoke the *word*. The sphere of vision snapped back into crystal clarity.

"Well, Bertros, while your company is always welcome," Malagyros bowed politely to his elder companion, "you *did* say you had some information you wished to share with me. Please feel free to begin at any time."

Bertros looked gravely at his young host and put his wine cup down on a little porphyry side table. Then he fluffed his white beard, cleared his throat and looked uncomfortably around the room.

"Don't worry," Malagyros said with a smile, "I assure you, my rival cannot penetrate the spells that protect my privacy."

Bertros opened and then closed his mouth. Frowning, he looked at his hands, clasped together on his stomach.

The younger man cocked his head sympathetically.

"I know she's a friend of yours. If you'd rather not, there's no reason to tell me whatever it is." He looked askance at his friend. "You're not carrying a message from her, are you?"

"No!" Bertros frowned more deeply still. "I was just thinking you're more alike than different, the two of you. I wager you'd like each other if you met. You've got a lot in common."

"What could I possibly have in common with some slum girl with grandiose ideas?" Malagyros asked contemptuously.

"Well, to begin with, you both steal rare, magical objects. Though you do so for mischief, and she for gain. What grandiose ideas are you talking about?"

"I've seen her. Comely enough, but she wears her hair like some statue of the Foam-Born. Perhaps she has her professions confused." Malagyros laughed lightly.

Bertros looked like he'd swallowed a whole duck—sideways.

So he doesn't know that I'm listening, Aphonea murmured, aware that only Bertros could hear her.

"No, I haven't told him anything yet," Bertros answered her aloud. "I was waiting on your attendance." He turned to Malagyros, who was looking startled. "This visit," he explained, "is in fact a conference. Due to the influence of a spell-token that I wear—" he pulled the thing out from the neck of his tunic and held it up "—Aphonea is able to hear what we say to one another."

Malagyros's eyes widened in rage and he sat upright, swinging his feet to the floor. But Bertros raised a commanding hand to forbid any indignant outburst, and extended just a little power to sooth the younger man.

"This rivalry grieves your friends ... and the City's fences!" Whose groups overlapped considerably. "Bad enough that the loser in this ridiculous contest must leave the City. But *both* of you might die if you attempt the Eyes! Couldn't you just talk and settle your rivalry?"

"No."

No.

Bertros felt the touch of cold iron in their mutual refusal and sighed. "Then at least let us give you what information we have concerning the hidden temple and the cult of Nogra."

"I appreciate the help," Malagyros said quietly. "All I know now is that it can't be in one of the airborne palaces, since they must have earth around them to conduct their rites."

Is that all? That's pathetic, Aphonea mocked. *As to appreciating your help, so he should, since he's forever in need of it.*

Bertros smiled slightly and said with quiet emphasis, "I don't doubt that you *both* would eventually find out what we have to tell you. And, judging from past performance, virtually at the same time."

Malagyros grimaced and so did Aphonea in her workroom miles away.

"In a neighborhood not far from the Imperial Palace,

yet fallen on lesser times, as sometimes happens, is a small palace of black marble."

Appropriate, Aphonea observed.

"At one time it was the residence of the ambassador of Azbakhasia. He still owns it, but now it's rented to a wealthy businessman from the Old City." Bertros shook his head sadly and pulled a sheaf of maps and notes from a pocket in his dalmatic.

"I wish you'd chosen some less vicious cult to rob. Can't we arrange a contest that wouldn't risk your lives?"

"Such as drawing straws?" Malagyros teased, smiling. He shrugged. "Perhaps I need to prove something, my friend."

Due, no doubt, to his complete lack of magical ability, Aphonea sneered. *Or perhaps it's his gender. You men always have* something *to prove.*

"It is sheer hubris, in *both* of you!" Bertros insisted. "These people are evil. And so is pride when it leads you to foolishness."

"I have faith in my abilities," said Malagyros seriously.

As do I.

"Then go forth and conquer, my young friends," Bertros said with a resigned shake of his head. "But come back to us alive."

Aphonea studied the palace of Marcus Licenius Severus. A small palace perhaps, but an enormous house; unlike most, there was a space of open ground between the perimeter of the property and the outer wall of the main building—probably a custom of the Old City, she thought. The main block was two-storied, constructed entirely of black marble and looking as sinister as it did elegant. It seemed to *smell*, in some non-physical way, a spiritual essence that was dank and musty like an old cellar room.

Glowstones in brackets placed every ten paces or so illuminated the entire length of the palace. The grounds surrounding it were scanty and overgrown with bushes and small trees. That surprised her. Men of the Old City were usually such sticklers for imposing order on their surroundings, clipping and mowing even nature into submission.

Aphonea crouched on the top of the wall, her thigh muscles straining, holding to the shadow of a tree. She was nearly invisible in black clothing—eastern trousers and a tunic—with her pale hair hidden beneath a scarf worn low on her forehead and pulled across the lower half of her soot-streaked face. Her narrow, soft-booted feet were cautiously placed between pieces of sharp glass and rusting nails cemented into the wall. She had her full share of sorceror's arrogance, but Aphonea was also a pessimist. One born gifted with the talent should not have to rely upon mere material things like dark clothing—but one born to ancient nobility shouldn't have to steal for a living, either. Nobody *gave* you rare talismans, or money for that matter.

Cupping her hands over her eyes she whispered a spell, then did the same with her ears and her nose. When she opened her eyes she could see the protective spells that warded the house and grounds of a supposedly innocent Old City businessman.

They were vile. Her magical senses revealed a roiling green fog that smelled of decaying meat. She could hear cries and moans that tightened the skin on the back of her neck. Suddenly, the eyeless ghost of a young man flitted by on a wind she couldn't feel.

The breath stopped in her throat from shock. She'd read of such spells, but had never before seen them in use. There were two of them in action here and each one required a bloody and agonizing sacrifice to erect. There wasn't a legitimate magician in the City who would consider using them.

For a fleeting moment she felt dread anchor her to the wall and she entertained the idea of living in Lady's Gift, her family's original home. *I could buy an olive orchard. Teach at the Academy. Maybe study philoso-phy . . .*

Then she remembered Malagyros's voice mocking her hair and wondering if she'd mistaken her profession.

Aphonea drew her darkened athame from its sheath at her hip and pricked her finger, letting a drop of blood fall upon a leaf picked from the tree that hid her. She spoke, gesturing over the leaf, then sent it fluttering into the garden below with a puff of her breath.

It fluttered along like a butterfly, in idle patterns, threatening to light, then moving on. The fog and the voices and the ghosts rolled after it, leaving a brief open-ing for her to run through.

"It's enough money to buy your freedom, and your family's, from Marcus Licenius's," Malagyros said. "*And* buy a shop down in the Horn."

The slave licked his lips and glanced around the low, smoky den of the little tavern. Drops of sweat rolled down his forehead, the smell mingling with the ripe scents of fish sauce, grease and spilled wine.

"As much as me life is worth," he said, with a thick Erus accent. His hair was the color of bleached tow and his face flat and snub-nosed. Barbarian looks . . .

"Is your life worth that much? Marcus Licenius is so good a master?" Malagyros didn't think so; not from the number of fines the man had paid for slaves unaccount-ably dying. The City charged for those; about enough to cover the cost of exorcism for the angry ghost.

The slave's dull blue eyes kindled. He spat into the sawdust-covered floor—the latest of many such, by the looks.

"That for Licenius!" He glanced to either side again. "Here's what we'll do . . ."

Malagyros smiled at the memory. The bag he handed over to the slave chinked dully, the sound of coined sil-ver. The man fumbled off the amulet he wore and pushed past the thief without speaking. A robed woman followed him, holding an infant in her arms. Any slave could find sanctuary in a temple ... provided he could deposit the cash value of his purchase price, as recorded by the master for tax purposes. That kept the appraisals reasonably honest, and furnished slaves a tiny sliver of hope.

Bertros' plans showed the traditional mansion layout, built in four blocks around two central courtyards; but it showed no entrance to the cellar they knew was there.

"The palace was built over the site of another house," Bertros had told them. "The former owner was famous for his wine cellar. Apparently it was enormous, even larger than the house itself. And it's supposed to be as deep as the present house is tall."

Malagyros was certain the entrance lay hidden in one of the rooms in the front of the house. One frequently used by the owner, where privacy would be taken for granted, such as a study.

He was also dressed in black, his shoulder-length hair bound back with a cord, and around his waist was a wide leather belt fitted with holders for a series of small containers. He pried one loose and smeared the contents over his eyelids, nose and ears. Then spoke the words that activated the spell; you didn't need the Talent, if you could buy its services. Opening his eyes he saw the same loathsome spells that Aphonea had discovered and blinked in disbelief.

He'd thought the cult of Nogra was the usual set of wealthy degenerates, finding in some exotic religion a new excuse for debauchery.

I was wrong, he thought. Whatever else they were, this crowd weren't amateurs.

The window was narrow and deep in shadow from the untrimmed bush that lay between it and the nearest glowstone. Aphonea placed her long, slender fingers against the shutters, and closed her eyes. In seconds she felt the vibration of a vastly more powerful spell beneath the warding. A few moments more relayed the heavy, oily flavor of evil in it.

There was something beyond, but she couldn't catch it. Fortunately, it was far enough away that it shouldn't have to be dealt with immediately. She countered the simple warding on the window, then cracked her knuckles, made several gestures that seemed to knot her fingers together like a squid's tentacles and muttered a *word*. Like many, it seemed to consist entirely of consonants— nobody knew why. The greater warding parted seamlessly; she grimaced, feeling as if it had left a coat of rancid oil on her skin. The latch clicked back as she moved finger and thumb, and she stepped gingerly over the low sill.

Beyond was a small drawing room, furnished with dark-cushioned, spindle-legged couches and painted sculptures. *Mostly second-rate,* she thought with an old-money connoisseur's sneer. Except for a five-foot human-oid cat with a curved sword and flared helmet. *Exotic.* A closer look showed that it wasn't a statue after all. It was *stuffed*.

"Gahh," she whispered.

The wall paintings showed satyrs cavorting with nymphs among the flowers. A painting that made her uneasy for some reason. After a moment she thought she saw a satyr, whose head was turned away, move slightly. It was a particularly muscular satyr and the nymph he had in his grasp didn't look like she was enjoying herself at all.

Aphonea decided that her counterspell wasn't going to last forever and crossed to the door.

The door was also warded. *That's what I felt from outside. Lady Moon, the extravagance!* A more compli-cated spell than that on the window, obviously intended to keep something inside this pleasant little room.

Interesting. If the mage who created these spells wanted something to remain in here she was inclined to agree with his sentiments without having to know the reason for them. She certainly didn't want anything breaking out and following her.

There was a soft, enquiring growl from behind her. Glancing over her shoulder Aphonea saw that the satyr in the painting was now looking in her direction.

It had the face of a minor demon, the hairy, under-slung jaw crowded with razor-sharp teeth. Its gleaming red eyes didn't seem to see her yet, but slid past and around her without focusing. The nostrils in its moist snout worked busily and apparently with more success than its eyes, for the face was turned unerringly in her direction. It made another deep-throated sound, one of pleasure this time, as though scenting a favorite dish.

Aphonea worked quickly but carefully on the warding spell. Not to counter it, but to hold it in abeyance, so it could be closed behind her with a *word*.

She heard the demon's arm coming out of the wall with the sound of a snake sliding over dry tiles, and gratefully felt the spell respond to her command. Cautiously, she opened her senses to the hall beyond the door, seeking other spells or the presence of humans.

Aphonea's neck prickled, and her back felt terribly exposed. She risked a glance behind her. It had one horned hoof on the floor and its squamous hand was reaching for her. It smelled like a ferret a long time from its last bath.

Nobody's out there, she assured herself and opened the door, burst into the hallway and pulled it closed behind her in one quick movement. She spoke a *word* and the spell smoothed into place just as something collided with the door. There was a sharp *snap*, the smell of ozone, and a small, wounded "meep!" from within the room.

Looking around her, Aphonea realized she'd been right, there was no one here. A slight frown creased her forehead. Her sources had informed her that Marcus Licenius had a large number of hired guards. Where were they?

*　　*　　*

Malagyros chose a well-lit window in the front of the palace. *Nobody would break in here. Ergo, a light warding. Easier to fool guards than spells.* Spells didn't sleep. They also didn't drink the three crates of wine jugs delivered "by mistake" three hours earlier. In his experience, mercenaries *did* do that sort of thing, on a boring assignment. They'd check the wine for poison and sleep-spells, but that wouldn't stop the entirely natural effects. People in the service of sorcerors tended to forget that sort of thing.

The window *should* have been guarded. Rumor gave the westerner at least thirty men. But he'd watched the palace and grounds from the roof of a neighboring villa for hours and had seen no movement at all.

Not until he'd used the salve that let him see the spells protecting the place. He shuddered.

They must be inside, he thought. *I would be.*

There was definitely a warding on the window. He felt fear prickle along his nerve endings and an overwhelming sense of hopelessness assailed him.

Steeling himself, he drew another vial from his belt and pulled the stopper. Moistening his finger with the oil inside he outlined the window. Then he drew symbols across the shutters and when the final line was drawn the fear and sense of doom left him. He grinned in satisfaction. *You don't need to be a silversmith to buy a wine cup.*

Malagyros slipped a slender knife through the gap between the shutters and lifted the latch within. Without hesitation, he stepped into the dimly lit room beyond.

He found himself in a reception room, large and coldly formal in the Old City style, lacking the ornate comfort favored by Imperials. It was open to the hallway and Malagyros could see the sleepy slave who tended the door. He'd certainly taken advantage of the mistaken delivery; a jug lay by his head, spilling a little thick purple wine onto the tesseract mosaic of the floor.

The best Kheftu vintages were like that; they crept up on you.

Slowly Malagyros pulled the shutters closed and reset the latch. Then he stood in the darkness for a few moments, watching. The slave stirred, smacked his lips, snored.

Malagyros could see a doorway leading further into the house. He began to move very slowly across the room, letting his soft-soled boots down with a careful precision.

The next room was a formal dining room, filled with couches and low tables, the walls painted in murals of dead game and seafood. A glass skylight stretched overhead, and a gallery ran around the second story. The room was scrubbed clean and the couches pushed back along the walls, but there was a very faint scent of old wine, probably soaked into the marble flooring.

His office will be convenient to the dining room, Malagyros thought, *for those times he's entertaining clients*.

The door to the second room that he came to was firmly closed, and, judging from the colly-wobbles it gave him, it was also warded.

Excellent! He took out the vial of oil again and drew the signs that would dissipate the warding spell, allowing him to enter.

A small glowstone had been left burning in the room beyond, probably in case the master wished to use his study during the night. Its wavering light revealed a room some fifteen by twenty paces. Scroll racks lined the walls, the lettered tags dangling from each set of ivory handles. Nearer the desk were cases for the newer bound codex-style books, and several chairs. The desk was huge, piled high with papyrus and parchments and several heavy paperweights; one was carved from an emerald the size of his fist in an exotic Eastern style, showing a she-dragon copulating with a giant six-armed ape. Malagyros beat down temptation.

The wall behind the desk was decorated with a mosaic

of a weird sea creature, apparently eating a ship and waving the crew around with its many tentacles. The beast's six eyes were bulbous, scarlet things that looked like hot coals.

Malagyros smiled. *Eureka!* He lit another lamp and began to search for a means of opening the secret door he was certain the mosaicked panel represented.

Aphonea crossed the dimly lit hall and entered one of the rooms opposite the demon-inhabited drawing room, closing the door behind her. From the deep pockets in her trousers she withdrew a short, black wand painted with silver runes and dangled it from a purple cord. She spoke to it in a language that her father had taught her just before his death, in the increasingly rare intervals of sobriety; it always made her want to sneeze. The wand quivered three times, then pointed, straining against the cord like a dog against its leash.

Cautiously she slipped from the room and moved silently down the hallway, following where the wand pointed. It led her down one corridor and into another, until it clicked against a wall of the same black marble that made up the mansion's main structure, carved in low relief into the image of something squidlike.

Tucking the wand away, she positioned herself in front of the wall, both hands raised before her, fingers shaping symbols on the air. At length the squid's eyes began to glow a dull orange and Aphonea reached out and pressed them. The wall swung open onto a set of stone steps leading into darkness.

Malagyros paused at the bottom of the steps and looked around him. He stood upon a tiled floor, a dull black tile that hinted somehow at depths beneath and roiling water. He also saw that the lamp he'd brought was unnecessary, as glowstones burned at regular intervals down the length of the hallway. He almost wished they didn't; the walls were covered in mosaic murals, mostly concerned with the rites of Nogra. Red was the predominant color . . .

Blowing out the lamp, he set it in a shadowy corner near the steps, then stood with his hands on his hips and looked around, wondering which way to go.

He tried to imagine where he would want to place the hidden temple of an evil god. *Surely not under the dining room,* he thought. *You wouldn't want to give it ideas.* But not so far away that the god would be offended.

Mentally, he superimposed the plan that Bertros had shown him over what he was seeing. Then he struck out in a direction that should lead him away from the living quarters.

At length the corridor ended, branching left and right. He set off again, left this time. *Ten brings you one they'll always take the left-hand path.* Demon-god cultists tended to lack both humor and imagination; nobody with much of a sense of the absurd would get involved in this sort of thing to begin with.

The corridor ended in a doorway blocked by strings of beads . . . or to be more precise, strings of human knucklebones, each inlaid with a glyph in black gold. Its lintel posts were carved with symbols that moved before his eyes with an obscene sinuosity.

Damned if I know why someone hasn't lifted this before, he thought, mentally buffing his nails. With infinite care he nudged one string of knucklebones aside, using the point of his knife, and peered through.

Before him lay a large room with rough stone walls and a gleaming black marble floor. Opposite was a basalt altar in whose center burned a blue-white fire of obviously magical origin. Above the altar was a crudely carved statue with many arms and faceted red eyes that sparkled in the frantic light from below.

Nogra! Malagyros thought. His heart hammered, and he could feel his mouth go papery dry, sweat trickling down his flanks.

There was no guardian in sight, human or magical. He

walked boldly through the doorway into the empty temple, allowing the curtain to drop shut behind him.

Instantly, but too late, he realized his mistake. The room spun around him and he found himself opposite the doorway, across the room from it. He took several steps towards it and before his eyes it wavered and disappeared.

Malagyros looked to his left and there it was, just as far away, but in a different wall.

He walked back and forth for what seemed like hours, growing more and more alarmed. Only the position of the idol of Nogra remained constant. Or so it seemed, but he wasn't yet desperate enough to deliberately walk in that direction.

He tried closing his eyes and walking forward with slow shuffling steps. When he opened his eyes his hands were almost touching Nogra's altar and he leapt backwards with a sharply indrawn breath.

Next he tried walking to the wall opposite the door, the one that seemed closest to him. He couldn't reach it. He tried running, walking backwards, concentrating on something else, lying on his back and pushing himself along with his feet, none of it worked.

Twice more, Malagyros almost touched the altar, the rest of the time he simply never arrived at his chosen destination.

The longer he remained in the temple, the more clouded his mind became.

"Why am I here?" he asked himself, frowning. "This seems an unprofitable way to spend my time." The image of Nogra was distracting, and he looked away. For a moment he closed his eyes and pressed his hands to his face, the metal of his rings touching the skin in points of cold.

I'm here to steal the . . . eyes! His sweat turned cold. A spell of confusion, operating through sight. He *hated* confusion spells. All his adult life he'd been outsmarting magicians who relied on the Power. Striking at his wits just wasn't *fair*.

Malagyros thought, *It's my eyes that are deceived. I'm not seeing what's really there.* He fumbled at his belt and yanked free a vial containing the salve that would enable him to see through the spells around him, quite forgetting he'd already used it. Quickly he smeared it on and spoke the activating word.

The room reeled uncontrollably. He dropped to his hands and knees and became violently sick. Then he crawled away from the noisome puddle and dropped groaning onto his side, gasping, breathing in the stench of his own sour breath. Malagyros scrubbed the salve from his eyes with the sleeve of his shirt, covered his eyes with one arm and begged his head to stop spinning.

At last, totally exhausted, he slept.

Aphonea gazed into the darkness at the bottom of the stairs as though reading something written on the blackness. She stared harder, then harder still, until colored patterns floated before her sight.

No warding, no demonic guardians, no magic at all.

She frowned. That couldn't be right. This house seethed with magic. Why would the stairway to their holy of holies be completely unwarded?

Aphonea's neck prickled. She shrugged. Perhaps these stairs led only to a wine cellar, or perhaps they felt their god could take care of itself. Far be it for her to plumb the thought processes of religious maniacs. She was only a humble sorceress, trying to scrounge a modest living in a highly competitive world.

Well, all right, trying to scrounge a highly lucrative living out of a very crowded field.

Drink and gambling were time-honored aristocratic pastimes. Unfortunately, her ancestors had honored those customs rather too vigorously.

Aphonea started down the stairs. On the fifth step the stone sank beneath her foot and with a gasp she stepped backwards, flailing for balance. At the same time, with a grating of stone, the black marble door slid closed behind her, locking her in darkness. She remained quite still, straining her ears for further sounds until her witch-sight was able to reveal her surroundings.

Looking down, she saw that the next four steps were missing. Leaving a hole whose smooth walls fell into darkness even her magical sight couldn't penetrate. *Perhaps you're supposed to die of thirst before you hit bottom*, she thought.

She probed. *No spell*. Just a damned counterweight and chain, set off when somebody stepped on the tread. *How crude. Just what you'd expect of a westerner like Marcus Licenius*. They were a bunch of peasants, for all that they'd founded the Empire. The City had been ancient long before the Imperial capital was transferred here.

She walked back up the stairs and tried to open the door again. In spite of several spells and quite a bit of heaving and shoving the door remained solidly closed. Apparently it simply wasn't designed to be opened from this side. Kicking it didn't do any good either, and hurt her toe.

Turning around she gazed thoughtfully down the steps. *Well, that leaves me only one direction to go. Two if I get really depressed*. She looked at the wide, dark square in the middle of the stairs.

Rushing downwards she leapt, and thought as she sailed out and over the gaping hole, *What if the other side is counter-balanced to dump me into the trap?*

Aphonea landed solidly and her momentum carried her down three steps before she could stop herself. She glanced over her shoulder and laughed a little hysterically, grateful that the followers of Nogra lacked her nasty imagination.

Then she shuddered, remembering the spells that protected the palace grounds. *Yes*, she thought, *they're quite nasty enough without my little contributions*.

She continued to descend. The staircase had walls on either side, sometimes farther apart than her spread arms could reach; at other spots a large man would have trouble passing.

It was an unusually long staircase and the backs of her calves began to hurt. Still, she took her time and tested every step before putting her weight on it. But there seemed to be no more traps. She began to feel as though she'd passed some sort of test, and wondered if this was some mock mystical passage that all acolytes needed to travel before being accepted as full members. *That would make sense, you wouldn't want to risk killing all of them.* At least, the leaders of the cult wouldn't. Most of the rest of humanity would probably prefer that they did.

Down and down she went, until her legs burned and her breath came hard. Sweat ran down her back and sides, sticking her tunic to her flesh.

How deep can this go? she wondered desperately. *I'm going to meet the Iron Limper coming up from his forge if this goes down much further.*

At last she couldn't go on and collapsed in a heap. Aphonea rested her head on a cool, smooth step and lay still, gasping, the blood pounding in her head. Pulling out the stopper in a small flask she drank a little water, then poured some into her hand and wiped it over her hot face, drying it off with a corner of her headscarf. Lying back, Aphonea stretched her aching legs out before her and closed her eyes.

I'll just take a moment, she thought. *Until my head stops pounding.*

"Aaahhh, looks like we've caught us a thief, Fesros."

Malagyros was startled awake. *Very* awake, as if some pressure had been released from inside his skull, something that had been crowding thoughts out of his mind.

He lay still on his side, listening to Fesros and his friend advance into the room. So far, there were only two sets of footsteps.

"Faugh! What a smell. Tsk, looks like our guest here had an accident. Who's gonna clean that up? That's what I want to know. Not me, I'll tell you that."

"Some luckless slave'll take care of it," Fesros muttered tiredly. "Whadda you care, Rabba?"

Malagyros heard them approaching and forced himself to stay loose-limbed, breathing evenly. He considered his options and decided they weren't good. There seemed to be only two men, but there were probably more waiting in the corridor. On the positive side, they could at least get him out of this damn room. The point of a sword touched the side of his neck coldly.

"Wakey, wakey," Rabba said cheerfully.

Malagyros opened his eyes slowly and looked up at his two captors. Despite the situation, it was all he could do not to grin.

Many a rich man amused himself designing elaborate uniforms for his personal guard, with varying degrees of success. But Malagyros had never seen anything to equal this!

Both men wore cheap, knee-high boots of garish, scarlet leather that doubtless left their feet and legs orange when they were removed. Brilliant blue tunics were sashed with rumpled bands of a contrasting red, while cloaks of yet another red hung limply from their shoulders. Upon their heads was a glittering travesty of a helmet. A thing that left the face unprotected and probably wouldn't stop a blow from a half-heartedly swung fist.

No wonder they don't patrol the grounds, Malagyros thought. *I wouldn't want to be seen in public in that uniform either.*

The two soldiers glanced at each other.

"He's polite," Fesros observed, "I give him that."

"Or smart enough to be dangerous," Rabba muttered. "You better come with us," he told Malagyros. "Someone's waiting for you." He winked cheerfully.

*   *   *

Aphonea shifted in her sleep, and started to slide down the stairs. She woke with a start and a gasping cry of alarm. The fall was easily stopped, but her heart pounded for a full minute before it calmed. Wearily, she rose to her feet, wincing at the stiffness of her legs.

I've slept a while, she thought with regret, and some apprehension. *I really should get out of the study more.* She went to the women's gymnasium three days a week. *Well, three days a week most of the time.* Running around sweating was so *boring* compared to real study.

Then she continued her descent, having no other choice. At last, she came to the bottom of the steps and stared down a narrow passage that turned abruptly about ten paces from where she stood. The air smelled of mold and earth and patches of nitre glittered on the walls. They were rough fieldstone, the mortar between them crumbling with age.

With a sigh, she set off down the winding passage, her eyes and sorcerous senses alert for traps. After only a few moments one of those senses stopped her in her tracks, her eyes widened in surprise.

Aphonea had an acute sense of where the sun and moon were in the sky, and she was suddenly aware that it was near midday!

How could such a thing have happened? Surely I didn't sleep that long. But the ache in her legs confirmed her instincts. Aphonea's eyes narrowed. *Bertros said this cellar was two levels deep. But I must have walked miles down those stairs.*

She let out her breath in an exasperated huff. She'd set off a trap spell. One that kept the victim in a trance, standing in one place lifting their feet up and down as though actually walking, running . . . or descending a staircase.

No doubt it was set over the pit at the top of the stairs. While leaping over it her mind had been occupied with all sorts of possibilities, her body gripped by an excitement that easily covered the sense of springing a well-laid trap.

The only reason she'd escaped was because she'd fallen asleep and slipped out of its influence.

Well, this complicates matters nicely, she thought irritably. *Better find someplace to hide while people are up and about their business. Then tonight I'll find the temple, get the Eyes and leave.*

But in her heart, she was certain that Malagyros had been and gone, carrying the eyes off with him. Leaving her to be caught in his place when the theft was discovered.

I really do hate that man, she thought wearily, and forced herself to continue down the corridor.

She'd followed its winding course for only a short while when it ended in a doorway spilling light and laughter into the corridor. Aphonea crept cautiously forward until she could see into the room.

Rough-looking men, most of them roaring drunk, occupied themselves with willing women, or gambled. The room was dirty and crowded with benches and tables, smoking torches sputtered in wall niches.

These would seem to be Marcus Licenius's missing guards, she thought with disapproval. *Whatever he's paying them, it's excessive.* Then she saw a door on the opposite side of the room from her.

She withdrew down the corridor and sighed mentally. This was going to take some hard work.

Usually an invisibility spell was placed on a muffling cloak, or something of that nature, leaving the mind free to deal with the wearer's surroundings. Placing one directly on herself and keeping it there was going to take great concentration.

She took a deep breath and began her incantations.

Rabba and Fesros led him through twisting corridors until they came to a ring in the floor.

"Yank on that," Rabba snapped.

Malagyros bent over, grasped the ring and pulled. The stone it was set into came up with a rush of damp, odorous air, revealing a black pit below.

"Strip," Rabba said.

Malagyros hesitated.

Setting his jaw, Rabba poked Malagyros's arm with his sword's point hard enough to draw blood.

"Just do it," Fesros advised wearily.

They examined every article of his clothing thoroughly, tossing each down into the pit when they were through with it. Holding back only his knife, lockpicks and belt of magical potions.

"In you go," Rabba said cheerfully when they were finished.

Malagyros looked dubiously into the darkness below him.

Rabba was readying himself to deliver another sharp poke, when Fesros spoke up, "It's not that deep. Let yourself down to arms length and drop, you won't hurt yourself."

Malagyros looked at him and saw not kindness, but a bored desire to have things go smoothly. He nodded and took the man's advice.

He landed on a smooth, moist surface, with his knees flexed. Fesros had been right, it wasn't deep.

The stone was fitted back into place above him, plunging the cell into darkness so complete it was almost unbearable. It could be felt, it could be heard and, irrationally, it gave him the feeling that he was going to fall.

Malagyros forced himself to gather up his clothes and get dressed. Then he explored his cell, pacing it out, feeling the texture of the stone wall until he felt he knew every inch of it.

He found a hole just above the level of the floor, large enough to allow access to a medium-sized dog.

He stood up and thought about that. Unpleasant thoughts that refused to go away.

Then he noticed it was growing lighter, and glanced

up at the ceiling to see if the trapdoor was being quietly opened. But it was still in place, and the pale light grew. *I doubt it's here to make me feel better,* he thought.

There was a scuttling sound from near his feet and he pressed himself against the wall, looking down at the hole he'd found. Silence descended again. Malagyros waited, sweating, concentrating on keeping his breathing regular and slow.

The thing exploded out of the hole with a violence that shocked him. Even expecting it, Malagyros nearly froze in horror at the sight of the giant brown rat. It rushed at him squealing angrily, beady black eyes bulging redly from its sockets, yellow teeth viciously bared.

It leapt and hit him in the chest, knocking him off balance, but not down, digging its claws into his shirt and the flesh beneath, snapping at his face.

Malagyros had it by the throat, and for a while it was all he could do to keep it at bay. He screamed with pain as the strength of his own arms dragged the gripping claws through his flesh. Flecks of foam spattered his face and he thought frantically that it must be mad.

Desperately he ran into a wall with all his strength, the rat's body shielding him from the impact. Again. Again. Again, and the razor-edged chisel teeth gaped in a scream of pain. Finally, the creature weakened enough that Malagyros was able to tear it free from its grasp on his clothing. With all his strength he rammed it back against the wall, until he felt neckbones parting and at last the rat hung limp in his grasp.

He flung it away in disgust and abruptly, the light went out.

Aphonea entered the guard-filled room stealthily. Even though they couldn't see her, she needed to avoid touching the men, or making any inexplicable sound. She also had to be careful of how the light hit her, lest she cast a shadow. Men were fools, but light had its own laws and didn't confuse easily.

She slid gracefully around a grappling couple, ducked under a thrown goblet and tiptoed towards the door.

A fat, hairy little guardsman lurched up to her, reeking of wine and foul odors.

"Who're you?" he demanded, small red eyes glittering, "What're you sneakin' around for?"

Aphonea blinked. Then she reached out with one finger and touched him in the center of his forehead.

"You do not see me," she said, gazing into his eyes compellingly.

He slapped her hand away.

"I do too!" he insisted.

Reaching out he snatched her headscarf off and his face brightened in appreciation of her beauty. He looked around happily, as though expecting applause for this conjuring trick. But his fellows were lost in their own exploits.

Perhaps I can lure him into the corridor, she thought, wondering if he was unaffected by her magic because he was so drunk. She smiled at him.

Encouraged, he grabbed her breast and gave it a playful squeeze.

Changing her plans, Aphonea punched him in the nose, knocking him onto his fat behind. Then she tried to leap over his prone body. His hand flashed out and caught her ankle, bringing her down on top of him.

"Theeeve!" he bellowed. "Thieeeeeeffff!"

Like old battle horses responding to a clarion call, his sodden companions raised their heads all around the room. In seconds Aphonea hung from several strong, if unsteady, grips.

She didn't even try to fight them; she was too stunned. Not as much with terror at being caught, as by the fact that her magic wasn't working.

"The westerner'll wanna see her," one suggested.

"Might be a bonus in it," said the little fat one, wiping blood off his upper lip. "Da boss'll be happy."

"Yeah," said another, studying her lewdly, "I bet he likes her."

They all laughed uproariously and half-dragged, half-carried each other and Aphonea from the chamber.

Malagyros sat in the dark for what seemed like hours. He slept, or thought he did. The dark left him uncertain if his eyes were opened or closed.

Are they coming back for me? he wondered. There hadn't been any bones or other debris to indicate a previous prisoner. He knew the rat might eat bones if it were hungry enough, but surely there would have been some sign of a body—cloth, or hair . . . fingernails. He wrested his mind from that avenue of thought. It was a fair bet that prisoners, or their bodies, were taken away.

In which case, I'd better be ready. He considered the rat's carcass, lying somewhere in the darkness. Perhaps he could break its jaws and use the teeth as a weapon. But he was certain the animal had been mad and was reluctant to risk cutting his hands on its mouth. *Perhaps I could sharpen one of its bones.* He shuddered in disgust.

Just then, the stone was lifted and light poured into the cell like molten gold.

His eyes smarted from the sudden light, but he had to suppress a whimper of joy at the sight of it.

A knotted rope dropped down, and Rabba's face appeared overhead.

"Hey?" he shouted into, to him, impenetrable darkness. "Ya there?"

After a moment, Malagyros stepped into the light. He stood blinking up at them and thought Rabba looked immensely relieved to see him.

"Get yer bones up here," Rabba said. "The boss's mage has a job for you."

Malagyros raised a sardonic eyebrow, then wound the rope around his waist and began to climb. He pulled himself out of the hole and rested on his hands and knees while he studied his captors.

Fesros held a torch, and looked less bored than he had been.

Malagyros noticed for the first time that the witch lights lavished on the deserted corridors were no longer burning. Wondering why, he glanced at Rabba.

Rabba's sword was in his hand, his face tight and nervous as he looked back at his prisoner.

"Coil up the rope and hang it over there," Rabba snapped, indicating a ring on the wall to which the rope was attached.

Malagyros stood slowly and turned his back on them, pulling up the rope with a great show of reluctance.

"Mithra!" Rabba swore. "Move it, you bastard! Ya don't keep a mage waiting if ya know what's good for you."

"It's because I know what's good for me that I'm in no hurry to meet this mage of yours," Malagyros said dryly.

"I said *move it!*" Rabba snarled, stepping closer.

Malagyros took a grip on the rope and swung, hitting him full in the face with fifty pounds of stiffened rat. Rabba went down like a sack of grain. Malagyros swung the rat again and caught Fesros on the side of the head with a meaty *thwack!* The guard staggered, his eyes unfocused, and Malagyros dropped the rat and grabbed Fesros's head, yanking it down to meet the force of his own upthrust knee. Then he tumbled him into the open cell. He caught Rabba under the arms and dropped him in too.

Then he closed the trapdoor, picked up the sword and torch and went exploring.

He spared a last glance backward. Intriguing. Those were, perhaps, the only men in all history to be bludgeoned to death with a rat.

Marcus Licenius Severus's drunken guards dragged Aphonea along a series of winding corridors until they came to a set of bronze doors, defended by a pair of men in . . . uniforms.

Aphonea blinked at the sight. No wonder the off-duty guards didn't wear them. They were a blinding shade of blue, with mismatched red accoutrements.

The men defending the doors crossed their spears to bar passage and tried to argue their fellows out of the idea of breaking in on the Old City man at his leisure.

Her little fat guard moved in close to the doors and kicked them hard several times before he could be stopped.

Silence descended.

Then, in a voice pitched high with rage, a man called out, "Who dares to disturb my pleasure?"

Suddenly, every man was sober, and aware of making a serious mistake.

"Enter!" the voice shrieked.

With a glare at their comrades, the men on duty opened the doors and Aphonea's captors brought her forward with much less enthusiasm than they'd been showing.

They entered a large room, which Aphonea was startled to see resembled the Emperor's audience chamber, down to the silver and gilt tilework. The room was lit by the fragile light of hundreds of candles, and their scent filled the air. At the head of the mock audience chamber was an oversized replica of the throne of the City, expanded to the size of a bed. On it sat an obese man in a linen tunic. His elaborately curled hair gleamed with sweat and his mean, close-set eyes glittered with fury.

At either hand sat a naked woman. Both looked mildly apprehensive, but not the least embarrassed to be in a room full of men.

At that moment an elderly man parted the curtains behind the throne and swept to Marcus Licenius's side.

"What are *you* doing here?" Marcus snapped in exasperation. "Light," he said and gestured. Nothing happened, and he flashed to his feet.

"LIGHT!" he bellowed.

Again, there was no response and he turned to the old man, his lips thinned as he awaited an explanation.

"The magic has stopped, Lord."

"I've noticed," Marcus sneered. "What did you do, Persus? Is this one of your experiments gone wrong?"

"The whole City is without magic," the mage replied in the same even, cool-toned voice. "The sky palaces have fallen, houses of illusion have vanished, leaving their occupants smashed on the ground." He shook his head. "There was no warning, nothing. The magic just . . . stopped working."

Marcus grasped Persus's shoulder.

"Quickly, we must . . ." He stopped and glared at the men who had disturbed him. "What are you doing here?" he asked coldly. "How dare you filthy, disgusting swine thrust yourselves into my presence?"

Only a westerner could manage to sound prissy and bullying at the same time, Aphonea thought.

The fat guard was pushed forward, his eyes starting in fear.

"I . . . we . . . I"—he glared at his fellows—"have caught a thief." He reached out and caught Aphonea's sleeve, dragging her forward.

Marcus's little eyes narrowed and he stepped forward slowly, his nostrils pinched and white. Then he paused, looked excitedly at Persus, then back at Aphonea, and smiled.

"My acolytes," he said to the two nude women, "take her and prepare her to meet the god."

"Yes!" Persus hissed. "How very wise, my Lord."

And only an Urda could be fawning and condescending in one breath, Aphonea thought as the "acolytes" took hold of her. *Just let me get a grip on one of these brainless sluts and I'll—*

One of them jabbed a slim, bejeweled dagger into the soft skin under her jaw, and she decided to accompany them without a struggle.

"The rest of you get out." Marcus said. Rubbing his

hands, he turned to his mage and began a whispered conference.

Malagyros wandered the hallways, testing the occasional door, finding them all locked. He bitterly regretted the loss of his lockpicks. He was very glad for the torch, though; all the glowstones seemed to be out, for some reason.

He came to a branching in the corridor. Judging by the dust on the floor, he chose the path less traveled by, hoping to avoid notice as he searched for a way out.

After a while, he came to another door and half-heartedly tried to open it. It was locked.

Then, in the distance, he thought he heard voices and began to apply his weight to the door as he struggled to open the latch. Rust flaked off in his hand and he realized it wasn't locked at all, but merely frozen, he redoubled his efforts. At last, the latch began to lift with a high-pitched metallic squeal.

He thought the voices in the distance were closer and was certain they could hear him as well. He heaved his weight against the door and it gave with a screaming of hinges.

Malagyros closed the door behind him and moved quickly into the room, hoping the light from the torch wouldn't show under the door. He glanced back at it and heard a sound from deeper in the room.

Turning back he caught an impression of "spear" and dropped to the floor without thinking. There was a twang and the rush of air over his head; then with a solid "thunk" the spear lodged itself in a beam holding up the ceiling.

Looking back and forth between the spear and the launching mechanism, Malagyros wondered, *Why would they set up something like* that *in a empty room?* He looked about. The room was indeed empty, containing only a collapsing rack for holding barrels and the shattered remains of one that had fallen.

Ah! he thought. *A little jest from the previous owner. Apparently he had a problem with the servants tippling.* He looked at the spear again. The iron head was double flanged and eight inches long, followed by a seven-foot shaft. *Seems a little severe. But then, any man with a two-story wine cellar was probably a bit fanatical.*

He moved over to the mechanism, and glancing down, realized that the darkness below wasn't mere shadow, but went down for some way.

Thrusting the torch through the opening he saw a room apparently filled with stone benches.

The temple! he thought in excitement. He dropped the torch and with a certain amount of wriggling, followed it down.

Picking it up, he held it over his head and realized with disappointment that he was not in a temple, but a mausoleum.

What a bizarre thing to have under one's house, he thought and shuddered. Then remembered the warding around the palace and realized the westerner wasn't a man to fear the evil ghosts might bring.

Malagyros looked around for a door. Seeing one, he strode rapidly towards it. Then stopped, the hair rising on his neck. He was certain he'd heard a man's muffled voice coming from one of the tombs, shouting, "I'll get you for this, you bitch!"

Marcus Licenius leered at Aphonea as two burly acolytes dragged her towards him. The two females who'd led her from the throne room, each nursing livid bruises, glared at her from their places beside the westerner.

Stupid of them to put the knife down, Aphonea thought.

They'd taken down her hair, which hung to her waist in a thick curtain that gleamed softly in the torchlight. And they'd stripped her of her clothing. Dressing her in a garment that hung to her hips, made up of fine chains that held magical amulets over her body's energy points.

It was intended to make her docile, draining her strength and leaving her in a trance. But it wasn't working now and she kicked and struggled fiercely, trying to bite the men who held her.

Despite her fury and her fear, she was aware that Marcus Licenius's bad taste extended to his ecclesiastical gear. He and his followers were dressed alike in purple satin gowns, bound at the waist with sashes of cloth of gold decorated with symbols picked out in red silk. They wore scarlet slippers with pointed toes, from which a tiny silver bell hung. Upon their brows, no doubt intended to represent the Eyes of Nogra, six orange globules of paint were smeared. Around each neck hung a carved jet replica of the idol behind the altar, set with six glittering red stones for the eyes. They seemed to imitate Marcus Licenius' diet, too—unlike the guards left upstairs, they were *all* severely overweight.

Her eyes fell on the altar behind him. It was crudely hacked from a block of limestone, with runnels carved into its top, leading to a hole. Beneath which was a carved niche holding a silver bowl hung about with glass goblets wrapped in silver mesh. In the center of the altar lay a mallet with an egg-shaped stone head, crossed by a long and sharply pointed curved dagger.

Aphonea swallowed hard.

Above the altar presided an obsidian statue of Nogra. The creature seemed possessed of thousands of warty tentacles, some held aloft in mystical postures. The head looked like nothing so much as a scowling tar bubble with six glittering scarlet eyes.

"O, Nogra," Marcus Licenius was praying, "give to your servants the power of magic. Deny it to all others, we beg you. We swear to reward your aid with a sea of blood to slake your mighty thirst."

He spun around to face Aphonea, and his little eyes glittered with lust as he looked at her nearly naked body.

"You have been found pleasing in the god's sight," he

intoned and licked his lips. "Now do I bestow upon your mouth the Kiss of Affirmation."

He grabbed two handfuls of her hair and pulled her towards him. Covering her lips with his, he thrust his sour-tasting tongue into her mouth. Aphonea thought seriously about vomiting, but decided on a more direct strategy.

Now do I bestow the Teeth of Ferocity to your tongue and the Knee of Retribution to your groin.

Marcus's eyes bulged and he pulled away from her with a weird little gurgle, spraying blood through writhing lips and clutching at himself with both hands.

Then his eyes flamed and he grabbed her by both arms.

"I'll get you for this, you bitch!" he screamed. And with surprising strength he flung her onto the altar.

I'll-get-you-for-this-you-bitch? Malagyros thought. Puzzled, he went over to the talking tomb and laid his ear against the top. There were many voices down there. One, louder than the rest, kept shouting, "Get her! Hold her! Grab her, *someone!*"

He shoved at the marble slab laid over the crypt until it was pushed half off the tomb. It had a hinged wooden bottom with a small brass handle. Lifting it, he found himself looking down into Aphonea's furious, terrified face.

Several weirdly dressed individuals were forcibly holding her onto a stone slab, and at her head, a dark-haired man was raising a stone hammer and shouting incantations. Marcus Licenius, in the robes of a high priest of the cult.

With only the fleeting thought, *I'm going to regret this*, Malagyros picked up the sword and leapt into the tomb, breaking his fall on Marcus's fat back. His feet seemed to sink into a foot of blubber, with india rubber at the bottom. Marcus dropped like a sack of grain and didn't get up again. The mage dropped to the floor beside him, twitching and foaming at the mouth in the grip of some sort of fit.

Malagyros swung on the worshipers with his sword and they released Aphonea, trying to run or fight as the spirit took them. Aphonea leapt from the altar and tackled one of the acolytes, pounding the woman's head on the floor until she stopped struggling.

Malagyros turned, his body and arm moving in the automatic patterns a thousand hours of practice in the gymnasium had taught. *Cut*-thrust-twist-turn-slash. Panic drove him, a vision of *both* their bodies stretched over the altar when sheer numbers bore him down. Soft, heavy resistance met his blade, and the jarring thump of the edge hitting living bone.

But the blade found a target every time he thrust. *These people have no idea how to defend themselves, they're just getting in each other's way.* One thrust another onto his point and leapt at him with an ornately curved knife. He jerked the point free and swept the blade in a roundhouse slash that severed the priest's lower jaw.

I wish I hadn't seen that. I wish they'd run, *dammit!*

The other acolyte came up behind Aphonea with the sacred dagger raised over her head. Her shadow betrayed her and Aphonea spun round. Grabbing the woman's wrists in both hands, Aphonea fell onto her back, planted her feet in the woman's belly and threw the acolyte over her. The woman landed on her head, and even over the screams of the others, Aphonea heard her neck snap.

Malagyros stabbed yet another purple-robed man and yanked his bloody sword free. He stared into the mad eyes of his final opponent.

It was obvious that, despite overwhelming evidence to the contrary, the man believed his god would allow him to defeat the invader.

"Go away," Malagyros said quietly, "or I'll kill you."

The man's eyes flickered with doubt, then he smiled.

"I don't think so," he said smugly.

Malagyros shrugged, "Your choice," he said.

The man lunged and Malagyros thrust with his sword, slicing through the man's chest. The man gave a weird little shriek and Malagyros heard it echoed behind him. Yanking his sword free, he spun round to confront the staring eyes of Marcus's mage, the sacred hammer falling from his grasp.

Malagyros looked over the mage's shoulder into Aphonea's eyes.

"You've bewitched him?" he asked softly.

She raised one brow.

"Not necessary," she said. "That's because"—she gave a tug, and the mage's body slowly fell—"the best symbol for a sharp knife"—she held up a bloody athame, the sorceror's ceremonial dagger—"is a sharp knife."

He grinned and then he really looked at her. Aphonea was naked but for a net of jewels held onto her by a pattern of fine gold chains that formed a deep fringe around her hips. Her breasts gleamed like pearls in the torchlight. He swallowed hard.

She pulled her hair forward and folded her arms across her chest.

Annoyed by both their reactions, he forced his eyes to her furiously blushing face.

"I like your dress," he taunted.

"Could you loan me something to wear?" she asked, her eyes angry, but her voice cool. Then she helplessly indicated the bodies around them. "I just can't wear theirs."

He could understand it; they were drenched in blood. For that matter, he'd have been reluctant to wear those robes himself. Still, he was exasperated as he tugged off his tunic and tossed it to her.

"None of them got away," she said pulling it over her head. "So there'll be no alarm raised. Now all we have to do is get out of here."

"Not quite," he said, looking at the idol, then at her. She gasped.

Then, as one, they both leapt for the statue, clambering up onto the altar and digging at its face with sword and dagger.

In the end, they each got three of the Eyes.

Malagyros scowled.

"If you were fair-minded you'd give them to me for saving your life," he said.

"If you were fair-minded," she snapped back, "you'd remember that I saved yours."

"Pah! It wouldn't have needed saving but for you. This whole stupid situation is your fault." He tucked the Eyes into his pocket. "Let's get out of here," he said and headed for one of the doors.

"Just a minute," she said following him. "What do you mean this is all my fault? What are you talking about?"

He grabbed a torch from a wall bracket and marched down the corridor without answering.

Nonplussed, Aphonea watched his muscled back disappear around a corner. When he said this was her fault, he obviously meant something deeper than their immediate situation. *But it was he who began our rivalry,* she thought in frustration, and started after him.

One day she'd suddenly found herself in competition for any magical object upon which she cast covetous eyes. She'd very quickly learned who was stealing things right out from under her hands, but never why. His father had been a *banker's* slave, and very successful indeed after he'd bought himself free. Malagyros gave the objects away as often as he sold them. Meanwhile, her income had dropped precipitously.

He was trying to open a door when she caught up with him.

"Malagyros, what did you—"

"Open this," he said curtly and stepped aside, looking over her shoulder down the corridor.

She blushed, aware that she would probably fail. She was also growing increasingly annoyed by his attitude. But he was right; they had to get out. So she stepped to the door and tried to probe the lock. She felt nothing and bit her lower lip. Then she tried her most powerful opening spell and let out her breath in something dangerously close to a sob when it didn't work.

"Get on with it!" Malagyros snarled, his eyes blazing with impatience. "Someone could come down this way any minute."

"I can't," she said; her voice almost failed her. "Magic isn't working any more."

"What?"

"A few hours ago, magic ceased to work. The Old City noble's mage said the sky palaces had fallen."

Malagyros's eyes narrowed.

"What kind of game are you playing? I never heard of such a thing."

She sighed, "I have, and it's no game. Sometimes a ship's captain will come into port complaining that a spell that moved his ship without oars or wind had suddenly stopped working. They often have to drift quite a way before the spell takes hold again."

He looked askance at her.

"It's true!"

"I haven't got time for this," he said. Then he gathered himself and hurled a mighty kick at the lock.

The door opened with a crash and hit the wall behind it with a resounding smack.

"Good job," she said sarcastically, "no one will ever notice that."

"Your fault," he muttered, closing the door behind them, "you're the one who wouldn't open it."

Her eyes flashed.

"Well, I didn't think spit and fingernails would do it! And while we're on the subject of 'my fault' what did you mean by that remark back there?"

He looked coldly at her and then continued down the hallway the door had opened on to.

"I think this may lead to the outside," he said. "Notice how the flame is behaving?"

He was right; the torch was reacting to a flow of air that drew flames streaming behind it.

"Don't turn your back on me!" she snapped.

"Or what? You'll turn me into a toad? Oh, you can't do that anymore can you?" he said in mock sympathy. "Magic doesn't work. What *will* you do?"

"What ordinary people do, I suppose," she said, glaring at his back. "Make cryptic remarks and then walk away from them."

"Daylight!" he exclaimed.

They hurried forward and saw that an enormous corner of stonework had plunged into the corridor, breaking off a portion of the ceiling, leaving it open to the afternoon sky.

They gazed upwards. Aphonea felt her jaw drop. *Odd. I thought that was just a figure of speech*, she thought, closing it with a snap. An enormous tower leaned over them, threatening to collapse and crush them at any moment. The air was thick with powdered dust; they both blinked and sneezed.

Malagyros dropped the torch and gripped her about the waist.

"I'll give you a boost up, then I'll follow."

Thinking of her unclothed lower half she slapped at his arms.

"You're not nine feet tall, you'll never make it. I'll give you a boost up," she said, "then you can pull me up."

"You're right," he said reluctantly. "It's not as though you could just go for help, since we're not supposed to be here."

She smiled, "Not to mention the fact that we've killed the master of the house and all his friends, while we robbed him."

She turned to the wall and braced herself against it, the tunic rose with the motion of her arms, revealing the curve of her buttocks.

He licked his lips and sighed.

"Well, I suppose that tower isn't going to hang there forever," he muttered and began to climb.

He pulled her up with ease and they fled to the wall, turning to stare in awe at the sky-palace that had crushed the westerner's house like a toy.

"The magic *is* gone."

"Yes," she said sadly. Then stubbornly, she asked, "What did you mean, that this was all my fault?"

He looked at her in astonishment, then gave a snort of amusement. "The world has ended," he mocked, "but about that remark you made ..." Then his smile faded. "When I first saw you I asked a friend to introduce us. I was standing behind you when you told him that you had no interest in meeting the son of slaves."

"Oh," she said, looking stricken. She bowed her head, blushing furiously and worked at the knot that bound the Eyes of Nogra into the hem of her tunic. "It was jealousy that made me speak so," she said. She looked up at him. "I apologize." Then she took his hand and placed the Eyes in it.

He smiled, reached into his pocket and placed his three in her hand. "The City wouldn't be the same without you," he explained.

There was a tremendous rumbling and they turned to the sky palace, expecting it to fall apart at last. Instead, it wobbled, like a drunk rising from a fall and slowly rose into the air. They watched it, amazed. Then they felt a change in the jewels they held and looked down at their hands.

The scarlet gems pulsed and flowed together. With one cry the two thieves flung them away in disgust. The Eyes splattered like overripe fruit and then flowed together. Malagyros and Aphonea backed away from the disgusting sight. It was enough to distract them from the hippo-like form squeezing itself through the broken wall.

Marcus Licenius stood glaring at them, a cavalry sword clutched in his heavy hand, his robes stained with blood.

Evidently the protective spells had returned before he could *quite* complete the messy process of dying. He took a ponderous step forward, and his slipper-clad foot squashed the red pulsing mass that had been the Eyes of Nogra.

"I'm going to kill you," he said, his eyes glinting madly. The little monstrosity he'd stepped on flowed unheeded up his leg. "You blasphemed my god, you killed my friends, you struck *me!* That bitch *bit* me. You're going to pay." Marcus took one step towards them, then stopped and began to emit a high-pitched scream. He hopped and wiggled and clutched himself obscenely as he screeched in terrible agony.

Then he stilled, and when he opened his eyes they were scarlet, with neither pupil nor sclera showing.

"At last!" he said in a voice like syllables of burning ash.

"After six hundred years of being drenched in blood I had no use for, I have what I've always wanted."

He ran his hands over himself in sensual delight. "My own body!" He grinned at them. Things moved at the back of his throat. "My master was too proud of creating me to destroy me when he realized how dangerous I could be. So he divided me into six parts and placed me in the face of that monstrous idol. How I have tried to get my stupid worshipers to give me my own body. But I was too weak. And now"—he hugged himself—"in thanks I shall slay you first. Your blood shall be the first to nourish me. Be thankful I spare you the eternal torment that shall be the lot of all the rest of humankind," he said.

The body that had been Marcus Licenius picked up the sword and came towards them. "I feel your Talent, witch. But it will avail you nothing; you are as helpless as this mundane lump."

Aphonea raised her hands. *I can't!* she realized. The binding of flesh and demon was too powerful to break as long as the flesh was whole.

And the flesh had two feet of entirely unmagical steel in its hand. The edge would make her less than whole very quickly indeed.

Marcus-Nogra's face wore a puzzled expression when Malagyros stepped forward, long sword held in both hands. It took off his head with a whirling stroke.

As though he truly couldn't conceive of anyone not wanting to feed him, Malagyros thought, as the momentum carried him staggering half a dozen paces. *Evidently demons don't study swordcraft.*

"I killed it!" he shouted.

The orange creature that was Nogra began to emerge from Marcus's body.

"Oh, shit," Malagyros said, backing up rapidly.

Aphonea stepped forward and plunged the Old City noble's sword through it, chanting the most powerful spell of un-making that she knew. Nogra began to bubble and spit like a peach on a blazing fire until it lost cohesion and began to sink into the earth, leaving only a pinkish slime behind it.

"We've got to get out of here," Malagyros said, putting his arm around her. "Chaotic as things are, we should pass unremarked, even dressed the way we are."

"Yes, what a fortunate disaster," Aphonea murmured dazedly. She found herself quite willing to let him choose their direction for the moment and wound her arm around his waist. "I heard what you said about my hair," she said.

"And I heard what you said about my parents."

"Why don't we start fresh?" she suggested.

"Exactly what I was going to propose."

A DAY IN THE LIFE

Laura Anne Gilman

Akif lounged against the cold stone wall of the tariff house, begging bowl clenched firmly between his knees. The early sunlight was only now creeping along the walls of Byzantium, and the wharf was already loud with servants and fishmongers about the business of the day. A troop of soldiers marched past, arrogant and precise, led by a Captain-Mage even more arrogant in his purple-striped tunic. Akif's lip curled in disdain, but his eyes followed them wistfully. In a city set in lockstep by social codes, the army was the only way to rise above humble beginnings. Anyone could become a soldier, earn his daily salt, become a recognized member of Byzantium's society. Anyone, that is, with a parent or patron to pay for training, weapons, regular meals. Some days Akif could barely scrape together enough coins for a skewer of meat from Padakis's stall, half price for burnt skewers.

The old man couldn't sell the meat elsewhere, yet he would never simply give it to the boy. Akif scowled. There was no charity on Market Wharf, not for a half-breed brat of a port whore and a Krymean trader. And without steady meals, Akif's growth had been less than optimal. His frail body was barely able to keep itself warm some nights, never mind form and sustain the muscles needed to lift a sword.

Life, the young beggar told himself without bitterness, *is damn unfair. But it could be worse. It could always be worse.*

Akif was shaken from his thoughts by a scuffle of rough cloth next to him. Celestine settled her rags about her legs in a parody of modesty and began untying her hair from its sleepknots.

"Anything astir?" she asked in a harsh voice, the result of a scuffle with drunken soldiers early in her life. Akif shook his head, picking up his bowl and running a finger along the worn-smooth rim. 'Lestine was the best pick-thief in the port, and always willing to share her takings—for the price of information. "The 14th sneered their way though just now" he responded, "but they weren't looking for anything more than trouble. Nobody passes wind in their face, it should be a quiet day." He tilted his head slightly, the thief's point. "Ishy burned a tray this morning."

'Lestine nodded her understanding. A burnt loaf was not only unsalable, but the aroma would keep customers away. It would be in the baker's best interest to get rid of the loaves as soon as possible. Akif would have little difficulty convincing the man to give him a loaf as an act of pious almsgiving.

The boy slid bonelessly up from his slouch, holding the bowl out slightly ahead and at an angle to his body, gnarled shoulder hunched to maximum advantage, peach-fuzzed face schooled to a nonthreatening pitifulness. Shuffling his way through the wooden and cloth stalls to where the baker had set up shop in the direct path of sailors long at sea and hungry for fresh foods, Akif heard the sound of a coin being placed in his bowl. Looking up, he saw only the brush of a wizard-woman's caftan pass by. He risked a glance into the bowl, always keeping most of his attention on the crowds around him. Almond-shaped eyes widened in surprise. The coin was small, but a treasure nonetheless, if he could only hold on to it, and not be robbed. Akif quickly fished the coin out of the bowl and secreted it in the pouch tied about his waist, under his ragged trousers. If Ishy saw the coin, he would demand it in exchange for the bread, and piety be damned.

Bread secured from the baker without too much effort, Akif returned to where he had left 'Lestine, only to find the spot now occupied by Piotr. Akif nodded to the old man but kept moving. Stopping would have meant sharing the blackened loaf, or fighting the other beggar off, and Akif was in no mood to do either. No doubt 'Lestine was busy finding better things than an honest beggar could bring in. He only hoped she had the sense to stay away from the market today—the Blues had been torching market stalls lately, and that always meant trouble for those who couldn't afford protections, magical or otherwise.

It was too early to go back to the wharf and find a corner—he always did better in the afternoon, when the sailors started leaving their ships. With his light skin and pale eyes under a heavy shock of soft black hair, he was so obviously the child of a foreigner, that the equally foreign traders were often more generous than they might be to a flea-bitten street beggar. Some of those foreigners had even tried to take him off the street, teach him shipboard ways, but he had no desire to see other lands. Byzantium was his home, it was where he belonged.

Bolting down the remains of the bread, Akif turned down one narrow street and then another, poking at the piles of refuse thrown there in the hopes of finding something useful among the trash. He had found his bowl there, several months back. Before that, he had been forced to beg with his hands, like a child.

Luck was with him again today. Kicking over one particularly pungent heap, Akif saw the gleam of blue cloth. He reached down and pulled the material free. It was a shirt, torn down one sleeve but otherwise wearable, if one didn't mind the smell of midden. Akif didn't mind. He wouldn't be needing a shirt until cold weather came 'round again, but he knew a place where he could stash it until then, and be reasonably sure the rats wouldn't nest in it. Stuffing the cloth under his belt to prevent anyone else from taking an interest in it, Akif continued his search until the heat of the sun warned him to find shade and water.

Retracing his steps out of the alleys, the beggar found himself by the Lyceum Musica. The students here were not as rich as those of the Lyceum Magica, but were more likely to let a poor beggar stay in the shade of their arcade, and perhaps allow him to draw some water from their fountain. Those of the Magica would as soon toss him into the fountain, and use their skills to hold him under until he drowned.

Sure enough, there was already a sizable crowd gathered around the immense crystal fountain. The fountain, a gift from a patron, sparkling with colored waters that splashed from curving tubes which twined about themselves in an intricate pattern understood only by the mage who had created it. Not even the Magica could boast of such a beautiful piece, although they made sure that their effects were far grander.

Akif skirted the courtyard, bowing and ducking through the groups of students, until he saw Riis and Jussim. Scooting in next to them, he swiped the bowl of water as they passed it between themselves.

"Hey!" Riis protested, then subsided, seeing who it was. "Oh, you. Didn't think to see you so far from the smell of brine," he said, taking the bowl back and draining it. Riis had been a better man once, until a chariot accident crushed his legs. There was no demand for crippled horsemen, and without a patron he had no access

to any healer who could do him any good. And so he
found himself among the company of those he would
have lifted his feet to avoid a few years before. Jussim
carried him about, receiving only abuse for it. No one
knew why the immense man stood for it, or why he
hadn't thrown Riis from a rooftop years before. Some
whispered Riis had put a spell on him, but common
sense scoffed at that. Riis had no money. If he did, it
would be used for healing, not portage. The two were
an oddity, but the society they moved in had more
important things to worry about, and thought nothing of
the past or the occasional rumor except when other gossip was slow.

Akif pulled the shirt from his belt and showed it to
the two older men.

"A nice piece of work," Riis approved, running the
cloth between two fingers. "Material's quality, stitching
should hold. That'll be a good find, come winter."

"I just can't figure why someone would throw it out,"
Akif said, taking the shirt back and poking a finger
through the rip in the sleeve. "This could have been
sewn up, look almost good as new."

Jussim snorted. "Don't ask why Buyers do anything,"
he advised. "It'll drive you mad." Riis threw up his hands
in disgust at Jussim's words. His action dislodged the
water bowl, splashing what water was left on the sun-
warmed cobblestones. Akif caught the bowl when it
bounced, and stood to dip for more water. Behind him,
he could hear the two men arguing.

Buyers, Jussim called them. The lucky ones, with
wealth enough to buy the magics which made life easy.
From storekeepers to nobles, they were the lifeblood of
trade in this city, bringing the money and magic together
to create the glory of Byzantium. How Akif envied them!
There was no point in envying the Magic'd—they simply
were, like the Emperor, or the sun and moon, and nothing would make them him, or him them. But the Buyers
. . . there was a dream. To have coin in hand, enough to

go beyond food and shelter, to buy a cooling charm to carry during the long summer days, or a love token to ensure a night of pleasure . . .

Akif shook himself. *There's no need to court heatstroke, standing in the sun with such thoughts,* he told himself sternly. *You're not Magic'd, and you're not Buyer. You're . . . Unluck'd, is what you are. You and all your sort, and there was nothing to be done for it. Not a damn thing.*

He dipped the bowl into the now-clear waters of the crystalline fountain and went back to where the two, tired of their argument, were discussing the relative merits of the legs on one of the Musica students. Akif shared the water around, then left them to their amusements. They worked the taverns at night, and so could laze the day away, but Akif had places to go, and people to beg from while they were still contented and lazy from the mid-day meal.

Normally Akif would find himself a corner in the outskirts of the city's center market, perhaps by one of the temples where people might be more motivated by piety. But that was where the chariot groups held sway. Akif had no desire to find himself in the middle of yet another riot sparked by spoiled nobles over the merits of their charioteers, riots in which anyone with the misfortune to be wearing the wrong colors was trampled. The youth spat. Hadn't they anything better to do, he wondered, than make other peoples' lives miserable over horses running in a circle? If the Emperor hadn't forbidden it, they'd still be casting magic at the horses to make them run faster. Such underhanded usage of magic had gone unchecked until Hyperion, the Emperor's current favorite, had died of such abuse, the magic draining his spirit until he could no longer go on. Now, the nobles might do as they wished with the chariots, and the charioteers, but the horses themselves were off limits. An incident over a spelled chariot, in fact, was what had started the recent bout of riots, bloodier than any in recent years.

With that in mind, Akif took a left turn down the

Avenue of Heroes, finding himself in a residential area
lined with coolly beautiful buildings of stone and mortar—some of them floating several feet off the ground.
This was unfamiliar territory to the beggar, and he kept
a careful eye out for soldiers or, worse yet, the private
guards these rich enclaves ofttimes hired to patrol their
streets. Soldiers might kick him around, or might ignore
him, depending on how their day had been. From the
Guards, with no Captain-Mage to control them, he could
expect at best a beating. At worst, well, not all the bodies
found floating off the docks drowned accidently. The
wealthy could afford to be generous to a harmless beggar,
but generally the risks outweighed the reward. As soon
as he could, Akif found his way to a busier area, away
from those houses that smelled of dangerous wealth.

Finding a small courtyard where several servants were
gossiping, he settled against a smooth-trunked tree and
curled into a comfortable hunch. The women stopped to
look at him, decided that he was no threat, and went
back to their gossip. Akif breathed a sigh of relief. It
looked like he might be allowed to stay. Once reassured
on that point, he began his spiel, tapping the rim of his
bowl with wiry fingers each time a possible patron came
into view. Most of them pretended not to see the small
figure, but a few stopped long enough to toss small coins
into the bowl, for which Akif would call after them
"Blessings upon your house, Mistress" or "Fair wind to
your business, Master." They always liked that one, even
if they weren't in trade. One man, wearing the wrapped-
leg trousers of a desert trader stopped to speak a few
words to Akif, dropping a well-worn coin, oddly shaped
and obviously foreign, into his hand for the recommendation of a quiet hotel that wouldn't overcharge too dearly.

Akif had barely hidden these coins away in his pouch
with the larger one from that morning when a noble
woman, came up to him, reaching down to tilt his face
upward with one slender finger under his chin. Satisfied
with what she saw, the woman tossed three coins into

his bowl and walked away, the folds of her silken caftan swaying behind her. Her companions giggled, hurrying to catch up with her. Akif looked down, jaw dropping when he saw the glint of gold against the dark wood. Gold, even adulterated, could keep him and 'Lestine warm all winter, warm and fed and with some left to save in his oh-so-hidden cache!

Scurrying to capture the coins before he woke from this wondrous dream, he accidently dropped the bowl. Jostled, the oddly shaped pieces shimmered, and three hand-sized lizards scampered out of the bowl where the metal had been only seconds before.

Akif swore in disappointment, but still managed to recover in time to catch one of the lizards. Breaking its neck swiftly, he put it aside. Not much by itself, but roasted on a stick, it could hold off hunger for another night. Nothing could be wasted in his world, not even a magic prank. Akif closed his eyes briefly, thinking of the life it would require to spend money for a magic of such low importance. A magician wouldn't have done that— only a bored Buyer, with too much time and money on her hands. Not for the first time, he wished for a body that was agile and tough, so that he could be a pickthief like 'Lestine or Marcus, and have a chance at some of that. But his mother had schooled him too well before she died of the wasting plague. Regrets were even more expensive than magic, and of less use to one of the Unluck'd.

The afternoon wore on, and Akif plied his trade on the corner. The servants went on their way, and were replaced by two off-duty soldiers wrangling over what to do with their time off. Akif listened with half an ear— the places the soldiers frequented were likely to become popular with the merchants soon after, following the path of money being spent. Knowing where those places were before anyone else meant a head start in taking their coins. But the soldiers, soon joined by others of their cohort, had little new to suggest. It was almost summer,

and everyone was feeling lazy under the waves of heat.
Akif himself had almost drifted off, his bowl tilting dangerously to one side, when the first screams started.

The soldiers, their argument forgotten, took off at a
run. Akif scrunched himself into a smaller ball, hoping
that whatever whoever was doing to cause those screams
would be satisfied with the soldiers, and not come looking for more victims. There was a series of yells, and
then a loud, rumbling crash. The ground shook once,
and then again in rapid succession. From a distance, Akif
could hear other noises coming from all over the city.
Dust sprinkled down over him and he looked up, only
to fall to the ground in shock, his arms covering his head
as he cowered there.

The sky is falling, he thought to himself. *We have
offended the heavens and they are come to destroy us.*

But Akif hadn't survived the streets for almost two
decades by being superstitious, and soon he risked
another glance upwards. The sky, normally blocked from
view by the castles of the Magic'd, was clear. Even the
usual steady stream of carpets had ceased. The dust he
had felt . . . The beggar put events together, and came
up with the impossible. The castles had fallen. That crash
he had heard . . . the buildings he had passed were held
up by magic. They had fallen.

It's impossible, Akif thought, but he was already on his
feet, begging bowl forgotten. His body screamed, *Run!
Hide!* But his mind was already wondering what he
would see, once clear of this pleasant corner which, he
noted thankfully, had been laid early in the life of the
city, not relying on any magics other than human sweat.
He could stay here and be safe—probably. A body with
half a brain *would* stay here. If buildings were falling in
the Buyers' quarter, he didn't want to think what had
happened to the port, or the huge stone tariff house.
That part of the city was held together only by magic,
the better to impress heathen strangers from the cold
countries.

Even as he was thinking this, Akif found himself moving cautiously through the streets. The soldiers had disappeared. Faintly, Akif could hear the bells ringing, calling the City Guard to order.

My father's gods, Akif thought in amazement. *We're being invaded! The Muslims have found a way to stop the magic, and they're finally invading.* He wasn't sure how he felt about that. To be sure, his father's blood had done him no good in this city, but would it help him any more once the city was overrun? And overrun it would be, of that he had no doubt. Soldiers were soldiers, and good at killing, but everyone understood that the magic was what kept the city walls unbreached.

Akif looked around cautiously, as though he expected to see the Muslims riding down the streets on their fine-bred horses already. There was no one in evidence, even those folk who would have normally been out and about on such a day had gone into hiding. *That might not be such a bad idea,* he thought to himself, still walking down the street. *Looting's bound to start soon, if I know this city, and it'd be best for a poor beggar boy to be out of sight and out of trouble until it all calms down—one way or the other.* Even as Akif thought this he was moving, dodging to one side to bypass a crack in the magic-paved street, or swerving to avoid a late-crashing piece of palace. *Romanus must be very angry. The General always made such big speeches about the glory of Byzantium . . . To be overrun by Muslims will cause his heart to burst, if the Emperor doesn't get to him first!*

Akif was vaguely aware that such thoughts were close to blasphemy, but he couldn't bring himself to stop thinking them. *There's no magic in the entire city. None. The Magic'd will go elsewhere, and we'll be as we were. But what will the Buyers do without magic?*

Akif stopped, looking at the pile of rubble in front of him, blocking the street. The grey and white pattern looked familiar to him. *It was a house I passed,* he realized. *The one with the stone gryphons guarding the door.*

Akif sniggered, hardly recognizing the sound as coming from him. *Shouldn't have built with magic!*

The house next to the remains of the gray and white building still stood, its intricate ironwork gate hanging ajar where the magical restraints, spelled to admit the owners, and keep all others out, had dissolved. Some magic, but they hadn't relied on it.

Akif looked at that doorway for long moments, fingers absently stroking the cloth of the blue shirt still tucked into his belt, listening to the echo of bells and distant shouts getting louder. They'd loot the fallen buildings first, most likely, and the Muslims would be too busy to worry about Buyer houses until much later. Coming to a decision, he straightened his shoulders as best he could, stepped over the rubble, and marched through the gates pretending that he had every right to be there.

Walking into the antechamber, Akif could see where the magical protections had been only from the descriptions in 'Lestine's stories. There was nothing on the walls now—no smoking ruins, no carved-out remains. Nothing to indicate magic had ever touched the flat tiled surface. It was as though the magic had disappeared completely, rather than being blocked. But that was impossible. Wasn't it? Shaking his head, Akif moved up the shallow stairs, bypassed the open sitting area and atrium, and opened a heavy carved door. It was made of a solid dark wood, and therefore imported. Akif figured that anything of interest would be behind such a door.

The room inside was dominated by a long, gleaming table of the same wood as the door. The table was set for dinner—no doubt the servants had been preparing the evening meal when the Muslims attacked and had run for safety. Then Akif noted several pieces of plateware lying on the floor, dropped as though in midflight from cabinet to table. Human servants would have placed the plates on the table itself, just in case this was a false alarm and their master would be coming back to punish them. The beggar drew his breath in sharply as he took in the designs on the walls. This was a house of the Yecenia family. Powerful in the Emperor's court, they would not have risked human servants who might sell an overheard bit of conversation and destroy months of negotiations or plotting. Rumor on the streets said they used magic to perform all household tasks, from washing to cooking to showing guests to their rooms. Akif could only shake his head in amazement. And when the magic went away, so did all of their servants. Unfortunate for whoever was being served!

Without thinking, Akif slipped into one of the over-sized chairs and picked up a silver goblet. It was empty, but he could close his eyes and imagine a glittering servant coming forward to fill his glass, could imagine himself toasting his guests and gesturing broadly to begin the passing of platters heaped high with fresh-cooked foods, all done to perfection. Silent servants, glimmering with magic, would stand behind each guest, awaiting their every desire, be it for more wine, or another serving of roast hen, or a dish of pistachios to finish the meal. *I could be a Buyer. I could do this*, he thought with glee.

As though in a trance, Akif rose from his seat and walked over to the ironwork curtains separating the dining area from the next room. A touch of his hand was enough to swing the curtains apart, revealing a gilt and ivory ballroom, its floor a dizzying mosaic of cream and gold tiles spiraling around in to the center. A raised dais hugged one corner of the room, the family's golden camel blazoned across the top.

Musicians would play there, Akif decided, trying to picture the scene. It was harder than before—food he had experience with, if not in such quality. But dancing? Music? There wasn't much of that in the port, only the stumbling jigs, accompanied by a badly-tuned zither, that one heard on particularly rowdy nights in the taverns. After a few minutes Akif gave up trying to imagine the guests, and concentrated on the music. He had heard of magicians who could pull music from the air, as though commanding the wind to play for them. But all he could create was a memory of the reedy sounds of a flute, and the irregular beat of drums, sounds that would echo oddly in this ornate hall. His attempts only served to emphasized the fact that he did not belong here.

Retreating, Akif closed the curtain carefully, and returned to the equally exotic yet familiar atmosphere of the dining room.

Shaking his head, he turned to explore other portions of the house, hoping to find a few items of carryable size. The owners, he rationalized, would never miss them. *And wouldn't 'Lestine be so surprised!*

Turning the knob of the wooden door, Akif felt a tingle on the back of his neck. Turning slowly, he saw, out of the corner of his eye, the plate still lying on the floor rise, as though being picked up by a tired, weakened servant. Distantly, Akif heard the noise of doors shutting, and alarms going off.

The Muslims have failed, he thought. *The General has managed to restore the city's magic.* Akif felt a moment of panic. If that were so, the Buyers who owned this house would be back soon. This was no safe place for him to be.

He put his hand on the doorknob again, then stopped. Turning, he went to the table and grabbed one of the goblets off the polished surface. *They'll never miss it,* he assured himself quickly. *They'll be so grateful to have their house and money—and the magic—they'd have given it to me if I were begging when they came home.* But the silver weight seemed to burn his hand as he walked through the house. Every step he took echoed too loudly on the cool tiling.

Just then, Akif felt a soft breeze waft across his bare back. A breeze like a boat moving across water might make—or a person moving quickly! Turning on one callused heel, Akif yelped in fright at the sight of a tall, graceful form forming out of the ether. His thoughts froze within his head as he watched the servant become solid. Its elongated head turned to face him, great glowing eyes boring into Akif's soul.

"Who enters my master's home?"

As though the silent words were a knife that cut the bonds holding Akif in place, he turned and ran down the stairs, his feet barely touching the cool stone steps in his flight.

Skidding to a halt at the foyer entrance, Akif swore at the sight of another servant—*it couldn't be the same one!*—rising between him and his chance at freedom. Taking a deep breath the beggar turned once more, running heedlessly down the hallway.

Mother of Storms, I will bless your name forever to the winds, but get me out of here! he thought, barely checking his speed to look into open doorways as he passed. No hope of escape in those, since most of the rooms on this floor were given over to storerooms and the like. No doors to exit, no windows to squeeze through. And all the while Akif could feel the magic'd breeze of the servant coming closer and closer.

The smell of warmed spices pulled him to the left when the hallway branched. Not stopping to consider his choice, Akif followed the scent down a corridor marked by coarser stone underfoot and a lack of hangings along the walls.

Before he could do more than note these changes, he felt the burning-cold touch of the servant at his midsection. Yelping in terror, Akif jumped forward. The rope holding his trousers to his waist parted under the strain, leaving the servant holding a pile of ragged cloth and twine, and Akif standing nude in the center of a large, overwarm room.

The kitchen! Akif thought, then swore in disappointment. There were plenty of places to hide, true, but the servant was standing there in the doorway, watching him. Akif took a deep gulp of air, watching the pale, shimmering figure with apprehension.

Nowhere else to run, boy, he told himself. *And there's*

nothing you can do against a magic'd creature. Nonetheless, his gaze roamed the cluttered kitchen, looking desperately for something—anything—to aid him. The
display of knives he stopped at, then passed over. What
good would even the best steel do against magic? What
he needed was a distraction, something to keep the
damned creature occupied while he slipped by it and out
the door.

And what if there are others? Akif shushed the voice
in his mind. If there were other servants up and about,
he was as good as skewered and over the fire already.
Best to assume that only this one had recovered.

Akif picked up a bundle of dried dates from the long
wooden worktable behind him. Weighing it in his hand,
the beggar tried to determine the best place to aim it,
calculating how long it might possibly distract the servant. Were his captor human, Akif would have had the
encounter timed to the second, but this was a new experience for him.

This will teach you to stay away from magic! he
scolded himself, then stopped. Something wasn't right.
Several minutes had passed since he had turned to face
his pursuer, but the creature remained in the doorway,
hovering slightly over the stone floor. The servant resembled nothing so much as a towering skeleton made of
the finest silks, draped and flowing with the wind, with
only those terrifying eyes to indicate that it was anything
more than a mannikin. But silks could bind and tie, and
Akif was sure this creature was stronger than it looked.

*So why hasn't it come after me? Why is it just standing
there in the doorway?*

A half-expected breath of wind made Akif jump to his
left. Another servant stood there, calmly observing him.
He had waited too long. Cold sweat broke out along the
nape of his neck.

"What are you waiting for?" he shouted. "You caught
me, now take me."

Still they stood there, waiting. Akif shifted the bundle

of food in his hand, then looked down at it as though he had never seen it before. All of a sudden, it made sense. Servants were magic, and magic had to be bound to something, be it a person, a charm—or a place. And if these servants were bound to this house, then others must be allowed in to deliver packages. That was why they were waiting. Before, he had been an intruder. Here, in this place, with food in his arms . . .

"Bless you, Mother of Storms," he said, hefting the bundle as he had seen human slaves do along the wharves. But where did those mortal servants come in, and how could he get out?

Spotting a small doorway in the stone wall, Akif moved slowly towards it, keeping one eye on the servant closest to him. Passing by a workbench, he snagged an old leather apron to tie around his waist, mourning the loss of the blue shirt and his coin purse, still in the first servant's skeletal grip.

"It's been a delight passing the hour with you," Akif said, reaching with his free hand to push open the door. "But I really must go now."

The creature in the doorway, its job done, turned to leave. "And you, who came late to the game," Akif said, feeling more secure the closer he came to freedom, "you can just go on your way as well."

Slipping out the door, Akif dropped the dates and slammed the door shut, breathing a sigh of relief. Only now did he realize how close to collapsing his body was.

Collecting his wits, Akif turned and strode down the alley between the house and where its neighbor had once stood as though he had every right to be there. More proof that the magic was back—the grounds were still and quiet despite the crowds Akif could see gathering down the street a ways. All the more reason to escape, before more servants, less easily fooled, arrived.

Akif noted from a safe distance that the magical gate-keepers had yet to reappear. That was something to remember—'Lestine would be grateful for that information.

But more than that, think of the stories he could tell! He, Akif the beggar, thought good only for a few coins in pity, had outwitted not one, but two magic'd servants! No one could possibly match his story, even if they had seen the Muslims ride up to the walls themselves!

Akif walked out into the din and confusion of the streets, whistling cheerfully.

ELEMENTAL TACTICS

Roland J. Green

To Alexandros Vutsuius, Second Procurator of the
Obrizam Squadron

From Markos Celtios Nilo, Prefect, Office of Thalassic
Studies, Lyceum Bellum

Greetings:

I send this letter by way of a trusted servant, so that
you will have some warning of my probable arrival on
your doorstep or deck. We have been friends much too
long for me to wish that you find me one morning, like
an unwanted child set out for exposure!

I am rejoining the Fleet because of what happened
the Day the Magic Stopped. You have doubtless heard
more than enough about the matters known to all, and
I can add little myself.

Less well-known to anyone not in the City at the time
was the outburst of crime. Many of our most reputable
criminals (if one may call them such) were moderate in

their use of spells. This is partly because of the well-known phenomenon of certain spells clashing disastrously with others, to the great danger of anyone in the vicinity. (Robbing a house can mean the galleys or a labor band on the frontier; burying its owners in its rubble means impalement.)

It is also because cheap spells are seldom strong and often worthless. Costly spells, beyond the means of many thieves, will do as one expects—always provided that the mage who sold you the spell will not have reported you to the authorities for the purchase of a spell with criminal intent.

But I digress, my old vice. You always said that a ship could be on the rocks three times over before I could finish phrasing an order to the rowers to back water.

Well, the Day the Magic Stopped I found myself on the rocks in a most uncommon manner, having nothing to do with orders or rowers. I also found myself dealing with piracy in an equally uncommon manner.

The affair had begun some months before, when those of us with friends at the Thalassocrat's Office had heard rumors of a diving vessel that a noted mage was building or causing to be built or planning to have built.

I continued with my classes, my courting of Helena Hymanos (I still miss Maria, perhaps more than ever now that Remus is serving out of the City, but a man of my age is not meant to sleep alone), and my attendance at the Thalassocrat's petty court. If you ever think that sailors ashore intrigue less than nobles, think again.

A day came when the Thalassocrat himself summoned me to his office. I went in an exalted mood that quite took away any distaste for the ceremonial involved. The night before, Helen and I had consummated our betrothal, drunk deeply of excellent strongwine, and driven away the aches in head and stomach with a spell that left me feeling like a boy—a condition I promptly put to use.

My buoyant mood did not survive more than moments alone with the Thalassocrat.

"Markos, you are looking well."

"God smiles on my affairs in many ways, Excellency."

"I hope this will continue. I wish you to be the observer for this office in the trials of a diving vessel."

"Then—the tales one hears—"

"Are quite true. Ioannes Philippos Magus has devised a vessel that he says may travel underwater for hours of time and leagues of distance."

"To what purpose?"

The Thalassocrat shrugged. "He says it will be valuable for both defending our harbors and attacking those of the enemy. Since no barbarian folk have had a respectable navy for some while, I permit myself doubts. However, you know mages. They seem to know little of anything outside the Lyceum, but do useful work in spite of this."

"Then I am to see what use might be made of this vessel?"

"Quite so. You were the best man I could find available for the work, having experience of both the practical and the theoretical aspects of the sea. Once you have descended in this craft a few times—"

My jaw sagging or a catch in my breath must have drawn the Thalassocrat's attention. "I trust your health will permit that?" he said, in a way that made it plain that if I was fit to be out of bed my health *would* permit it.

My visions of lounging upon a breezy deck and watching the Magus's diving vessel play about me like a frisky porpoise vanished abruptly. One might even say they sank.

"My health is excellent," I said. "I was about to ask what 'observing' meant, and you have answered my question in the way I hoped for."

"Curious to see the sea from underneath?" he asked.

"Now that it seems that it may be possible without turning sponge diver, for which I am a little old—yes."

"God be with you, then. The Procurator of Finance

will arrange your travel and allowances, if you will see him on your way out."

That evening I departed aboard one of the Thalasso-crat's galleys, bound for the Eastern Shore where Ioannes Philippos was at work. It was swift, the weather was fair, and the rowers sang in tune. The voyage would have been a pleasure if Helena had been with me and a most curious mission had not lain ahead.

We reached our destination in the night, but I remained aboard the vessel until dawn. At that point I discovered that our underseagoing Magus was less mad or perhaps only wealthier than I had thought.

He was working aboard a curious vessel, assembled from two elderly galleys joined together by a stout wooden deck. Below that was a second deck, joining the vessels a cubit or two below the waterline, and on this deck rested the diving machine.

I call it a machine because at first glance it looked like nothing fit to cross an ornamental pond, let alone navigate a harbor fit for seagoing ships. It resembled nothing so much as two large, bronze horse troughs joined together face to face—the *very* large kind, as you see in the stables of the Guards' cavalry.

I estimate its length as some twelve cubits. At what I will call the stern I saw a wide-flanged Archimedean screw thrusting out of a hole in the bronze. Both forward and aft was a pair of fins, rather like those on a fish except rectangular and also made of bronze. They seemed to be hinged, as if intended to be capable of movement, although I assumed that the screw was the propulsive device.

Forward was a dome set with small glass-covered openings, shaped like a helmet but of a size suitable for Goliath or at least Samson. Toward the stern was an arrangement of bars and ropes, which seemed incomplete, as though it was intended to receive some further apparatus.

I looked about me, my eyes having adjusted to the gloom on the lower deck, and saw two men—freemen, with guild badges on their headcloths—at work on a large bronze buoy, or perhaps a barrel. It seemed about the right size to fit the stern arrangement, and I hailed the men to satisfy my curiosity.

Their answer came back:

"Who wants to know?" (I censor their reply.)

I gave my name.

They replied, "Oh, him."

I had no immediate reply, but a voice from the shadows said, "He has the right to an answer."

By this time I was practically on top of the men, standing in the narrow space between them and the edge of the lower deck. The men looked at each other and grunted. "It's the float for the Greek fire," one of them said.

"Oh." As I spoke, I took two steps backward, not reckoning on where I was going. As I took a third, my heel came down on empty air. I toppled backward and struck the water with a mighty splash.

To make matters worse, I inhaled as I struck, and came to the surface thrashing and coughing desperately, to get the water out of my lungs or at least some air into them. The men had to drag me out of the water. I was spared the ignominy of needing to have an air elemental conjured into my lungs, to restore my breathing.

I was leaning back against a coil of rope when I became aware of a man in magus's robes standing before me. I could not make out their color, but he had the sash of a Doctor at the Lyceum Magus, and I knew that I faced Ioannes Philippos.

Ioannes Philippos is a small man, and of course he abandoned his family name when he entered the Higher Studies at the Lyceum Magus. But I would wager much that there is Celt in his ancestry. He possesses a most imposing mustache, and it is an easy exercise of the imagination to imagine it drooping down both sides of his mouth instead of merely crowding his upper lip.

He is also uncommonly polite for a mage. He returned my bow, then dismissed me to obtain dry clothing, suggesting that I borrow a set from his workmen, as more suitable for entering the vessel.

This we did as soon as I was dried and clothed. Upon crawling through the hatch in the helmet (which the mage called an observation cupola), I knew I faced one certain problem in executing my orders.

I am uneasy or worse in confined spaces. I could easily see myself spending every voyage in this diving vessel in a state of perpetual uneasiness apt to turn into crippling fear. For the moment, however, my fear was within reason, and I was able to listen to Ioannes Philippos discuss his creation by the light of a small oil lamp.

The interior of the vessel was so crowded with mechanisms that there was barely room to turn around. The main features were a steering wheel under the cupola, two sets of levers fore and aft for the operators of the horizontal diving rudders, and the propulsion position.

This last consisted of six seats, rather more comfortable than rowers' benches, each convenient to a large crank. The cranks were linked in some manner that I never quite understood to a shaft which they caused to rotate, and the rotation of the shaft caused the rotation of the Archimedean screw I had seen projecting from the stern. Its wide flanges pressed against the water, and propelled the boat forward.

The most ingenious feature of the vessel was invisible. I now had enough assurance to speak, and commented that there seemed to be rather less space inside than one would judge from the vessel's exterior dimensions.

"Oh, of course," the mage said. "I have been quite forgetful. Above us is a tank of breathing air. Below are three tanks now containing air, but with valves that may be raised to admit sea water."

"Is that how the boat rises and sinks?" I asked.

"Largely. On the surface, the main tank is filled with water and the other two with air. When one wishes to dive, one fills the other two partly with water, making the boat so heavy it can be driven below the surface by the screw combined with manipulation of the diving rudders. To return to the surface, one simply reverses the process."

"And the air is supplied by—?"

"Elementals, my dear Prefect. Two lesser ones in the small tank, a greater one for keeping the phlogiston level in the air high, and the greatest in the main tank. *It* may be needed to blow that tank empty, so that we can rise in haste."

I considered that after a watch or two in the depths no one would gladly rise any other way.

"I judge then that the crew is nine humans and four elementals?"

The mage smiled. "Your powers of deduction are respectable."

"But why a human crew at all?"

That was a bold question on slight acquaintance but Ioannes Philippos took no offense. "That is also a matter of elementals. I can contrive no spell to drive the vessel without weakening my command over the air elementals. Any mechanical propulsion would have needed a fire elemental. Fire elementals both consume air and are hard to control.

"One does not wish to ask air too much of one's spells in a diving vessel, my dear Prefect. Time may be of the essence, and the circumstances which produce disaster may outstrip the casting of a complex spell."

I was delighted but held my peace, to not seem patronizing. Ioannes Philippos was clearly not one of those vainglorious mages who believes that only lesser mages fear juggling half a dozen potent spells at once. I would not willingly come within several stades of such, let alone go down under the sea in a diving vessel with them.

* * *

I went down under the sea in the vessel three times before the Day the Magic Stopped. Twice we went with the full crew (the cranks were turned by six stout fellows apparently chosen more for strength than for wits). Ioannes Philippos himself both steered and controlled the elementals.

The third time, Ioannes Philippos handled the stern rudders and left steering to his assistant, a sober man of middle years named Kybalos, with the mark of an old Fleet sailor all over him. Only four men were at the cranks, but we were towing our weapon.

The weapon was that barrel of Greek fire that had frightened me into making a fool of myself. The diving vessel would tow the barrel at the end of a long line, as it dived under a hostile vessel. Progressing forward, the vessel would draw the barrel against the enemy's bottom. At that point either a mechanical device activated by a second line or a small spell would ignite the Greek fire, causing violent pressure against the ship's planks. Leaks were certain, a quick sinking not impossible.

"It works against small boats, I know," Kybalos told me. "The mage is working on a compound that will ignite if seawater touches it. Then we can put little glass horns on the beast and when one of them breaks off—poof!"

"Glass?"

"Strong against pressure, brittle against a blow. I wouldn't have been Alexandros down in that glass sphere of his for a satrapy." Kybalos seemed to have complete trust in his master, which spoke well for the mage—old sailors are notorious skeptics.

Oh, yes. I had not mentioned my fear of enclosed spaces to them. This is because I had discreetly gone to a local mage and asked for a protective spell against it. His price for the spell was considerable, his price for discretion outrageous.

The mage had a merchant's eye, however. He suggested an alternative—that I have a certain potion compounded, that would allow any half-trained healer to cast a mild version of the spell on me. He recommended three reliable alchemists who could compound the potion.

I took both his advice and the potion. (It smelled vile and tasted worse, and was so expensive that I am sure the alchemist was sending some of his profit to the mage.) However, it did as it was supposed to, and the local healer gave me a useful piece of advice.

"Take a canteen of the potion, diluted with wine to cut the smell, when you are going into tight quarters," he said. "If you start feeling uneasy, take a good swig. After the second or third casting, the spell will begin to linger in your psyche, and the potion will bring it out when you need it."

Now we come to the Day the Magic Stopped. I will try to be brief, or I shall be in Obrizam before the letter is!

We were towed out of harbor before dawn, behind a light galley that carried the crew and their supplies as well. A small boat was lashed to either side of the diving vessel, hiding it from curious eyes.

There were plenty of those about; the sea approaches of the City have not grown bare of ships since you took up your duties in Obrizam. Galleys of the Fleet, of friendly realms, of realms that were friendly as long as their ships in our waters were hostages. Merchant vessels of every nation able to build, buy, rent, or pirate a ship, carrying everything from silk and purple dye-shells to loads of building stone. Pleasure craft, fishing vessels, wealthy men's yachts large enough to sail the open sea, a thousand schemes of hull paint and as many different markings on sails and oars. . . .

It was splendid.

But enough rhapsodies. We reached our planned diving point, some leagues out but still in shallow water, by noon. We ate lunch, pickled squid, barley cakes, and cheese, as I recall, and drank lightly of well-watered wine.

Then we all used the heads. That was an inflexible rule of Ioannes Philippos, and I can assure you that it was needed. The diving vessel does have a chamberpot, but I think you can imagine the consequences of doing one's business in a completely enclosed space. Even the air elementals can only moderate the stench, and perfumes or herbs are useless.

We were to test the Greek fire device that afternoon, so we could only cast off after it was ready. The two boats that had been our disguise took their position, each with four rowers and several skilled sponge divers, ready to carry lines down to us if we could not rise of our own accord.

The boats then towed us away from the galley. Ioannes Philippos was the last man in, and he and Kybalos latched the hatch in place. Then we all took our places, the crankmen began their work, the air-supply elemental whistled as it poured phlogistinated air into the vessel, and we angled down into the depths.

It was the mage's intent to make a long triangular voyage, possibly as much as three leagues, testing how well he could observe and identify ships underwater. I had suggested that I might be of some assistance, with my Fleet experience. As there was room in the observation cupola for two, he graciously allowed me to join him.

The bottom here was some nine fathoms down, safe enough for a vessel proof against the weight of the water at a depth of fifteen fathoms. Our major concern was running afoul of someone's anchor cable—even worse, having someone cast their anchor atop us. The vessel's hull was stout bronze, well-brazed by shipwrights who had used the most expensive fire elementals. But the observation cupola and the Archimedean screw were less robust.

The day was sunny and the spring dose of silt carried down by the rivers long-since sunk to the bottom. So through the glass of the observation ports, I could see a good deal through the green dimness outside. Boulders, some scoured clean, some weed grown. Patches of bare sand and mud, others overgrown with weeds taller than a man. When we passed over a wide patch of weeds, the mage adjusted the bow diving rudders so that we angled up a trifle. (He did not wish to have the screw tangled in the weeds.)

Old amphorae, some intact, some in fragments. Bones—one unmistakably a human skull. The barnacled timbers of long-lost ships. A shadow on the bottom, that must come from a ship above and ahead.

It was at that moment that the magic stopped.

Now, from the fact that I am writing to you from this world and not the next, clearly we did not immediately suffer disaster. Indeed, it was some time before we realized that anything was wrong.

I was first aware of a change when I realized that the flow of phlogistinated air into the vessel had ceased. I also realized that the smell of sweat (mercifully, nothing more potent) was stronger.

I climbed down from the cupola, took my flask of potion, and emptied it. At least it did not taste as vile as usual.

Then I became aware that there was a faint whistling from the deck below, and what felt like a current of rising air. I also noticed that the boat seemed to be sinking deeper, and wondered if the mage was maneuvering to avoid the ship ahead.

Then we struck the bottom, or rather, we floated down on to a patch of sand and landed feather-light, with the bow angled slightly up.

I saw surprise and the beginnings of dismay on the faces of the crew. I confess I wondered if my own face mirrored theirs. Indeed, I felt bold enough to tug at the hem of Ioannes Philippos' robe, although I knew that if he was trying to remedy our situation he would not thank me for the interruption.

Instead he looked down at me, a mild frown on his face. "You should have fallen to the deck for that."

"Your pardon, mage, but—"

"No. That was not to criticize. I was trying to regain command of the air elementals. The spell was potent, and touching me while I attempted it—"

"We don't have no air?" one of the crew said. He was at least trying to command his voice, but without great success. He did succeed in getting all his mates out of their seats, shouting and gesticulating.

"Quiet!" Kybalos shouted. His voice boomed through the confined space like a god's war cry in the tunnels under the City. The mage flinched, but the men gave way. Some of them even sat down. Kybalos and I glared at the others until they did the same.

"We have air," the mage said, with the air of a teacher instructing a class of witling children. "We merely will receive no new air until I can command the elementals again."

That seemed to calm the men somewhat. I withheld my own questions about how long this would take and how long the air would last without the elementals. There was also the matter of rising to the surface, if the vessel needed more air to do so.

How long we waited, I do not know. Certainly it was not much more than a quarter of an hour, but it seemed to me that the air was already growing foul.

Then I saw the mage beckoning to me. Stepping up into the cupola, I saw what disturbed him. Debris was floating down from the surface, including at least three dead men—and dead by violence, not drowning. One had clearly been some rich man's private guard, from his dress, but he had no weapons and showed bloody gashes in both throat and belly.

"That will draw sharks," I said, lacking the wit to say more.

"Sharks are the least of our worries," the mage said. "I think magic no longer has power in our world."

Perhaps the potion that I had drunk had not departed with the other magic. Perhaps, also, knowing that a leader must have self-command aided me, or even my brief prayers to the patrons of hopeless causes.

"I have tried every spell that it would be safe to cast within this vessel," Ioannes Philippos continued. "None of them have the slightest effect. Meanwhile, I believe lawless men are taking advantage of this—circumstance— to rob and murder. Our friends of the galley may be too busy defending themselves to come to our aid."

I concealed my impatience. Analysis of a disaster is all very well, but it seemed to me that extricating ourselves from it demanded more immediate attention.

"Before we grow too weak from lack of air, we must swim to the surface, steal a boat, and row to safety," the mage concluded.

I thought then that Ioannes Philippos Magus was offering a general solution but leaving the details and the labor to others. From their faces, so did the men.

In the next moment, I learned I was wrong—much good that it did me! The mage blithely continued.

"Now, since a sufficient pressure of air will balance an equal pressure of water in the ballast chambers, why should it not do the same thing in the cabin?"

He seemed to want a reply. Kybalos and I looked at each other. Kybalos nodded. "It ought to."

"It *will*. But we cannot command the air elementals to make more air. We must increase the air's pressure some other way, such as by letting water into the cabin. The less space there is for air, the higher its pressure. In time the pressure within shall equal the pressure without, and then we can open the hatch and float to the surface as lightly as bubbles."

It had not occurred to Ioannes Philippos (nor, I confess, to me) that not everyone would be as blithe about filling our only refuge with water and then stepping out of it far below the sun and the air. One man promptly vomited. A second went to help him, another snatched a crank out of its socket, and a last drew a knife. The two with weapons came at me, probably because I was the closest target.

That also gave me the task of stopping them, if we were not to have dire trouble. I sidestepped the first's swinging crank and punched him in the stomach. It was a hard stomach, but my hours at the pankration were not altogether wasted; my fist was harder.

As the first man doubled up, the second thrust hard with his dagger. It struck the potion flask on my hip, piercing the bronze but leaving my flesh intact. The next moment, Kybalos drew a short club from behind a piece of equipment and brought it down on the man's head. He fell to the deck and lay still.

"Did you need to hit him so hard?" Ioannes Philippos said. "A senseless man cannot swim well."

Kybalos and I exchanged looks again, freighted with our thoughts about mages who could neither cast spells nor stop brawls. Then Kybalos shrugged.

"The water should revive him. If not, I will help him."

It was easier said than done, getting the water into the cabin. The ballast chambers had valves for letting water into them, but no means of passing the water on into the cabin.

Fortunately one seam in the main chamber was already partly sprung (that was the whistle of air we'd heard). We had to hack at that seam with pry bars and beat on it with crank handles before it would make a decent opening. The air had grown foul with the reek of vomit, so we went at it with a will, forgetting the fear that had been so close to destroying us, in our desire to breathe clean air again. At last we had a respectable fountain of water from the chamber.

The water rose swiftly, from our ankles to our knees, thence from our knees to our waists. By the time it was up to our chests, our ears were hurting as if someone were holding hot needles against them. I felt my stomach twist and swallowed hard against the urge to vomit.

As I swallowed, something went *click*, like beads rolling together within my ears, and the pain diminished. I swallowed again—it diminished further. I shouted as well as I could with my mouth only fingers above the water.

"Swallow! Swallow! It helps your ears!"

The men started swallowing as if they'd been handed cups of the finest wine. Even Kybalos did so, for all that he was froglike inside the cupola, loosening the fastenings of the hatch.

Then the squeezed air inside the diving vessel became stronger than the water outside it. The hatch was wrenched not only out of Kybalos's hands but off its last fastening. The water inside leaped up to swallow us. I had just time to take a last deep breath before I shot through the hatch and found myself hurtling up through green dimness toward the surface.

We had no attention to spare for what was happening on the surface for some time after we reached the air. All of us made the journey safely, but the man who'd been knocked senseless could not keep afloat unaided. The mage surprised us all by swimming easily, so we were free to seek a floating oar and tie the man to it.

We now saw ships all around us in greater or lesser disarray. Whatever had stopped the magic below had done the same on the surface. Ioannes Philippos had been right about our needing to save ourselves by our unaided efforts.

Close at hand, we saw a high-sterned merchant vessel, with men running about her decks like mice in a burning kitchen. A second look showed us the glint of steel, and a second ship alongside. The second one was a lean, rakish two-master, the kind barbarian corsairs favor, except that she was painted up like a wealthy man's toy.

We were looking alternately at the ships and at one another, so not all of us saw the woman leap on to the railing of the larger ship. Her scream carried across the water and turned all heads. We all saw her leap overboard—and we saw the archers run to the railing and shoot until she sank from sight.

Then we all looked at one another, and I have seldom seen nine men of a more united mind.

Kybalos and a Porsinian crankman dove at once, and on their second dive released the Greek fire. Meanwhile, the rest of us had found an overturned boat, righted it, and were bailing the water out and retrieving oars.

Soon we were under way, carefully keeping out of bowshot. There was no wind, and most of the pirate yacht's oarsmen should be on their victim's deck, seeking loot and captives. Our prey should not flee before we reached her. Now, if we could only find a reliable method of firing the barrel. . . .

If I ever again sit in an open boat with a barrel of Greek fire between my knees, improvising a way to set it off, you may call me a madman. You may *treat* me as a madman!

We had done the best we could by the time we rounded the bows of the ships. With a clearer view to the north, we could see smoke clouds that hinted of other piracies. The City's Fleet would soon be along to restore order to the seas, even without magic, but not soon enough for our ships!

Kybalos estimated the current and wind, with some help from me and more from the mage, who knew more of such matters than I'd expected. He had managed to retain not only his garments but his wits, as well as much dignity as possible when a man's mustache is drooping over his mouth and he has to blow it clear to speak.

The barrel went over, and we paid out the two ropes. We watched it drift down toward the two ships, barely visible above the surface. We wished we were as invisible as the barrel, because we were well within bowshot.

"Not to mention that bastard running us down,"

someone muttered. Indeed, it seemed that the pirates were returning to their own ship.

Time came and went—enough now gone to eat a quick meal and gulp a cup of wine. We could no longer see the barrel, but it had to be between the two ships— and no fire. No fire—and the time for the burning fuse already passed.

Kybalos jerked on the second rope, attached to the flint-and-steel igniter. Still no fire. I cursed. The mage raised his bushy eyebrows. Kybalos jerked again, and cursed loudy enough for three. Then he threw down the rope, jerked off his tunic, and rose to leap over the side.

The gesture drew the pirates' attention. I held Kybalos back, the pirates shot, and arrows whistled about us. In a moment Kybalos, Ioannes Philippos, and I were the only ones in the boat.

I resolved that the moment Kybalos came to his senses, we would take the mage and join our comrades. I tightened my grip on him, and in that moment the barrel erupted.

I do not exaggerate in using that word. It was more like a small volcano than the common ignition of Greek fire. A ball of flame rose from the sea between the two ships, washing over both of them, climbing higher than the mastheads. The smaller ship went over on her beam ends and had barely recovered before the mainyard of the larger one swung down like a butcher's mallet.

It struck the pirate like a mallet striking an ox, driving through the deck and the bottom like a stone through parchment. The pirate, already burning amidships, began to list. The fire had barely time to start spreading before the rising water quenched it, and a moment later the pirate was gone in a whirl of foam, wreckage, and bobbing heads.

Some of those heads were making their way toward us more purposefully than I cared for. "Get back aboard and start rowing," I shouted at our swimmers. "We aren't enough to help."

"No need to row," Ioannes Philippos said, sneezing as his mustache went up his nose. "Tell them to hold on tightly, please."

Almost before the men obeyed the order, the boat was moving. With neither sail nor oar nor Archimedean screw, it raced away toward the shore, the men silenced by fear or the effort of holding on.

We did not stop before the big ship was engulfed in flames from stem to stern, and a Fleet galley was creeping toward her. The mage looked dubious.

"I suppose we could go back. But any Fleet mage should be able to levitate enough water to put out that fire. Best we mark our own vessel with a buoy, so I can conjure the air elementals back into the tanks with as little delay as possible."

We did so, and after salvaging the diving vessel, learned what had happened. The magic had returned, and with it our air elementals. By some aspect of the laws of affinity, they sought the nearest part of the diving vessel, which happened to be the Greek fire barrel. This created an immensely potent combination of air and fire—perhaps even the equal of a fire elemental. So potent that it ignited by itself, with enough force to devastate both ships.

Ioannes Philippos hopes to be able to duplicate this effect, preferably in an uncrewed small vessel that can be launched from a larger, crewed diving vessel. The small one would be propelled by an air elemental turning an Archimedean screw and detonate Greek fire against the hull of an enemy's ship. But I will leave such matters to him.

For better or worse, the "pirates" were the servants of the cousin of some barbarian king (Fritharik is the name I recall), who took advantage of the lapse in the magic to seek easy prey. They had found it, when we intervened.

Our intervention, however, destroyed both ships, and

the larger one was owned by a merchant with extensive Army contracts. Also, good relations with Fritharik are worth more than completing the prosecution of his servants (the cousin is dead).

So we of the diving vessel have all been richly rewarded, sworn to silence, and offered honorable posts at a safe distance from the City. Thus I come to Obrizam, and hope I find you in the same good health as I am at this writing.

Oh, one last blessing. It seems that I added no potion to the wine I drank in the sunken vessel. With neither potion nor magic, I overcame my fear of confined spaces!

God grant that this will continue.

Hail and farewell,
Markos

*dis*ILLUSIONS

Mike Resnick and
Lawrence Schimel

They were gathered in the Great Hall when Edward looked up with an expectant smile on his face. An instant later it started raining toads *inside* the castle.

As the guests began screaming, Edward waved his hand, and suddenly the rug itself became a thousand mouths, each gobbling up one or more toads. But as the last of the toads were eaten, the mouths became insatiable, and started gnawing upon the furniture.

Another wave of Edward's hand, and the furniture turned to solid gold. Teeth cracked against it, mouths withdrew, and, sprouting wings, the furniture began hovering a few inches above the rug, daring it to test its strength once again. The mouths vanished, the furniture gently came to rest upon it, and golden legs metamorphosed into wood as Edward grinned and bowed deeply for his applauding audience.

Vivian sighed, wishing she were elsewhere, but she displayed no outward sign of her boredom, laughing along with the other assembled members of the Thirteen Families. She tried to recall when it was that the magic had faded from her and Edward's relationship. There was a time when his every trick delighted her, simply because they were *his*. Now, when they made love, she murmured cantrips she pretended were moans of ecstasy to disguise his appearance with that of another man, *any* other man—she didn't care.

Somewhere along the way, things had come undone.

Her heart, which once had felt as buoyant as the Emperor's sailships, now felt as if it were a splintered wreckage of silken sails and ebony timber, as if the spells which had kept it aloft had malfunctioned, now that Edward's sorceries no longer amused her. He seemed to send the craft hurtling earthward once again, into the mud. All of Constantinople looked muddied to her now, the bright and glittering splendor eclipsed by her mood, as if the sun had become blotted out by a cloud of dust, or had simply stopped shining altogether.

An intricately patterned python engulfed Edward in coils from behind his chair. Edward opened his mouth wide enough to accommodate the snake's thick body and swiftly consumed it as the assembled elite erupted once more into laughter, like giddy schoolgirls over some tidbit of gossip. Vivian was so tired of it all, and of Edward in particular. Something was lacking in him, something which she desperately craved from him, though she could not pinpoint precisely what was wanting. She wondered, not for the first time, what he was truly like beneath his illusions and spells—if perhaps, accidentally, she might once have seen the true Edward even as she gave him other men's faces to wile the time away, might have seen the man he was beneath his young and virile exterior. Vivian herself augmented her looks, retarding the vagaries of aging with spells and illusions, but she imagined the true Edward to be a void, as if he were nothing more than his elaborate and powerful sorceries.

Though young, and not merely young-seeming, he was

unquestionably the most powerful magicmaker in the city, and therefore the most celebrated member of the Thirteen Families, who were Constantinople's most accomplished magicians and who enforced that status with a swift and iron fist (although always from afar, and via their magic, so as never to sully their own fingers). It had been a coup for Vivian to attract his attentions, and even more so to have kept them this long. Although, knowing Edward as she did, Vivian found the task simplicity itself. For all his sorceries, Edward seemed lacking in all artifice in life, easily swayed and manipulated by her cunning. Vivian spent long hours concealing his naiveté, protecting him, and her own position as his consort and lover, from others who would exploit him. That was reserved for Vivian alone.

But even that privilege had long since paled in its thrill, and was now more of a chore than anything else—defending her throne from any and all assailants, petty and overt.

Of a sudden, Vivian's chair dropped through the floor, which had opened a hole as quickly as a champagne bubble bursting up from the glass' bottom to crack the surface with fizz. She idly wondered whether to cast about for some spell to save her life, lest she fall to her death from the heights of the castle they'd been visiting, but she trusted Edward would spare a moment's thought for her and save her (if this were not in fact another of his own pranks).

Vivian took the moment to enjoy her respite from the society of her fellow members of the Thirteen Families, who in their aggregate sum she found quite tedious and sadly droll. She stared down at the city from her aerial vantage: the Grand Concourse, hub of Constantinople and gate through which all visitors passed, the golden globe that shined down from above its dome an earthly sun, and a short ways to the left, the Cathedral, equally majestic in its non-magical splendor of stone and human construction that rivaled, nay, dwarfed, the magical fabrications which had sprung up along and beyond the road that stretched between the Grand Concourse and the Cathedral, puny and insubstantial flights of fancy.

Her reverie was interrupted by Edward wrapping his arms about her from behind the chair and squeezing her tightly, almost like a python he had produced earlier. "Were you not even the slightest bit concerned?" he asked, burying his face in her long, curly black locks and running his hands up along her belly to her breasts. "You looked so ravishing up there, I couldn't help stealing you away. Let's make love in midair," he whispered into her ear.

"For the world to see, like some common sailor and his whore?"

"We're invisible," he said, fumbling at the laces of her dress, and Vivian knew that in that moment he had indeed made them so.

"Please, Edward, you know it's not that I don't trust your spells to keep us aloft, but I really do prefer the comforts of solid ground beneath my feet, and a bed, and—" Vivian had a long catalogue of her preferences, hoping she might thereby be able to put him off, but they were suddenly back in Edward's terrestrial palaces. For all his sorcerous might, he had constructed his home of natural substances, though equally elaborate and plush as the wholly dreamed airborne castles of his peers. If Vivian needed to suffer the emotional discomforts of making love to him, she would rather it occur among the creature comforts she had grown accustomed to as his consort. Edward lifted her in his arms and placed her upon the thick, feathered comforter of the bed they shared, climbing atop her. The words to the spell which would change Edward's appearance began running through her mind, and at the first opportunity she uttered them, her fingers clawing Edward's back as she twisted them to form the proper signs. Edward mistook the signs as Vivian goading him, and was further aroused. He no longer bothered with the clasps and stays of her clothing, but made the entire contraption disappear in an instant, leaving her body naked beneath him. Mercifully, it was over in a few minutes, and Edward fell promptly asleep.

The moment he began to snore, Vivian extracted herself from beneath him and pushed away from the bed. She went into the bathroom, locking the door behind her, though she knew such a safeguard meant little to Edward, or practically any of Constantinople's inhabitants for that matter. In this city of magicians, it was simplicity itself to cause a lock to undo itself with a spell most children learned before they had stopped wetting their pants. Still, it was something Vivian felt compelled to do, an emotional signal to herself that she was locking him and them out. She let the illusions fall from her body, and stood regarding herself in the mirrored wall before stopping to run hot water into a basin and scrub his scent from her skin with sponges and soaps. It was a long time before she again felt clean.

Vivian toweled herself dry, though she might as easily have spelled herself so. It was not that she disdained magic, or its benefits; like all the other inhabitants of Constantinople, Vivian's life was thoroughly saturated with magic. She practiced it daily, casting spells and illusions almost before thinking; and that was why she preferred to dry herself, and to perform a hundred other tasks manually, lest she become so dependent on magic that she lose herself to it. It kept her alert to consciously not use her magic to handle the minor details of life, and it was that alertness of mind and attention to detail which was how she had been able to attract and keep Edward's infatuation all these years.

Staring at her image in the mirror, Vivian had to ask herself if the effort was worthwhile. Not the honing of her consciousness—that she would not forsake even for all of Edward's powers—but Edward himself. True, while she lived in Constantinople, his presence in her life gave her access to a society and privilege to which she could not otherwise hope to aspire. But, having now climbed her way all the way to the top, up, even, to their airborne palaces which floated high above Constantinople's towers, Vivian found herself bored.

Life was too easy.

That was perhaps what bothered her about Edward; because of him, there was no longer any sense of competition in her life, no challenge for anything. Edward could by force of magic do or give her anything she desired. And, since he was so easy for her to manipulate, he did. Vivian had nothing left to stimulate her, and her frustration was driving her to distraction. Though she was free to roam throughout Constantinople, she was trapped by her relationship.

She looked at herself in the mirror, saw how she was getting so much older, despite the care she took with her body. Her once raven-dark hair was now heavily graying beneath her illusions. How much longer could she live like this? Vivian felt she would die, suffocated by the tedium of this life and illusion. She almost thought she would have been more content to have stayed far from the city, to have become some farmer's wife, the two of them forever battling with nature to eke out a living for themselves and their family. Vivian knew, of course, that such positing was idle, especially surrounded by such pampering splendor as she was right then, but she would at least have felt alive every day in such a life, she thought. Bitter perhaps, but she felt bitter now, and with less reason.

But could she give it all up?

Relinquish her status, the power at her command through Edward ... the feeling of overwhelming boredom and discontent she felt of her life.

Vivian wasn't quite sure. All her life her mind had been set to climbing to this pinnacle. To climb down now seemed too much like a defeat—and besides, she had no new goal to replace this one.

She sighed, and left her bathroom, hurrying quickly

through the bedroom where Edward still snored beneath the rumpled blue comforter. In her closet, she put on a light dressing robe, and was about to leave their apartments and find some more secluded part of the castle, perhaps overlooking the ever-changing mosaic of the city, to ponder further her dilemma—when she spied herself in a small wall mirror and noticed she had forgotten to put on her illusion of her younger self. The words to the spell leapt immediately to her lips as she reached for the doorhandle, but Vivian paused. She wondered what it might be like to walk about as her true self, to discard her despised life in this small trial. It was not as if she would be seen by anyone of import: just a few servants, if anyone at all.

Pleased with herself, Vivian reveled in the sensation of being free of cloaking illusions as she walked through the familiar halls of Edward's palace. These walls, too, were authentic in their substance. The stone floor was cold beneath her feet. Hardly any other palace in Constantinople could boast the same; they were all fabrications. Her naked foot would tread upon illusions of soft rugs or stones that were always the proper warmth. But Edward, as a show of ostentation, had foregone a magic-made palace, and instead used his magic to command a vast wealth of natural substance into his abode. The other members of the Thirteen Families thought it eccentric, and odd that he chose to remain so terrestrial, while all of them had set their palaces drifting among the clouds. . . .

But its simplicity, its genuineness, not to mention the incredible magic it took to construct it, manipulating that which already existed rather than summoning from nothing what was desired, were what had attracted Vivian to Edward in the first place. She stared from a window at the city spread below her, and all the cluster of fanciful and impossible buildings illuminated by the golden globe which hung above the Grand Concourse. She had loved him once, that she couldn't deny; but something had happened, and that love had simply vanished, like one of his illusions. Pop, and it was gone. As if, Vivian thought, staring at the shining golden globe, as if one day it simply vanished.

And, as if in mute response to Vivian's thoughts, the golden globe did just that.

Vivian blinked against the sudden dimness and wondered, awed, what had happened. Had she caused it to go out? How furious everyone would be! She felt a momentary giddy delight as she surveyed the city, now cast into twilight. There was still light coming from somewhere . . . ah, yes, the sun. How easy to have forgotten that it still shone, eclipsed by the brighter, magical sun that had been created ages ago, and which was held in place by the collective unconscious of Constantinople. Vivian was awed that she, by herself, had been able to counteract that force of will, which all these years had kept the golden globe in place. . . .

And suddenly, staring at the city in the dimness, Vivian realized that it had not been her at all. The fanciful and impossible buildings which had clogged the streets were gone. In their place stood sordid and dilapidated constructions of plain wood and brick. As she watched this diminished city, a sailship fell from the sky, and splintered into rubble.

Vivian tried to cast a spell, to bring her customary illusions into place, a spell that was so ingrained into her mind that she could maintain it even when unconscious. But her body would not grow younger and her hair stayed gray, picking up what little light there was.

It had not been Vivian at all, who extinguished the golden globe, but rather the fact that throughout the City the magic had been used up!

The thought delighted her. She imagined the airborne castles of the Thirteen Families plummeting like the sailship she had seen, in great, disastrous wreckages.

And Edward? Now he was just an ordinary mortal, like everyone else. All his powerful sorceries were gone, vanished on the winds. Vivian could not help wondering

what he truly looked like without his disguises, if there
was any substance to him at all. She hurried back along
the corridors, feeling along the walls with her fingers
since the magical lights which once had illumined them
were absent now. Their bedroom, at least, would still be
lit from the large windows that looked out over the
gardens.

Vivian paused before the door, savoring the moment,
delaying it. She had wondered for so long what Edward
truly looked like, she did not want to diminish her discov-
ery by rushing through it. She imagined how he would
look as her fingers turned upon the knob, positing some
obese and slobbering old man in her mind, the way the
grand and fanciful buildings had reverted to rundown
tenements without the magic to support them. How
much easier it would be to hate him, knowing his true
and repulsive form!

Vivian thought she was braced for anything he might
seem, any repulsive, disgusting form that she found lying
in her bed, a form that she knew she had made love to
hundreds and hundreds of times. She had thought she
was braced for anything, but what she found took her
completely by surprise.

Edward had not changed at all!

The sheets only partially covered his finely-sculpted
naked body. Even his teeth were perfectly straight. She
could not resist pulling back the covers, to learn that even
there, his endowment was no illusion, but his natural-
born manhood.

And suddenly Vivian understood what was wrong with
their relationship; Edward was all surface. With him
there was nothing else, nothing deeper, no soul. He had
the thin veneer of society, with which he had been born;
good looks, good breeding, and that was it.

She laughed out loud, but softly, not wanting to wake
him. She wondered how he would feel, suddenly helpless,
when moments before he had been the most powerful

person in the city. He would be crippled without his sorcery, she was certain, like a month-old baby.

Vivian did not know how long she stood, staring down at him, pitying both him and herself. She made plans, now that Constantinople had crumbled, and was grateful that Edward had constructed his palace rather than imagining it. They would likely have been killed by the fall, had he followed the fashion of the other members of the Thirteen Families. Vivian wondered how many of them still survived. She could not say she regretted their imagined deaths. And Edward's physical palace would provide the means to establish a life elsewhere; she would take certain objects with her when she left, items that were portable yet valuable: the silver, a gold vase. But even the thought of sudden poverty did not dismay Vivian. She was brimming over with excitement, and stayed only for the pleasure of watching Edward's face when he awoke and discovered that he was powerless.

Then, suddenly, light flooded the room. The globe was back, and so was the city, restored to its original ostentation of imagination. As Vivian watched, reassembled palaces climbed slowly back into the sky as her plans and hopes sunk.

Behind her, Edward woke and, dreamy-eyed, reached for her. Vivian found herself suddenly, magically, in bed with him, cuddling beneath the covers. "I had the most awful dream," Edward whispered in her ear, running his hand down her back and along her buttocks. "I dreamed that the magic had gone away." He laughed, and began kissing her neck.

The magic had returned. But staring at Edward, who held her in his strong and powerful arms, Vivian knew that the magic was still gone.

WHAT PRICE MAGIC?

Teresa Patterson

Ragnar, Prince of the Rus, gazed upon the glory of the Golden Gate that marked the entrance to the City of Kings, the pride of Constantine, Theodosius, and Justinian, and felt despair. The dull iron of the manacles and chains that bound him clashed with the gilded icons and glowing wards of the massive archway. Brightly dressed and bejeweled citizens stared as the captive prince headed the ragged parade of Varangian prisoners that streamed past them.

The prince knew that behind their impeccably manicured hands they remarked upon his now-matted long red hair, and his rugged build beneath the remnants of his armor. He knew they called him "barbarian." Their eyes burned him much as the mage fire had done during the disastrous last battle. His skin was scorched and blistered from that fight. But bad as the pain was, the searing pressure of the magic was much worse.

And magic was everywhere. The air itself seemed to seeth with it. Wards and spells glowed on every building. Mythic creatures and magical constructs shared the streets with mortal men and women. Churches and palaces floated above the ground, serene in their ethereal majesty, while below them beggars rested in their shadows and children played at spell casting.

Only among the *Volkhvi* priest-sorcerers of his homeland had Ragnar felt anything approaching the potency of Constantinople's magic. And it was the *Volkhvi* who first taught him to hate magic users and their craft.

He was still young when the High Priest had come for him, declaring him gifted and naming him as one of their own. His family had dared not refuse. The sorcerers convinced him that it was his destiny to be one of the few Varangians to become *Volkhvi*. Promises of power and glory assisted their seduction and he became an initiate. But when he faced down his fear to touch their magic, he discovered within a formidable hunger determined to consume him. The magic would grant the user anything, for a price. And that price was his soul.

In that moment, he also saw that the sorcerers wanted him, not as an equal, but as a gifted pawn used to wield forces they themselves feared. He rejected the sorcerers and their necromancy, swearing never to touch magic again. In retaliation they used their dark powers to kill his family, slowly and horribly.

The experience had left him sensitive to all levels of magic, from the most benign cast to the most complex conjuration. The potent energies he felt as he trudged through the streets of Constantinople burned his inner senses with its seductive and deadly promise.

Ragnar gritted his teeth against the pull. No wonder Prince Igor had wanted to take this city. The very ground here was power incarnate. Even the cursed *Volkhvi* would be awed by it. But the power had been too strong for the Kievan fleet, and now Ragnar would pay the price. Many of his comrades already had.

He glanced up at the ornate chariot that floated above him. It was drawn by a beast with three heads, those of a lion, a ram, and a serpent. The creature was quite docile now, nothing like the grotesque animal that had dropped from the sky to engage his fleet, three heads belching flame while mage fire flew from the hands of its master. He could not see the chariot's occupant clearly from below, but he knew that the engineer of his defeat, General Kurkuas, rode within.

The crowd cheered as the chariot glided by, even as they gawked and jeered the prisoners below it. Kurkuas was the one factor that Grand Prince Igor of Kiev had neglected to take into account in his conquest of Byzantium. That and his magic. For Kurkuas was a master mage as well as a brilliant general. His magic had reduced the entire Kievan attack fleet to burning timber in one short afternoon. With the fleet gone, it had been a simple task for the Byzantine dromons to sweep in and defeat what little resistance remained. The Grand Prince had escaped, thank the gods, but most had not.

Ragnar shuddered, remembering how the quiet waters of the Bosphorus had suddenly erupted like a living thing, tossing his ships like children's toys while leaving the defending dromons unscathed. He could still hear the screams as men fell around him, green mage fire writhing over their bodies like hungry serpents, its flame undiminished even as they sank beneath the roiling water. He remembered his own terror as his longship lurched and died beneath him, devoured by an enemy he could not fight. No amount of training or weapons skill could match the deadly power of Kurkuas' magic. No sword was a match for the three-headed beast that hovered just out of reach. Even a prince's courage had not been strong enough to stop the fear as the green flames came for him. And no hate could match the fury he still felt remembering Kurkuas' laughter as the cold fire engulfed him, sending him screaming into the embrace of the Bosphorus.

He did not remember when the burning stopped, or exactly how he had been pulled from the water, but he remembered being sickened by how few of the brave

warriors that had followed him from the north had survived. As he approached the massive Hippodrome at the
center of the city, he wondered whether the men left
behind might be the lucky ones. The Byzantine people
were weak, softened by the ease and convenience their
magic allowed, but they were notoriously unforgiving of
enemies of the state. Especially pagan enemies. With the
Amulet of Perun, god of Thunder and Lightning, clearly
visible where it hung from a thong around his neck, Ragnar had no illusions about his chances of survival.

The floating chariot banked overhead to land beside
the Varangian prince. Ragnar flinched involuntarily as the
team's serpent head snapped at him. The tall dark-haired
man within saw this and smiled. "Do you know why I
saved you?"

Ragnar forced himself to meet the mage-general's
green eyes, not bothering to disguise the hate he felt for
this man, and for all who wielded magic.

"You have the gift. You can feel the power. Can you
not?"

The prince gave no answer. General Kurkuas nodded
once, seeming satisfied, then touched his whip to signal
his foul beast forward. The gilded chariot surged into the
arena, fire bellowing from the three hideous heads of its
team as the packed crowd cheered wildly. Ragnar and
the other prisoners had no choice but to follow.

Once within the Hippodrome, Ragnar attempted to
hide his awe at the huge central *spina* that divided the
arena, topped with glowing columns of gold and silver
light. Each column was a moving display that celebrated
the rule of a popular emperor. The galleries, also supported in part by lighted columns, were filled with people
there to stare at the prisoners and celebrate another victory for the Empire. Over the top of the northeast wall,
Ragnar could see the massive domes of the Hagia Sophia,
the great cathedral built by Justinian, as it floated just
beyond the square outside the Hippodrome. The domes
glowed with golden mage fire, emitting a light that

gave competition to the midday sun. He tried to imagine a god that required such a place for worship—and failed.

Kurkuas drove to the center of the arena and dismounted, releasing his chariot to a handler. He directed the prisoners to fall in behind him. No one offered any resistance. Ragnar knew most of his men were exhausted from their wounds and the long walk. They were simply glad for a chance to stop.

A sudden fanfare of trumpets erupted from the royal box. The people in the galleries stood as one, cheering loudly as they waved and pointed skyward. Ragnar followed their gaze to see another chariot, this one glowing like a miniature sun, approaching from the east. At first he thought it was drawn by a huge bird. But as it drew nearer, he realized the bird was actually a magnificent white horse with huge wings.

There were two men in the chariot, both dressed in elaborate jeweled robes, one of brilliant purple, and one of gold. Ragnar knew that only Emperor Constantine himself, would dare wear a robe of purple. He surmised that the other man must be Romanus, Constantine's father-in-law. Both men ruled Byzantium, but only Constantine was *porphyrogenitus* "born to the purple." Though Ragnar had heard that it was Romanus, Constantine's father-in-law, who held the true power. Rumors of serious battles between the two had spread throughout the east. Ragnar knew that discord was the wedge Igor had counted on when he planned his attack. Obviously, the conflict was not as great as they had been led to believe.

The glowing chariot approached the grandstand to hover before the *kathisma*, allowing the emperor to alight into his box. The chariot then gently floated to the sands of the arena with its lone remaining occupant. Romanus dismounted from the chariot, made a stiff bow towards the emperor's box, then strode to meet General Kurkuas. The general, who had bowed as the emperor arrived, kneeled to Romanus before he stood to greet him. Ragnar wondered if this could be an intended insult to the emperor, or simply mutual respect between the two warriors. The men whispered together briefly, then Romanus gave Ragnar a long appraising look. The Varangian met his gaze unflinchingly. A prisoner he may be, but he was still a prince.

Another blare of horns pulled his attention to the *kathisma*. There, Constantine, now seated in a golden jewel-studded throne that sparked fire in the sunlight, rose from his box, throne and all, to float down towards the arena floor. A chorus of voices erupted in song, impossibly loud for the size of the area, as a group of amazingly beautiful winged women and boys, gowned in iridescent robes, spilled out of the surrounding galleries to hover around the descending throne.

The other prisoners recoiled in awe and fear, but Ragnar stood his ground. He could feel the magical energies being drawn into the emperor's ostentatious display. His nerves tingled painfully with it, but the emperor was not its master. He scanned the crowd in the royal box until he saw a man in dark blue mage robes with a look of extreme concentration on his face. There was the true power wielder.

Ragnar felt nothing but disgust for a ruler who relied on such tricks to inspire loyalty. Much better to trust a man's honor of the strength or his sword arm than something as precarious as magic. With magic always came the vagaries of the gods who granted it. At least his men followed him because of true loyalty, not because of any false show or sorcery.

"The Pantocrator has granted us victory over the pagan infidels!" Constantine's voice boomed throughout the Hippodrome. Many of the prisoners fell to their knees at the voice of a god issuing from the slender bearded man on the floating throne. It was more Byzantine magic. Ragnar stood his ground.

"Hail Constantine. He who is victorious!" The chorus chanted. The crowd repeated it.

The emperor's throne floated to hover above General Kurkuas, who dropped to one knee, head bowed before his emperor. He gestured slightly with his hand and Ragnar felt himself shoved to the ground by an unseen force. With effort he twisted his head to see that Romanus still held his feet, though he had inclined his head respectfully towards the emperor. He saw the emperor scowl at his father-in-law, then turn his attention to the general and his prisoners, obviously attempting to ignore the insult.

"God has granted us victory through *you*, General Kurkuas."

"Thank you, my Emperor, but it was the tactics of Romanus that enabled us to prevail." Ragnar could tell that Kurkuas was using his own magic to be certain his words were heard by all.

Constantine glared at Kurkuas, clearly irritated by the attempt to include Romanus in the glory. "And where is the barbarian who dared lead the assault on my empire? Did you bring me the infidel who calls himself Grand Prince of Kiev?" The emperor made a show of scanning the assembled prisoners.

"I regret that Grand Prince Igor managed to escape us, Exalted One." This time Kurkuas did not bother to enhance his words with magic.

Constantine ran his fingers through his carefully coifed beard, letting a long silence fall as the general knelt awkwardly on the ground before him. "Then my father-in-law's tactics were not so foolproof after all." He ignored Romanus's sharp glare. "What prisoners *have* you brought me then?"

"I have brought you the prince of Chernigov, cousin to Grand Prince Igor. It was he who commanded the Varangian fleet."

Ragnar was startled to hear his title and lineage. He

did not remember giving it to anyone. They were obviously better informed than he had imagined.

"Then he will have to surrender in Igor's name."

The invisible pressure suddenly increased, forcing the prince's face down into the rough sand. He struggled, but only managed to turn his head enough to free his nostrils from the sand. Out of the corner of his eye he saw the legs of the gilded throne touch down, then the emperor's elegantly slippered feet as they approached and stood inches from his prostrate body. Ragnar could feel the texture of the emperor's brocade robe against his cheek. The odor of heavy perfumes mixed with that of the warm sand as he felt Constantine place a slippered foot ceremoniously upon his head. Humiliation filled him as he tried to struggle against the magical restraint, tried to close his mind to the emperor's formal words of victory and the answering chant of the crowd. He prayed to Perun to give him strength to endure.

". . . So in the name of God and on behalf of your immortal soul, will you forsake your false pagan gods and accept the Pantocrator and his divine magic as your salvation?" The emperor stepped aside and remounted his throne to better hear the captive's answer.

Ragnar felt the pressure release him enough to allow him to rise to his knees. Defiantly silent, he sat up and glared openly at the emperor.

"Those who refuse to deny false gods must face the full penalty of death or slavery. In your case, Varangian, you have proven much too dangerous to live as a slave. I ask you yet again, will you accept the True Faith and allow the Divine Magic to enter your soul?"

The final choice had come. For Ragnar it was no choice at all. He had known the moment he was captured that it would come to this.

"I am sworn to Perun. And to Volos. I want no part of a god who devours men's souls. Your god preaches peace while killing from afar with his magic. I want no part of a god who values cowardice over courage!"

"How dare you!" Kurkuas advanced, red-faced with anger. Romanus grabbed his arm and held him back, speaking quickly to him as he glared at Ragnar. The galleries were in an uproar.

"If I do not speak the truth—prove it." He looked straight at Kurkuas. "Face me in battle without your magic. If I am to die—let it by your hand. If your god is truly all-powerful, will he not aid you even without magic? Or have you no courage of your own?"

"This is preposterous!" Constantine waved his hands. "Execute him at once and be done with it."

"No, my Emperor." Kurkuas broke from Romanus to stand before the floating throne. "I will face him. For the glory of God and the City at the Center of the World."

Constantine looked doubtful.

"Surely he has earned that right with his victory over the Rus?" Romanus advanced on the throne, placing one hand on Kurkuas' shoulder. "Or," he gestured towards Ragnar, "would you have this barbarian's insults cause doubt in the minds of the people?"

Constantine glared at Romanus. Ragnar could tell there was certainly no love lost between these men. Of course, all that mattered was that he be given a chance to die like a warrior, by steel, and not like some trussed and fatted calf.

"And if Kurkuas should lose?" The emperor asked quietly.

"To a wounded barbarian? Quite unlikely. But if he does, you will be rid of one more of my mage-warriors, and you will have provided grand and unusual sport for the population." Romanus bowed deeply, the first sign of true obeisance Ragnar had seen.

The emperor considered for a moment, a hint of a smile beneath his beard. "Very well. We will allow this challenge. We will prove that no pagan dare stand against one of God's chosen warriors."

Ragnar found the pressure was gone, allowing him to climb to his feet. "I am honored." He sneered, "It seems you have at last found the courage to face me as a man. Show your own honor—if coddled Byzantines have any— grant my men freedom when I best you."

"You ask a lot, barbarian." Kurkuas spat.

"Why? Are you afraid you'll lose and have to grant my wish?"

"When the Bosphorus runs dry and Hell is covered in northern ice!"

"Then swear it."

Ragnar's gaze locked with Kurkuas'. He barely noticed as his men were led away. Out of the corner of his vision he saw the emperor and Romanus pull back to watch from a safe distance, Constantine still floating in his throne.

Kurkuas finally relented. "Very well. I so swear that your men will be given their freedom—*if* you defeat me."

Another fanfare sounded as one of the winged women flew to Ragnar, carrying a short sword. As she handed it to him she smiled shyly, her golden hair spilling over her jeweled slave collar. Ragnar wondered if she were a magical being or a real woman. Surely no real woman would find anything to smile at in his current unkempt condition. She gently removed his chains, her touch causing him to wish she were a real woman. Her perfect curves under the iridescent fabric reminded him of his own wife, far away. She smiled at him a last time as she gathered up the shackles and glided away. He was not one of these Greeks, but he understood enough about their concepts of winged deities to appreciate angels.

Experimentally he hefted the sword, admiring its balance and the waving patterns of folded steel shimmering within the blade. Damascus steel. He had heard of its like, but never before seen it. Best of all, there was no hint of magic within it. The sword was clean and deadly. Silently he commended his sword to Perun, that he might strike with the strength and speed of lightning, and his soul to Volos that he might be welcome in the afterworld should he fail. Dropping into attack position he advanced on the general. Kurkuas stood calmly waiting for him, his own sword relaxed but ready.

They feinted and counterfeinted. Ragnar was slow, his body still worn from the battle the day before and the long march, but Kurkuas was sloppy. He lacked the edge of a man who knows his life depends on his blade.

Kurkuas attacked. Ragnar easily deflected his blade, trapping it with his own for a moment. Green eyes met gray ones, both filled with hate.

"Now!" Romanus called out.

Suddenly Ragnar's vision blurred. He staggered back, sick with vertigo. The general did not follow, even though Ragnar was open for attack. A strange ringing filled his head. The ringing blended into music, then into voices.

For a moment he was no longer standing on the sands of the Hippodrome, but was floating in light, wrapped in the soft arms of a woman he could not see. He was so tired. But now he could rest. It was all over. He could have peace if he would just relax and give in to the caressing voices. The pain was gone. The hate was gone. He felt new strength within his body, new energy infuse him as he surrendered to the light.

The Hippodrome rematerialized around him, but the feeling of euphoria and the sound of the voices remained. The voices promised him joy and freedom, he had only to surrender completely. They wanted something from him. Just a little thing in return for all this power. He felt ripples of energy flowing throughout his mind and body. He had never felt so strong. He was a god. He could do anything.

He looked around the arena until he saw the emperor, a purple heap of dung sitting in that ridiculous floating chair. Hatred ripped through him. This man must die. And he could do it so easily. It would be like slapping a gnat. The energy sang through his body . . . so easy—just release the energy and the emperor would die. Just relax and focus the hate and burn him where he sat. So easy. So . . .

"NO!" Ragnar wrenched himself free of the spell to find himself sprawled on the sand. He grabbed his blade edge until it cut into his palm, using the pain as a focus to force the seductive vision away. Scrambling to his feet he saw Kurkuas glaring at him. He had no doubt who had done this. No wonder the general was fighting badly. He had been preoccupied with his magic. The fight was a sham to keep Ragnar too busy to notice the spell building. He had simply become a convenient pawn in the royal power game. He did not want to think about how close he had come to being devoured by the magic.

"I won't let you use me!" He advanced on Kurkuas, shaking with fury.

"Kill him!" Romanus shrieked. "He must not speak!"

Ragnar dove towards Kurkuas. Before he could complete his attack the air exploded in front of him. He was thrown backwards to slam onto the hard sand. Stunned, fighting to regain his wind, he looked up to see the angry general advancing on him, tendrils of green and white energy coalescing around his fists.

So, it was to be death by magic after all. Ragnar was not surprised. He understood that they could not allow him to live now that their plot to use him had failed.

"I see now the value of Byzantine honor!"

'Be silent, dog! Fight if you can, but your sword is nothing against the power of God's magic."

Ragnar crawled slowly to his feet, grasping the Damascus sword. His breathing was ragged. His chest ached as if kicked by a mule. He advanced again on the general, who smiled.

"At least I am no coward!" The Varangian wheezed.

Green flame blossomed from Kurkuas' fist in answer, leaping toward Ragnar to slam him again into the sand. He felt something give inside, and tasted the salty copper of his own blood. The odor of hot sand, and his own burning flesh clashed as the mage fire closed around him. Trying to ignore the pain, he clenched his teeth. He would not scream. He was a Varangian prince. He would go to Volos as he had lived, with courage and honor.

Suddenly the mage fire faded, bringing a wave of relief as if a great pressure had been removed. Ragnar braced himself, wondering what new torment would replace it. Looking up, he expected to see the general closing for the kill. Instead Kurkuas stared with horrified amazement as the fire faded from his hands. A strange shimmer replaced the fire, quickly enveloping his whole body. He screamed as his tall straight body convulsed. He fell to the ground, writhing as if it were he who burned. Ragnar could only gape in astonishment as the mage's long elegant bones bent and twisted. Flawless skin melted into misshapen scars.

Screams drew Ragnar's attention from the fallen general towards the galleries in time to see the emperor's floating throne plummet to the sand. The emperor was thrown from it like a rag doll. Retainers rushed to surround him before Ragnar could tell if he was injured.

Something was happening to the magic. It receded from his consciousness like the ocean at low tide. The lighted pillars and decorations within the Hippodrome faded out, one by one, just as the mage fire had faded. Glowing columns and ornate jeweled mosaics dissipated to reveal old and cracked masonry, or, in some cases, no structure at all. The Hippodrome had been originally built of stone, centuries before, but now looked as if all the subsequent repairs and ornamentation had been done exclusively with magic.

A deep rumble began, almost inaudible at first, building to a deafening roar. The ground beneath Ragnar trembled as the entire structure of the Hippodrome sagged and buckled. Shearing stone cracked like thunder as ancient structures, deprived of their magical support, shattered into dust and rubble.

Perun himself could not have created a more awesome display. Only gods could create such havoc. Ragnar hugged the shaking earth and prayed that his gods, if this frenzy was their doing, take care to avoid destroying him as well.

People screamed, running to avoid being caught under the crushing stone. Some leaped from the upper galleries onto the sands of the interior arena. Many of the jumpers did not get up.

A new sound, much like rending glass, drew his attention to the northeast wall where the Hagia Sophia slowly sank from sight. Ragnar was surprised that it had not already fallen, but perhaps the Byzantine god's magic was stronger there. The golden domes darkened as if their light was being slowly consumed, then shattered, leaving gaping holes as the massive cathedral settled out of sight.

In a few moments it was over. An unnatural stillness settled over everything, occasionally punctuated by the moans and cries of the wounded. Clouds of dust raised from falling debris partially obscured the afternoon sun, creating a bizarre twilight. Everything felt different. The magic was gone. All of it.

The prince closed his eyes where he lay on the sand and tried to feel it. But the insidious clamor that had so chafed at his senses since his arrival in this cursed city was now gone. The sand was only sand, and the land was only rock, stone, and earth. Clean and pure.

Slowly he opened his eyes to look for Kurkuas. If the magic was gone, then so were the mage's defenses.

Kurkuas was looking around himself with large wild eyes. His formerly tall body was bent and twisted, as if bones had broken and healed, but not correctly. His eyes came to rest on Ragnar.

Slowly Ragnar smiled and reached for his fallen weapon. He watched Kurkuas blanche as the mage realized his danger, his hands involuntarily moving in what must have been a warding spell. Nothing happened.

Kurkuas looked at his hands as if they had betrayed him, then turned to run. His shambling stumble bore no resemblance to his former liquid grace.

Ragnar started to rise and give chase. Sudden pain

lanced through his body, forcing him to lean on his sword for support. He needed all his concentration just to gain his feet. The ache in his chest made breathing difficult. Thick dust caught in his throat, threatening to suffocate him. Kurkuas had come very close to killing him. But close was not good enough. So long as he had breath he vowed to show the mage what a Russian wolf could do.

He started after his quarry, but found that his injuries would not allow him to move too quickly. By the time he reached the ruin of the main tunnel out of the Hippodrome, he had completely lost sight of the general in the chaos beyond.

Feeling very tired and frustrated, Ragnar collapsed upon a large chunk of broken masonry. Most of the tunnel's arch had fallen into pieces that now littered the path.

A small whimpering noise caught his attention. It sounded like someone was trapped in the rubble. He sat up, squinting through the dusty gloom as he tried to find the source of the cries. Then he saw it. A pale form, illuminated only by a thin shaft of sunlight through the broken roof, huddled in the debris. Slowly, trying not to jar himself and reawaken the pain, he moved closer.

The form cried out and pulled back at his approach. Large eyes, wide with fear, gazed at him from a perfect, though dirt-streaked, face. A torn gown of shimmery material clung to the unmistakably feminine figure. Disheveled blond hair fell about the girl's shoulders. The wings and smile were gone, but Ragnar recognized the sobbing girl as the slave who had removed his chains.

"So, you are a real woman after all." He stowed the sword in his belt, attempting to look less threatening. "Are you hurt?"

"Please, lord, do not look upon me. I am hideous."

Ragnar glanced at himself, his torn armor and blistered body. "If you are hideous, then I must be truly horrible beyond words."

His attempt at humor did nothing to calm the girl.

She really did remind him of Olga, though he had to admit that his wife's features were not so perfect.

"Let me help you." He began to move the larger pieces of stone from around her, trying to see if she were hurt or trapped. "Can you walk?"

"No! Leave me. You must leave me! I am being punished!"

Ignoring her protests, the prince lifted her from the rubble. He tried to set her on her feet, but she only collapsed to the ground, crying. He tried to lift her again but she rolled away from him. Her torn robes parted, revealing a withered and shrunken leg. Ragnar stared in surprise. The poor child was a cripple.

She saw him staring at her useless leg, and tried desperately to pull her gown back into place. Fresh tears spilled from swollen eyes. Ragnar wondered at the cruel irony of a master who would turn a cripple child into an angel. Gently he approached her.

"What is your name?"

"I am called Serapha." She whispered, refusing to look at him.

"I want to help you, Serapha."

"You cannot help me. Take me to my master. He is powerful. He is the only one who can forgive me and give my wings back."

"But you don't have to be a slave anymore. You can go free." Ragnar reached for her collar to remove it. She pulled back, grabbing it protectively.

"Easy. I will not force freedom upon you. But I cannot give your wings back. The magic is gone."

Fresh tears poured from the girl as she began sobbing hysterically. He reached for her, trying to give comfort, and suddenly found her clinging to him. He awkwardly brushed her hair from her face, feeling helpless.

After a while her sobs subsided. She slowly wiped her eyes and looked at the Varangian prince.

"God can give my wings back. God will forgive me."

Ragnar started to ask which one, but caught himself.

She gently touched his chest, tracing his wounds and blisters. "God can heal you as well. God's magic is all powerful."

Ragnar started to tell her that the magic was gone. But he could not bear to make her cry again. She would understand soon enough. For now it would be sufficient to take her to a place of safety.

"Is there some place you can go? Some place safe? I will take you there."

She looked up at him and smiled, a gesture that illuminated her entire face. Ragnar though that, wings or no, she was still an angel.

"Take me to the home of the Pantocrator. Take me to the Hagia Sophia."

At first Ragnar did not understand what she meant. But she pointed across the Augustaeum square towards the fallen cathedral. He peered through the clearing dust to see the building, still standing, if a bit lopsided, beyond the Augustaeum. She might be safe there. A small chunk of disrupted masonry fell from the remains of the tunnel's arch to bounce painfully off his shoulder. If nothing else, the church was probably safer than the tunnel.

Carefully he stood, cradling the girl as he fought back the protestations of his damaged body. He was glad that she was so light. He would be able to carry her to the church, but not much farther.

They stepped out of the tunnel into chaos. People were running and shouting, buildings were burning. Some were completely gone, leaving bodies and furniture sprawled in their place. No one paid any attention to the barbarian in their midst.

Where are you now, Igor? he thought. *Now this city would fall to us like fatted goats. Without their magic these people are helpless.*

Ragnar skirted a cracked marble slab. Probably once part of a larger building. Just beyond it a white horse lay thrashing on the ground, screaming piteously. As Ragnar

drew near he saw the animal was still harnessed to the
twisted remains of a chariot. The horse's legs were obviously broken, giving way each time the panicked creature
tried to rise. Sweat and froth stood out on its pale coat;
its eyes rimmed white with pain and terror. Seraphia hid
her face from the sight. The remains of a man could just
be seen beneath the broken wheels. Ragnar remembered
the emperor's chariot with its winged horse. He did not
want to think about how many other men and animals
might have fallen from the sky when the magic faded.

Carefully he sat Seraphia down, just out of view of the
suffering animal, then returned and mercifully dis-
patched the horse with his sword. Men deserved their
suffering, and usually brought it on themselves. But animals did not deserve to suffer at the hands of men.

After cleaning his blade, Ragnar retrieved Seraphia and
continued to work his way through the wreckage towards
the church. They found several other dead bodies, both
human and animal. Here and there, a few impossible
creatures writhed on the ground, dying without the magic
to sustain them. Seraphia hid her face in Ragnar's shoulder and cried quietly, unable to face what had become
of her city. Ragnar drew his strength from her need of
him, knowing that it must be worse for her than for him.

They finally reached the Hagia Sophia. The great
cathedral listed badly to one side; its eastern wall had
partially collapsed from the impact, but on the whole it
was surprisingly intact.

Many other people were also gathering at the church,
some carrying their dead and wounded, some looking for
lost family, and some just wandering as if in a haze. Only
a few seemed brave enough to actually enter the sagging
building. Most seemed content just to be on the grounds,
kneeling in prayer as they looked skyward towards the
shattered domes.

Ragnar did not feel safe among so many enemies in
his weakened condition. He had seen crowds turn ugly
before, and judged that these people might be quick to

vengeance, if they should decide that he was a threat, or worse, a scapegoat. He could not fight them now, it was all he could do to stand. Far better to brave the interior of the ruined church.

He quickly searched for a door that was not jammed. Finding one on the west wall, he carefully entered.

Inside, the marble slabs that had once covered the floor were cracked, and in some cases, lifted out of place at odd angles. But most of the main structure seemed solid. Ragnar set Serapha down on a fallen block and leaned against a pillar. His breathing was labored and ragged. He needed rest, but could not afford it just yet. He scanned the cavernous interior of the cathedral for a safe haven. Shards of mosaic tile and translucent glass littered the buckled floor. Along the wall mosaics looked like washed out lepers with huge chunks of the tiles missing from each design.

"I cannot carry you any further," he gasped.

She looked around, in sudden fear. "Please. Do not leave me here. At least take me to the altar. There is healing magic there."

He looked at her face, and could not refuse, even though he knew the lie of her words. "You will have to help me then; you must try to support yourself." Carefully he grasped her waist, and helped her place some weight on the stronger of her legs. Her brow beaded in sweat as she concentrated on trying to walk. He was still carrying most of her weight, but even the slight difference helped.

As they entered the central nave they saw that the great dome was almost completely gone. Gaping holes allowed the afternoon sunlight to stream into the cavernous chamber in brilliant shafts that illuminated the altar. It glowed golden almost as if it still held magic. Decorative banners on ceremonial lances flanked the altar as if awaiting a ceremony. Ragnar had to admit, that even in ruins, the building still had some mark of beauty on it. Approaching the altar, he noticed a figure kneeling at its base gesticulating wildly. The man cried out, and Ragnar's blood burned. That voice! It was Kurkuas.

Carefully but firmly, he set Serapha down on the marble floor, ignoring her pleas. Calling on his gods for one last gift of strength, he drew his sword and advanced on the general.

"Why have you forsaken me?" Kurkuas screamed at the altar, "I have always slain the unbelievers. I have cleansed the land of the heathens and apostate! I have defended the land! Why have you taken back the power?"

"Your god does not hear you. Your magic is gone. You have sold your honor. What have you left?" Ragnar's words echoed hollowly beneath the broken dome.

The figure at the altar stiffened and whirled to face the prince. "You! How dare you bring your pagan blasphemy into this place!"

"It is over. I have won our battle. I give you a chance to redeem your honor and keep your life. Free my men as you promised."

"Free your men?" Kurkuas started laughing hysterically, his eyes wild with madness.

Forcing his legs to continue to carry him forward, Ragnar tried not to let his pain and exhaustion show. "You have no magic. You are no match for me without it. Keep your bargain and free my men."

"No magic? I am a *tribute* to magic! Look at me!" He gestured to his bent and scarred body, cruel parody of the tall elegant man he had been "This is the mark of magic! Honor God! Use the magic he has given! Defend the faith! And this is the repayment." Bitterness edged his voice. "The magic burns you out until nothing is left but the power itself." He threw his arms wide, spinning to face the altar. "Fail that power once . . . only once!" he sobbed, "and it will all be taken away." He dropped his arms like one exhausted, slowly turning back to the prince. His contorted features softened as his green eyes focused on something beyond Ragnar that only he could see.

"And yet—there is no greater glory than when the magic runs within you. To feel the burn as it consumes you, knowing that nothing can stand against you. Knowing that, for at least that moment, you are God!" Slowly, the mage collapsed to his knees, a broken marionette, hysterical laughter welling from him as he opened his arms for the killing blow.

Ragnar stopped just short of the general.

"No! Please don't kill him!" a feminine voice screamed.

Ragnar turned to see Serapha, trying to force her legs to work as she half crawled toward him across the nave floor.

"Don't kill him. I beg you! I need him! I need his magic! You cannot kill him!"

The prince looked at the lovely girl, begging for the life of this miserable rodent, and was moved. She was right. He couldn't kill him now. There was no honor in the death of an unarmed broken man. He lowered his blade and turned away in disgust.

And felt fire erupt in his gut.

Serapha screamed.

Looking down in disbelief he saw a bloody lance tip protruding from his belly. He sagged to the ground, gasping as Kurkuas jerked the ceremonial spear free. Useless hands clasped the wound in a vain attempt to staunch the flow.

Kurkuas stood over the prince, holding the spear triumphantly as Ragnar's blood ran over the silk banner still mounted on it. "Did you really think a mere barbarian could out think a civilized warrior?" He laughed, a crazed sound that echoed in Ragnar's head. "And as for your men, it was much too late. I had them killed before we even began our little contest. The City of Kings is no place for uncivilized pagans."

White-hot fury blended with the searing pain in Ragnar's

gut. He tried to reach his sword, but his body was sluggish and refused to respond. In his blurring vision he saw Kurkuas turn toward Serapha.

"And you, fallen angel. Did you conspire with the devil to take my magic? I know you! You are a demon in disguise. That is why you must crawl on your belly like a worm. God will give me back his favor when I have slain you all!"

Serapha tried to scrabble away, but he caught up to her easily.

"Please, just give me my wings back!" she begged. "I will do anything. Just give them back and let me go."

"Only if you can fly in Hell!" He raised the lance, ruined silk banner still fluttering from it, and struck her.

Ragnar tried to cry out, but there was no breath. His body was growing numb and unresponsive as his life-blood drained away. Only the fury kept him conscious. He could accept his death—he was a warrior prince, born to risk death—but not the butchery of this girl. It was the *Volkhvi* massacre all over again. It all came back to him, the helplessness, the despair as he watched innocents die.

A slow tingle touched his spine, growing to spread quickly over his body. The familiar energy hummed along his nerves, briefly superseding the pain.

It took a moment for his fogged mind to realize what was happening. Through fading eyes he saw the dull mosaic walls begin to glow, as if illuminated from within. The magic had returned. Its seductive call grew louder within his dying mind.

This time he did not fight it, but opened himself to it completely. A euphoric rush surged through him as he welcomed the power, instinctively channeling its burning to meld with his fury. He could feel his body healing even as the energy began to feed on him. His sight cleared. He saw Kurkuas, apparently oblivious to the returning magic, standing over the screaming girl, his

eyes blind in madness as he swung the heavy lance high
in the air for a final killing blow.

"NO!" Ragnar bellowed. His voice reverberated with
newfound energy. But the general was deaf to all but his
personal demons. The lance streaked downward.

Almost without thought, Ragnar released his fury. A
white hot bolt of eldritch energy shot from his hand to
slam into the mage, knocking him from his feet and
deflecting the lance. Kurkuas hit the marble screaming.
His body writhed and convulsed as the mage fire eagerly
devoured him. The stench of burning flesh fouled the air.

When Ragnar was sure that the general had stopped
moving, he called the energy back. It hungrily returned
to him, burning within him even as it sang its song of
power and glory. Slowly he rose from the floor, bathed
in the magical glow from the golden altar and sparkling
mosaics. The pain was gone. His wounds were gone. He
felt strong again.

He strode to Serapha and offered her his hand. She
shrank away. She had not been afraid of the ragged barbarian prince, but cowered before him now. Awe and
terror disfigured the face that had once smiled at him.

He looked sadly at his hands—hands that had used
mage power to kill. He could sense all the lines of power
within the great church; he felt the City's lifeblood
returning around him.

He could feel the magic laughing within him as it
began to exact its price.

THE SCAM

Brian M. Thomsen

Apprenticeship's End

The apartment was at the edge of the sprawl surrounding the city. On one side sat a warehouse and on the other a small wineshop. A shoulder-high fence separated the property from its neighbors. Half a day from the seaport of Melantias and not far from the road to Constantinople, the almost miniature villa was not in a prime location, but it had been chosen years earlier for other reasons. Its two rooms were comfortably furnished and the brick and stone house was set far enough back from the street to give a sense of quiet. More importantly, the entrance to the door was sheltered from view by a high hedge, and each room featured no less than three escape routes. Just inside the entranceway, two men stood a few feet apart. Both were well-dressed. The conversation paused as their eyes adjusted to the lesser light of the main room. The younger man spoke with some animation, but in low tones that were impossible to hear from even a few paces away.

"Why do I have to be the outside man this time? You

yourself said that I was the best grifter in these parts for nigh unto three years now," beseeched Jon Hookah. "Sure, I still have a lot to learn, and sure, I'm no match for the city trade, or the mage gangs . . . but damn it, Othello, why can't I be the inside man this time? Even a junior scam caster has some rights. It's not like you've never let me be the inside man before. Hecuba! I've been on the inside more times than you have been for the past few months. Please?"

The graying Moorish scam master fingered his beard and shook his head. A wisp of gray hair fell across his eyes; Othello sighed. This was not going to be easy for either of them, but the time had come. The elder grifter's prime had passed, and he had to tell his student the truth. It was never easy letting an apprentice go, or accepting retirement, for that matter. This would be their last game together. The youth could handle the inside position better than men twice his age with three times the experience. Still, even a gray old cuss like himself deserved a swan song. Hookah would have to realize that.

"Jonny," began Othello One-Eye to his soon-to-be released apprentice, "you are right. You are the best grifter in these parts . . ."

"Yeah, and? . . ." interrupted Jon, figuring a "but" was on its way.

"Hecuba, you have done put me to shame the last few times."

"And? . . ." reiterated Jon, growing even more impatient.

"And, as you have mentioned, even a junior scam caster has some rights."

"So? . . ." replied Jon, tired of hearing his own argument recapped for him.

"And one of those rights," Othello said softly, "is to be told when the time has come for him to break out on his own, to be his own master, and that time has come."

"Huh?" said Jon, thrown by the curve this consensual altercation had taken. His face went through a range of fleeting expressions before settling back to one of well-trained neutrality.

Good, the elder thought in approval of the young man's quick recovery, *he's ready*.

"You are no longer an apprentice. The lessons are over, and I can teach you no more. It is time to find a new teacher, and start the next phase of your education," Othello confessed, trying to hold back a tear he felt forming in his left eye (his only eye, for that matter, since the other had been plucked out by a dissatisfied mark thirty years ago).

"But, Othello, surely you . . ." interrupted the young grifter, scared about where the conversation was leading.

The older man knew how his charge must feel about the direction of conversation. He had felt the same way when Seludius had cut him free almost fifty years earlier, scared and unsure. Had it really been that long?

"No interruptions, now," insisted the graying scam master, just stern enough to assure the newly released scam caster to let him finish his say. "When you get to be my age, you don't like to see a lot of time wasted with silly arguments. I'm getting old, through no fault of my own, of course. Every man owes time its due. But I'm getting awfully slow."

"You're not . . ."

Othello continued, uninterrupted. "True, I haven't embarrassed myself, at least not yet. But in our game, embarrassment can sometimes be more than unpleasant. Sometimes it can be fatal, and a master, even a small-time one such as myself, has to know his own limitations . . . his time to retire. And my time is about to arrive."

"But, Othello, you're not too old," Jon insisted. "And no one can do the ruby-dung marble swindle the way you can. I'll never be the scam master you are. Not in a million years."

"Your flattery is appreciated, and you are right. No one can do the ruby-dung marble swindle the way I can," agreed the soon-to-be-retired master of the arts of distraction and deception, "and that's why I want to be the inside man for just one last time, sort of as my swan song. Even a graying old coot like myself deserves the chance to take a final bow. Don't you agree?"

"But . . ."

"I knew you would," continued the master, "but you're wrong about one thing. You are ready for the city trade. True, you're not up for taking on any of the major mage gangs. You don't want to step on their toes, after all. The bosses of those gangs are powerful, and they're mean . . . and none is meaner than Doyle Hussan. He's got the City Guard in his hip pocket, at least enough of them to keep the rest at bay, and all transient and nontransient, small-time grifters in line . . . but you're good. Better than the others, at least in these here parts. Yes, indeed, apprenticeship is over, and it's time for college."

"Surely you don't mean the Lyceum Magus?" Jon asked incredulously.

"Of course not. That's for marks. However you do need a new teacher, and that's why I've written you a letter of introduction to another former apprentice of mine, one who's left the small-time grift behind in favor of the big scam. Hecuba, Pall Gondor wasn't much younger than you when he took off for the city."

Jon was shocked when he heard the name.

"You think I'm ready to work with Pall Gondor?" he asked.

"None better," Othello answered. "You'd be wasting your time hanging around these parts. You were meant for better things, bigger scams . . . much bigger than ruby-dung marble swindles."

"But I like ruby-dung marble swindles," he insisted. "And I'm not sure I'm ready for the city."

"You're ready for the city alright," Othello assured, draping his crooked ebony arm over the youthfully strong shoulders of his former student, "and the city is ready for you too; and with Gondor's help, you'll be fine."

Othello reached into the folds of his multipocketed robe and withdrew a letter.

"Here it is. A letter of introduction from me to Pall. He'll take you on. He owes me at least that much. The address is on the envelope. You'll find him easy enough."

Jon inserted the envelope into his robe, still not quite comprehending the great passage in his life that had just taken place.

The old scam master straightened up, or at least as much as his bent old bones would allow him to, and quickly moved on to the next subject at hand.

"Now, my former apprentice," Othello orated, in the self-assured voice that Jon had grown accustomed to. "It's time for my grand finale, my last curtain call, the final scam before I retire and you move on. Now hand me that mound of dung from a recently gelded stallion that I ordered you to fetch."

The former apprentice complied, savoring Othello's theatricality.

"Now remember, there is no reason to expend more power on a spell than is absolutely necessary. Power and prowess are needed to instigate it. The veldt maintains it, until the power runs out, or is interrupted, and all things continue on from there. Now also remember, scams only should last for as long as you need them to. There is no sense in tying up a lot of your power in maintaining a spell after you've already made your getaway. It's hardly worth it. After all, if I wanted to cast a spell that would turn a mound of dung into a ruby marble forever, why would I bother to scam it? Also remember, any change that is needed to alter a spell, whether to recharge it so that it will last longer, or manifest some sort of physical change, will always require more power than the initial spell itself. Agreed?"

"Agreed," said Jon, still in awe of his former master, despite the evidence of the ravages of time upon his beaten ebony frame.

"Now, I will utter the words of power over this worthless pile of dung. *Ookah, KaKa, Rubah*, and behold!"

As Jon had seen on numerous occasions prior, the mound of brown had turned into a deep red ruby marble, larger than a man's fist. Othello carefully wrapped it in a silken cloth, and placed it in a samite pouch, and said, "Now, it is your turn, young man on the outside. Adorn me, so that that foolish old merchant Durnang will believe that I am indeed a prosperous and respectable old merchant like he imagines himself to be."

"Yes, teacher," replied Jon, for what he anticipated would be the last time in their relationship. *"Sachsus, Brooksus, Bloomsus."*

"Now, my former apprentice," Othello, now magically bedecked in the finest robes available this far from the city, instructed, "you wait here maintaining the disguise spell, while I go inside, and conduct my business with the old skinflint Durnang. I'll be out in no time. After all, am I not the best scam master in town?"

"Of course," Jon replied.

"And is the ruby-dung marble swindle not my specialty?"

"Why certainly!"

"What could go wrong?"

The two grifters agreed, parting ways to take their appropriate roles in the swindle, blissfully unaware of the potential, and likely, danger that lurked ahead in the form of a visitor who had arrived at Durnang's minutes before they had.

Had Jon not slowed his and Othello's walk with his totally now-out-of-place argument, there was a good possibility that Othello might have recognized the other visitor, and would have called the whole thing off ... but such was not the case.

The Visitor

Obese and pockmarked, old Durnang ushered the disguised Othello into a back room that he reserved for his more discreet transactions, inquiring with great urgency, "And are you sure that you haven't been followed?"

"But of course," Othello replied, then adding while gesturing to the silks and sculptures that adorned the old fence's abode, with one of his own faux-bejewelled hands. "One doesn't become as successful as ourselves without being careful."

"Agreed," Durnang replied, escorting Othello to a plush divan. "Have a seat. I shall return in a moment."

Durnang waddled through a curtained-off doorway, into a neighboring chamber, giving Othello a chance to take in his surroundings.

Without a doubt, Durnang was a most successful fence. His chambers breathed auras of opulence that reeked of city-earned wealth. Rumor had it that he had connections in very high places in the city, but Othello had dismissed such stories as fabrications. Durnang appeared successful, but like Othello himself was to the local grifters, only in relation to the local competition.

Durnang was the most successful fence in the area, but nothing compared to what the kid would meet in the city, Othello thought. Durnang, despite the size of his ego, was just another small-time hood . . . small-time just like himself.

Durnang returned, and sat next to Othello on the divan, facing a marble table set up against a curtained backdrop of two fauns frolicking.

"Now that we are comfortable," the old fence commenced, "it is time for business. You have brought the ruby marble?"

"But of course," Othello replied, removing it from its wrappings, enjoying the resultant widening of Durnang's eyes in gleeful greed, then adding, "and you, of course, have brought the gold?"

"But of course, my friend. But of course," he replied. "But first, may I touch it?"

"Surely," replied Othello, handing the rube fence the faux ruby marble, confident that his naive powers of perception would not penetrate the expertly cast disguise spell.

Durnang carefully examined the gem, drooling in anticipation of its acquisition.

"This is the largest ruby marble I've ever seen," the fence commented.

"I promised nothing less."

"Of course you didn't . . . and we are both men of our words."

"Of course. Now if you will be so kind as to give me my agreed upon compensation, I will be on my way. My caravan awaits."

"But of course. Funny thing though, a recent visitor of mine, the client for whom I was acquiring this gem as it turns out, was wondering how you got here since *his* was the only caravan to arrive these last three days."

Without blinking an eye, Othello responded. "That is because I've been here five days. I had other business to attend to before coming here. You know the lot of traveling businessmen."

"But of course," Durnang verbally agreed, but still did not come across with the gold. He added, "Ours is a lonely lot."

"Agreed," Othello responded, hoping that Durnang would hasten through this recent onslaught of bathos, and hand over the gold.

"That is why I thought you might want to meet my client, a businessman like ourselves."

"I really don't have time," Othello insisted, trying to stand, but finding himself incapable of making his legs respond to his mind's commands.

"Oh, yes, you do," insisted Durnang, who with less effort than one would anticipate from one with such girth, came to his feet, and strutted to the curtained entrance from whence he came, drawing the curtain aside with a flourish to reveal its previously concealed occupant. "I'd like you to meet an associate who has convinced me to enter into a mutually beneficial partnership with him, making my business one of his regional offices. He's from the city, and perhaps you've heard of him, Doyle Hussan."

There stood Doyle Hussan, the most arrogant, yet powerful, mage mobster within earshot of everyone Othello had ever known. He looked to be eight feet tall, and built like a stone idol of some legendary hero of the arena. His stern visage was accentuated in meanness by a razor-thin mustache that drooped into two slender threads of hair that outlined the sides of his unbearded chin.

Othello tried to remove himself from the enchanted divan but couldn't, and realized that the one slim hope of salvation lay in his continuing the charade.

"Master Hussan, it is a great honor," he offered. "I would like to shake your hand, but, unfortunately, find myself unable to come to my feet."

Hussan ignored him, instead outstretching his hand to Durnang, ordering, "The ruby! Hand it to me!"

Durnang complied, as Othello looked on.

Hussan strode around the room, the ruby marble bouncing in his hand. After a few moments, he approached the divan upon which the old scam caster was imprisoned, and tossed the faux gem to Othello.

"It is as I suspected," boomed Hussan.

As the gem came to rest on Othello's palm it began to glow, a sure sign that the jig was up

"It is a swindle," Hussan continued. The ruby marble melted into its natural state of excrement, staining Othello's palm and faux robes. "Well done for some country bumpkin rube, but a swindle nonetheless. And nobody swindles me."

"But Master Hussan," Othello pleaded, "I had no idea."

Hussan ignored the gray old grifter's response.

"You are obviously not acting alone. Someone of your limited expertise can not possibly carry on more than one charade at once, and a dung dealer like you could never afford such finery.

"Therefore, I will return you to the back alleys from whence you came, so that you might act as warning to others. *Felix, Morris, Minx.*"

Othello felt the grip of the divan release, as he felt his own bent frame contract.

In a matter of moments, he was shooed from Durnang's chamber, skittering away on all fours.

With great pain from his now increasingly arthritic limbs, he rejoined Jon in the back alley.

"Scat, you mangy old feline," Jon insisted, trying to shoo the recently arrived cat away.

The cat refused to leave, looking up at him with its one doleful eye.

"Scat," Jon repeated. "First I get this tremendous blast of pain in my head as if someone ripped through my concentration with a mace, then Othello doesn't show up. . . ."

The graying kitty interrupted with a loud series of meows.

"Shush!" Jon answered, and for the first time actually looked into the feline's tearful eye. He recognized the glimmer of intelligence and insight that rested trapped behind its feline form as that of his former master and teacher.

Taking the graying puss into his arms, Jon offered it the warmth of his closeness.

"Othello," he implored, "what has happened to you?"

Just then a very human and powerful voice issued forth from the feline's throat.

"Look upon the work of Doyle Hussan, and cower, you knaves," the voice boomed. "This sorry back-alley scoundrel has tried to swindle me, has paid the consequences, and will spend the rest of his days as the true creature of the back alleys that he is. Let this serve as a warning to all others who seek to undermine the minions of Doyle Hussan."

The voice ceased, and was replaced by Othello's own helpless meowing.

Jon continued to carry his former teacher, pausing in the village only once to pick up a sling and blanket, with which to wrap and carry his arthritic feline charge.

By nightfall, the two were within two days' journey of the city.

Jon only stopped to rest and sleep a few hours each night, and occasionally to catch some food for himself, and his feline companion, who was too old and inexperienced in the catlike ways to hunt for itself.

One thought occupied Jon's mind.

Revenge.

. . . but first he needed some help, and hopefully, Pall Gondor would comply.

Or, at least, Jon hoped he would.

He owed Othello that.

Both he and Gondor did.

Whatever it took.

In Othello's name revenge must be attained.

Country Grifter Meets City Con

The city was as beautiful and opulent as the most treasured gift Othello had ever given Jon.

Jon still remembered that evening of luxury and pleasure. It was his fifteenth birthday, and Othello had hired the village whore to usher him into manhood . . . but that was not all. His teacher had cashed in numerous favors and debts to remove any trace of tawdriness from the affair. The middle-aged bawd was transformed into a virginal princess, eager yet demure, pure yet experienced. The homespun draperies and straw mattress of her chamber became a bejewelled bower of silks and splendor . . . and the planned-for sexual assignation was carefully transformed into a chance meeting between two young people sharing a single night of passion and pleasure on the long and winding road of life. Jon had been amazed at how easy the seduction had been, assuming that Othello's gift had been some sort of glamour that had enabled him to seduce the fair young heiress. He had never found out how far Othello's glamour had extended.

The naive eyes of the young grifter were filled with wonders that recalled that nostalgic event, while the wizened feline eye of his former mentor cynically recalled the same.

At first Jon was surprised at the incongruity that seemed rampant within the city walls. Everyone was dressed in opulence, yet beggars were starving in the streets.

Unbeknownst to himself, Jon had entered the city via the poor section, and as the realization of the situation around him became clearer, he began to realize that things were indeed alike all over. Only the scale was different.

"I had always heard that the city glittered," observed Jon to the feline companion he still bore in the sling across his chest, "but I now realize that all that glitters isn't gold, and no matter how gaily you paint and bejewel a building, a slum is still a slum."

Othello meowed.

Lately Jon had convinced himself that he understood the kitty's replies.

"You're right," he answered the feline, "it is strange that a big-time scam caster like Pall Gondor should be in such a downtrodden neighborhood. Maybe you got the address wrong?"

Othello meowed.

"No, I don't doubt you. Well, we'll find out soon enough. It should be somewhere in the next alley."

Othello purred.

"You're right. This is the address, so this must be the place."

The two companions had stopped in front of a small bathhouse, where a mud-wrestling match was taking place in a courtyard vestibule.

A maid of indeterminate age approached them and

instructed, "Half a piece of silver to watch, a whole piece to take part. You'll have to leave the cat outside though."

Othello meowed, giving the maid a wink with its one good eye, slightly taking the maid aback.

"We're looking for Pall Gondor," Jon explained.

"Never heard of him," the maid insisted. "Be on your way. There are others willing to pay good money to slosh around in the mud."

Jon started to leave, saying to his feline companion, "You see, Othello. I knew that we'd never find Pall Gondor around here."

Just then the maid interrupted, "What did you call that cat?"

"Othello," Jon replied.

"Othello, as in Othello One-Eye?"

"Yes . . . and I, uh, have a letter of introduction to Master Gondor from him."

"Come inside then, and set a spell," she replied. "That's Pall wrestling in the mud right now. I'll send him in to you once he gets all cleaned off."

Jon and Othello had been sitting in the salon of the bathhouse for a little while when a roguish fellow of early middle age entered, toweling off his still damp head.

"You looking for Gondor?" he inquired.

"Yes," Jon replied.

"Kim said something about a letter of introduction?"

"Here," Jon said, slightly reluctant to believe that this obviously down-on-his-luck rogue was the legendary Pall Gondor.

"I'm Gondor," he said as he read the letter, then looking up, continued, "and I know what you're saying. What a dump! Well I've had a little run of unfortunate luck, and I just got out of the gaol. Kim said she'd front for me until I got something together. How's Othello, that flea-bitten old coot?"

Othello hissed, and spit.

"Ask him yourself," the young grifter replied.

Pall looked at the aged feline, recognizing the gleam in the one good eye, a gleam he had not seen for close to two decades.

"Othello," he cried, "what happened to you?"

Though the question was not addressed to him, Jon replied. "He wanted to pull just one more swindle before he sent me on my way. It was the ruby-dung marble swindle. He said it would be his final bow, and that I needed a new teacher. You."

Pall turned his attention to the young grifter. "So, what went wrong? I mean he knows that scam like the back of his hand."

"We didn't know that Doyle Hussan was involved."

"Doyle Hussan?"

"Yeah, and now Othello has to live out the rest of his years as a cat."

Pall fingered his beard in contemplation.

"Given a cat's life expectancy around this city, that might not be too long. We have to do something, and do it fast."

"What can you do? Othello and I were doing better than this out in the sticks. I doubt there is anything that you can teach me that I can't learn on my own."

Othello meowed.

"No, Othello," Pall answered the cat, "let me handle this." He then turned his attention back to Jon, while continuing to pet his former mentor. "This city will eat you alive, and Othello doesn't want that. Besides, I can't take on Doyle on my own, and the little help you'll be is better than none at all."

"You're going to take on Doyle Hussan?"

"No, we are. It will be a big-time scam like this city has never seen before. We owe it to Othello."

"Do you have a plan?" Jon asked, realizing that Pall had just voiced his own early sentiments.

"No, not yet," said the down-on-his-luck scam caster, "but just give me a chance."

Con-to-Con Conversation

Jon spent the next few days catching up on his rest, and nursing the infirm kitty that had been Othello.

Their journey from the suburbs had taken a lot out of them, even more than one would have expected from the old gray cat.

Pall had not been kidding when he said that they would have to do something fast. Though Othello in his prior human form had just been beginning to feel the ravages of late middle age, Othello in his feline form was more than ancient, and showing more evidence of decline as each day passed. It is entirely possible that cats might have nine lives, but they were obviously much shorter than man's. Jon began to worry that he and Pall would be seeking Othello's revenge in memorium, long after the cat that had been their teacher had already passed away.

Pall never seemed to be at home, leaving the running/ proprietorship of the bathhouse to Kim, who assured the young grifter and scam caster that this was typical for him when he was trying to come up with a big idea.

Unfortunately Pall's return each evening was usually marked with depression as some new great plan had again and again failed to surface ... and even more so as Pall began to drain progressively more and more sacks of mead.

The time had finally come for Jon to say something.

"This is really great! Othello wanted to send me to you in order to continue my education. Well, master scam caster and con artist extraordinaire Mr. Pall Gondor, I already knew how to drink and embarrass myself in public, and I have no desire to pursue a career in the learned sciences of running a bathhouse or mud wrestling. Back when Othello and I were working together we would have come up with six or seven scams by now, and Doyle Hussan would be shaking in his boots. We should never have come here. Hecuba, you've just gotten out of prison. I've never been arrested, and

Othello had never been arrested. Only losers and marks get arrested."

Pall Gondor sighed, and put down the wineskin.

"How long have you been on the grift, kid?" he asked the holier-than-thou former apprentice.

"Five years," Jon replied.

"So Othello picked you up out of the gutter, too."

"I was getting by."

"Sure you were. As was I. Did Othello ever tell you how he lost his eye?"

Othello let out a large meow.

"Hush, you old coot!" Pall ordered, and turning his attention back to Jon pressed on, "Well, did he?"

"He said it was carved out by a dissatisfied mark when something went wrong with a con. He said he messed up."

"He didn't mess up. I did!" Pall insisted. "I was twelve years old, and almost as full of myself as you are now. I'd been living on the streets for as long as I could remember. Othello had taught me a few tricks of the trade, and I had assisted him in a few minor scams, up until the time I had figured that I had learned enough, could get by on my own, and didn't need anyone's help anymore. There was no reason to split the booty. I was twelve years old, and I was self-sufficient. I immediately set out from Othello's hideout in search of the perfect mark to provide me with a stake that I could take to the big city."

"You were only twelve?" Jon interrupted.

Pall continued his tale without answering.

"I set my sights on an old merchant who specialized in jewels from the sea, and I followed him back to his stall. I was going to use the old dissolving pearls trick, figuring I could cash them in for gold, and buy passage on a passing caravan. Well, the merchant kept asking me questions like 'What is a beggar urchin doing with priceless gems?' and 'How did you come by such riches?' I lost my nerve. I hadn't planned on the old geezer not accepting my first and only line of persuasion. 'You want some pearls, cheap?' I had asked. Well, everything that could go wrong did. I lost my concentration, my disguise, and my control, and the pearls melted back into sand. The old geezer was a lot stronger than I thought; I was sure he would have wrung my neck, except that Othello arrived on the scene. It seems he had been following me all day, and had been watching my little exchange from afar. He threw himself on the merchant's mercy, asking that I be spared. The merchant made him swear that he would keep an eye on me so that I didn't cause him any more trouble. He did, and I was released. Othello then took me back home to continue my education. I had already learned that I wasn't as smart as I had thought, and that I hadn't spent enough time in planning the scam before I put the trick in motion. The next time I didn't leave until Othello told me I was ready, and that was four years later."

"But what about Othello's eye?" Jon asked.

"The merchant had cut it out, so that Othello wouldn't be as prone to distraction, when he was keeping an eye on me."

Othello meowed.

"I owe that cat my life," Pall continued, "and I can't afford to screw up."

Othello purred, nuzzling his former student of twenty-five years past.

"What happened recently? I mean, that you wound up in prison."

Pall leaned back, and put his hand to his brow.

"What do you think?" he answered. "I screwed up."

"How?"

"It's not that I didn't plan enough, or keep my back covered. All of the disguise spells were in place, all of the right guards paid to roll over, the proper stooges set up, everything. It was a thing of beauty."

"So what happened?"

"I screwed up. I made it real apparent that all of a

sudden I was rolling in the gelt. The mark noticed, paid the City Guard more than I was willing, and hauled my butt off to the gaol. I'd still be there if the mark wasn't afraid that I would make a big production out of my incarceration."

"The mark was scared?"

"No, he was embarrassed. I mean I can't blame him. I may have screwed up, but he was just plain stupid. I mean imagine an alderman mage falling for the old flying camel derby shutout scam. Let alone, not having another mage in his employ to check for secondary spells, and enchantment. He was the perfect mark: arrogant—'Oh, no problem, no one can pull the cowl over my eyes'; greedy—'No, I think it would be better if we were partners, share the risk, as well as the profit'; and unpopular—'Who cares what the rabble thinks, this is my decision.' "

A smile came to Jon's lips, as he realized how much Pall's sarcastic mimicry reminded him of Othello.

"The mark sounds a lot like Doyle Hussan," Jon offered.

"All marks are the same. Doyle Hussan included."

Just then Pall brightened as if a torch of an idea had ignited his mind.

"All marks are the same. Doyle Hussan included," he repeated. "That's right."

"What's right?"

"What does a mage mobster fear most?" Pall quizzed.

"I don't know. Another mage mobster? Someone more powerful, perhaps."

"Almost, but not quite." Pall explained, "The code of the underworld is clear. There is no shame in backing down to a superior force or individual, especially when defeat is unavoidable. Of course, you are expected to take him out as soon as his back is turned, but that's not important now. No, what a mage mobster fears most is simple—it's embarrassment,"

"Embarrassment?"

"Sure. Mage mobsters come to power through respect, and embarrassment jeopardizes that respect. After all, you're not usually afraid of something that you can laugh at."

"So? . . ." Jon queried.

"So," Pall continued, "all we have to do is find a means of embarrassing Hussan in such a way that it would be important enough for him to bargain with us, say returning Othello back to human form, in exchange for our silence and/or the incriminating evidence."

"But how?"

"One of us will instigate the situation, and the other will threaten to expose it. And if we play our cards right, he'll never catch on that we're working together."

"On what?"

"I haven't quite figured all of the details out yet . . . but it's coming to me. We'll need lots of help, too. Scam casters, spell seducers, aura recorders, the works. Thank god, Othello here has plenty of friends still prowling these streets. Friends who owe him their stock in trade— you know, that first leg up in the scam trade."

"And they'll all help us?" Jon asked, slightly incredulously.

"Sure they will," Pall insisted. "Favor owed is a favor owed. Scam casters never forget . . . and those who don't owe Othello or myself personally will jump on the band- wagon when they hear about the situation. One thing that preys on every con artist's mind is the fear that he will scam one con too many, and that just like Othello here, it will catch up with them. We'll appeal to their deeper instincts on a con-to-con level."

Othello meowed.

"Of course, we'll call in Kid Abdul, and Lance Shield, too."

"You really think it will work?" Jon asked, slowly jump- ing onto the bandwagon of excitement.

"Hopefully . . . but even if it doesn't, what choice do

we have? I can guarantee you one thing though. We'll show this town the greatest scam it's ever seen."

Othello meowed.

"Right," the two con artists agreed, and all three shook hands on it, very gently to avoid aggravating the graying cat's arthritic paws.

Othello smiled for the first time since his transformation.

The Briefing

Jon was greatly impressed at seeing Pall in action. The legendary scam master was like a whirling dervish darting through back alleys of the city like a fox with a fiend on its tail. He bore little resemblance to the despair-ridden wino of just a few days ago. He was a man with a mission, and the clock was running.

Pall seemed to know everyone in the city. He'd enter two or three shops on a given alley, and within minutes a new recruit would have given notice to his previous employer, and assented to a rendezvous at a later hour at the bathhouse which had become the headquarters for the entire scam operation. (Kim had even hired some old friends whose outward appearance, though no doubt masking a heart of gold, would scare off a rabid tiger, let alone an eligible and lonely young male in search of a slosh in the mud, thus assuring that business would be down, and that preparations could continue undisturbed.)

Pall was also not shy with sharing the workload, as Jon soon found out. First, he was sent off to look into the renting of air barges, and when his results were determined, by Pall, to be cost-prohibitive, he was sent to the junkyards, and ship graveyards in pursuit of the perfect wreck that was large enough to throw a really big party on.

Jon searched high and low, but was unable to find a suitable vessel to meet with the older scam caster's approval. The seafaring craft were too bulky, and the airworthy ships were too small. He was about to give up hope, and accept the disappointment of having failed in his first big con assignment when the vague miasma of an idea crossed his mind.

"Does it really have to be an air barge?" he asked Pall.

"What would you suggest instead?" Pall answered.

"Well, since I know you are rounding up some crack levitators, I was wondering if maybe something else could be substituted."

"Like what?"

"How about a small building, sort of like the bathhouse?"

Pall scratched his head for a moment, and then shrugged.

"Why not," he replied. "Do you have one in mind?"

"How about your bathhouse?"

Pall shook his head.

"It's too easily traceable back to us ... but as I recall there is another one on the other side of the square. We ran them out of business with the mud wrestling tourneys. Yes, that one will be fine."

The bathhouse in question was quite run-down, with lightweight wood slats showing through its gilt enchantment. Like Kim's, it followed the arena style of architecture with a blown-glass tank at its center.

Pall nodded, and patted Jon on the back, saying, "Good work. Welcome to the big con, and just in the nick of time. We're getting the entire gang together tonight to start putting the plan in motion."

"What is the plan?"

"You'll find out tonight."

The gang started to show up just after sunset, and an odd lot they were. Kim's friends, the obese and craggy female wrestlers from the courtyard, played hostess and greeted each arrival, showing them to a seat. The visitors were equally courteous, and everyone seemed to get along fine.

Pall turned to Jon and said, "Well kid, never before has so much confidence been manifest in a single location."

"Confidence?" Jon queried.

"It's just another word for the grift, the scam casting, the confidence trade. Don't worry, you'll get used to it. It goes by many names, but it's all the same. Let me introduce you to the masters."

And with that Jon was introduced around.

Caleb Two Hands, the crack levitator, was there. He was called Caleb Two Hands because he had been caught stealing twice. It was only through a crack disguise spell on his already missing appendage, that Caleb was able to convince the guards that he was a first-time offender. Afterwards he figured that it was time for a change in focus, and after much intense study, he became the crack levitator of confidence.

Kid Abdul, despite the moniker, was no kid at all, and was in fact older than Othello. At one time he was a master of the large-scale disguise. Now he specialized in spell detection and distraction, providing the mosquitos and gnats that would distract a mark while the queen bee was moving in for a sting. Despite his advanced years, no one was better, or more discreet.

"You know, Pall," Abdul explained. "I owe Doyle one. His chief disguise detector used to work for me. He was very showy, but also very dense."

"No doubt you can handle him," Pall offered.

"None whatsoever," the elder statesman of scam replied.

Lance Shield specialized in low-cost escort services, everything from making a small gathering look like a mob scene, to cosmetological enhancements of beauty and youth. Kim's heavy-set friends quickly latched on to him, and they quickly established themselves as the amour cell.

Jon was in awe of the company he was now keeping. Some of the names he remembered from Othello's tales, others from new stories, and still others from popular folklore. He had had no idea that Othello was so tied in to the big time. He was further baffled by the amount of respect the crowd showed Gondor. On the exterior he was still the same down-on-his-luck ex-con con, but in this company he was treated as a master caster to behold in awe. Once again, Jon realized, looks can be deceiving.

"Hey kid, c'mere," Pall called from across the hall. "Let's get this plan on the scam now!"

Jon took his place at Pall's side with Othello resting on a pillow behind them.

"Okay, everyone settle down," Pall instructed. "We all know why we're here."

Othello meowed.

"Right," Pall continued. "Revenge is sweet, but we can't lose sight of our ultimate goals. One—obtain a means of embarrassing Hussan; two—get him to lift the feline imprisonment spell from Othello; and three—survive to scam another day. Now all of these goals are extremely risky, and I think it's fair to say that the accomplishment of all three with the requisite discretion required to avoid anyone's exposure as part of the con is exceptionally unlikely. Knowing that, does anybody want to withdraw at this time? No one will think the less of you, and everyone will respect your instincts for self-preservation. Anyone?"

The chamber was filled with a deafening silence.

"Okay, then," Pall commenced. "On with the briefing."

The Plan

The plan was genius in its simplicity.

Doyle Hussan was a big mage mobster, in more than one way. He controlled more than fifty percent of the city's vice/goniffery/corruption industries, with strong financial and magical interests in several legitimate businesses as well. He was alleged to be a major benefactor of the Lyceum Magus, and a open political supporter of the City Guard publicly, and a surreptitious fiscal supporter privately. He had managed to construct a public facade as a likeable rogue/robber baron whose shadowy interests tantalized the ladies, and intrigued the men. It was open knowledge that if you had any interest in affairs of a gray nature, magical or otherwise, Hussan was the man to see . . . or else.

Pall had realized that Doyle's position of imposing and threatening strength was carefully balanced on the teeter-totter of public opinion. Thus, as he had proven with his harsh retribution to Othello, he could never tolerate any person or matter that threatened to expose a weakness in his omnipotence, for without the public opinion of power, his entire underworld empire would come tumbling down. No one respects a buffoon, and once a mark, always a mark.

Thus Pall's immediate intent was to successfully play Hussan as a mark, and for this he had chosen a variation on the old Murphy scam, with a little of the backroom casino gig thrown in to give the scam the necessary panache.

The old abandoned bathhouse would be turned into an airborne betting palace, redone through a combination of theatrical sets, balloons, and curtains, and a mixture of enchantments, glamours, and disguises (manned by a crack team of no less than five outside spell casters under Kid Abdul whose sole concern was to keep the illusion up and running). The physical props and facades would serve to distract Hussan's entourage of magic observers, not unlike the inclusion of a sample authentic gold piece on the top of a stack of pseudo-gold pieces.

The scam that would be presented to Doyle by Jon would be as follows. Jon wants to buy out the airborne palace of decadence from its current owner and needs financial backing for the deal. The hook that was to be dangled before Doyle was that Jon had worked out a scam to bilk customers out of further gambling losses by still accepting bets on the upcoming Sow's Ear Derby while the "clients" were aloft in the casino even though the races had been finished. Jon would be getting the results levitated to him via a contact at the local bookie joint who would share in a piece of the action. The "clients" would land, find out the race results, and settle up their losses. Further income would be obtained through informed shill side bets with some of the heavy hitters, thus doubling the profit on each loser. Doyle would see the profit to be made, put up the capitol to buy the ship, and then demand a controlling interest in all future proceeds, as he had done in numerous cases before. Jon would then "be forced" to sign over the casino to him.

Part two of the scam would take place on the following day. Pall, in disguise, would approach an emissary of Hussan with evidence that both the head of the City Guard and the Lyceum Magus (both expertly played by Lance's impostors) were among those bilked on the prior day, and unless Doyle recalls the spell on Othello, two things will happen: Doyle will be exposed as a cheat to his very influential friends, and as the owner of a broken-down bathhouse. Doyle will have to give in, not wanting to be made a mockery of, Othello will be changed back, and the conspirators will all scatter to the four winds, free to scam cast another day.

Othello meowed in approval.

The Set Up

It was hard to believe, but in less than a week's time from the initial briefing at Pall's bathhouse, and the presentation of the plan du jour, all of the initial contacts had been made, roles practiced, and tricks put in place.

Kim and her wrestling friends, in collaboration with the redecorating genius of Lance Shield, had spent numerous hours converting the dilapidated bathhouse into a wonderfully tacky second-rate den of sin, complete with colorful festival streamers and balloons. Under Lance's "glamourizing" it would become a palace to behold, rumored to have been flown in from some far-off kingdom to cater to the city's well-heeled gambling circles.

Likewise, Pall and the gang had begun the all-important circulation of rumors around town that an exotic casino airbarge was on its way to take up residence in their fair land (for which Jon was busy practicing an exotic, yet understandable, accent from some unknown tongue of some yet-to-be-discovered far-off land).

Preliminary contact had been arranged with Hussan through numerous slow-witted emissaries of the feared mage mobster, all of whom were either duped, coerced, or seduced into cooperating with the plans of the gang. Eventually, an audience had been cleared for Jon with the mage mobster himself.

Jon, decked out in a caftan of silks and satins from other lands, appeared in the hall of the dreaded Doyle Hussan, a perky breasted beauty of indeterminate youth on one hand, a seer's crystal globe on his right.

"I have heard great and wonderful things of your exploits and power, great and marvelous Hussan," Jon intoned in his best pidgin common. "And have I got a deal for you!"

Hussan was not amused. This was his fifth petitioner of the day, and he had a good mind to incinerate him and his buxom morsel on the spot. He lifted his eight-foot frame from his throne, and was about to utter the magical words of power, when his major domo interrupted.

"Master," the domo beckoned, "he is the one from the ship."

"Really," said Hussan. "Is all as it seems to be?"

The domo turned around, and concentrated on the visitor, and his bimbo, and laughed.

"Not to worry, Oh great one," the domo replied, "for there is a glamour at work here, but one that he seems to be blissfully unaware, for the young . . . uhum . . . lady is actually a rather fey gentleman."

"Perhaps he is his type?"

"Oh, no sir. He pervades the hall with an aura of ignorance. You know how these foreigners are."

"Quite," said Hussan, and returned his attention to the visitor. "You! You have a proposition for me."

"Yes, Oh great Doyle Hussan. I come from a far-off land, and I seek your assistance in buying the flying betting parlor, the Cloud of Chance," Jon offered with all the sincerity of a bazaar pitchman.

"What's in it for me?" the mage mobster demanded.

"A share in the gelt, my lord, but we must act now!"

"Why?"

"I have a plan that will make us richer than our wildest dreams."

"My dreams are quite wild, thank you . . . but you still have not explained why I must help you today."

"If I do not tell the ship's owner that I will be purchasing the ship, he will have it move on to other lands, and we will miss the Sow's Ear Derby."

"And why should this concern me?"

Jon scratched his chin, and reluctantly shook his head.

"I guess I'll have to let you in on my plan," Jon said, motioning the bimbo to leave. After she had left, slinking off in a manner that brought much amusement to Hussan's guards (not to mention the major domo), he resumed his presentation. "Everybody knows that there is a lot of action with the high rollers on the Sow's Ear Derby. Well, I figured that these same heavy hitters would love to go for a ride in the Cloud of Chance during the race. Unfortunately, once we are airborne, a fog will come in obscuring our view . . . a local fog caster owes me a favor . . . and as a result we will continue to take bets on the race we can't see, even though the actual race is over. We will only accept the losing bets, of course."

"And how will you know what the losing bets are?"

"A local bookie who owes me a favor will levitate them to me once they are in. I figure I can keep the crowd afloat for a good two hours of sure-thing betting before anyone is the wiser."

Hussan was impressed by the plan, and also by the honesty of the dishonesty of his visitor.

"But why do you need me?" Hussan pressed. "Why

don't you just tell the owner of your plan, or better yet, why don't you tell him you will buy the ship yourself, and then pay for it tomorrow out of your winnings?"

"We come from an honorable land, and the owner reveres honesty in all games of chance. He worships the goddess of fairness, so there is no possibility that he will play along. As to my doing it on my own, he will not trust me, and will figure that I am up to something. But if the great and noble Doyle Hussan was to express an interest in buying the ship, how could he refuse?"

"Indeed," Hussan replied.

"Here," Jon pressed, handing the ball of crystal to the major domo. "Is she not a beauty?"

Hussan gazed upon the ball, and floating within was indeed the likeness of an airship, capable of carrying a large gambling den.

Hussan came forward and shook Jon's hand.

"We have a deal, partner," he said. "I will bring the requisite amount tomorrow, and will even attend your gambling fete with my entourage, so that we can split the proceeds at our earliest convenience."

"Thank you, O great Hussan," Jon extolled, backing out of the hall, while taking a bow with each step, "I mean, partner."

When Jon was out of earshot, Hussan turned to the major domo and said, "What an honest, dishonest fellow with quite a profitable plan!"

"Yes, master," the domo replied, "I did not detect a single untruth uttered from his lips. He spoke both his mind and his heart at all times."

"Yes," Hussan continued, "tomorrow will be quite profitable for me. I wanted to do something different for this year's derby. Too bad I don't need a partner."

The major domo had never gotten used to Doyle Hussan's fiendish laugh, and this occasion was no exception.

Several blocks later, Jon was escorted to a back-alley room by his bimbo companion Lance Shield. There he was met by a mesmerist who removed the spell of honesty from him, and then by another mesmerist who removed the false identity spell from him.

A liar lying out of ignorance is not lying at all . . . and Lance was sure that Doyle Hussan had fallen for it hook, line, and sinker.

The Magic Goes Awry

The day of the Sow's Ear Derby had finally arrived, and all of the gang of scam casters, grifters, and con men were primed and ready to go.

It was a beautiful day in late spring. The weather was warm, and the sky was clear. No one would expect the onset of fog, or the possible obscuration of the view of the race. The expected clients of the Cloud of Chance had already been coached in just the right amount of surprise and indignation they would have to show in order to convince Hussan and his entourage that they were not "in" on the scam.

As it was midweek, there were very few observers milling around the perimeter of the old bathhouse. The Sow's Ear Derby was always held on a weekday, for only those with the proficiency to turn a sow's ear into a purse of silk, and then back again were allowed to enter, or to even attend. Though many audition, and easily accomplished the initial transformation, only the truly gifted were able to successfully reverse the change in the time allotted. As a result, an airborne observation vessel, complete with gambling, vice, and decadence, was bound to be popular.

Kim's wrestling heavyweights had already been transformed into beautifully svelte courtesans of the highest calibre, and they spent the remaining hours practicing lying around and looking seductive.

The bathhouse had been fully renovated for its temporary facade as an airborne casino, and just awaited the scam caster's disguise spells that would succeed in "glamourizing" it into the latest exotic wonder of the world.

Pall was prepared to play his part as archmage of the Lyceum Magus, who had turned down his box seat at the races in favor of more accommodating company, (the actual archmage had taken ill that morning, and had confined himself to his bedchamber until the disturbance in his stomach passed, thanks to an old friend of Othello's who now worked in his kitchen), and was currently being helped into his collegiate robes by Kim.

"You know the place looks pretty good," he commented, "even without the glamour."

"It's those lighter-than-air balloons," Kim offered. "Imagine that, they float in the air on their own, without any magical help whatsoever."

"If you ever left the grift, you could always become a decorator."

"Not on your life," she replied, pecked him on the cheek, and took off to help the girls with their lounging.

Jon, also now in costume, approached Pall who was now partaking of a few puffs of smoke from a slightly run-down hookah.

"Do you think I need the mind spell again?" he asked.

"Nah," said the older grifter, "he thinks he's taking you. Why should he worry? Remember, the first mark of a prime mark is arrogance. I wouldn't be surprised if he just showed up with some of his strongarm goons, and left the brain boys at home. And don't you worry about the goons. The girls can handle them."

Pall continued, "After today your part is done, and all you'll have to do is lay low till the rest is over. Once I show up with my entourage of big mouths tomorrow, threatening to expose him as a liar and a cheat, we'll get our way. And then it's on to greener pastures."

"New lessons to learn," said Jon.

"New scams to cast," added Pall.

"New cons to con and bees to sting," they finished together.

Jon and Pall then shook hands, and took their places as the illusionary crowd began to form.

* * *

Doyle Hussan arrived right on time, and as Pall predicted, with only a few strongarm goons in tow. He quickly sought out Jon, greeting him with the predatory smile of a tiger prepping for lunch.

"The gold arrived, as promised, I presume," the mage mobster offered.

"But of course," Jon answered. "You are now the proud co-owner of this opulent flying pleasure palace, partner."

Hussan continued to smile, as his stooges took off with some of the local hostesses. Hussan could not find it in his heart to tell them that, given the real identity of Jon's bimbo from the day before, they might be in for a rude surprise should they find themselves getting too involved. He kept his place at Jon's side, taking in the palace's opulence.

"We should be levitating shortly. It is almost mid-afternoon. Plenty of time for the race, eh partner?"

Hussan, still smiling, placed the iron bar that was his arm on Jon's shoulder. "Tarry a moment, good sir," he said, "I'm afraid that there has been a change of plan. I've decided I don't really need a partner. My boys will collect the proceeds of today's venture upon our return. But don't worry, I'm sure I'll keep you on, as a cabin boy perhaps."

Jon put on his best faux rage.

"But you said," he cried in a hushed whisper.

"I lied," the mage mobster explained, "something which I am quite good at. I am also good at taking out my wrath on those who lack an acute grasp of the obvious, as in who has the upper hand, if you catch my drift. Now, see to my guests, and get this ship on the clouds. After all, clients in an establishment owned and controlled by Doyle Hussan cannot be disappointed."

Jon sulked off to join Kim behind the bar, hoping that he had been convincing. As he crossed the room he began to notice that it didn't seem as crowded as it had before, or as opulent even.

That was when he noticed that Pall now looked like Pall, and the girls like the goons' worst nightmares . . . and then the casino floor that they were standing on lurched to the side, settling at an uneven tilt on the no-longer-magically-smooth foundation. This levitating gaming parlor wasn't going anywhere.

"What happened?" he cried to the older scam master.

Kid Abdul, who a moment ago had been drifting in a controlled pattern over the gaming floor, held aloft by magically navigated hot air balloons, ready to direct the casino's ascension, dropped from the air, his fall cushioned by a pile of dung that had formerly been a fountain of gold. Regaining his feet, he tried to collect his composure, unsure of how many marks were in the immediate area, and finally burst out with, "You're not going to believe what I've seen! I was drifting around the periphery doing the usual amount of tricks when I decided to look out over the city. I couldn't believe what I was seeing. A wave of destructive chaos seemed to pass over like the shadow of doom. Our once beautiful city of illusions had become a junkyard of dirt and spittle. Airborne castles were crashing to the ground. Carts and carpets ground to a halt. I couldn't believe what was happening around me, and then, poof, down I came."

"Something must have gone haywire. A spell overload, or something," Pall conjectured.

Just then a familiar voice piped up from behind the bar.

"I'm back," said the resonant human voice of the ebony-unto-gray spell caster named Othello who had only seconds before been a cat. "What happened?"

"I don't know," Pall replied, "but it's good to have you back."

Kid Abdul ventured an opinion.

"I've heard about instances out at sea where sailors

have come across dead spots where magic doesn't work. Perhaps one has descended on the city."

"What about Doyle Hussan?" Jon cried. "We're all doomed."

All heads turned to the spot where Doyle, the eight-foot-tall, iron-bar-strong, mage mobster had been standing, everyone fully anticipating his oncoming wrath. What they beheld instead was quite a surprise.

Standing in his place was a bent and broken old crone, cowering at the masses.

"Go away," she cried, "I am Doyle Hussan, the great and powerful. Feel my wrath. Experience my lack of mercy."

Even Doyle's stooges had to laugh, as the crone further shrank in humiliation.

"Wait until the boys see this," one of the goons shouted in a high-pitched voice that revealed his eunuch origins. "C'mon guys."

The strongarm eunuch took the crone in his arms and followed by his companions, took off for the palace of Doyle Hussan, the formerly great and powerful.

Epilogue

Though the magic returned in about an hour, the ensuing chaos went on for days.

No one ever heard of Doyle Hussan again, and the city was none the poorer for it.

Othello remained in human form, probably owing to no one reinstigating the transformation spell in Hussan's absence, and decided to try his hand at some easier sleights of hand in the surrounding suburbs.

The gang, satisfied at a job well done, even if it finished differently from the originally intended plan, split the gold that Hussan had delivered for the purchase of the bathhouse, and went their separate ways, back on the grift, in search of the perfect con.

As for Jon and Pall, this was the beginning of a beautiful friendship, one built on mutual trust (in each other and their abilities—but in no one else).

ALTERNATIVE MEDICINE

Judith R. Conly

"Kurrush, you're in my light again," Zoë snapped. "Can't you—" Her assistant dodged as she reached past his broad chest to seize the handle of the glass-bottomed oil lamp that was the sole source of illumination in the storeroom. Holding the lamp in the air at shoulder height between herself and the wall, she told it, "Stay put," and released it to the spell that would keep it suspended until someone's hand moved it. That was better. "We could use another lamp in here," she said with an apologetic half-smile that softened the strong lines of her face. "In this light I can barely tell rosemary from pine needles."

"But they feel completely—" At Zoë's scowl, which brought her dark brows together over the nose that dominated the rest of her features, Kurrush cut short his puzzled comment. Past experience should have kept him from irritating his employer any further when she was already on edge from being enclosed in a small space, even for the time required to unpack the latest shipment of herbs, both medicinal and culinary. After all, it had not taken long for him to realize that his head-and-a-half advantage in height was a benefit only in that it gave him easy access to upper shelves, and that the muscular good looks that made him so popular with the neighborhood girls only attracted Zoë's attention when she needed him to lift something.

"And they've shorted us on the willow bark. Of all things." She gathered her long black curls in one hand and used them to fan her neck. "I could use some myself for the headache I've got from deciphering their packing list. I wish willow trees weren't so hard on water pipes. I'd grow my own. The joys of being a city healer ..." She sighed. "I suppose I shouldn't complain. At least we didn't lose the whole inventory in the fire."

She closed her ebony eyes against the sting of tears. *The only thing we didn't lose.* The fire that had cost her parents their lives just ten months ago remained as fresh in her mind as this morning's breakfast. *This time last year, I was not alone.* The structural walls of the house, magically warded against fire and wind, and the climate-controlled storeroom were all that had survived the blaze that had swept through the two-story dwelling late one summer night. Once in a while she still fancied that she caught a lingering smell of smoke, even though she had personally approved the cleansing that the house had been given before she could bear the idea of refurnishing and moving back into it.

"Patient in the waiting room!" the front door announced.

Zoë's eyes snapped open, instantly cleared of memories. She flashed an evil grin up at Kurrush, like a child who has found an excuse not to do chores, and slipped out of the storeroom.

In the waiting room sat Zoë's neighbor Irene, a timid woman of about thirty, and her youngest son, Michael. The boy was covered with dirt from head to toe, except for his cheeks and chin, which his tears had washed clean. He supported his left forearm gently with his right hand. His face wore the set expression of an eight-year-old in considerable pain but determined to be brave in front of the grown-ups.

"Michael!" Zoë exclaimed. "What have you—what happened to you? Let me see. Kurrush! Get me a bowl of water and a cloth for washing."

She settled herself into the chair next to the lad and looked at the arm that he held out for her inspection. The dirt did nothing to disguise the wrist-to-elbow swelling. A cursory cleaning revealed purple bruises concentrated midway between wrist and elbow.

"Now, Michael, can you move your fingers for me? If you can't, don't worry," she cautioned, as the attempt made the boy bite his lip against the pain.

"Is it broken, Healer?" Irene asked anxiously.

"It certainly looks that way," replied Zoë, "but it's nothing I can't fix." She gave mother and son a confident smile. "How did it happen?"

"I was playing Magic Carpet," Michael answered. "I finally got it to go high—up by the roof—and Bastos jumped on and broke my con ... conce ..."

"Concentration?" suggested Zoë. Bastos the cat doubled as the Sphinx when Michael played Egypt.

"That's it. Con-cen-ta-tion. And the carpet fell, and so did I. Bastos is fine," he assured his mother, who gave Zoë a look that said, *What can you do with a child like this?*

"Well, I'll tell you what. You sit still, so I can keep my 'concentation,' and I'll make your arm as good as new." He nodded his head vigorously in agreement, wincing when the movement jarred the limb.

She sat back in her chair, put the palms of her fine-boned hands together, and intoned, in the language of her ancestors, the prayer with which she began all but the direst of emergency healings: "Blessed art Thou, O Lord our God, King of the Universe, Who has sanctified us with His gifts of healing." Thus calmed, she reached for the magic that was, paradoxically, both within and around her, and directed it into the broken arm, which Michael had resting across his thighs.

Both bones were broken, but the breaks were clean, and the bone ends had shifted only slightly out of alignment. The magic extension of Zoë moved them back into correct position and lent Michael's body the extra energy it needed to accelerate the knitting of the bones, until they were literally as good as new. Then she restored the circulation that had been damaged in the fall and drained the excess fluids responsible for the swelling directly into a magical elsewhere without causing further tissue damage with their passage. She retained just enough magical energy to replace what she had spent from her own reserves and released the rest to return to its source.

Michael's dark eyes were wide with amazement. "Healer, Healer, I felt how you did that! Really, I did," he added to his mother when she tried to quiet him.

Zoë looked at him assessingly. "You know, Mistress Irene, I wouldn't be surprised if he did. His magical abilities have consistently been ahead of his age level. Look at his trick with the 'magic carpet.' And remember when he gave his father a halo? He was only four."

The boy was torn between pride at his accomplishments and annoyance at being discussed as if he weren't there. "I bet I could do it myself," he interjected.

"Don't you dare, young man!" his mother warned.

"Your mother's right. Healing's not a game. If you don't know what to do, and why, and in what order, you can do more harm than good."

"How long does it take to learn all that?" the lad asked.

"Well . . ." Zoë considered. "My father started teaching me when I was six, and I was fifteen before he'd let me do anything more complicated than closing cuts without his supervision. That was eight years ago—about the time you were born. Of course, he let me do more and more on my own, as I showed him that I knew what I was doing, but he still had things to teach me when he died last year." *I will not cry. I will not cry.*

The young face fell. "I'll *never* learn it all!" Both women laughed.

"I probably won't either," Zoë admitted, rising to her feet. She fetched a finger-sized packet from a moisture-sealed jar on her desk and handed it to Irene. "There may be a bit of residual stiffness or ache in that arm. This should be enough willow bark to take care of it. If he's still uncomfortable tomorrow morning, let me know."

Michael grimaced. "Willow-bark tea. Yuck."

"If you'd be more careful and not hurt yourself, you wouldn't need it," Zoë pointed out mock-sternly.

"Thank you, Healer," Irene said, twisting the belt of her tunic nervously around her fingers. "About your fee. My husband—Nikos gets paid today. I'll send him around with the money when he gets home tonight. And . . ." She hesitated. "I miss them, too," she blurted out, and all but ran for the door, pushing her son ahead of her.

Zoë stared after her. *She has known me since I was Michael's age. When did I become intimidating?* Zoë's mother, who had been both midwife and housewife, had assisted in Michael's birth, and the boy was named after her father, who had been friend as well as healer to most of his patients.

"Mistress?" Kurrush's hesitant voice made her conscious of the frown that furrowed the olive skin of her forehead. "Mistress, shouldn't we finish—"

A crash of breaking glass brought them racing to the storeroom. Flames were beginning to spread across the oil from the lamp, which, impossibly, had fallen to the floor, to the discarded wrappings from packets of herbs.

Zoë froze in horror, unable to break the grip of memory. *"Jump, mistress, jump!" Kurrush called from the safety of the street. She hesitated on the edge of her second-floor balcony, the smell of smoke from the bedroom behind her stinging her nose, then jumped toward her father's assistant and the small group of neighbors. Pulled off-balance by someone's helping hands, she landed on the side of one foot and felt her ankle snap. Swallowing a scream at the pain, she turned back toward her home. Flames billowed out of the waiting-room windows and doorway, and out of her own bedroom window. From the master bedroom, closed against what her old-fashioned parents considered the contagion of the night air, a few curls of smoke escaped between the slats of the shutters. She cried out and tried to move toward the house, but her ankle gave way at the first step, and she almost fell. Firm hands gripped her shoulders. "Mistress, it's too late." Sensible Kurrush. For a moment she hated him. Then his strong arms lifted her off the ground, and she buried her face in his shoulder, unable to watch the late-come firefighters at work or to look at the human remains they eventually brought out of the shell of the house that was now hers alone.*

Familiar hands moved her gently out of the storeroom doorway. After a few seconds, Kurrush returned with a pot of sand and dirt, which he spread deftly over the burgeoning flames. By the time he finished inspecting the oily mess to be certain that no pockets of fire remained, Zoë had returned to a shaky approximation of her usual composure.

She drew a deep breath, tried to form words, shook her head, and let the breath back out. The second attempt worked better. "I don't know what I'd do without you."

Kurrush's cocky grin crinkled the corners of his gray eyes. "That's what I'm here for, mistress. Hewer of wood, carrier of water, putter-out of fire . . ."

"Cleaner-up of dirt," she concluded, glowering at the filth in a bad imitation of a strict employer. "Where did it come from? I didn't think dirt was something we kept in the house."

"Remember the dwarf potted-palm tree that Mistress Helen gave you to help redecorate? The one you put behind the waiting room door?"

Zoë's grimace was not unlike Michael's reaction to

willow-bark tea. "We could forget about it until it's too dead to be repotted, couldn't we?" she asked hopefully.

"Forget about what?" Kurrush's look of innocence was totally unconvincing.

"At least until we figure out how a lamp with a permanent 'stay put' spell on it could fall." She poked gingerly at the pile of dirt with one sandal-clad foot until she unearthed the edge of a piece of the lamp. She pulled out the fragment with delicate thumb and forefinger, shook off the worst of the grime, and carried the relatively clean shard into the kitchen, where she did her best thinking.

Setting her prize on the table, she sat in her favorite chair, and asked the morsel, "How could you have worn out a simple 'stay put' spell, laid and guaranteed permanent by the best statis spell master in the whole city of Constantinople, in less than a year? Hmm?" The glass trembled slightly, as if in answer. "Let's take a closer look. . . ." She reached for the magic and gasped, her breath stolen by shock. "Kurrush, it's gone. The magic. It's *not there*."

"Mistress?" His voice cracked with confusion and disbelief.

"The magic is gone," she repeated, as if each word were a leech that had to be pulled off her tongue. "Try it yourself. You have more than enough ability for that." She waited while he did his own variety of reaching several times.

He shook his head. "Gone. Completely gone. Mistress, what will you do? Your healing . . ."

"Indeed. My healing. And the people who rely on it. On *me*." Her narrow jaw was set grimly.

The lamp fragment quivered again, and the cooking utensils that hung from a frame over the table swung back and forth as the ground trembled beneath the house.

"What was that?" Kurrush asked in alarm, springing to his feet.

"Earthquake? No, I'll bet . . . oh, God. Think of the palaces of the Magically Gifted—think of the Emperor's palace—held up in the air by magic. What's holding them up there now?"

"Nothing," he whispered.

"Nothing," Zoë agreed. "Think about . . . how much of the City is substance, and how much is . . . was just magic. How much is left?" She rocked back and forth in her seat, thin arms wrapped around her middle as if it too might suddenly decide to disappear. "Where are you going?" she asked Kurrush, who was striding out of the kitchen.

"To see how much of *our* neighborhood is left," he threw back over his shoulder. She scrambled to join him at the front door. "It's not too bad, actually. Not what you can see from here, anyway." They took a few steps outside to get a better view.

The most obvious absence was the alabaster surface of the street, whose creation and maintenance was the responsibility of the city government. The newly-revealed cobblestones showed the signs of many years without repair, but the magical layer that had lain above them had provided enough protection for the road to remain passable.

The buildings themselves were mostly privately owned and showed little damage. The middle-class owners, lacking the wherewithal, both magical and financial, to indulge in large-scale flights of fancy, had taken great care to keep the substance of their property in good condition. True, the jeweler's sign was now dingy paint instead of glowing gold and gems, and the florist's window displayed asters and chrysanthemums instead of orchids and lotus blossoms, but the basic structures were in no danger of collapse.

With a sigh of relief, Zoë returned to her own sturdy home, noting in passing that her red-and-white caduceus sign was overdue for a new coat of paint. Kurrush followed her back to the kitchen, where she dropped into her chair and rested her chin in her hands.

"Now what?" she demanded of the air. "Everything I spent three-quarters of my life learning—every skill—everything that qualified me to be a healer, and not just a healer's daughter—gone. Just like that. And the people who have learned to accept me as a healer ... What can I do for them now? When they come to this house—to me —expecting to find healing, what do I do?" Her fingers slid up into the hair at her temples and tugged, as if to pull an answer out by the roots.

"Your mother used to make your father camomile tea for his nerves," Kurrush suggested, a deliberate *non sequitur*.

"That sounds good ... But the firestarter won't work!" she wailed, distracted from the self-pity that had threatened to escalate into hysteria.

"Relax, mistress." He patted her reassuringly on the shoulder. "I was a country boy, remember. Getting dragged off to the Big City hasn't made me forget how to start a fire the old-fashioned way." He rummaged around in a drawer for flint and steel, muttering to himself, "Fourteen years in the hind end of Persia has to be good for *something* ..." He never had the chance to find his tools.

A young man, whose fine Egyptian-cotton clothing identified him as a servant in a well-to-do household, burst into the kitchen, breathless and disheveled. "Healer, come quickly!" he gasped. "The master—his heart—he—oh, please, come quickly!"

Zoë sprang to her feet, eyes wide with alarm. "Oh, dear God, Master Chrysander's heartbeat spell. It doesn't work any more. What—" She paused, pushing her thoughts to greater speed, then dashed into the storeroom, grabbed a small bottle, and ran back. "Got your breath back, Alexis? Good. Let's go. Don't just stand there, Kurrush. I need you. Come on!"

The normal ten-minute trip to the higher-class district

where master contractor Chrysander had chosen to build his own house seemed to take a lifetime on the uneven surface of the street. Twice Zoë, whose mind swung like a pendulum between fear-born emptiness and kaleido-scopic thought fragments that dispersed too fast to be useful, almost lost her footing entirely on the newly unfa-miliar pavement.

Chrysander was one of her father's oldest patients and friends. Since the fire, he had been almost a second father to her. In his youth he had worked his way up from construction worker to contractor and had later made his fortune in the short-lived fad for houses made of real materials that had amused the Magically Gifted two decades before. He had also taken charge of restor-ing the interior of Zoë's house after the fire, trusting her to repay him gradually as she earned the money.

If he dies . . . Zoë blinked back the tears that blurred her vision and forced her thoughts to focus down to one: *It's up to me to see that he doesn't. But* how? *How can I help—how can I determine what would help and what would harm—when I no longer have a sure way of per-ceiving what is wrong? And yet . . . How could I forgive myself if I did nothing? How could I live with myself, much less continue to function as a healer, wondering if my fear of failure killed him? No. If making my best effort to help means that I must risk harming him, that is a chance I have to take. Taking chances is part of my job. Cowardice is not.*

The familiar facade of Chrysander's mansion was unchanged by the absence of magic. His wife, Euphemia, met the trio at the front door. "Thank God you've come. He's upstairs in his study. He collapsed there, and we didn't want to move him until you got here," she explained, practically dragging Zoë up the majestic front staircase.

"You did the right thing," Zoë confirmed. She freed her wrist from the older woman's painfully tight grip and moved ahead, into the study, where an overdressed man in his early thirties, assisted by three servants, was preparing to lift a prone male form on a sheet. "Leave him alone!" she ordered, hurrying to her patient's side, almost throwing the bottle of medicine onto a nearby table as she passed.

"Well, well. It's the little healer, come to help poor Papa," drawled the heir to the household, smoothing his fine silk tunic over the beginning of a paunch. He extended an arm to block her passage and leaned toward her in forced intimacy. "I told you last time: Marry me, and you can be his full-time nurse. I *am* overdue for a new wife," he murmured in a voice too quiet for anyone else to overhear.

"You take your name *much* too seriously, Theodoros," Zoë snapped as she pulled away, eyes flashing with fury. *Gift of God, indeed. Gift to God would be better—preferably as a eunuch monk!* She had forgotten neither ten years of such advances nor the old bruises that had mottled his late wife's body in addition to the broken neck from the fall that had killed her. "Kurrush, clear the room. I can't work with all these people in the way." Euphemia started to protest. "I'm sorry, Mistress Euphemia, you too. Here—you're in charge of making sure that we're not disturbed. By anyone." The responsibility seemed to satisfy the worried wife, and with the aid of her authority it was only a matter of seconds until the healer was alone with her patient and her assistant.

At Zoë's touch, Chrysander's eyelids lifted, and he struggled to speak. "Z-zo'—good hands."

She frowned. "Don't waste your strength talking, or you might find yourself out of everyone's hands." He was not the type of man who responded to coddling.

"Not waste." He fought for another breath. "My will—house is yours. Gift."

"No, it's not," she replied emphatically. "You're going to live to collect everything I owe. *If* you shut up." She placed one gentle finger on his quivering lips and shook her head. He snorted and surrendered, closing his eyes as if each lid weighed as much as one of his building blocks.

She sat back on her heels and wondered where to begin without the magical vision that allowed her to see inside the body. *Start with the obvious.* She put one hand on her own chest and located the place where the heartbeat felt strongest. She found the corresponding spot on Chrysander's chest and felt ... so little. She leaned over and pressed her ear to his chest. The beat was weak and alarmingly irregular, and even that slight pressure affected the rhythm of his breathing.

"Kurrush, bring me that medicine and a glass of water. Quickly!" She added a few drops of medication to the water and smiled thanks to her assistant for thinking to provide the shaft of a pen to stir the mixture. "Now lift him up for me. Getting this into him could be tricky."

As Kurrush raised Chrysander's shoulders, the waxy-skinned head fell back slackly. "No!" Zoë cried in anguish. "Put him down!" Again she listened for his pulse. Nothing. Incoherent thoughts chased each other around like leaves in a whirlwind.

"Mistress?" Kurrush looked from her to the door.

"No. Not yet. I'm not giving up so easily." *Remember Papa's first commandment: thou shalt not panic. You are a healer, not a silly little girl.* Her nails dug into her palms as if the sheer strength of her grip could force her recalcitrant mind to calm.

What would her father do? She could almost hear his voice. *"Think, Chaya,"* he would say with the loving exasperation that usually accompanied his use of her Hebrew name. *"What is the purpose of this procedure? Why are you doing it?"* Why had she created the spell that had kept Chrysander alive for the last several months? To remind his heart what its rhythm was supposed to be. Why? To keep his blood circulating throughout his body. Why? Because there was a ... something ... in the blood that he needed to stay alive—a something that entered the body through the lungs, with the breath, so at this point simply stimulating the heart would not be enough. Her mind's eye could almost visualize what the magic would have shown her so clearly.

First, supply some of the element that the body requires. *I hope there's enough left in the air I exhale.* Zoë knelt at her patient's head and opened his mouth. Suppressing a brief, incongruous flash of modesty, she placed her lips over his and breathed confidently. A stream of air from his nostrils tickled her cheek, and his chest remained motionless.

Close the nose, Chaya, or it will let out what you put in. She pinched his nostrils closed and, with a wordless prayer for help, breathed into his mouth a second time. She was gratified to see his chest rise with the air that she supplied. She gave him one more breath, for luck.

Now for his heart. She surveyed his broad chest. Her heartbeat spell had applied gentle rhythmic pressure directly to the heart whenever it faltered. Without the magic, the inside of Chrysander's body was no longer accessible. What could she do from the outside to achieve a similar result? *Think fast, Chaya.*

... The heart lies under the breastbone, there. She identified the spot with the fingertips of one hand, then replaced the tips with a wide-spread hand, realizing that she would need a larger surface to receive the required weight. *If I press there, in rhythm, like his pulse—my pulse ...* Finding her own heartbeat was easy. Halting her actions long enough to capture and remember its speed was not.

"One-two-three-four," she counted under her breath. *Like a march. A triumphal march.* "One-two-three-four." She placed both hands firmly on her patient's chest and leaned. "One-two-"

Crack. A rib snapped under her weight.

"Damn!" If his ribs were not strong enough to hold her, what was? The breastbone itself was her only option. If it, too, proved too weak ...

Zoë shifted position so the heel of one hand rested

squarely on the breastbone, then placed the other hand on top of the first. She resumed her count. "One-two-three-four." Much better.

She did three more counts of four, then realized that Chrysander had gone too long without air. Returning to his head, she gave him two breaths, followed by another round of chest compressions. Then more air. Then more pressure. The third time, Kurrush was in position and supplied the air. She wanted to hug him in gratitude but was forced to settle for her biggest grin.

After they completed a total of six breath-and-pressure cycles, Zoë stopped them to listen for a pulse. Nothing. They did another six cycles. She listened for a pulse. Nothing. With less optimism, they did another six cycles. She listened for a pulse.

"Yes! It's weak, but it's regular. He's alive, Kurrush! He's alive!" Her whole body glowed with joy.

His shining face mirrored her enthusiasm. "You saved him, mistress."

"*We* saved him," she corrected. "I couldn't have done it without you. And he's not exactly stable yet. I'd feel better if we could get that medicine into him, but we need him conscious for that. I don't want to risk choking him."

They did not have long to wait. After a few minutes, during which short time Chrysander's breathing and pulse both grew considerably stronger, his eyes opened and struggled to focus.

"Zoë?" His voice was barely audible.

"I'm here, Master Chrysander." She bent over him to catch his words.

"Am I—?" He ran out of breath and frowned in frustration.

"Going to live? Of course, you stubborn old man," she replied, as if his survival had never been in doubt.

His hand groped for hers, and she gave it to him. "Good hands," he said, squeezing weakly. "Father—" *breath* "—would—" *breath* "—be proud." *Deep breath.*

Rendered speechless with surprise, she returned the pressure of his hand.

"Mistress?" Kurrush stood over her, holding the glass of water and medicine. Sensible Kurrush. For a moment she loved him. She relieved him of the drinking vessel. He knelt at Chrysander's head and lifted the patient's head and shoulders to lean them against his thighs.

The older man drank the liquid without argument, sipping slowly until the glass was empty. Then he was restored to his prone position, exhausted by even that small effort.

Zoë checked his pulse once more and, satisfied that she could leave him under her assistant's supervision, decided that she could not postpone facing the crowd outside the study. She slipped out the door and closed it quietly behind her.

A chorus of voices greeted her. It stilled almost immediately at her raised hand. "He'll live," she stated simply.

"Thank God," Euphemia said, and burst into tears.

The healer put an arm around the other woman's shoulders and glared at Theodoros, whose mouth was open, no doubt to say something clever. "You can all go about your business. Your mistress will tell you more later, after I tell her." To her amazement, they all accepted her high-handed order.

She drew Euphemia into the study after her. The distressed wife, eyes still streaming, ran to look down at Chrysander. Zoë leaned against the door and allowed Kurrush the honor of preventing their hostess from throwing herself on her husband's chest.

By the time Euphemia regained control of her emotions, Zoë was completing written instructions for the continuing care of her patient. "This should cover all eventualities for the next week or so. Pay particular attention to his medication. Tincture of foxglove is a very powerful stimulant, and if it's used improperly, it can do more harm than good." *Translation: it can kill him, but that's not something a nervous relative needs to know right now.* "Don't move him more than absolutely necessary. If you have a litter that will fit through the doorway, you can carry him into the bedroom on it. Otherwise, bring a mattress in here for him to lie on until I tell you he's stable enough to be moved farther."

The older woman's eyes were troubled. "You make it sound like he's not out of danger."

"He's not," the healer confirmed, "but he will be soon as long as you follow instructions." She looked pointedly at the piece of paper in Euphemia's hand. "I'll be back tomorrow to check on him. In the meantime, just let him rest." She spoke with a confidence that she did not entirely feel and was relieved to see her client's face lose its tension. The problem with the healing magic's instantaneous results was that it made anything less dramatic seem inadequate.

The medical team made a hasty withdrawal while the lady of the house was distracted by questions from son and servants. The walk home passed in companionable silence, except for the occasional observation of a change caused by the absence of magic.

The kitchen had never looked better to Zoë, even if the hanging pots and pans no longer had ornately inlaid bottoms. She dropped into her favorite chair and pillowed her head on her forearms.

"Hungry, mistress?" Kurrush asked.

"Hmm? Now that you mention it, yes." She watched as he got the stove started.

"What would you like to eat?"

"What's the most perishable, now that our cold closet isn't? Fresh meat, eggs, butter, milk . . . We'll be feasting for a few days. After that . . ." She shook her head. "So many changes, and no time to prepare."

He pulled an assortment of foodstuffs out of the erstwhile cold closet, and laid them on the counter near the stove. "That's not all. How long do you think the city will be able to go on providing gas for cooking?" He put a pan on the stove and threw in a chunk of butter. As it melted, it was followed by other ingredients that hissed and crackled as they met the hot pan.

"God bless my old-fashioned mama. She told me once that everyone thought she was crazy for insisting on a stove that would burn wood as well as gas. It won't be the same, but at least we'll have hot food." Thoughts of her mother brought feelings of nostalgia and regret, but remarkably little pain.

Kurrush sprinkled in pinches of two spices from the jars on the counter, thought a moment, and added a third. Zoë lifted her head and sniffed the air with interest. "Where did you learn to cook like that?" *And how could I have not noticed before?*

The young man shrugged. "I've always known how. It's easy. It's all in the spicing. I just know what goes together. You know. Like the herbs for healing."

Zoë's mouth fell open. "But, Kurrush, I don't *just know* what healing herbs do. Most people don't. Most people have to study them—we spend years studying them. Didn't anyone ever tell you?" A thought struck her. "Maybe that's why Papa . . ." Her voice trailed off as she tried, and failed, to find a nice way to say, "why Papa bought you."

"Don't worry, mistress," he said reassuringly. "My past doesn't bother me any more. Your father freed me as soon as he could. And I've had four years to forgive my father for selling me when the crops failed. If he hadn't, I might still be down on the farm, trying to get rocks to grow." He ducked his head and turned back to the stove. Perhaps the frying pan really did need immediate attention, or perhaps he was not quite as free of bitterness as he behaved.

The dishes were in a cabinet near Zoë. She put two plates on the table. Her stomach growled as Kurrush served his creation. Out of habit, he collected the unused portion of his ingredients and opened the cold closet to put them away. She stopped in mid-chew as he exclaimed, "Mistress, it's cold! The cold closet is cold again!"

She swallowed hastily. Then, still fearing the worst, she reached cautiously for the magic; the look of concentration on her assistant's face told her that he was doing the same. The old familiar tool and ally, so sorely missed in the last hour, had returned.

"Thank God! And yet ... Suppose it decides to go away again?" Her confidence, once shaken, was not so easily restored.

"Heaven forbid," muttered Kurrush.

"But if it does," she persisted, "shouldn't we think about alternatives? Shouldn't we be able to prevent ... falling lamps, for example? A hook in the ceiling might not be quite as convenient as a 'stay put' spell, but it's a lot better than a lamp falling on a patient!

"And the healing ... Kurrush, the prayer I say talks about 'gifts of healing'—gifts, plural. Not just magic. Papa understood that. I didn't, until today. What about *planning* more procedures like the one I had to ... improvise today? What about your instinct for herbs? What about—"

"Patient in the waiting room!" Was it Zoë's imagination, or did the front door's voice sound more cheerful than before? She grabbed one last hasty bite of her meal before abandoning the rest.

Life was back to normal.

THE BEGGAR'S REVOLT

Michael Scott

"Of your charity, lord . . . lady?"

The thrusting hand was ignored as the elegantly dressed couple swept past. Stiicho was about to mutter a curse in their wake, but he only had a few left and he decided to keep them for someone more deserving.

The beggar turned back to scanning the crowd streaming out from the great cathedral, his single rheumy eye expertly sorting through those who might give, those who definitely would not, those who could, but wouldn't and those who shouldn't, but still did. He saw one of his regular patrons wending her way through the crowd towards him, cruel black eyes fixed greedily on him, thin lips pursed in what she imagined was an expression of pity.

A handful of copper tinkled into his woven basket.

"Aaah, my lady, you honor me. The gods will surely smile on you." The beggar's voice was thick with phlegm, the words broken, and when Stiicho raised his head, the livid scar where his throat had been cut was clearly visible on his scrawny neck.

270

The woman gathered in her skirts and crouched on the step beside him. "Did you hear about Maggot?"

Stiicho nodded. "Aye, I heard," he said softly. Maggot had worked the West Gate, close to the river. He'd fallen asleep under the bridge as usual, but at some time during the night, the upper reaches of the Bhosphor had over-flowed and had driven the water rats out of the sewers.

Mercifully, the old man had never woken up.

"You could end up like that," the woman hissed.

Stiicho glanced sidelong at the woman. "Like what, my lady?" he asked bitterly.

"Torn apart. Unmourned ... except by beggars like yourself. And in two days you will have forgotten about him."

"He will not be forgotten," Stiicho said simply. "And I do not fear death. My days are numbered by the gods, likewise the manner of my death."

"But it doesn't have to be like that. Come with me. I can offer you shelter, food ..."

"And religion," Stiicho said with a crooked, broken-toothed smile. "Isn't that what you're offering in return? Faith for bread. I heard you've taken to converting the beggars to this new religion from the east." He laughed wetly. "I can't put much credence in a religion which finds its converts on the streets."

The hard-eyed woman surged to her feet and, for a moment, Stiicho thought she was about to kick out at him. Then she composed herself. "My god is offering you redemption. When He comes again, He had promised to make the least of men, the greatest, and to throw down those in authority."

Stiicho suddenly understood. "So that is why you are collecting the beggars! So when your god comes, he will turn them into kings ... and they will repay you." He threw back his head and laughed, until his breath caught in his lungs and he began wheezing, tears flowing down his pitted cheeks. When he wiped his eyes on the back of his sleeve and looked up again, she had gone. The beggar laughed again. Half a year ago, the woman had been caught butchering cats—because her auguries had told her that a cat would carry pestilence into the city. The Lady Lisel was mad, but she was not out of place in this city of madness: only the sane were looked upon as freaks and wonders, and only the mad thrived.

Stiicho checked over the crowd again, and decided that he might as well take his midmorning break now. He could be back on the cathedral steps in the early afternoon and, if the weather remained mild, he could stay late. Coming to his feet, he decided he'd check in on Einar, the weather caster, just to see what weather he and his fellow casters had decided for today.

The inconspicuous beggar hobbled back toward the Grand Concourse, allowing the atmosphere of Constantinople to wash over him. Although he'd lived in the City at the Center of the World all his life, it still had the capacity to amaze and delight him. Constantly changing, forever altering at the whim and fancy of the Magically Gifted, or in accordance with the latest architectural fashions, many of their palaces hung suspended in the air, decadent examples of their incredible power.

While almost everyone in the city had some magical ability, a few were the Magically Gifted, the overlords, those people chosen by faith or gifted by the gods with a magical ability a hundred times more powerful than normal humans. Anyone could become one of the Magically Gifted, but in the last few generations the Thirteen Families had been breeding amongst themselves in an attempt to retain control. A season ago, the city had been in uproar when all the new-born male children were snatched by the elite Sere Warriors. All but two of the children had been returned to their parents. No one knew what had happened to the other two, though it was commonly believed that their Ability was incredibly powerful and that they had been adopted by one of the Families. Stiicho, however, believed that they had been put to death. He knew how the Families worked.

The beggar passed under the shadow cast by Ya-Sah's palace and quickly made the Sign of Horns, closing his right hand into a fist, extending index and little finger, warding off evil. The majority of the Magically Gifted were neither good nor evil, but Ya-Sah was one of the exceptions. On the nights of the full moon, he delighted in sending harpies down into the city to hunt for sport.

Stiicho turned into a blind alley, and ran his right hand along the weeping, foul-smelling wall. Although it looked like solid stone, his fingers touched wood, and then a metal handle. With a quick glance over his shoulder to ensure that he was not being watched, he pushed open the door and then slipped into his simple room and locked the door. If anyone had been watching, it would have seemed as if he had stepped through solid stone. The spell was a simple blind and Stiicho renewed it monthly for a dozen coppers.

Once inside the room, Stiicho straightened to his full height, and spoke the arcane *word* which allowed the body spell to fall off him ... and Stiicho the ancient, crippled and ugly beggar was replaced by a tall, raven-haired young man. Stiicho stretched, twisting his neck from side to side, working the kinks out of his muscles. The glamour gave him the appearance of an old man, but it still required quite a bit of acting ability to play the part day after day, night after night. However, it was a living.

Stiicho scooped the handful of coins out of his beggar's basket, shaking them in his big hands. One sounded wrong. Holding it up, he tilted it to the light. His lips curled as he look at the face on the coin: he was told he bore a remarkable resemblance to his cousin, Dagus, the emperor. Stiicho dug his nail into the metal, below his cousin's throat. Seven years ago, his cousin had sent two assassins to do exactly the same to him. His blunt nail imprinted a half-moon into the coin. Counterfeit. Stiicho flipped it across the room ... but it never reached the wall.

The wall vanished. Door, walls, ceiling simply disappeared. The floorboards beneath his feet were replaced by packed earth. He was standing in the street . . . except that the street had also vanished, whole rows of tenement houses disappearing, winking out of existence, one by one, bodies hanging poised in midair before plummeting to the ground, too shocked even to scream.

Numb with horror, Stiicho spoke the *word*, pulling on the body spell like armor.

It didn't work.

He spoke the spell again—it was a new one, two days old, good for another ten days—but still nothing happened.

And he realized what was happening. The magic was leaving Constantinople.

Stiicho was running even before the thought had flashed through his head. "Move, move. Run. Away from here!" He pushed his way through dazed people—some of them naked, their magical garments lost—past confused lovers, who could suddenly see their partners for what they truly were. An enormously obese old man was standing by one of the fruit stalls holding a rotten turnip in his hands, looking blankly at it. Moments earlier, he had been a slender youth, triumphant because he had discovered a prize pineapple amongst the fruit.

Standing in the middle of the fruit market, Stiicho threw back his head and bellowed. "Run. The magic has gone. The sky palaces will fall. . . ."

Even as he was speaking, there was a thunderous detonation across the city as one of the Magically Gifted's palaces plummeted onto the streets. Another and another followed. Stiicho looked upwards. Ya-Sah's enormous palace of black stone was visibly trembling. Then it began to oscillate. Spinning slowly, it descended onto the streets. But as it fell, the dark walled building disappeared, the soaring turrets and ornate arches vanishing, until only a saucer of earth and stone remained. Streamers of cold fire spun off the disc, visible evidence that someone was attempting to keep the disc in the air. But still the disc fell, until it was just above the level of the rooftops, then the saucer tilted, one edge sheering through a three-story building—built with brick and mortal on solid ground—slicing through the upper floors, cascading wood and brick and bodies into the street.

Stiicho turned away and began pushing people out of the marketplace, driving them before him with words and blows. He hauled a wizened old man to his feet and pushed him towards the street. Stiicho recognized his clothes: he was Solon, the dealer in slaves. Formerly he appeared as a tall, elegant, foppish youth; now he was revealed in his true identity, old and diseased.

A woman stumbled before Stiicho, her child falling from its pouch on her back. Stiicho caught the babe before it hit the ground. Catching the woman he hauled her upright and hurried her from the square, still carrying the child.

The remnants of Ya-Sah's palace finally settled on the market square, tons of stone and soil crushing everything beneath it, the thunderous sounds echoing and re-echoing through the city. In the long silence that followed, the wails of the injured and dying seemed unusually loud.

"The magic is gone," Stiicho said aloud. He stopped, realizing that he had shouted, and that the people standing around were turning to look at him. The baby in his arms began to cry and he handed the child back to its mother.

"The magic is gone," he repeated.

The Lady Lisel pushed through the crowd. Without the magical spells to enhance her appearance, she looked old and haggard, her luxurious mane of raven hair now revealed as gray wisps on a pink scalp. "The day of judgement is at hand. The Lord is coming."

A series of elongated shadows darted across the sky as the metal skyships that were the Emperor's pride and joy, fell into the city, close to the river. Plumes of flame and black smoke erupted upwards.

"It is the prophecy fulfilled," Lisel continued, eyes wide with delight, spittle flecking her lips. " 'The city shall crumble to dust beneath the wrath of my gaze.' "

The crowd began moving uneasily.

"My god is coming . . . and He is a vengeful god." Lisel hopped from foot to foot. "Abase yourselves now, pray to Him for protection."

Some of the crowd were beginning to kneel, when Stiicho snapped, "Get up. This is not the end of the world—simply the end of magic." He pointed towards the Grand Concourse. "Those fools have used all the magic in the world, wasted it by their excesses." He gestured to the destruction behind him. "Look again. It is only the magic that is gone. The magical buildings, the magical garments . . ." he touched Lisel's strawlike hair ". . . the magical appearances. And if the magic is gone—then the Magically Gifted are no more. All men are equal. Do you not see what this means?"

The crowd looked at him blankly.

"It means that we can now make our own destinies. A man shall be judged on his merits, and not by some quirk of fate that gifts him with magical ability."

"I know you," Lisel suddenly whispered, raising a sticklike arm to point at him. "I know you."

Stiicho ignored the woman. "This is the beginning of a new age for Constantinople, an age of reason, of science . . ."

"You are Stiicho, the Pretender!" Lisel backed away from him, eyes suddenly wide with fear. The emperor had declared Stiicho a wolfhead, the size of the reward an indication of just how much Dagus wanted him dead.

"Stiicho . . . Stiicho . . . Stiicho . . ."

The name ran around the growing crowd in a rising murmur. Finally, Solon the slave dealer looked at Stiicho. "Are you Stiicho, Pretender to the Throne?"

"I am Stiicho. But I am no pretender. My cousin

Dagus assumed the throne because his magical ability was stronger than mine. I argued that science, and not magic, should rule the City at the Center of the World." He raised his hands as the dust settled and Constantinople, in all its ruined glory, was revealed. A few houses of stone remained standing amidst empty shells or abandoned lots where, formally, fine houses and palaces had stood. "And see, I have been proven right. I wanted all houses to be built of stone, not magical constructions. But my cousin tried to have me assassinated, and when that failed, claimed that I had attempted to assassinate him. He declared me wolfhead and drove me from the city. But I returned. I've lived here, watching, waiting."

It was almost the truth. In the beginning he had thought about leading a revolt against the palace. He'd entertained grandiose schemes about assuming his rightful place ... but as the years had gone by the dreams had faded, until he had finally come to accept that he could never stand against Dagus and the rest of the Magically Gifted.

Until now.

"You could lead us, Stiicho," someone said from the heart of the crowd, as if reading his thoughts.

"Yes ..."

"Lead us ..."

"Lead us ..."

"Emperor Stiicho ..."

And suddenly he was moving, hurrying down the narrow streets, heading back to the Grand Concourse, and the crowd was behind him, growing, swelling, and they were taking up his name, repeating and repeating it until it swelled to an mighty uproar.

"Stiicho ..."

"Stiicho ..."

"STIICHO!"

He strode out onto the Central Avenue, tall and straight and proud, numb with the realization that a lifetime of dreams was about to be realized. The magic had

gone away ... and with it the emperor's power, the
menagerie of manticore and werewolves were gone from
the grounds, the ravenous serpents vanished from the
moat, the walls of fire that protected the throne room
would have been extinguished, even the minotaur, the
emperor's personal bodyguard, would be no more. Dagus
was just another man, petty, weak and spoiled, worthless
without his magic. Stiicho, who had never had magic of
his own to rely upon was the stronger now.

The crowd swept past the steps of the cathedral where,
less than an hour ago, Stiicho had been begging. The
stone building was untouched, but its magical stained-
glass window, which showed ever-changing images of the
Emperor, was gone. Stiicho considered it an omen.

He turned once and looked back at the crowd—and
was shocked by its size. The handful of people from the
marketplace had swelled to many hundred, and more and
more were joining.

Stiicho threw back his head and howled his triumph.
Harald the Seer had foretold that this would be a week
to remember, "momentous events" the wild-eyed fortune
teller had predicted. Momentous events, indeed. He had
opened his eyes as a beggar this morning, but he would
sleep an emperor.

The emperor's palace of jade and gold was at the end
of the Avenue of Stones, which was lined with frozen
statues of the emperor's enemies. Occasionally, he
removed a limb before turning them to stone so that
they could remain alive but forever in agony. The statues
were gone, the plinths empty except in one or two cases
where a slumped body was bleeding its last, its agony at
an end. The released statues were standing bemused
along the edges of the road.

"Join us," Stiicho called. "The magic has gone. Claim
your revenge on an unforgiving emperor."

The warriors acted first, stepping out to join the crowd,
the artists and politicians following them. The warriors

who had displeased Dagus or his father or his father
before him, took up positions on either side of Stiicho.

"Where are we going," an eagle-eyed veteran, wearing
armor of the previous century, asked.

"To the palace," Stiicho said. "To overthrow the
emperor."

"You have the Family's looks," the warrior remarked
shrewdly.

"I was a cousin—without magic. I was considered
inferior."

The warrior smiled. "But no longer it seems."

"No longer."

With the arrival of the warriors, the rabble fell into
more orderly rows, and an air of determination settled
over them. By the time they reached the end of the
avenue, they were almost completely silent.

The emperor's palace was a tumbled ruin, the shell of
stone looking forlorn and decayed without its magical
mantle. Hundreds of people—courtiers and servants—
wandered the suddenly overgrown lawns, looking lost. A
terrified Dagus ran through the wild gardens, scraps of
clothing clinging to his corpulent body. His lips were
moving, hands waving in the air as he attempted to call
back the magic. He ran out through the Peacock Gates—
the thousand of brilliant feathers wilted to dust—and
stopped when he saw the crowd. Even from a distance,
Stiicho saw his cousin's eyes widen as he recognized him.
His mouth opened and closed, but his voice was swallowed by the sudden sound of the crowd: a roar of triumph, a baying of beasts. And then silence. Stiicho
stepped forward, conscious that his entire life had been
leading to this place, to this time, when he could confront
his cousin and set everything to rights.

"What does it feel like," he shouted, voice echoing off
the stones, "to be ordinary? What does it feel like to be
without magic, to see your city crumble around you, your
magical edifices, your constructs, your glamours and
shades vanish? What does it feel like to see yourself as

you really are? Don't answer. You will have the rest of your life to think of an answer." Stiicho's voice rose in triumph. "An hour ago, I was a beggar . . . and now? Now I will be the emperor of the City at the Center of the World!"

In the silence the sudden sound of stone cracking was clearly audible.

Stiicho turned. The warrior standing beside him was holding up his hand, eyes and mouth wide with horror as the flesh hardened to stone. He brought his hands to his cheeks and touched granite skin. When Stiicho looked back at his cousin, the palace gardens were altering, shifting, changing, the rank weeds vanishing, ornamental shrubs and delicate topiary reappearing. Somewhere across the city a clock was tolling the hour.

The magic had returned.

JACUS THE SLUG

John Mina & William R. Forstchen

"Jacus! Jacus, you damned slug, get in here!"

A tremor of fear tightened Jacus' heart. Furtively making the holy sign, he clutched the relic of Saint Sergius, a genuine toenail paring of the blessed saint himself, contained in a tiny brass reliquary, which Jacus kept concealed beneath his tunic.

"Another day, grant another day," he whispered, a ritual he had engaged in now for fifteen years.

Jacus, dragging his next-to-useless clubbed foot behind him, hobbled into the study chamber of his lord master, the dark priest Halkosus. With bent head he approached, willing his knees not to tremble, and as always, they did not obey.

"Look at me, slug."

Jacus looked up. Behind the desk covered with ancient scrolls stood Halkosus, nephew of the Emperor himself. That power alone would cause any mere slave to tremble, but it was not his blood line that engendered fear, it was something far more terrifying and sinister that filled Jacus with horror and loathing every time he was in the presence of his master. Halkosus the Pig, as everyone called him when he was far away, stood before him, his pink blotted face and squinty tiny eyes indeed reminding Jacus of the pigs his wife tended in the barn.

Jacus struggled to assume what he called "the face," the look of heartfelt respect tinged with loving awe that was the key to survival.

Halkosus gazed at Jacus, his features wrinkled in a sneer. There was the heavy smell of opium-laced wine in the room. His master had been at it again, Jacus realized. Sometimes that was for the good, most times it was not.

"Slug, sometimes I want to vomit at the mere sight of you," Halkosus growled. "You're ugly, despicably ugly."

"Yes, master."

There was no denying the truth of that, Jacus realized, even when the words came from Halkosus the Pig. He was indeed clubfooted with a hunch to his shoulders that caused some to look the other way and make the holy sign when they passed him. And yet, perhaps the deformity was a blessing, Jacus always tried to reason.

His unknown parents, in the land of the Bulgars, had set him out in the woods to die on the day he was born. Brother Ionus, returning from a mission to the Bulgar king, had thus found him, and brought him back to the monastery and there the monks had adopted him. Born healthy he would later reason, and he would have lived, and most likely died a Bulgar pagan, ignorant, laboring in the fields, and dying unsaved. Unable to do labor they had taught him instead to read and write, opening to him, in the sunlit corridors of the scriptorium, the joys of philosophy, history, poetry and even the hidden arts of alchemy and magics.

It had even been discovered that he had some small talents for the latter, nothing that would ever make him a great practitioner but enough to amuse the children of peasants who worked for the brothers. Brother Ionus had even allowed him to briefly visit and study with Binyamin ben Gibb, who though not a believer of the new faith, was held in high esteem by the monks as a conjurer who was a wise, just and holy man.

Brother Ionus had hoped that he would one day take the holy vow but, as the kindly brother would later say, if all took the vow, there would be no children born to sing the praise of the Creator. There was a young peasant girl, Tirra, who became the object of his fascination. And to the amazement of the villagers, many of whom believed that his foot and shoulder were a mark of cursing, she had been drawn in turn to his inner strength, his kindness, his self-deprecating laugh and gentle smile.

They had lived thereafter outside the monastery gate, for after all, one who was married could not very well live within the monastery walls, a realm in which no woman was allowed. Somehow, in his naivete, Jacus had come to assume that this was all that the world would ever be, a loving wife, a daughter born the year after their marriage, and working in the scriptorium. He believed the dream until the coming of the Third Time of Troubles, when the emperor died, some say murdered. The abbot of the monastery, being allied closely to the former emperor and being a little too vocal in his protest of the new, found his lands taxed beyond the ability to bear until one day the emperor's cataphracts had arrived, escorting the tax collectors. And on that day Jacus discovered just how far-reaching and cruel the world truly was.

Brother Ionus, being a monk, and his abbot were of course not touched, for to do so to a holy man was a great sin, but all who lived beyond the gate found that through a fine technicality of the law they were liable for the new taxes that were owed. Before that day was two hours old, Jacus and his entire family were taken into slavery, for "failure to pay debt." Within a week he was presented to the emperor's nephew as a token of esteem, a good scribe with the gift of a fine hand being hard to find.

Halkosus stirred in his seat, emitting a sonorous belch, and stood up.

"Tomorrow afternoon is ceremony day, slug. I want the proper scrolls in order; the list is on my desk. See that all are in their proper place on the altar. I go to see my uncle; I expect everything completed when I return. Make sure the steward receives my selection for this evening's feast as well."

Jacus dared not look up. Tonight was the night he had waited and prayed for so many years, the sole reason he had endured, without a murmur, all the abuse and scorn of his master without complaint.

Halkosus left the room and Jacus momentarily leaned on his master's desk until his knees stopped shaking. He looked down at his master's desk and examined the list of summoning spells, all the time clutching the holy relic concealed beneath his tunic.

The selection was more ghastly than usual. Going to Halkosus' gold-inlaid trunk, he opened it up with the key that was kept in his master's desk and one by one pulled out the master copies of the scrolls.

He carried the scrolls over to the desk, sat down, and pulling out a sheet of vellum from a storage bin he carefully trimmed it into half a dozen small squares and then, while muttering prayers to ward off evil, he copied each of the dark incantations down for the ceremony with a fine flourishing hand. Finished with each of the spells, he sprinkled sand on the vellum to blot the remaining ink and then placed the master scrolls back in their trunk. After years of copying them he knew each and every one by heart, with all its dark obscenities that Jacus would never dare to repeat, even when the sun was shining overhead. He knew even the most powerful of the spells, a spell that the mere possession of would have terrified Brother Ionus, for it was the spell that kept the forces of darkness locked in their burning hell, a spell that supposedly Saint Constantine and Saint Sergius himself had used to cast demons out of the land when the true faith had come to replace the old.

He looked down at the box that contained so much

evil, wishing yet again for the nerve to simply stick a burning ember in and to purge the world of the dark powers that Halkosus controlled by the dark and obscene words. When the spells were recited aloud, with the proper blood offering, evil could walk again in the land, but in the process the spell itself was consumed by flame, thus it had to be copied down fresh each time.

He knew that Brother Ionus would turn his back on him for the help he gave Halkosus. But then Brother Ionus did not have a daughter coming of age who needed protection. By custom the children of those sold into slavery were traditionally released once they reached their sixteenth year, if their parents loyally served without complaint. By custom and not by law, but it was all that Jacus had.

He sat back behind the desk for a moment, allowing himself the one small entertainment of the day. Halkosus had a most wondrous marker of time in his office. It struck him as curious, for after all a man had to but look out the window, except on the cloudiest of days, to know what the time was, but Halkosus was rich and could afford such trivial toys.

It was a glass ball and contained within it was a tiny man dressed in wondrous ropes that shimmered with a strange unearthly light. Jacus still wondered if the man inside the ball was actually a real living being, or merely an illusion, for the clock, as Halkosus called it, kept time through magic. The little man held a staff, with which he pointed to the markings of the hours. But at each hour, before he moved his pointer to the next marker, he would perform some magical trick. Perhaps it was to juggle tiny balls of fire, or conjure birds from out of the emptiness which would then fly around inside the ball. It was nearing the hour and Jacus settled back to watch the show.

He had often waved to the little man, had tried to talk to him, but the marker of time never seemed to notice him at all.

He waited patiently, and from across the bay he heard the first pealing of the bells marking the noonday hour. He stared at the little man, and then, there was the slightest of tremors, and Jacus held his breath. The earth shook, ever so imperceptibly. He had known such things up on the border of the Bulgar lands. The little man started to move and then seemed to freeze and then he simply seemed to disappear for an instant. Just as suddenly he was back and for a moment Jacus thought that he actually looked confused.

Strange. It was as if the magic had suddenly died for an instant. He watched the little man intently, but he was again carrying on with his antics and Jacus rose up from behind the desk; there was still so much to do before Halkosus returned, and today of all days, he could not allow even the slightest complaint.

Placing the scrolls into a leather container he left Halkosus' office and made his way down the long flight of stairs which led to the back of the altar. With the key entrusted to him he opened the door and stepped out behind the dark altar. Again there was the prayer to Saint Sergius as he stepped out behind the black stone and into what Halkosus called "his church."

He dared to look up for an instant at the three-fathom-high statue of the Dark Lord. The fire within the belly of the statue was cold; tomorrow morning the slaves would pile in the wood and oil to set the blaze burning so that by the time of the ceremony the black iron statue would be glowing red-hot with dark smoke belching from its mouth. He looked up at the evil thing, its mouth opened in a perpetual grin of dark lust, its four taloned arms extended, holding in each the writhing form of a human offered in sacrifice. For fifteen years he had served as the scribe to the high priest of this monstrosity which was allowed to flourish within the very sight of the great cathedral. Only the nephew of an emperor could be allowed to do such a thing, a nephew who undoubtably had some dark and sinister information that kept the emperor from striking him down.

Jacus placed the scrolls upon the altar for Halkosus and turned to look out on the nave of the temple. Long wooden benches were arrayed for the "worshipers," who would fill the room tomorrow after making an appropriate offering to the coffers. The money Halkosus had thus taken in, by pandering to the perverted lusts of some of the most illustrious nobles and ladies and the richest merchants of the land, was supposedly uncountable. Though Halkosus was too lazy and often too drugged to remember his own spells, he would entrust to no one the counting of the offering once the ceremony was over.

Jacus looked at the posts that were arrayed before the altar, where tomorrow the poor tormented slaves and criminals who would be the food of the dark lord would be chained. Some, he tried to reason, deserved such a fate, and Halkosus made sure that the jails were rarely filled, but more than one was simply an innocent who had crossed the wizard and that was why he had placed such special trust in Saint Sergius, who had thus far spared him and his family across fifteen years of bondage.

Jacus lowered his head and turned away, wondering if, when his day finally came, Saint Sergius would meet him at the gate and offer intercession for all the evils that he had been a part of, no matter how unwilling.

Tonight, at least, would be a partial reward, for tonight his daughter would go free.

Jacus felt the hand of his wife tighten in his as the last of the plates were cleared from the table. Halkosus, sitting at the end of the great feasting table, finished yet another tale of court intrigue for his appreciative guests who laughed at all the appropriate moments. Beside him sat his son, Cletus, who looked every inch his father, and was back from a yearlong holiday of debauchery on the islands to the south.

"A rare day tomorrow," Halkosus announced, while raising his goblet and spilling most of the wine on his heavily stained golden tunic.

"Tomorrow the boy here will run the service."

The guests nodded appreciatively and Cletus beamed, his piglike eyes squinting.

Jacus, standing with the other servants at the end of the room, waited patiently, looking over at his wife and especially at Lavinna, who was radiant in her white gown which they had worked more than a year for, doing extra jobs late at night, so that on her sixteenth birthing day she would look like a fine lady. She gazed at her parents and nervously forced a smile. Tomorrow, Jacus thought proudly, tomorrow she will have her papers of freedom and can leave this hellhole forever. Brother Ionus had already pledged her protection. She could read and write and perhaps she would seek a life in the nunnery or would find some young man of intelligence who would see her great worth.

"Slug, where the devil are you?"

Jacus nervously stepped out from the line of servants and dragging his leg he walked up to where his lord sat. Halkosus looked down at him with disgust.

"It turns my stomach that I have a servant so ugly," Halkosus announced, looking over at the fine lords and ladies for sympathy and they nodded in ready agreement.

"Some day soon I'll replace him, but a good scribe is hard to find."

"I have an extra one, my lord," one of the guests announced with a languid air and Jacus felt his heart freeze. He dared a sidelong glance at the speaker. It was a young upstart from the provinces who had frequented Halkosus' temple of late, obviously seeking to ingratiate himself with a member of the royal family.

"He's a fine-looking boy," the guest continued, "if you

know what I mean and I know you can appreciate such things."

Halkosus chuckled, his interest aroused.

"And writes a fine hand, trained by his father. I've no use for him, one scribe is burdensome enough at times. He's yours, my lord. I'll send him over tomorrow, a gift offering to a friend."

Jacus remained silent, head lowered, feeling as if his heart had gone to ice.

"Well, Slug, you have a rival," Halkosus rumbled.

Halkosus looked back at his guest.

"Send the boy over. The piece of filth I now own can train him."

Jacus waited, not daring to say a word, and Halkosus turned away as if diverted by something else. Finally he looked back at Jacus, as if remembering a trivial detail.

"Oh, your daughter," Halkosus announced, "bring her forward."

Jacus looked back at Lavinna and motioned for her and his wife to come forward. They approached the dais and Jacus heard more than one comment from the guests about his child that sickened him. Jacus dared to look up at Halkosus and saw him leaning back in his chair with a bored expression. But it was not Halkosus who suddenly struck fear into him, it was his son, Cletus, who was now leaning forward, gazing at Lavinna with a strange intensity.

"Amazing, isn't it," Halkosus announced. "A creature so disgusting could sire such a child. Perhaps it's evidence of how unfaithful his wife must have been. This child definitely came from the other side of her bed."

The crowd laughed and Jacus looked over at his wife, seeing the hurt and rage in her eyes. He ever so slightly shook his head.

Say nothing, he prayed, say nothing for Lavinna's sake.

Lavinna stood in silence, daring to look up at Halkosus and she appeared, to Jacus, to be like a regal princess who could float above the filth and corruption.

Halkosus started to raise his hand, as he usually did when making what he felt was an important pronouncement.

Cletus, however, grabbed hold of his father by the shoulder and leaning over, whispered into his ear. Halkosus paused, and suddenly in his heart Jacus realized that all his years of prayers were coming to naught because of a momentary whim of another.

Halkosus listened. He looked down at Jacus and then over at the young noble who had just given a gift. He smiled.

"You know, Jacus, that the freedom of the child of a debtor slave is not mandated by law, simply by custom."

"Yes, my gracious lord," Jacus whispered.

"She could still have her freedom though—" and Halkosus paused dramatically "—for a price."

"What price, my lord?" Jacus asked, his voice trembling.

Halkosus smiled and looked over at Cletus.

Cletus stood up, leaned over the table and beckoned to Lavinna.

Her features pale, Lavinna looked over at her father, who nodded woodenly for her to obey. Her mother started to reach out but Jacus grabbed his wife by the hand.

"Don't!" he whispered hoarsely.

Lavinna approached the dias and Cletus leaned over.

"I think you'd be fun for a little sport," Cletus announced and he grabbed Lavinna by the hair, twisting it and pulling her towards him and the words he now whispered to her were lost.

Her features started to redden, tears coming to her eyes. Jacus looked over at the audience who were intently watching the drama, more than one with wanton gazes of lust.

Cletus, laughing, looked over at them.

"Perhaps, after I'm done, the rest of you can have some sport with her as well before the night is finished."

And joyful laughter broke out. "She'll be broken in by then and might even enjoy it!"

Lavinna started to scream, trying to pull away from Cletus' grasp and he laughed the louder, his other hand reaching out and tearing her gown.

"Bastard pig!"

The cry was an explosive roar, a scream of hatred and anguish pent up across fifteen years of torment.

Jacus leaped forward, in spite of his infirmities and sweeping up a knife from the table he drove it into Cletus' arm, pinning it to the table. Cletus let go of Lavinna with a howl of pain, struggling and crying as he tried to wrench his arm free. Jacus picked up a bowl of stew and hurled it at Halkosus, the bowl shattering as it struck his master in the face.

"You're all bastards, you're all pigs!" Jacus screamed. "I pray that the Dark Lord drags all of you to hell. Saint Sergius above! Send them all to hell!"

From the corner of his eye he saw Lavinna, standing defiant, gazing with pride at her father, his wife holding their child in a tight protective embrace. He never even saw the blow that came from behind and knocked him near senseless to the ground.

Halkosus, roaring with anger, was over the table and fell into kicking Jacus on his hunched back and deformed leg and then raised his hand to blast him into oblivion.

"No!"

It was Cletus, clutching his injured arm.

He came around from behind the table and stood over Jacus who looked up at him, speechless from the blow.

"Save him for tomorrow, uncle," Cletus hissed, "save all three of them. Food for the Dark Lord. I promise you a show no one will forget."

Gasping for breath, Jacus the Slug leaned over and struggled to keep from vomiting, as the fresh scent of blood and torn entrails washed over him. Even though the victim had long since lapsed into the final silence, his screams still tore at his soul. He was vaguely aware of the laughter coming from the audience in the temple behind him, but at the moment he was too sickened to even care, to take offense, or even to feel hatred.

The Servants of the Dark One, wearing their black masks, came prancing out from behind the temple altar, followed by two slaves bearing a stretcher. The Servants cavorted and leaped high in the air, while the slaves picked up the fragments on the temple floor—part of a leg, a flame-scorched head and pieces of offal, piling them up on the stretcher. Done with their task they hurriedly ran back behind the altar bearing the food of the Dark One. The Servants, finishing their ceremonial dance, followed them and the audience started to grow restless in anticipation of the next act.

Jacus watched in silence, aware that his daughter was still crying in terror, her arms wrapped around his waist. He reached down absently, the chains binding him rattling loudly, and patted her on the shoulder. He spared a glance to his wife.

"At least it's over," she whispered, reaching out to touch him. "Saint Sergius will join us together again in paradise."

Jacus looked up at the dark statue that towered above him, dominating the temple. The eyes of the statue glowed with an unearthly red glimmer, its mouth open, in a silent howl of lust, its four hands holding a writhing victim aloft as if about to tear its latest feast asunder.

From a small platform near the statue's mouth, the Servants now reappeared and, pulling the human fragments from a sack, they tossed the bloody offering into the Dark One's open mouth, the audience in the temple thundering their approval as greedy flames shot up out the statue's mouth, thick oily smoke roiling out and wafting into the back of the temple, where the more delicate of the devotees started to cough and gag.

Jacus looked back over his shoulder at the crowd. They were already drunk, bestial, eyes rolling, some already tearing their garments off, inflamed by the sight of blood being offered to their Dark God, and by the stimulants that heavily laced their wine.

The temple was packed to overflowing today for word had raced across the city about the grave insult Halkosus and Cletus had suffered at the hands of the Slug and all had come to see what special torment was now in store for the offenders.

As he looked back more than one saw him and, laughing, they taunted him.

"Slug, Slug, Slug!"

Jacus pulled futilely on his chains which were locked to a ring bolt set in the temple floor. It was useless. Wearily he looked at the lock which was sealed by a dark magic. His daughter, still crying, buried her head against his shoulder and he held her tight.

"I should have done what he wished," she whispered. "The two of you, at least, would be safe."

Jacus stroked her hair and held her tight.

"No, my child. Your mother and I love you more than life. Would you not have done the same and fought back if someone tried to hurt your mother and me?"

She looked up, tears in her eyes, and smiled.

He looked around at the other "offerings," chained like him to the floor. Sometimes, for sport, Halkosus would condemn someone to be an offering and have him chained before the altar. Only to let him live for two, three, even half a dozen ceremonies before finally picking him at last. Clutching the relic of Saint Sergius, Jacus silently prayed that the blessed saint and protector of slaves would intervene and at least spare his family this day. And yet, there was another thought, a cold wish, that it would not be so, and that their suffering would end today. For they were doomed, and to not be chosen today was simply to postpone the inevitable.

A deep thundering boom echoed through the temple and the mob, which had been degenerating into a lust-filled orgy, grew quiet, going down on their knees, raising their hands up over their heads.

"Come to us; Come to us, O bringer of pain, O bringer of joy."

Jacus watched them, sickened by their bleating chant. Some were lost in a dark ecstasy, others, "the tourists" his old master called them, who had come out of curiosity or for a dark thrill, looked around nervously but joined in the chant nevertheless.

The deep thunder of the kettledrums continued and from behind the statue two men appeared, dressed in robes of black that were trimmed in silver, the billowing robes unable to conceal their heavy, bloated forms. Their faces were concealed by masks that mimicked the lust-filled features of their lord.

The masks were supposedly to conceal their identity, for after all the worship they practiced was illegal, but all knew who they were, and none would dare to lay hands on the high priest Halkosus and his son Cletus the Pig, the nephew and grandnephew of the emperor. Jacus knew their features all too well and he could imagine their dark grins of lust and amusement as they surveyed their "flock" for the day, already picking who would be their companions when the ceremony reached its final frenzy.

Halkosus walked in front of the altar and bowed low, placing his hands upon the altar and taking from it a ceremonial whip, with golden handle and light silken cords, his son Cletus doing the same. They then whipped themselves lightly on their shoulders and back. Out in the audience more substantial whips had been passed out and some of the faithful fell to with a strange joyful frenzy, flogging themselves, while the tourists, choosing the light whips with silk cords, gently flogged themselves so that they would not bruise their skin or tear their fine garments.

The two priests turned and looked back at the

audience, motioning them to continue with even more enthusiasm.

"It is with blood that the Dark Lord is aroused," Halkosus roared. "Make your sacred offering!"

Jacus covered over his daughter's ears so she could not hear the screams of lust and pain that now echoed through the temple.

He saw Cletus looking over, and Jacus sensed that the Pig's gaze was lingering for a moment on Lavinna.

Would she be next? Jacus thought, his heart filled with rage.

The two stood near Jacus, Halkosus taking his son by the shoulder.

"Now remember," Halkosus whispered, "this is much more involved than a lesser summoning. You were sloppy with the last one. He almost got away from you. The mob might not have noticed it but the fine connoisseurs of such sport will," and he nodded to where the honored guests of the ceremony sat in a side balcony, watching those down on the main temple floor with amusement. More than one of the guests wore a mask to conceal their identities as members of the royal family or high government bureaucrats, who the next morning could be found kneeling in the great cathedral sanctimoniously chanting their prayers.

"Maintain your highest level of concentration at all times."

He spoke the words harshly, Cletus nodding nervously.

Jacus looked over at Cletus in silent rage.

He's nervous, Jacus thought, *we're the ones who're dinner and he's nervous.* He wanted to laugh at the irony of it all, but knew better than to draw attention.

"If you lose control, it'll turn on you. It's not intelligent, but it's strong-willed. It'll lure you. You'll think it's torpid, divert your attention to something else and then it's at your throat. So nothing fancy, just bring it through and then keep your focus."

Cletus, looking sidelong at his father, said nothing.

"I'll be right behind you in case anything goes wrong. But if I have to step in to save a student, even if he is my son, I lose face before the families. And if I lose face . . ."

His words trailed off and Cletus visibly cowered. The fat one turned away from his son, his gaze sweeping around the temple, his arms extended with a show-manlike flair, and the crowd, which had finally tired of whipping itself, was back on its feet in anticipation, eager for the ceremony to resume.

It was the time of the choosing and Halkosus and Cletus now stepped down from the high altar and started to walk down the line of chained prisoners in order to choose their offering.

"The Slug and his family!" someone shouted and the cry was picked up.

Jacus watched silently as the two made a grand show of their sport. They stopped before a chained thief, as if about to chose him, the thief groveling for mercy. The two laughed and continued on. They approached another thief from the city prisons, who was on his knees, pite-ously begging. With a disdainful flick of his finger Cletus marked the man out. He began to scream hysterically and after the chain was released by Halkosus it took several servants to drag the man to the open circle before the altar. Halkosus waved his hand and the thief's feet seemed to be frozen in place so that he could not take another step, his wild cries echoing in the temple.

The two continued their walk, finally approaching Jacus, who this time did not avert his eyes, his hatred showing.

"How are we today, slug?" Halkosus said with a grin, and with a backhanded blow he slapped Jacus across the face.

Jacus remained silent.

"I was sick of you anyhow. With the offer of the new scribe I at last had a means of getting rid of your dis-gusting presence."

Cletus started to lean forward as if to fondle Jacus' daughter, and Jacus pulled her in tight.

"Keep your bloody hands off her, pig," Jacus snarled.

Cletus fixed Jacus with his gaze and there was a moment of blinding pain, as if a fire had erupted beneath his skin.

"Not yet," Halkosus snapped angrily and the pain dropped away. "Let's have some fun with him first."

Halkosus stepped back and with a dramatic flourish he pointed at Lavinna. The audience roared their approval as the chain was struck off.

Jacus struggled to grab her until a servant, armed with a staff, struck him across the side of the head, knocking him down to his knees.

As Lavinna was led to the sacrifice circle she looked back at her parents, and through his tears he saw her smile.

"Soon all of us will be free," she said softly even as Halkosus pointed to the ground, binding her feet to the temple floor.

"Take me!" Jacus screamed, "Take me. I'm the one that's guilty. Take me!"

The mob behind him, watching the drama, started to laugh.

"Oh take me, please take me!" some of them started to chant, mocking Jacus' agony.

Halkosus looked over at Jacus, laughing.

"First you'll watch your family die, slug, then there'll be time enough for you later."

Jacus turned and looked back at the audience, the aristocrats, the fat merchants, the nobles who crossed the Straits and came to Halkosus' hidden temple down in the district of brothels to enjoy the forbidden religions of old. They were on their feet, laughing and pointing. He wanted to scream his rage, his protest, but knew that such as they fed on his anguish.

Though some of the richest of the empire, they were the scum of it, knowing that here, just a short ferryman's ride across the Strait, they could satiate their perverted pleasures, free of any fear of arrest. For here, out of all the Empire, such perversion was allowed to flourish since not even the emperor would dare to challenge the sack of corruption that was his nephew.

He watched Halkosus, the grand priest, as the fat one continued to strut before his dark altar, arms raised up to the statue of the Dark Lord, chanting now in some dark, obscene and forgotten tongue. Halkosus started to shake convulsively and Jacus knew that this was all part of the show, the ritual.

Halkosus staggered about before the altar like one possessed, now shouting dark obscenities, the audience joining in, screaming the foulest words as part of what they believed to be the ritual of conjuring to call forth a minion of the Dark Lord. Jacus looked back up to where the highborn guests sat, leaning over the balcony railing, some of them laughing and pointing, others watching intently, a few drawn back nervously, their senses rebelling against the darkness.

There was a subtle nod from Halkosus to Cletus. Cletus went up to the altar and took one of the scrolls that Jacus had copied only yesterday, never dreaming of who it would be used upon. Cletus started to read from the scroll, making large sweeping gestures with his arms. A shimmering fog appeared in front of the younger wizard. Smoke started to pour from the scroll, and Cletus threw it into the circle, where it burst into white hot flames. Jacus averted his eyes at the brilliance. The flames disappeared and in its place there was a dark shape, like a heaped up mound of rotting flesh, green with corruption. A gasp echoed from the audience, followed by a round of applause for the conjuring of such a rare and loathsome thing.

"A Slug for the Slug's daughter!" Cletus announced, and many in the audience roared at his joke.

The giant slug seemed harmless enough as it slowly slithered about within the circle, a rounded head crowned with a single antenna waving back and forth. It seemed to focus on Cletus, who pointed to where the two prisoners waited and the thing gave off a bubbling hiss, spun around, and started slithering toward the horrified victim at a remarkable speed.

Jacus barely heard the hysterical screaming of his wife, or his own screams of rage, so loud now was the roaring of the mob. The beast slowed for an instant, its snaillike head weaving back and forth as if trying to decide. Cletus looked over at Jacus, grinned, and shouted a command.

The slug turned to the right, coiling itself around the legs of the thief, who was struggling, waving his arms, his feet pinned to the floor of the temple so that he looked like a nightmarish tree being lashed by a storm as he waved back and forth. The slug continued to wrap itself around the thief's body, slithering upwards, coiling around his midsection so that only the upper torso of the thief was visible.

The thief started screaming, at first in fear, but the tone quickly changed to screams of pain, as the slug's head reared upwards, revealing a gaping mouth that was as black as night. The mouth came down, wrapping around the thief's right arm, pinning it tight. A sick sucking and slurping sound was coming from the creature and the thief's voice rose to a high, hysterical shriek of unworldly terror.

The slug let go and the mob gasped in astonishment. The man's arm had been digested so that only bone, trailing pieces of muscle and tendons, remained.

The slug now lowered its aim, clamping down on the thief's legs, the temple filled with a ghastly slurping sound as the slug now settled down to its meal, devouring the thief a piece at a time. The legs were consumed, and Halkosus, with a wave of his hand, fused the joints on the thief's body so that he remained upright. Miraculously the man was still alive, howling insanely, until at last, the slug reared up and covered the man's head. A moment later it withdrew its hold, and the crowd broke into a thunderous applause at the sight of the skull, its mouth open. The slug finally concentrated on the midsection and then withdrew, the entrails of the thief spilling out around his feet.

The slug drew back, its head weaving back and forth, as if looking for its next meal. Cletus looked over at Jacus and laughed.

"It's always a sloppy eater with its first course. It'll take ten times as long with your daughter before it's done."

The slug turned as Cletus waved his hand and pointed at Jacus' daughter.

Lavinna, who had kept her composure for so long, finally broke down and started to scream.

Jacus buried his wife's head against his shoulder and looked back at the mob as if somehow there would be a voice of pity that could save his child. But he could see there was none.

He raised his head up, looking up at the dark statue that dominated the altar, smoke pouring from its mouth and closed his eyes.

"Saint Sergius, hear me!"

His scream echoed through the temple as if an obscenity had been shouted in the land of darkness.

The laughter and cries of the mob stilled.

"Saint Sergius, save my daughter! Saint Sergius, let the Dark One take everyone here to hell!"

There was a tremor, ever so faint at first but he could feel it slowly starting to build. The audience was now deadly silent, his cry of anguish still echoing.

The tremor continued to build. Jacus heard a faint snick, and looking down he saw that the lock that held him and his wife to the floor had snapped open.

The beast, which was now only inches away from reaching out to embrace his daughter, started to waver and then, in a flash of light and smoke, it was gone. Halkosus and Cletus looked at each other in surprise, as if the other one were at fault for the disappearance of the monstrosity that had been conjured.

Jacus staggered forward to the circle which contained Lavinna. She was free and raced to his embrace, sobbing hysterically and he quickly passed her to his wife.

"Flee!" and he pointed to the door behind the altar that led into Halkosus' living chambers.

But Halkosus was starting to recover and he advanced towards Jacus.

"Saint Sergius! Answer my prayer!" and he pointed a menacing hand at Halkosus.

He sensed in his heart that he was bluffing, but there was a hope beyond hope that somehow the holy saint had heard his prayer from out of the pit of darkness and had decided to intervene. Jacus reached into his tunic and tore the relic free from around his neck and held it up as a talisman against Halkosus.

There was a moment's pause, the ground beneath them still trembling. All were silent.

Halkosus waved his hand as if to ward off the charm and to strike out with pain . . . but nothing happened.

He tried again and still nothing.

He stared at Jacus, wide-eyed, and then a look of rage clouded his features.

"I can still crush you with my bare hands, slug!"

He began to advance, Jacus holding the relic up, praying intently, hoping that at least his wife and daughter were escaping.

There was the sound of something cracking, of metal groaning. Halkosus paused, looking up behind Jacus and his piglike features blanched, his squinty eyes growing wide in terror. A wild shriek erupted from the audience, the mob starting to back up, falling out of their seats.

Jacus turned and looked up.

The statue of the Dark Lord had moved. Its head turned, flames belching out of its open mouth, its fiery red eyes now alive, turning, looking, gazing down hungrily. It reared its head back, a dark howl of lust and primal joy and hatred bellowing out of its iron lungs and flame-filled stomach.

The mob broke in mad terror, running for the rear door, piling up against it. But it would not open, as if the magic that caused the great bronze doors to open and close had somehow failed, locking it shut. The mob started to tear at the door in a mad frenzy, clawing over each other in a blind insane fear.

The Dark Lord tore its left foot free from the floor of the temple and stepped forward, bringing it down with a clanging thunder. It then tore its right foot free and brought it down, stepping straight over Jacus, who was looking up at the devil which was now loose upon the world.

Well, if this is the judgement of Saint Sergius and his means of intervention then so be it, Jacus thought with a grin.

He held the relic up high as a protection and the devil swept by, as if not seeing him, and leaped into the nave of the temple. The crowd was now insane with fear, running back and forth in blind terror. The devil reared its head back, laughing cruelly. It raced forward, trailing fire and smoke. Its four arms reached out, dropping the bronze images of victims and with iron talons scooping up the first of its real victims, plunging them headlong into its open mouth. Laughing, it grabbed one after another, smoke and fire engulfing each of his offerings at the touch of his red-hot pincers. Some, it lingered over a minute for its amusement, tossing them back and forth through the air, tearing them asunder, or simply stomping on them with its iron feet. Others it picked up and flung shrieking against the wall or tossed high in the air to then gulp down as they fell back into his open mouth.

Like cornered rats the mob ran back and forth, squealing and crying, begging for mercy so that even Jacus was sickened by their final anguish. Somehow a few managed to finally tear the door open, and ran shrieking out into the street. The devil snatched up the last of them and then kneeling down it placed its mouth against the door and blew a jet of flame out into the street.

It then stood up, looking around hungrily and started back towards the altar. Jacus turned and looked. Halkosus and Cletus were gone!

The demon continued to advance and then paused to turn its attention on the highborn nobles who occupied the balcony, which had but one exit down to the floor of the temple. The nobles were piled upon each other in terror, writhing and screaming. The devil looked at them and laughed; leaning over it blew out its hot breath and they ignited into flames. It then plucked the shrieking torches, one by one, and devoured them all. Hot greasy smoke was now pouring out of its mouth, filling the temple with the stench of burning flesh. The wooden roof was now on fire, the rafters engulfed in flames.

Jacus continued to look around the temple for his two tormentors. They had not been consumed. But where were they?

And then the realization hit, they must have fled through the door behind the now-shattered altar. How much time had passed, he could not even say, perhaps they had already escaped. He turned and hobbled towards the door.

"Saint Sergius, guide my vengeance!" he shouted, looking back at the demon.

Ascending the stairs he found all in chaos, servants running, screaming in terror. He caught a brief glimpse out an open window and saw that the city across the straits was in chaos. Great buildings had collapsed, fires were breaking out, and over all could be heard a loud commingled roar of terror rising up from a million voices.

Perhaps Saint Sergius was going too far, Jacus thought, but the city was indeed a sinful place and who could challenge the judgement of a saint?

He continued up the stairs, heading for Halkosus' chambers and flung the door open. Huddled in the corner of the room he saw his wife and daughter . . . held by the wretch Cletus, with a knife poised at Lavinna's throat. At his side was Halkosus.

"Don't move, Jacus," Cletus screamed, "don't take a step closer."

Jacus held up the relic and Cletus pressed the blade in tighter so that a thin trickle of blood coursed down Lavinna's throat.

He lowered the sacred relic.

"None of the magic works!" Halkosus bleated. "What have you done, slug?"

"I called on the holy saint the way I should have the day I was first given to you," Jacus snapped, all terror gone, his voice now filled with authority and command.

He looked over at Cletus.

"Let her go!"

Cletus hesitated.

Jacus held the relic back up.

"Let her go, I say, or the demon will come and devour you too."

Cletus started to lower his knife.

"Don't let go of her!" Halkosus cried. "The magic's gone, that's why the Dark Lord is loose. He was bound to his hell by magic conjured by the saints and now he's free. Jacus, command the magic to return and then we'll let her go."

Jacus hesitated. He looked over at the clock and saw that the little man inside had disappeared, just like the day before. Could it be that the magic was really all gone? If so, what had he done, he wondered.

He looked back at Lavinna.

"First, my daughter," Jacus said quietly, "or the demon will come right for you, Halkosus. And if you two kill her, I'll make sure your torment is doubled."

Cletus hesitated.

"Let her go now!"

The knife dropped away from Lavinna's throat and Jacus hobbled forward, grabbing his daughter away from Cletus.

"Now go!"

Halkosus looked at him, his eyes narrowing.

"How dare you command me?"

"How dare you challenge me," Jacus hissed.

Halkosus stood silent for a moment.

"First my spells," and he pointed to his trunk, Cletus tearing the lid back and scooping the spells out.

Halkosus looked over at Jacus, as if hesitating, and then reaching over to a panel behind his desk he pushed upon it. The panel slid back to reveal a document hidden within and he started to pull it out. There was handwriting upon it and Jacus recognized the script . . . it was the handwriting of the emperor himself. Somehow, that document was the dark secret which had allowed Halkosus to indulge in his perversions for so many years without fear of reprisal.

The slightest of tremors shook the building and suddenly, within the clock, the little man seemed to appear for an instant, and then disappeared yet again. Halkosus saw it as well, even as he pulled the document out. He looked at the clock and then over at Jacus.

"Slug, I suspect you don't even understand what has happened. You don't control any of this at all."

Jacus held his holy relic up.

"Saint Sergius!"

Halkosus looked around nervously, but nothing happened.

Halkosus laughed hoarsely and putting the document down on his desk he reached to his belt and pulled a dagger out. He looked over at Cletus and grinned.

"Let's have our revenge," Halkosus snarled.

Cletus hesitated, blanching as Jacus pointed the relic at him. But nothing happened.

Cletus recovered his courage.

"Just save the girl for me," Cletus hissed and he started to advance on the three huddled in the corner.

The high window behind Halkosus' desk shattered and

a long glowing arm reached into the room, grabbing hold of Cletus.

The son of the Pig let out a shrieking howl as the red-hot talons dug into his flesh. The arm started to pull him out through the window. Cletus grabbed the sides of the window pane, his hands lacerated by the shards of glass. He kicked and screamed, begging for mercy. The demon pulled Cletus loose and with a roaring laugh threw him screaming into his mouth.

Halkosus looked out the window and then back at Jacus.

"Slug, Slug, save me! Save me, I beg you!"

Jacus stood silent, arms folded as the hand came back through the window. The burning fingers wrapped around the Pig's head and Jacus was amazed that at that moment Halkosus really did sound like a squealing pig being dragged to slaughter. His fat chubby legs kicked and thrashed as he disappeared through the window and down into the burning maw of the demon.

Jacus looked back at his family and then, with holy relic raised, he advanced alone towards the window.

The demon looked in at him and laughed.

"Begone foul one, back to your hell," Jacus commanded, trying, and not too successfully, to keep the trembling from his voice.

The demon grinned.

"By the Saints, slug, you amuse me," the demon growled.

"Begone."

The demon threw back its head, a loud laugh echoing across the city.

Again there was a tremor and Jacus saw, from the corner of his eye, that the little man was again appearing within the clock.

He climbed up on to the broken window sill and held the relic up.

"I command you to be gone!"

The demon looked at him, now filled with annoyance

and he started to reach out ... and then he simply disappeared.

Jacus stood in the window, suddenly aware that the streets below were filled with terror-stricken citizens who were gazing up at him with awe.

With a dramatic flourish he held the relic of a toenail paring of Saint Sergius aloft.

"Saint Sergius has spoken!" he shouted. "Let all who are sinners take heed!"

A loud cheer erupted. Bowing, he climbed back down from the window and looked over at his wife and daughter, who came rushing into his arms, and the three dissolved into tears.

He was still holding them when the door into the room was flung open, revealing a Varangian guardsman who stood before him, gape-mouthed.

"Who are you?" the guard asked.

Jacus looked at his daughter and wife, and then down at the scroll lying on Halkosus table.

Trying to act calm he walked over to the desk and sat down, and reaching over he took the scroll up, opened it and scanned its contents. A thin smile traced his features.

"Can you carry a report to our emperor?" he asked, looking at the guardsman.

"I was sent here from the palace when the report came that a demon was loose. The entire city's in chaos, madness has broken out all over. Some are saying that it started here."

"Tell his most gracious emperor that Saint Sergius, at my calling, has saved us and rid us of a great evil." He paused, looking back down at the document.

"Tell the emperor that I am now the owner of what is left of his nephew's holdings by the power that his nephew once held. And tell the emperor as well that his secret is safe with me, as long as I am safe with him."

The guardsman looked at Jacus, and then down at the document. The thinnest of smiles creased the guardsman's features.

"Did the demon really devour all the slime here?"

Jacus nodded and the guardsman now started to grin.

"That'll cause a stir. Even Wotan would have been sickened by what was being done here."

Jacus nodded sagely, saying nothing.

"And you did it, of course, that's how I'll report it."

"Tell him that the noble Jacus," he hesitated, "the Slug, did this."

The guardsman, still smiling broadly, bowed and then hesitated.

"For your own sake, hide that document well," the guardsman said and then withdrew.

Jacus sighed, settling back in his chair and looked up at his wife.

"Tomorrow we shall arrange a birthing day feast for our lovely daughter and we shall see which suitors will come to pay court. Perhaps even a member of the royal family, I might think, but only the better sort that you find in church and who keep the holy rites. I think we shall give this place to the blessed Brother Ionus who can exorcise the demons and turn this into a monastery dedicated to the holy saint. How does that sound?"

"Jacus?"

"Yes, my love?"

"Did you really do it?"

Jacus simply smiled in reply. Taking the document, he tucked it back into its hiding place and slid the panel shut.

"Of course I did, my dear, Saint Sergius and me. What would even make you ask such a silly question?"

GRAND ADVENTURE
IN GAME-BASED UNIVERSES

With these exciting novels set
in bestselling game universes,
Baen brings you synchronicity at its
best. We believe that familiarity with
either the novel or the game will
intensify enjoyment of the other.
All novels are the only authorized
fiction based on these games and
are published by permission.

THE BARD'S TALE™

Join the Dark Elf Naitachal and his apprentices in bardic
magic as they explore the mysteries of the world of
The Bard's Tale.

(continued)